The Southern Belles of Honeysuckle Way

ALSO BY LINDA BRUCKHEIMER

Dreaming Southern

The Southern Belles of Honeysuckle Way

Linda Bruckheimer

DUTTON

DUTTON
Published by Penguin Group (USA) Inc.,
375 Hudson Street, New York, New York 10014, U.S.A.
Penguin Books Ltd, Registered Offices: 80 Strand, London WC2R 0RL, England
Penguin Books Australia Ltd, 250 Camberwell Road, Camberwell, Victoria 3124, Australia
Penguin Books Canada Ltd, 10 Alcorn Avenue, Toronto, Ontario, Canada M4V 3B2
Penguin Books (N.Z.) Ltd, Cnr Rosedale and Airborne Roads, Albany, Auckland 1310, New Zealand

Published by Dutton, a member of Penguin Group (USA) Inc.

First Printing, April 2004
10 9 8 7 6 5 4 3 2 1

Permissions appear on page 358 and constitute a continuation of the copyright page.

REGISTERED TRADEMARK—MARCA REGISTRADA

LIBRARY OF CONGRESS CATALOGING-IN-PUBLICATION DATA

Bruckheimer, Linda.
    The southern belles of Honeysuckle Way / by Linda Bruckheimer.
        p. cm.
    ISBN 0-525-94454-0 (hardcover : alk. paper)
    1. Real estate development—Fiction. 2. Mothers and daughters—Fiction. 3. Women—
Kentucky—Fiction. 4. Family reunions—Fiction. 5. Birthdays—Fiction. 6. Kentucky—Fiction.
7. Sisters—Fiction. I. Title.

PS3552.R79425S68 2004
813'.54—dc21   2003049247

Printed in the United States of America
Set in Perpetua
Designed by Eve L. Kirch

PUBLISHER'S NOTE
This is a work of fiction. Names, characters, places, and incidents either are the product of the author's imagination or are used fictitiously, and any resemblance to actual persons, living or dead, business establishments, events, or locales is entirely coincidental.

To the memory of Miss Allie,
who feathered the path
with sunshine and tall tales

I never met a Kentuckian who wasn't on his way home.

——Old Kentucky Proverb

Prologue

Rebecca
Somewhere Out in the Wild
Black Yonder

AUGUST 1999

I t is way beyond midnight, an oven-hot August evening, and I am drift-ing along a strand of Louisiana asphalt that I can't quite locate on any map. The wisp of a road bounces across an alligator-infested swamp, and the air is thick with the stench of stagnant water. Fluttering before the windshield like poison jewels and disappearing into the bayou are glow-ing, snapping insects. Several miles behind me was the last vestige of civilization—a weathered gothic church with a sign saying: FREE TRIP TO HEAVEN—DETAILS INSIDE.

The skyscape around me, though, is cloaked in summer finery: The Big Dipper's silver stars twinkle above the oak trees. A huge Japanese lantern of a moon illuminates the night. And there's the Milky Way, trailing across the sky in misty, billowy tufts like miles and miles of bridal veil.

An ordinary motorist would admit they were lost, or at the very least, misplaced or off-kilter. Lila Mae, my wayfaring mother and a utopian traveler, would simply call the situation "the scenic route." It is true that I don't know where I am at the moment. It is even, as an old song put it, a little worse than that: "I don't know where I've come from, 'cause I don't know where I've been." Or so the lyrics go.

If the accounts I've heard from gas station attendants and tollbooth operators are to be believed, it is not an opportune time to be drifting. Percolating somewhere in the Gulf of Mexico is a hurricane, one that's threatening to sweep ashore. Because of this, my nerves are drawn tight as the strings of a Stradivarius. But, there is magic in the night, and I am infused with excitement, as if the wings of some exotic bird were flapping inside me.

Sprinkled like melting snowflakes along this lonely trail and causing me to pause every few miles or so are the remains of Louisiana plantations, their Corinthian columns rotten, and the majestic allées of old, mere petrified soldiers of twisted bark. In the age-old grapple between purity and evil, their limbs climb upward as if reaching for the heavens, while their long arthritic roots burrow deep into the clay earth. Corroded iron gates lean in the wind; bits of their broken curlicues are hidden in the tall grass like Easter eggs.

I am both fascinated and repelled by this region, the Old South in its glory days of magnolia blossoms and bloodstained ground, where soiled Confederate gray and the boom of cannons still pierce the night. If I close my eyes, from some ancient crevice comes the tinkle of banjo music and the crackling of burning sugarcane and the *rat-a-tat-tat* of a thousand dancing belles.

Decades before, I wandered through similar fields and picked pearls of cotton, which I tucked into the pocket of my pink toreador pants, a trinket of my home turf to keep my dreams squirming with life. Perhaps these ash ghosts that rattle the cages of my memory are the exact mansions that caught my girlish fancy as I wished on stars and conjured images of the perfect future.

Officially, this current adventure is nothing more than a means to an end. My younger sister, Carleen, and I are on our way to Kentucky from California, where we will join Irene, our Baby Sister; Miss Olive, our grandmother; plus dozens of friends and relatives to celebrate Lila Mae's seventy-fifth birthday. Unlike the others who have chosen the lickety-split friendly skies, we have opted to leave a few weeks early, wending our way across the American landscape in a car—the scenic route, if you will—the exact route (if such an absurd thing is even possible) that Lila

Mae, our discombobulated mother, and her four young children took several decades ago when our family set out for California on Route 66.

The object of our desire is a glimpse of the good old days, before progress and the bulldozer ambushed our heritage. Simple as this task sounds, Carleen and I might as well be on all fours, scraping around for a misplaced gold doubloon.

At my side, darting in and out of consciousness, is Carleen. Cradling an assortment of road maps and nestled in bittersweet dreams, her blond head is tipped against the car frame. A tiny fractured robin, she is, with her feathery hair blowing across her face and the disappointment of her life somehow settling in her wings. She shifts and slides and twitches her mouth into a tortured smile. Every once in a while, she will bolt upright and say, "Where *are* we, Rebecca?"

Sound asleep in the backseat are our teenage daughters, Ava and Cassie, or, as Carleen and I refer to them when we don't think they're listening, Lolita Number One (mine) and Lolita Number Two (hers). They are adorned in grape nail polish, tank tops, and hoops that pierce various parts of their bodies, all of which clash with the notion that Carleen and I embrace of ourselves as strict mothers.

I roll down all the windows, turn on the CD player and select Johnny Cash. His voice—gravel spliced with black velvet—fills the air as he sings "Folsom Prison Blues." A second wind sweeps through the car as Carleen jumps up and the girls stir. We turn up the music and sing along, our lungs bubbling with the Southern humidity.

> *I hear the train a comin';*
> *it's rolling round the bend,*
> *And I ain't seen the sunshine since I don't know when*
> *I'm stuck in Folsom Prison, and time keeps draggin' on*
> *But that train keeps rollin' on down to San Antone.*

"*Sing, Johnny, sing!*" Carleen yippees and churns the dial until the speakers thunder. The girls, now wide awake and trussed in headphone wires, are plugging their ears and flashing their eyes to the heavens. Donning their metal headbands, they listen to CDs while Carleen paws the floor, searching for the Styrofoam cooler of Coca-Colas. She flips one open and hands it to me, our normal symbol of armistice when we've been bickering and want to reseal our sisterly bond. We've grown up believing that all rifts can be chinked with a Coca-Cola.

For the past few days, we have had *beaucoup* unfinished business, stemming from what is commonly known as "the sweating skull incident." The skull is nothing spectacular—an amateurish drawing on a concrete wall of an ice bag, a skeleton with beads of sweat flying from it, and a sign that says: WARNING—700 MILES OF DESERT.

It is flabbergasting, even to me, but the sign was the number-one item on my list of things to see on this trip. Because Carleen read the map wrong, we looped around with the last streaks of daylight above us, ending up nowhere near the skull. Missing it, I badgered Carleen, was tantamount to traveling to Egypt without seeing the pyramids, or Paris sans the Eiffel Tower, or Peru minus Machu Picchu. On and on I ranted, ending with one of my Homeric, "end of civilization as we know it" speeches. Fed up with my harangue, Cassie finally hollered, "Gosh, Aunt Beck, it's *only* a sweating skull!"

Through the day, I have lambasted Carleen for taking after the Stalkers, our mother's side of the family, who have the sense of direction of an amnesiac hummingbird, and she has crucified me for being high strung and demanding—Wooten tendencies. Had she only known, Carleen informs me, "that the Queen of Sheba would make me the reader of maps, pumper of gas, dispenser of junk food, snapper of photos, and tracker of funnel clouds, I would have taken the blasted plane to Kentucky."

The two Lolitas amuse themselves with their electronic paraphernalia, and drive us crazy with the incessant chant, "How far are we from the Smithsonian?" Unsuspecting bystanders might be impressed by the budding culture vultures, but in truth our young lasses have other interests at heart: seeing Sonny and Cher's bell-bottoms and linking up with two teenage boys they met at the El Tovar Lodge at the Grand Canyon who are now summer tour guides at the Washington, D.C. museum.

Suddenly, a panel of storm clouds moves across the sky. The wind tickles the willows, making a sound like the rustling of taffeta ball gowns. A bolt of heat lightning springs to life every few seconds, something that causes Carleen, a world-class scaredy-cat, to gasp and shriek. "Go back to sleep," I tell her. As unlikely as it is, Carleen has spotted a vagrant and slams her foot against an imaginary brake pedal. Nobody else can even see the man, but from yards away in the black night, Carleen swears he is the Night Stalker.

"I'm not kidding!" she insists. "It's him!"

I assure her that Richard Ramirez, the Los Angeles serial killer nicknamed the Night Stalker, had been sentenced to prison long ago. (It deserves mention that today alone Carleen has already spotted a grizzly bear, a wild dingo, a Gila monster, three funnel clouds, and yet *another* rambler who was Charles Manson's double!)

But, regardless of these far-fetched notions, Carleen, much like our mother, has a knack for getting everybody all riled up. In spite of ourselves, we begin talking about Martians, Tasmanian devils, and the killer nobody ever found who had strangled the schoolgirl in the lime-green socks and left her by the wayside.

Imagine, I think, if we were on a movie screen with an audience watching us, traipsing across the treacherous open road, two young daughters under our protective charge. Perhaps at this very moment, knowing there's a villain waiting to pounce, they are shouting warnings: "Stop! Wait! No!" It's possible, too, that they are snorting to themselves, "Morons, what did they expect when they hightailed it across country by themselves?"

Hovering over the treetops like a crown of rosebuds is the glow of an approaching town. In an empty field our headlights illuminate a white-robed Jesus standing like a lonely hitchhiker. PREPARE TO MEET THY MAKER, it warns. The Savior, crackled like an Italian fresco, stretches his arms east and west and stares us down with eyes pricked with bullet holes.

We zoom along the highway, passing motels with kidney-shaped swimming pools and coin-operated palominos. We pass roadside stands selling spiced pecans and a fireworks shack named *Big Daddy's*, which even in the wee hours, has a sizable crowd purchasing Black Cats and Killer Bees. "TURN AROUND," the girls holler. "STOP!" Carleen gives

in, rummaging through her wallet to find change. But I press the accelerator, making them pout, "We never do anything fun!" When I tell
them we can't keep stopping for this and that and the other, Carleen
chuckles, "You sound just like Mom," an observation that makes me
wince.

With that, from a peephole of my memory, I see our last innocent
decade. It is 1959 and there is a rickety Packard filled with four screaming meemies and a starry-eyed woman enveloped in Arpege. Above us
are the Texas stars as bright as Christmas ornaments and on the radio
Elvis is singing "All Shook Up." Behind the wheel Lila Mae is begging her
unruly kids to cut out all that racket, irked that "the Queen of Sheba's
too busy with them movie magazines to pitch in!" All the while, there is
talk of fresh starts and dreams of gold-cobbled streets.

When that trip, which should have taken several days, took several
months, Lila Mae's explanation for the delay came in a windfall of ver-
biage: I got waylaid, I was sidetracked, as if the expressions themselves
were the culprits that had ensnared her, not her own bad decisions.

Through the decades, Carleen and I have toiled in the garden—
hoeing, tilling, pulling all suspect matter by the roots, searching for
proof that we are not our mother's daughters. But, we are obviously
trapped in Lila Mae's gypsy footprints. As behind schedule as we are,
Carleen and I are easily coaxed, often pulling to the roadside simply to
marvel at the freight trains and summer thunderheads. We stop for chili
dogs in the Gator Cafe, a diner with an enormous alligator perched on
the roof like a bizarre bonnet. We stay in the Valdosta Arms, where every
room has a velvet painting of Martin Luther King, Jr. For hours, we
travel behind a grass-green Volvo that bounces like a covered wagon,
staring at the bumper sticker: VISUALIZE WHIRLED PEAS.

With the wind velocity approaching "ferocious," and dawn looming
before us, we enter St. John's Parish, checking into the Magnolia Plantation Lodge, an inn with faux Greek columns and a crystal-chandeliered
lobby. The female employees wear crinolines and the night clerk, a
marble-white man named Bud Coffey, is dressed as Rhett Butler.

Soon enough, we are in our room with its frizzy carpeting and che-
nille spread and a rackety swamp cooler. But, at least there is a televi-

sion that will give us an update on the hurricane. I open my travel book, thinking I will scout the pages for interesting sights along our path, but I am drowsy.

With the moonlight blanching the drapes, I drift to sleep, remembering places we stayed years ago, wondering if this might even be one of them. When I close my eyes, I still can't shake the image of Lila Mae, one that blinks to me from a movie screen in another galaxy. She is a chatterbox in deep conversation with a truck-stop waitress, then she's a confused figure hooked over a road map, a helpful filling station attendant at her elbow. I see the wind sweeping her print dress around her legs as she stands by an isolated roadside, waving a hankie, hoping for someone to help us with a flat tire or broken radiator. She is trying to avoid serious trouble, when all the while we suspected we were already in it.

Thinking her arthritic knee would slow us down and her singing would drive us crazy, Carleen and I have left her behind in California, cushioning our farewell with assurances and avowals: "Someday, you'll have to come along with us, Mom. It would be so much fun," I said to her, never explaining why she couldn't come on that particular trip, never defining when "someday" might turn out to be, acting as if the decision to stay behind had been her idea, even though the choice to come with us was never presented to her in any formal fashion.

"Oh, honeeee! I would love that!" She makes two fists and pumps them as if rooting for her favorite ball team. In the Los Angeles sky is a froth of coral smog and a hazy sun. Lila Mae stands shadowed by the crepe myrtle and a swing from my grandmother's porch and cheers, "I really would love that!"

"We should do it then, right, Carleen?" I say. "Absolutely!" she replies. Everybody realizes that this is a now-or-never trip, and we also know that there is still time for Lila Mae to pack—not in her usual way of taking every item she owns—but certainly enough notice to gather the basic essentials. But we remain dead silent, careful not to prompt her into actually joining us. Even as the tide of promise rises and buoys our spirits, sadness envelops me. We all know a trip of that sort is never to be.

"Don't forget to call me, girls. And you take good care of my little grandbabies," she laments. She is wearing the morose gaze of a convict facing the electric chair. "Who knows, this could be the last time we ever see each other again." When I tell her to cut out the dramatic stuff, that she's fit as a fiddle, she retorts, "Well, for someone who almost had both legs amputated, I suppose I'm doin' okay. Won't you be surprised if I *do* kick the bucket!" In her eye is a decoy of a thought, one that she's surrounded with velvet ropes. "You might not be celebrating my birthday after all . . . you could be gathering for my *funeral!*" She folds her arms and tilts her head in a queenly pose, thrilled to have the last disturbing word.

"Whatever . . ." Cassie drawls out a bored response. But my Ava, a delicate soul who is distressed by Lila Mae's possibilities, protests, "Please don't say that, Grandma! We'll see you at your birthday party. Love you!"

"Yeah," I remind them all, "let's don't get too choked up, we'll be together in a couple of weeks."

I take a good look at Lila Mae in her early-morning disarray—the matted pearly white hair, the supermarket bedroom slippers. This is certainly not the mother I thought I wanted—an empress in coronet braids and fox furs—a mother, who with one wave of her kid-gloved hand, could build castles and destroy kingdoms. Lila Mae is another story—a pastiche of ordinary traits and mind-boggling contradictions—a housewife whose own shadow frightens her, yet whose desk drawers contain correspondence from famous criminals and whose den is wallpapered with autographed eight-by-ten glossies of Leona Helmsley, O.J. Simpson, even the Boston Strangler.

"Now you girls have emergency supplies, don't ya?" She flashes us an impish grin. "I wouldn't want Metal Fang to get aholt of ya!"

Cassie snatches the bait, asking Lila Mae who the heck is Metal Fang. Lila Mae answers coyly, "Oh, just some foreign killer with one of them hook arms they *never caught.* . . . You ask yer mothers. Yes, if Fang's out there, you'll need flashlights and flares and the like."

"Mother! What are we, six?" I gripe with a huff and a spin of my eyes. "Anyway, don't you think I've thought of all that?"

Even as I protest her nagging, I realize that I—a Miss Lifetime Achievement for Organization award recipient, someone who spends hours quadruple-checking my list of things to do—did not bring an emergency kit. Instead of thanking Lila Mae, whose efficiency annoys me, I chastise her, then make a mental note to stop at a hardware store before we get too far away.

"Now you girls call me by Toos-dee; I'll worry myself to pieces if you don't," she calls to us as the car slides a few inches down the steep driveway. "There'd be nothing left, if I lost my girls. Nothing at all!"

"There she goes with the *dee* business," we joke. "Have a nice *dee!* What *dee* is my doctor's appointment again?" We even start crooning: "Night and *dee,* you are the one!"

"Well . . . you girls." She looks hurt and misunderstood. "I'll just shut my dumb trap, I guess."

"Oh, don't be so touchy," I tell her. "Can't you take a joke?" I release the brake and the car leaps backward.

We blow Lila Mae a kiss and promise to say hello to the Old Highway for her. We'll belt out her favorite songs, "Old Man River" and "Tennessee Waltz"; we'll rub the fenders of the Cadillacs stuck in the ground outside Amarillo, Texas. We'll give our regards to the Big Blue Whale in Catoosa, Oklahoma.

Moments before she disappears from view, she lifts her sapphire-veined hand. Like an actress taking an unexpected curtain call, we see her pink fingertips as she waves another good-bye. I yell, "See you in Kentucky!" although I'm not sure the words get through.

But, now, as the cheap motel blanket scrubs my cheek and I listen to Ava and Cassie horsing around through the plaster wall that separates our rooms, I wonder why we didn't bring Lila Mae along with us. Her lonely figure in the garden waving good-bye, the eucalyptus trees shifting and swaying overhead, and the curve of her smile, produce a haunting brew of emotions. I wonder why, just a mere week after saying good-bye to her, my brain is playing tricks on me, telling me how oh-so-easy—even fun—it would have been to have her traveling with us.

I call the desk clerk and ask for an early wake-up call; then I snap off the light. In the bed next to me, Carleen tosses and turns. I stare at the phosphorescent shadows against the ceiling and rejoin the words that still have me in their grip:

> *Well, if they freed me from this prison, if that railroad train was mine*
> *I bet I'd move it on a little,*
> *Farther down the line, far from*
> *Folsom Prison, that's where I want to stay,*
> *And I'd let that lonesome whistle blow my blues away.*

Unless Metal Fang or Charlie Manson gets us or we actually bump into the killer who murdered the schoolgirl in lime-green socks, we will be seeing Lila Mae in a few weeks' time. Most of the loves of her past and current life will be gathered in a big crepe-papered room. We will play her special tunes and sweep across the dance floor in slow waltzes and lively polkas. And we will feast on her favorite dishes: fried chicken and coconut cream pies. We will lift our spirits with crackling cold Asti Spumante. And in the dark morning hours before the Kentucky sun rises, we will sift through photo albums and swap Lila Mae stories, doubling over in laughter or shaking with tears, and there will be much celebration and merriment.

This isn't the way it really happened,
but this is the story anyway.

—Rebecca Jean Wooten Hamilton Mariani St. Clair

Chapter One

Rebecca
The Queen of Sheba

MAY 1999

Amere two months after the grand opening of Miz Becky's BBQ Shack in Blue Lick Springs, Kentucky, Rebecca's secretary, in total hysterics, pounded on the door, interrupting an important meeting with Rebecca's husband and their business managers. The girl was talking in such circles—heaving and waving her arms this way and that—but, finally, they got it out of her that Jimmy Buzz Burkle had just called. Burkle, the restaurant's manager, said that two men with pantyhose pulled over their heads—one fellow long and rough like a cornstalk, the other as thick and square as a butcher block—had showed up around closing time and tried to stick the place up.

"It was an armed robbery!" Tiffany, the secretary, kept repeating. Her bunny-rabbit-pink eyes blinked and enlarged as if adjusting to the shock of the information. "Something you'd expect in New York City, but in such a small town? It's just horrible beyond belief!"

Normally, Rebecca would have prayed for any disruption to a meeting where the big topic of conversation was the ungodly amount of money she'd been spending. But Miz Becky's was the ultimate touchy subject. The robbery was also the sort of mishap she feared would happen when she and David got the harebrained idea to open the restaurant, a business they knew nothing about (one that was twenty-five hundred miles away from their Los Angeles home to boot).

She told the girl they'd get the lowdown in just a second and tried to shoo her away. But Tiffany was as stubborn as a mule. She continued to stand in the doorway, the shadows from the blinds slashed across her linen suit like prison bars. "I mean, this is really a shock, especially after the way you built Kentucky up . . . shouldn't I try to reach Mr. Burkle?"

With so many people in the room, Rebecca was in no position to do what she really wanted to do, which was to double up her fist and threaten the girl. The secretary had been given specific instructions to hold Rebecca's calls, plus, it was the second time that day alone that she'd gone out of her way to do the exact opposite of what she'd been told.

Earlier, Tiffany had dropped the first bomb, informing Rebecca that the developer who'd been buying up property right and left in her hometown had his eye on her grandmother's farm. Tiffany knew the subject was one that struck panic in Rebecca's heart, but with a shudder of her skirt's kick pleat, she had dashed away, leaving behind just enough information to make Rebecca nauseous at a time when she had meetings and couldn't get to the bottom of things.

The worst part about the situation was that Tiffany had already managed to get some key players riled up. David, Rebecca's husband, took a deep breath and gave his head an irritated shake. "Great," he let out a puff of air. "Just what we need . . . St. Valentine's Day Massacre!"

Since he was the very definition of stability, a man who didn't jump to conclusions, his response was peculiar, especially since the massacre was an expression Rebecca herself always used to get her point across. Besides, nowhere in Tiffany's information—as earth-shattering as she tried to make it—was there anything suggesting the stickup was as drastic as all that.

As perturbed as David was, it was nothing compared to their business manager, Reginald C. Peepers, Jr. He and his associates at Peepers, Peepers and Fishbein were on hand for the monthly, and ghastly, financial meeting. After hearing the robbery news, Peepers, whose eyes were now all lit up like high-beam headlights, gave the table a hearty slap. "JUST WHAT I PREDICTED!" he bellowed. "Just what I predicted!"

The man, or Little Peep as everyone called him behind his back, was a five-foot pipsqueak with lollipop-pink skin and a mouse-brown hairpiece that sat on his head like a fried egg. "Yes, yes, we were afraid of something like this. One way or another the restaurant business will absolutely *kill* you. And don't say I didn't tell you so!"

"That's right, Boss Man! It's the toughest damned business going." On cue, Phil Bustamante, Peepers's chief yes-man, chimed in. "Nine out of ten joints are shut down within six months."

The rest of Peepers's posse—a lachrymose batch of sycophants and henchmen—had their ears pricked in curiosity like anxious German shepherds. They made grunting noises and shifted in their chairs as the stench of triumph wafted over their table.

Since Rebecca had been on the hot seat the entire afternoon justifying her business decisions in general, and Miz Becky's BBQ in particular, the timing of the robbery couldn't have been worse. Just as they did once a month, Little Peep and his lynch mob had marched into David's office with attaché cases, all bulging with financial reports and charts. Peep, passing out statements to each participant, had just spent the last hour reviewing every line and column. They had already pored through the stock portfolio, the household account, and the commercial investment statements. There had also been a review of the redecorating budget of David's corporate offices, a Spanish Inquisition that involved every piece of furniture and art in his voluminous facility. Peepers's eyes—cynical, investigative sickles—had wheeled around the room, taking in the Brazilian mahogany desks, the modern abstract oils, and the Art Deco bronzes. Moving his finger in a rainbow shape, he said, "It's attractive, all right, but expensive." Because Rebecca had overseen the project, he automatically—and erroneously—assumed it was an extravagant debacle.

After that, they spent the next thirty minutes staring at Little Peep's Grand Scheme of Things economic plan—some program that had them living like the Amish for decades then leading the life of Riley when they were eighty or ninety years old. It was propped up on an easel, a big multicolored chart, sectioned off like a pie and filled with arrows and stars and other symbols that were all Greek to Rebecca. To make it work—Little Peep always stared at her at this point—she had to cut her expenses by seventy-five percent. "Especially your Kentucky interests." He had glared at her with his pinball eyes at half-mast and added, "I am dead serious."

Probably to torture her, he saved the worst topic for last. This was the moment of truth Rebecca had been dreading since the previous meeting. A sheaf of papers an inch thick, the heading said: MIZZ BECKY'S BBQ SHACK: PROFIT AND LOSS STATEMENT. Rebecca made a mental note of the misspelling of Miz, something—as minor as it seemed—to use against Peepers if he got uppity.

Little Peep had cleared his throat the way he usually did when he was paving the way for a bombshell and said: "The firm has run the numbers for the barbecue restaurant and, just as I imagined, it is *not* a pretty picture. In fact, as any fool can see, it's an unqualified disaster."

"What *kind* of picture do you expect after such a short time: the Mona Lisa?" Rebecca, her arms plaited at her chest, had refused to give Peep the satisfaction of even glancing at the report. Besides, the man was like a broken record with his "run the numbers" diatribe. "We've run the numbers and I'm afraid—" "We'll get back to you after we've run the numbers," blah, blah, blah.

"I certainly don't expect miracles," Little Peep blared out, "not from this project! What I do expect is numbers that reflect promise. You could keep Miz Becky's open until doomsday and it still wouldn't matter!" When he was anxious or excited—usually when there was somebody else's bad news to discuss—his system sizzled and wheezed, as if you were hearing the motor running for all his organs. "My advice?" he roared, extracting a monogrammed handkerchief and mopping his sweaty forehead, "Cut your losses now . . . *dump it!*"

Rebecca, horrified and panicky, hopped up and said, "Over my dead body!" defending the newly opened business as one that would "practically run itself," and would be less trouble than all of their other business ventures put together. "Kentucky is not like Los Angeles. It has a completely different work ethic!" All this was uttered before she knew anything about the robbery and was accompanied by a Byronic speech singing hosannas in the highest to her beloved home state.

Miz Becky's wasn't one of his typical cold business deals, Rebecca reminded him. Families were involved—mostly relatives and old friends from the Blue Lick Springs crowd, whom you couldn't just abandon overnight. "If you ask me, we haven't given the restaurant a decent chance," she protested. "It's only been a couple of months, for crying out loud!"

"All the same . . . all the same . . . it's a couple of months too many. The handwriting is on the wall."

Not only did Little Peep's speech take gall, it was pure, unadulterated gobbledygook. First of all, he kept insisting that only a sentimental idiot would have invested in a rural town, a spot he assumed was draped in cobwebs and despair. But that wasn't true because CASTLECO, a huge development company, was swooping up property right and left. Plus, Peep's current position was the diametrical opposite of the advice he usually gave them. Time after time, he had convinced Rebecca and David to make one investment or another, then later, he and his accountants would march in swinging their Halliburton briefcases and making a million excuses why their bum-steer stocks or limited partnerships hadn't skyrocketed yet. "Stay the course!" he would bark like a determined ship's captain. "You can't expect miracles overnight." Now Little Peep had the nerve to demand that Miz Becky's, a brand-new restaurant, was supposed to be making money hand over fist, but the thousands they gave him to invest was supposed to be given the same treatment as a Mt. Everest climber—something you wished well, but figured you might never see again.

Rebecca positively refused to allow some weasly accountant to dictate what she and David should do with their own money. With her jaw clenched and her eyes set in a dark smolder, she announced, "I'm sick of these dotcom investments that we're stuck with until kingdom come. They're just worthless pieces of paper. At least Miz Becky's is something tangible." Rebecca wasn't sure David, who ordinarily played referee between her and Little Peep, felt the same way about it, but he was on the telephone, which was the main reason why she was getting by with the bickering to begin with. "Besides, if we end up in the poorhouse," she continued, "then *I'd* rather be the one who put us there, and I want the fruits of our bankruptcy efforts surrounding us!"

"If that's your aim," he hollered, "then trophies and Dom Perignon are in order. You're the fastest horse on the track, a Triple Crown winner!" Although Rebecca could tell the blue-cheeked Peepers was furious—he was all puffed up like a tuba player struggling to hit a high note—at least he didn't call her Secretariat. According to his bookkeeper, this was Rebecca's code name in interoffice memos.

"Investments should be made with your *head*, not your *heart*." Peepers plucked his suspenders with an exultant snap and added, "Just look at the numbers we ran. You'll see for yourself."

"Huh," she retorted, "there's more to life than numbers."

"Actually," he said coolly, "there isn't. If it doesn't work on paper, it doesn't work." He rapped his knuckles against the desk with the finality of a judge's gavel, turning right and left to include his cohorts. "This is a hopeless case!"

Even if Rebecca talked to the men until she was blue in the face, she had a feeling that it was Peepers, Peepers and Fishbein—not Miz Becky's—who were actually the hopeless cases. What did the fuddy-duddy accountants know about dreams and visionary plans anyway? When they made every point by referring to columns and graphs, they dismissed any project that didn't make money galore, and denigrated all purchases that were driven by emotions or instinct. Unfortunately, the latter described perfectly all the love children of Rebecca's investment philosophy—the antiques, artwork, old buildings, and property she collected like charms on a bracelet. She was attracted to feel-good and pride-of-ownership projects, three-dimensional items that could be touched, admired, or passed on to future generations.

If you did it Peepers's way, you'd be living in a shabby apartment in the slums with a slew of eye-popping bankbooks and financial statements—one of those human-interest stories highlighted on the evening news. After you'd kicked the bucket, neighbors would say, "Why, we always thought they were as poor as church mice!"

Truthfully, Rebecca hadn't seen eye to eye with any of their business managers—there had been dozens of them—but Little Peep took the cake. David wasn't crazy about him, either, but he claimed the man was a brilliant economic analyst and, therefore, a necessary evil. As the CEO of a corporation with divisions as far-flung as film, publishing, and cosmetics, David was the last person whose business judgment Rebecca would question. But, as far as she was concerned, Peep would have to be Einstein, Galileo, and Socrates in one to justify putting up with him.

Rebecca knew it was way too much to ask that her husband would defend the barbecue business in public, particularly since the robbery news, but she lobbied him for support anyway.

"David," she had pleaded, "aren't you going to say anything?" The way he had eyed her, you'd have thought he'd forgotten that the barbecue restaurant had actually been his idea. "It can't be as bad as everyone's making it sound."

"It might not be." His fingertips gingerly drummed the incriminating report. "But it sure isn't good." As usual, crisis galvanized all the angles and colors of his face to some stratospheric level of appeal; the muscles beneath his Italian suit were racing with adrenaline, the wheels were turning, the mental gears were shifting. "Well," he sighed, as if to adjust his perspective, "we knew it wouldn't be a picnic."

It didn't take much to picture the scene unfolding in Blue Lick Springs: The tiny Mayberry of a spot would be all atwitter with purring telephones and revved up hot rods. The American Gothics and tobacco farmers would gather their toddlers and grandmas alike to flock to Main Street. Pappy Bagler, the area's Paul Revere, would sputter down Hot Bottom Road on his electric lawn mower, shouting, "There's been a robbery! A BIG ROBBERY!"

Instead of doing what she usually did—which was to turn ordinary issues into cataclysms—Rebecca tried to add some positive angle to the mess. "Now, now, we know how ultradramatic Jimmy Buzz can be. It's possible that the robbery was nothing. Besides, we couldn't be in better hands. After all, he *is* the sheriff."

"Sheriff? Nobody ever told me *that!*" Peepers, his eyebrows like two eagles in flight, turned to Bustamante for verification. "Did you know about this, Phil?"

"Hell, no! Nobody told me a thing about it." Phil Bustamante shoved the air, his hands like two stop signs, as if to say, "Hey, don't pin this on me."

"This isn't exactly high treason, is it?" Rebecca boomeranged the dirty looks right back to the two men. "Haven't you ever heard of someone with two jobs?"

"It's not the number, it's the type for God's sake." Little Peep's bright red bow tie bobbed at his throat. "Barbecue and bullets? Quite a combo if you ask me."

Now that she knew how Little Peep felt about two jobs, she wasn't going to mention Burkle's third: He played the washtub for the Kornkob Mountain Pickers, a local bluegrass band. Anyway, they were stuck with Jimmy Buzz since it was his "world-famous" barbecue recipe Miz Becky's was using.

"Is there a reason why we're stalling?" asked Little Peep. "Get Mr. Burkle on the phone. We could have total pandemonium on our hands." You could tell by the way he was talking that havoc was just what he was hoping for.

"I'd be shocked if that was the case," said Rebecca, stopping to rustle around in her purse as if the robbery was the least of her worries. "*Very* shocked, actually."

"Well," said Tiffany, "that's not the impression he gave *me*. He said it was urgent, extremely urgent!"

The only thing going Rebecca's way was that they couldn't get through to the restaurant. "All circuits are busy." The woman on the recording made the announcement sound as if she were imparting good news. "Please try your call later."

Peep yanked at his shirtsleeve and checked his platinum Cartier watch. Seeing the hour, he flipped his palms into the air and fumed, "How can the circuits be busy? Are the Hatfields and McCoys at it again? Does *anything* in the sticks work?"

While the minutes ticked by and Little Peep's momentum mounted, Rebecca was in the advanced stages of hyperventilation. David still wasn't saying much, except "Just keep dialing the phone," but he didn't have to. Although they had an ironclad rule to maintain a harmonious appearance in public, she was familiar with the aura of catastrophe. A typhoon was brewing in her husband's eyes, one that turned them a ferocious turquoise. They were not exactly boring holes in her, but they were telling Rebecca that Miz Becky's losses were so drastic, the general situation so dire that, if she would just listen to reason, she would see it his way, or else. In other words, he looked like he wanted to brain her.

It was too good to be true that the phone would stay busy or that Little Peep would finally get fed up and leave or that Tiffany, who was *tsk-tsk*ing like an officious Mother Hen, would rush off to a hot date. Nor would David, running late for another appointment, suddenly say, "I'm outta here," and tell Rebecca to fill him in later. No, no, the fortuitous scattering of the witnesses would not happen. In a matter of minutes, the sheriff would be on the line and all the bloody details, like worms after a torrential rain, would come bobbing to the surface.

While everyone was preoccupied with red ink, Rebecca made a fast getaway into her husband's private bathroom. As she stood under the blue light, staring at the mirror, her chest heaved up and down in a struggle for composure. It was a pretty dismal sight: Her eyes were two olive nuggets suspended above cheeks as pale as lily petals and her hair, reddish brown and usually lustrous, was a droopy mop. The henna rinse, which was supposed to brighten and lift her face, could only do so much. After all, it was a hair dye, not a crane. Overall, it was a look that would have sparked her grandmother to say, "Whar the devil ya goin' lookin' lak that? Ragpicker's alley?"

Dumping the contents of her cosmetics bag on the counter, she grabbed her lipstick and the vial of Chanel No. 5, daubing behind each earlobe. Good old Chanel, she thought, her lifesaver. Two swipes of Russet Moon, a whisk of seashell-pink blush, and a fragment of allure reappeared. Trying to repair her mussed hairdo, she took her brush, giving her hair one hundred very deliberate strokes. She noticed that the lightbulb was flickering; plus, they were low on hand lotion and jasmine room spray, so she searched for a notepad, making a list of items for Tiffany to pick up. She opened every drawer and scrutinized every shelf in the medicine cabinet, ending up with all sorts of things to buy—cologned soaps and hair tonics—and even more reminders to call the painter to touch up the floorboard, the tile man to regrout the backsplash, and an electrician to install a dimmer switch.

She must have lost track of time, because David jiggled the doorknob and said, "Rebecca, are you okay?" She fibbed and said she was fine, although she was anything but.

There was an excellent reason why Rebecca was dawdling, why calamitious thoughts in two languages—coup de grace and final nails in her coffin—sprinted through her head. Somehow, she had gotten involved with three new businesses besides Miz Becky's, ones that her husband and Little Peep knew absolutely nothing about. None of them—namely a barbershop, confectionery, and bowling alley—were actually off the ground yet, but the trio of skeletons were thumping the closet door. So, it would be a total disaster if Sheriff Burkle filled them in on the robbery *and* accidentally spilled the beans. Since all lives in Blue Lick were an open book and nobody in town honored the psychological warfare of husbands and wives and accountants, this was not only possible, but highly probable.

Rebecca could hear it now—all the particulars about the shipment containing the antique barber pole and the decorative bowling trophies. There would be exclamations of disbelief about the flood of candy shop employment applications . . . and oohs and ahhs over the big, expensive marble counter being installed.

And, if bad karma and Lady Fortune were really in cahoots against her, Burkle could even start blabbing about Rosemont. For the past several months, Rebecca'd been driving everyone crazy with questions about the Greek Revival plantation and nobody ever had the scoop. This would probably be the one time she'd get the unabridged lowdown. Rebecca hadn't actually purchased the house yet—for the single reason that it wasn't for sale—but she wasn't going to let such minor details keep her from exploring the possibility.

Rebecca wasn't a fool; she knew David and Little Peep would find out about all the new activity sooner or later, but she wanted to dole out the information in her own good time and at opportune moments like the split second after the *Wall Street Journal* announced record profits for David's corporation, or—better yet—after she and her husband shared a bottle of Pauillac and a moonlit walk on Malibu Beach. Until then, she had no choice except to tell David and Little

Peep the same thing she always told the U.S. Customs officer: "I have nothing to declare."

At the moment, the mere suggestion that she was contemplating more activity in the one-horse Kentucky town could trigger Armageddon . . . well, she didn't think it would be *that* bad, but it would be tip-top mayhem all right. But the two men couldn't be any madder at her than she was at herself. She had played up the town as heaven on earth, only to have gun-toting hoodlums make her into a liar. She had even brushed aside her grandmother's and uncle's comments. "Oh, Blue Lick ain't as perfect as ya think! We got our problems, too, yessireebob!" Olive would poke her hickory cane into the freshly mowed grass and say, "We got hooligans lak ever'one else."

As usual, Rebecca had taken their comments as the high-pitched fits of small-town dramatists. "Their idea of a crime is a few dollars missing from a vending machine," Rebecca assured David, "or some stolen hubcaps."

All the romantic beach outings in the world wouldn't guarantee David's support for a project as ill-fated as the one Peep described. And she could lobby all night long about the barbecue restaurant being David's bright idea, but Rebecca had much more at stake, since Blue Lick Springs was her hometown.

While they waited to reach Sheriff Burkle, Peepers and his associates were already making more noise than the ringing of a Christmas Eve cash register. Bustamante was punching a laptop computer, some guy named Conklin was running numbers on his pocket calculator, and Little Peep was dictating a memo on his tape recorder. He kept fiddling with the financial reports, shuffling and fanning them around like a Las Vegas blackjack dealer. The last thing he said before they dialed Sheriff Burkle again was, "Yes, yes, we should take immediate steps to shut the place down."

When Rebecca didn't jump up and scream bloody murder, Peepers added, "I'm talking first thing tomorrow morning!"

"We'll see about that, won't we?" she muttered defiantly. She swiped a look at the despicable Peepers. He was holding a Montblanc ballpoint pen in his hand like a billy club. He beat out the *Dragnet* theme against the table and gave her an amused, deadeye stare. For all her big talk about Little Peep not having the upper hand and for all her threats about wrapping his pretentious satin bow tie around his neck and choking him until his tongue popped out, there was no denying that he was going to be very tough to deal with, very tough indeed.

Chapter Two

Carleen Raye Wooten Carlyle
The Middle Girl

MAY 1999

With all the starving children in China, Carleen certainly didn't have the nerve to gripe about her own circumstances, mostly because she couldn't put her finger on anything hair-raising enough to qualify her for *The Jerry Springer Show*. Plus, every time she mentioned dashed hopes and torched dreams, her friends would either roll their eyes or tell her to join the club! Regardless of her inability to clearly define her situation in ten highly dramatic words or less, things just hadn't panned out. As a result, Carleen walked around with a malaise that was too heavy for cocktail hour chatter but of no particular interest to the police.

The fact that she had complaints at all would have been puzzling to anyone reading the U.S. Census Bureau report. According to that document, she was a specimen of statistical perfection. Even though she looked good on paper, Carleen had the feeling that life was passing her by.

Each New Year's Eve, she'd remove the brass notepad from her drawer, the one that said: THE FASTER I GO, THE BEHINDER I GET, and write down her resolutions. She would stop dillydallying around and be more like Rebecca, squeezing destiny by the jugular and grabbing at all the merry-go-round rings. She was tired of those frightening thunderbolts of reality—a friend's funeral, another birthday, or a deejay's announcement: "And that was Buffalo Springfield from 1969." If the next thirty years flew by as fast as the last thirty, she'd have nothing to show for them but insignificant encounters with total strangers.

Carleen hated to add up the countless hours she'd spent listening to a waitress's complaints about a tyrannical husband or the amount of time she'd wasted on all fours in a shopping mall helping an elderly woman search for a lost earring. It was embarrassing how many grocery checkers' life stories she knew. And what about all the career pointers she'd dished out to restroom attendants, not to mention all the anonymous street-corner infants she'd cootchy-cootchy-cooed.

For Carleen, these incidents were more than random acts of charity; they were a second career. Lila Mae, who saw it as a good thing—meaning her daughter was a chip off the old block—told Carleen she should be proud, that she was a "people person." Friends and John Does alike agreed, referring to her as a bleeding heart and a Good Samaritan, but Carleen knew the truth: She was a plain, old-fashioned pushover.

One by one, her days were smashed into inconsequential shards by everyday acquaintances. There was Della Hedger, the school secretary who coaxed Carleen to serve hot lunch or sell raffle tickets, and Brent Randolph, a single father who lived hand to mouth. He convinced her to carpool his son, Cody, who lived way out of Carleen's area, and to fix the boy's lunch every day. There was also Anita Roundtree, her disabled neighbor, who had Carleen right where she wanted her: baby-sitting Danny Boy and Liberace, her two Doberman pinschers, anytime Anita wanted. According to Roundtree, Carleen was the only one who could do anything with the dogs.

"That's bullshit! And you fall for it," Nelson, her husband, told her. "Just tell the woman you can't do it . . . it's as easy as that!" When Carleen reminded him that Roundtree was the "poor crippled woman who lives all by herself," Nelson was unrepentant. "She has no business having pets if she can't take care of them."

It wasn't that Carleen was completely wishy-washy or incapable of taking a stand. In fact, she had strong opinions and, in some incidents, real gumption. But, before she put her foot down, she had to be boiling hot, on the verge of explosion. Dr. Lorraine Broadman, a popular Bay Area radio therapist, had called that reaction an "inappropriately motivated *no*." Broadman, to whom Carleen listened every day, advised her audience that, "Saying *no* on a day-to-day basis should be matter of fact, just as simple as saying *yes*." Broadman had also urged them to analyze how they got into their predicaments by spotting patterns, something to help them avoid repeat performances.

Carleen thought she was making progress when she was able to say "maybe" instead of "yes." But, Dr. Broadman, in yet another session, threw her for a loop when she declared, "*Maybe* is for wimps. It suggests possibilities. It tells the other person there's room for negotiation."

As cut-and-dried as Broadman made it sound, and as dead set as Carleen was to stand her ground, she still ended up in all sorts of hot water.

Her most recent dilemma was one that didn't fit any pattern, and one that proved that the situations were getting worse, not better. She had just gotten rid of the Jehovah's Witnesses when someone started calling her home and hanging up at all hours of the day and night. She had a pretty good feeling it was Smitty, the ex-con she'd met when she chaperoned a field trip for her daughter's civics class. The man, a former jewel thief, had spent twenty years in and out of Vacaville state prison for armed robbery, but according to the warden conducting the tour, he was supposedly fully rehabilitated. Normally, Carleen would complain to her mother, who was prone to such encounters herself, only to have Lila Mae say, "Oh, how sweet! You did the right thing, honey." This time, even she hit the ceiling and said, "Surely you've got more sense than that!"

The excursion to Vacaville, one Carleen had volunteered to help organize, was meant to discourage the preteens from leading a life of crime. Smitty had started out on the right foot, assuring the group that crime didn't pay, but one little boy asked him, "What's the biggest thing you ever swiped?" and in no time, the man was telling swashbuckling tales of Monte Carlo casino heists and James Bondian escapades. Naturally, his behavior had infuriated the warden and dismayed the parents— particularly Carleen, who felt somewhat responsible for the trip.

For all Smitty's gloating, he went out of his way to tell the students that he had never killed a man. "I mighta robbed 'em blind, but they're all alive and kickin'!" He threw out his chest in pride and the children even gave him a round of spirited applause.

In spite of his large, intimidating frame and shady background, the man seemed frail. His hair was frosty white and hung like icicles around his thin, lined face. One eye, a twinkling, chalky gray globe, roamed around as if searching for greener pastures. The other eye, which they found out was glass, stayed fixed to one spot.

While there was no question that the man had everyone at their wit's end, he had struck Carleen as a harmless sort. As they had walked the aisles of the prison block, Smitty, whose name was Arthur Smith, had told Carleen all about his only son, Leonard Slidell, who had been so embarrassed by his father that he kept his mother's maiden name. Leonard, a gifted violinist, had been forced to give up a Juilliard scholarship and a promising career in music so he could hold down the fort—the family's pest control business—while his father paid his debt to society. As the story unfolded, tears had fallen from the man's one good eye.

The school group had kept its distance, and the other chaperones had snubbed him, too. But now—three years later and through a chain of circumstances Carleen was hard-pressed to remember—the ex-con and his violinist son were coming to exterminate her house for termites.

Nobody was more shocked or agitated by this development than Carleen herself. It was ridiculous that the random meeting had resulted in a first-name-basis relationship with such an unlikely character, but that was hardly a first. It was the fumigation appointment that really baffled her, since Carleen was against pesticides altogether. Not only was she a card-carrying member of the Environmental Watchdogs, she had organized protest marches, and had written editorials condemning extermination. Worse than all that, the termite treatment was something she had talked several of her neighbors out of doing to their own homes and something that would make her the laughingstock of Apollo Drive when the bug company showed up with canisters of poison and a huge red tent to treat hers.

Unlike other activists who pumped placards and embraced ideals but had scant firsthand knowledge, Carleen was the voice of experience. Several years before, when she and Nelson hadn't known better, they exterminated their first home without batting an eye. They diligently followed the technician's safety instructions, leaving the house and returning three days later. They were shocked when they opened the front door and stalagmites of black, cottony dust greeted them. Carleen had wanted to turn around and leave, but Nelson, anxious to sleep in his own "God-damned bed," said it wasn't anything that Lysol couldn't handle. He told Carleen to open all the windows and spray everywhere with the antiseptic air freshener. Although she went along with him, Cassie, who had asthma, wheezed so badly that she ended up in Alameda Hospital's emergency room. Plus, two English ivy plants and Moby Dick, a goldfish that Carleen had forgotten all about, were deader than doornails. Even Carleen was nauseous and dizzy, a condition that could only be connected to the spraying. It was months before the odor diminished and their various illnesses subsided.

Nelson, suddenly a big supporter of chemicals, had said the "illness" was nonsense, a figment of Carleen's imagination. "You'd be on the cover of every damned medical journal in the country if everything you complain about was really wrong with you." In Nelson's book you weren't sick until you were Sunny von Bulow or unless you were Nelson himself, in which case hangnails were treated like inoperable cancer. As for Cassie, what did Carleen expect? Their daughter had asthma, obviously she'd have an occasional attack.

It was bad enough that lightning had struck once; but she was resolved not to repeat their first horrendous experience. So, when Carleen got a hunch that the Poseidon, their practically brand-new home, also had termites, she didn't say boo to Nelson. He had a grudge against their house to begin with—partly because that particular design was known as the "lemon" of Mount Olympus Park, but mostly because Carleen had chosen it. "You just had to have the Poseidon, didn't you . . . ? 'Oh, look at the cathedral ceiling and the willow tree,' " he would mimic Carleen's reaction that first day. So the termite discovery would be one more episode to add to the Poseidon Adventure. On top of the construction idiosyncrasies that irked Nelson, in the five years since they purchased it, they had watched while the Colossus, Titan, and Zeus—the three other model homes in the development—had escalated in value while the Poseidon was in a holding pattern, barely worth the two hundred and fifty thousand dollars they had paid for it. Guess whose fault Nelson—who had favored the Zeus—claimed that was?

Carleen knew they'd have to do something, but she was waiting for Dr. Zollinger's Poplar Extract Formula, a safe, highly effective organic treatment developed by a Swiss scientist. It sounded almost too good to be true in that it was the cure-all for everything from dentures to hardwood floors. But there was something about the concoction that drove termites crazy. In any case, the formula was scheduled to hit the market in a few months, which is when she'd decided to break the news to Nelson.

In the meantime, he found out about the termites, anyway. This was thanks to some bad luck and Carleen's rotten judgment. Knowing Nelson was dying to use his fancy new tools, she asked him to help her hang an oil painting, only he couldn't locate his hammer. A tinkerer extraordinaire, he had a Masonite board where he kept every gadget imaginable, each one with a silhouette drawn around it, each one—complicated drills and bits, spools of wire, electric screwdrivers—in its proper place. "Can you believe that?" He was prancing around like a high-strung show horse. "Everything's here except the one thing I need!" Before he went into orbit, Carleen asked him if a Salomon ski boot was heavy enough to do the job, but Nelson said, "Carleen, we have a hammer and I'm going to find it, by God!"

Normally when he said "by God" it meant that he would explore every nook and cranny of their house, so her heart was slapping against her chest in dread. The shed, a graveyard of secret purchases, was no man's land to a husband who neatly folded his dirty clothes before depositing them in a laundry bin. For starters, he opened the shed door and two drapery rods fell forward, bopping him right between the eyes.

"Jesus Christ!" he hollered, batting away the brass poles, then kicking them across the floor. "Junk, junk, everywhere I look there's junk!"

Although the hammer was still nowhere to be found, during his search and seizure, he rounded up two tole lamps, a Federal game table, a Windsor rocker, and several scatter rugs. There was also the plein air watercolor, an antique "Rebecca at the Well" teapot, a bamboo hat rack, a tortoise tea caddy, and an aquatint of Mt. McKinley.

"My God, Carleen!" Nelson yelled, heat coiling from his pores, his blood racing like engine oil. "We could have owned a Rembrandt with all the money you've wasted on this crap."

As usual, he started switching subject matter, going from the misplaced hammer to the party invitation that Carleen had forgotten to mention. He complained that his shoes hadn't been polished according to West Point regulations and that some "total, complete idiot" had stored the Christmas lights and the glass ornaments in the same box. "This place is a wreck, an absolute wreck!" All the while his eyes bugged, the irises swirling into raging kaleidoscopes. "No wonder you can't accomplish anything!"

It was true that Carleen wasn't the most organized person in the world, but she did the best she could and there were no Hortensias or Blancas or Rosas to help her out.

By the time Nelson found the loathsome hammer, which was back in the garage about two feet from its Masonite silhouette, he was like a boiler room explosion. He kicked a wastebasket that tumbled over the concrete floor. Furious that he had stubbed his toe, he got mad at the hammer for starting the whole thing. So, he chopped it through the air like a berserk Indian chief, yelling, "DAMN IT TO HELL!" Finally, he jerked his arm backward and pitched the hammer toward the rafters like he never wanted to see it again. It somersaulted a couple of times, bashed into a ten-speed bike, then completely disappeared. Carleen waited for it to go kerplunk!, but the next thing she knew, Nelson had yelled, "DUCK!" and they scrambled for cover.

As they watched the plaster fall in fine, steady shafts and listened to the shifting beams, Nelson moaned, "Not again! How many times do we have to go through this?"

"Go through *what*, Nelson?" Carleen knew full well what was wrong but she played innocent. "What *is* it?"

"Termites!" Nelson was panting, perspiration crescents blooming under his shirtsleeves, "God . . . damned . . . termites!"

Carleen begged him to check out the rafter situation with the binoculars, but he insisted on climbing up the ladder for a bird's-eye view. As he mounted the steps, his eye cocked in curiosity, he inspected the beams the way a customer checks a diamond through a jeweler's loupe. Also, his head had disappeared into a small storage loft where he was skulking around with the flashlight. Carleen couldn't understand him too well, since he was crawling on his belly like a soldier in a foxhole, but she heard him say, "For Christ's sake, they're in here, too!"

A terrible urge lashed across Carleen's brain as she noticed that Nelson's legs were pedaling the air like a bicyclist, trying to locate the top step. She wondered what would happen if something (or someone) happened to jostle the ladder? She tried to camouflage this embryo of a notion, hoped to cram it into some secret gully. But there it came at a hundred miles an hour—one big premeditated murder of a thought.

Soon enough, Nelson had his feet back on the ground, marching to, then fro, like a hyperactive prosecutor. "Oh, this is perfect, just perfect! You work like a damned dog to buy a house and it collapses in front of your very eyes! What does a man have to do to get rid of these damned monsters!"

What a sight for the Contra Costa courthouse, Carleen mused, her splinter-dotted, worldly attorney husband with his pewter hair and monogrammed shirt—howling like a longshoreman. She also detected yet another layer to Nelson's rage; the termite was much more than a household pest and the extermination was anything but a run-of-the-mill procedure. It was actually an antediluvian struggle pitting man against beast. She had seen that club-swinging, Neanderthal gleam in his eye the first time they fumigated.

To keep Nelson distracted, Carleen kept telling him things probably weren't as bad as they seemed, but the reason she had been fixed in one spot like a doll on a metal stand was because she had noticed a pile of orange sawdust underneath a wooden toolbox. When she took a better look, she saw that the entire leg was missing! She'd spread what she could of the dust on the ground, stamping it with her foot like she was putting out a campfire. Plus she was hiding another pile with her left foot.

Carleen kept making optimistic remarks like, "Maybe the termites are just in a few planks," but Nelson insisted that they needed to take "immediate action!" The issue was a Bunyanesque monster, a topic with second and third winds and Nelson was breathing down her neck with his "top priority!" talk. If he would only slow down, Carleen could wait for the organic formula.

Another thing that kept Carleen from jumping on the extermination bandwagon so fast was something their contractor told her. Apparently, there was a welded section of the garage gutter that had separated from the galvanized T-joint, which meant that rainwater was dripping down the load-bearing wall, which weakened the soldering, thereby creating stress cracks and leaks or some such. The contractor had put so much emphasis on "*eventually* this or that *might* happen" that Carleen hadn't seen the urgency to fix it. In any case, for all they knew, they might not even have a huge termite problem. Chances were that it was actually dry rot. At least that's what the contractor thought.

Just to placate Nelson and the ex-con, who somehow had gotten the entire story out of her and kept high-pressuring her, Carleen made an appointment with Smitty's A-1 Extermination Company. But, that was as far as she was going to take it.

Before the technicians arrived, Carleen would psychologically prepare herself, trying to dream up every possible argument to rebutt the fast talkers. If the men said this, Carleen would respond with that. If they told her such-and-such, she'd combat it with so-and-so. She would imagine that the fate of her loved ones was at stake. She pictured Cassie trapped in the wreckage of a car, her golden locks spread around her like a mermaid's tresses, sirens blaring, hysterical bystanders collecting around her. Finally, she'd pay homage to Dr. Broadman, memorizing certain power phrases to bolster her confidence.

All that misery could be avoided if Carleen stuck to her guns with the termite men. She knew she'd be up against it—slick talker that Smitty was—plus he was bringing his violinist son, so there would be two of them, but she would sleepwalk through their spiel, be polite, maybe even string them along if that's what it took. In any case, it would be a freezing cold day in hell before she gave the exterminators the official go-ahead.

Chapter Three

Irene Gaye Wooten
Baby Sister

MAY 1999

It just killed Irene that she had to take orders from an absolute nincompoop, but she was getting a divorce from her fifth husband and her attorney said it would look very bad if she didn't make some attempt to find a job. Every Sunday she looked in the *Los Angeles Times* Help Wanted section but nothing appealed to her. As she scanned the columns of the newspaper, the jobs seemed suitable for ditchdiggers or astrophysicists.

But, three weeks before she was to appear in court, Edgar M. Goldfarb, her attorney, left her an ultimatum on the answering machine: "Ms. Wooten, I can assure you that the judge will not look kindly on your employment status . . . unless you can prove you're medically unable to work. Of course I'll represent you to the best of my ability . . . but this is how I expect the judge to rule."

Irene called Goldfarb back, reminding him of her carpal tunnel syndrome, a condition that prevented her from doing simple tasks, one that was actually responsible for several aborted attempts at holding down a job. In the past year alone, she had been dismissed from the Carousel Video position for inadvertently destroying the *Armageddon* display; and there was also the incident with the overturned root-beer floats at

Tony's Hot Spot. Her efforts to branch out into a new field didn't help either. She was fired from Ding-A-Ling Beeper Corporation after the first week even though the owner, an asshole named Wally Polk, said the name of his company fit her to a T. She did a little better as a shampoo girl at the Kut Kastle, where she lasted one month.

The fact that Irene was sixty pounds overweight, had a body so lumpy it resembled tufted furniture, and wore nose rings and black nail polish didn't help matters. Neither did the purple-and-ruby-red hair that covered her head in porcupine spikes. None of that information fazed Goldfarb. He simply said, "Surely, Ms. Wooten, there is *something* you can do."

Whenever she pressed Goldfarb for some satisfactory conclusion to the messy divorce, she'd get another huffy speech. "What do you want from the poor guy, Ms. Wooten?" he'd scream. "He's already totally wrecked!"

It was those comments that reinforced Irene's suspicion that her own attorney wasn't even on her side, and the reason she was penniless, depressed, and disenfranchised was because she really hadn't gotten a fair shake. Goldfarb—a name, rank, and serial number sort of guy—never wanted any of the juicy information that could be favorable to her side. He wouldn't even get a restraining order against her soon-to-be ex, saying Irene couldn't establish a legitimate reason for one. Anytime Irene said, "I *think* I saw Darrell hiding—," the attorney would stop her cold. "We're not talking fantasyland. Either you actually saw him or you didn't. Now which one was it, Ms. Wooten? You can't slap a restraining order on someone merely to satisfy your thirst for revenge. It becomes part of their record."

Irene told Goldfarb that was the whole point. She wanted to ruin Darrell's life just like he'd ruined hers! Although she was kind of joking, the lawyer stared at her, twisting his black, bushy mustache and shaping his mouth into a lordly prune.

It was a different story when Darrell had accused Irene of shattering the windshield of his Hyundai with a baseball bat. A scarlet-faced Goldfarb had shrieked, "Now why in God's name did you do that?" Irene made the mistake of asking, "How did he find out it was me?"

"Baby Sister!" Rebecca scolded her. "That was a dead giveaway. You should have said, 'What makes him think *I* did it?' or 'How dare he accuse me of such a thing!' "

As if all that wasn't enough, Goldfarb had sky-high fees . . . not that she had actually paid any of them yet.

Anyway, that's when Lila Mae got the bright idea that Irene should take a breather and relocate out of state. At long last, Irene would link up with some of her connections, something Lila Mae had always been big on. "Kentucky would be good for you, honey, and you could spend time with your grandmother and other kinfolk." What her mother was probably thinking was, "Let them handle the total casualty for a while."

Through the years there had been so much fanfare about Kentucky that Irene had always felt like a hollow tree, one that had survived only because of its historical roots. When her family had left the Bluegrass, Irene was still Baby Sister, a mere infant, wrapped in a pink blanket like an ice cream cone, two dinky eyeballs gaping into the jeweled green landscape they were leaving behind. In the intervening years, she had heard story after story about Kentucky, and their trip across country with Juanita and Benny Featherhorse on Route 66. With every telling, the tales became more fantastical and highly sentimental. Oh, the stallions galloping across dewy bluegrass! Banjo-plunking gents wooing flounce-skirted ladies! The birthplace of Abraham Lincoln and bourbon and Man O'War and every other icon that made the country great! There was nothing like it in the entire universe!

Although Irene often asked, "What the hell are we doing in California, then?" Lila Mae's replies were vague, blaming the relocation on "this and that," and "one thing or another." There was even some flimsy story about a fly-swatter business deal that flopped. Shortly thereafter, it was California here we come!

Time after time they made Irene feel like a complete imbecile just because she didn't know all the words to "My Old Kentucky Home," and a clueless bystander when they'd crack jokes and reminisce about old times. They would touch Irene's arm and apologize, "It's a Southern thing," as if they were charter members of an elite club, one from which Baby Sister was doomed to be blackballed.

Irene was a cog in the wheel of bad timing, the Wooten girl who had reached Los Angeles just when the ghosts of the 1950s—poodle skirts and Hula-Hoops and Elvis Presley—had vanished. It was a sliver of time when Irene was a muse for disaster, and she romanced it the way most people courted prosperity. Irene was a dirigible floating in the polluted air of Los Angeles, tethered to reality by one thin strand. And that strand—her only hope for salvation, according to Lila Mae—was her background.

A sneak preview of what awaited Irene had revealed itself through the east–west procession of kin, a cavalcade of freeloading characters, who turned up through the years on the Wootens' doorstep. Back and forth they came: the car mechanics with snot-nosed children and green-toothed wives; the swindlers with screwy inventions and pie-in-the-sky schemes. Why they flocked to the Wootens for inspiration was anybody's guess, since the family had never achieved the wild success they had sought in California. Or, as Lila Mae always put it, "We had such high hopes, but things just haven't panned out."

The legend of Kentucky, as fascinating and entertaining as it could often be, dangled above Irene like a Damocles headdress and soon she began to loathe the family history, the way an adopted child would yearn to locate his mysterious birth parents and resent them at the exact same time.

Except for one trip to attend their grandfather Wooten's funeral, an overnight excursion attended by the entire family, Irene had never really set foot in Kentucky. She was bursting with curiosity, dying to scout around for some of those celebrated sights, but they had gone straight from the plane to Silkes's Funeral Parlor. Rebecca and Carleen had sobbed and touched their grandfather's worn pin-striped suit. Irene had merely stared at the waxy body, mummified by his best buddy—Jack Daniel's—while plumbing the depths of her emotions for some heart-felt connection to the stranger swaddled in pleats and mahogany.

That afternoon, the girls had ordered cheeseburgers from the Blue Gill Lodge, the family's favorite roadhouse. They linked their arms around one another's shoulders, and said, "Can you believe it? We're here! We're really here!" Even Irene was included in an exclusive soror-ity that in the past had consisted of only Carleen and Rebecca. The trip also revealed another side of her big sister, who was usually as moody as the Gulf Coast weather. In Kentucky, Rebecca was charming, giggly, and full of pranks.

Later, they borrowed Uncle Shorty's truck and rushed down country roads, red dirt flying from their wheels, as they marveled at waterfalls and peacocks and sunflower-lined paths. It was only when they stopped at the Pope Lick covered bridge, and Carleen recalled the time when Spitfire Youngblood had dumped the carcasses of three suffocated kittens close by, that the illusion of nirvana was shattered.

At dusk, they had gone to a relative's house for beef stew, and warm cornbread wrapped in a coarse linen cloth. After the get-together, they had kissed their grandmother's papery cheek and waved good-bye through the parlor's plate glass window. That evening they departed on the red-eye.

As the plane's engines whirred, Rebecca had given her home turf one wistful survey and sighed, "It's so beautiful, I hate to leave . . . everything about it is so Rockwellian."

"Yessireebob, that says it all." Lila Mae always agreed with Rebecca whether she knew what she was talking about or not.

"What the hell does that mean?" Irene, warming up the surly, Los Angeles version of herself, had given everyone her black-cloud glare.

"Beats me," their father said.

"You know, Norman Rockwell, the painter," Rebecca explained, always with the unspoken "you morons!" tone spiking her voice. "A picture-perfect town with soda fountains and blue skies and white clapboard houses."

In mere hours, the pure paint-box colors and oxygen charge of Kentucky had slowly disintegrated into a pudding of smog and traffic and the chop of a thousand planes and police helicopters. As they landed, they had all peered into the ugly rows of Los Angeles neighborhoods and drab warehouses, dreading the drive back to their home when they would become co-conspirators in the sprawling, polluted catastrophe.

In the coming weeks, Irene found herself picturing Blue Lick Springs, yearning for another look at this paradise she called her home state, the name she filled in on the place of birth blanks on questionnaires. She tucked away the thought, figuring it would blend in with the woodwork of so many other stray desires.

So, for that reason alone, Irene would not deny that the idea of getting away from it all, particularly to a safe, foreign haven, did appeal to her. Moving out of state would also solve—at least temporarily—the problem of the increasingly violent Darrell, who had obviously graduated to some higher, and more draconian, form of inebriation. He was already tottering on such a lofty rung of drug abuse that he was waiting for new pharmacological breakthroughs before he could advance.

During their courtship, those blurry days and jet-black nights, filled with Thunderbird wine and multicolored pills, Darrell had been so utterly charming, so fascinated by Irene and . . . oh so supportive. When she was a stick, he reassured her that thin was in. Not every man liked women with meat on their bones, he told her. When she put on a few pounds, there was more for a man to love. On restaurant napkins he would scribble juvenile, but endearing, poems, and often he'd surprise her with tea roses and Edelweiss chocolate.

How long ago and faraway those hearts-and-flowers days all seemed. They had been replaced by new scenes, scenes that had multiple performances of Darrell's little love pats and many curtain calls of deep, black bruises for her collection.

There were horrors touched off by nothing more than a forgotten trip to the dry cleaner when Irene had walked into their duplex empty-handed. A fuming Darrell was waiting for his black wool trousers, waiting as if they were the only pair he owned. "You didn't go to the cleaners, *did* you?" His face had twisted and contorted and the right shoulder was warming up with its involuntary twitch. She reached up to pat his cheek, but before she could open her mouth to say, "I'm sorry," the dreaded arm lifted up.

Darrell darted here and there, punching lamps, slashing upholstery, opening and slamming doors, pulling out every kitchen drawer . . . out flew the silverware, utensils, the butcher knives . . . all of it a whirling, metallic storm before her bloody, half-shut eyes. All around her, as her head exploded in pain, were pinpricks of blurry light. The room had swirled with objects as if the feathers of a hundred birds were flying be-

fore her, little slices of walls and ceilings and floors, all shifting underfoot like a ship on vicious seas.

To calm him down, Irene, wrestling for lucidity, her crescent eyes
rolling in the back of her head, her glasses lying in some unknown shrub
of debris, kept saying, "It's all right, don't worry . . . it's okay." She was
all too aware that the reassurances should have been the other way
around, but it was anything, anything to break his diabolical trance.

Still fresh in Irene's mind was the night she was trapped in a closet
for hours, listening to the intoxicated mutterings of Darrell in the middle of a drug deal with a gang member named Angel, a small, devil
dragon of a man, who had a diamond hoop in his nose and geometric
razor designs on his face, while she took shallow breaths and squeezed
her eyes together, waiting for some miracle and praying to a God she
wasn't even sure she believed in.

In the midst of these nightmares, when she could hardly keep her
wits about her, Irene always formulated a game plan, one involving
packed bags and twilight escapes. She had seen enough *Oprah*s and *Sally
Jessy*s to know where this road led—more broken bones, hospital emergency rooms, and worse.

Like clockwork, Darrell would apologize, appearing with expensive
colognes or African trade-bead anklets. Despite the absence of all con-
nective tissue to logic, Irene kept hoping these incidents were isolated
but, of course, that was never the case.

In her heart of hearts, deep down in the black soil where starry-eyed
notions were smothered, Irene had always known the situation with
Darrell was hopeless. That she had no other place to go, that she had
burned her traditional bridges, that in her wallet was her driver's license
and a one-dollar bill, and that she had made an absolute jackass of herself with everyone she knew in her very passionate defense of Darrell—
each was a wall or stone of her prison's architecture.

It was hard to believe that it was easier to endure Darrell's moods
and outbursts, to keep accepting the growing number of fractures and
bruises like little carvings on a lover's tree trunk, yet three whole years
had gone by, ripped out of her life, a life that had little to show for itself
except the physical space taken up by her body.

To keep her momentum high, Irene kept recounting the practical reasons why she should move to Kentucky, throwing some of Lila Mae's propaganda into the mix. When that wasn't enough, she reviewed the actual footage, keeping the embers of the Darrell catastrophe burnished in her head.

Irene couldn't be positive about such mysterious things, but somebody—God, Buddha, Mohammed, Lucifer?—seemed to be giving her little hints, nudging her ever so gently in Kentucky's direction. Every time Irene turned on the television, it was crammed with advertisements depicting small towns where everyone waved and knew your first name, towns exactly like Blue Lick Springs. She had even been stuck at a broken traffic signal, not budging for twenty minutes, right in front of the Van Nuys First Methodist Church. The slogan in the big, glass box was typical of the catchy phrases churches used to get the attention of gridlocked, heathen motorists. They were the exact type that usually caused Irene to roll her eyes in sarcasm and say, "Oh, brother!" But this one—WHEN YOU FLEE TEMPTATION, DON'T LEAVE A FORWARDING ADDRESS—really, truly seemed to have been custom-made for Baby Sister.

Chapter Four

Rebecca

MAY 1999

The horsepower that drove Rebecca's need to rehabilitate Blue Lick Springs had an endless supply of momentum from the development company that was mangling her hometown landscape. The man responsible for all the ruckus was Horace Clarence Castle III, the scion of a long line of developers who craved a world dominated by neon, concrete, and high-rise buildings. The old families of Blue Lick were outraged that CASTLECO had its sights set on the gothic courthouse, the Hanging Rock church, and the 1790 Olde Nelson Tavern, a hangout of Jesse James. Nothing was sacred—not even her grandmother's four-hundred-acre farm! For all the town's collective complaints, individuals continued to do business with Castle.

Nobody could honestly say what Horace Castle had in mind for Blue Lick; all they could do was check the damage he had already wreaked in the tiny towns surrounding Savannah, Georgia; Beaufort, South Carolina; and even Charleston, his own hometown. He had taken peanut farms and peach orchards and nineteenth-century main streets and transformed them into sprawling housing subdivisions and super Wal-Marts. His bulldozers were carving land away like Michelangelo hacking marble, only CASTLECO'S handiwork was far from a Renaissance masterpiece.

Rebecca's current state of affairs as the clandestine competitor of Horace Castle was something she needed like another entry on her list of things to do, but something that wasn't all that unpredictable. In the ongoing war of torn allegiance between California and Kentucky, Rebecca had been the last family member to finally accept Los Angeles, the first one to rush back to Blue Lick Springs every chance she got, and the one who had never loosened her grip on her secret hometown dreams.

Years before, when Rebecca had gotten wind of her parents' capricious plan to fly by night to Los Angeles, she had been saturnine and disconsolate. This was in spite of her mother's fables of the gold-bullioned pavement awaiting them at the California border. She had even begged to stay behind with her grandmother, but Lila Mae had said no decent family would allow such a thing.

On the road to California, through the dark highways that twisted through saguaro cacti and pueblo ruins or the sunny paths that scissored through snowpeaked mountain ranges, Rebecca sat with her head tilted against the window. She stared at the red feather clouds, wrapped in a somniferous dream of Kentucky, and prayed that her mother would come to her senses and turn around. Rebecca already missed those Evening in Paris nights when the radio played "Lavender Blue . . . Dilly Dilly" and she and Glen Buchanan, her steady boyfriend, gazed into a moody fall sky, searching for Sputnik. California would never replace her world of senior proms and homecoming games.

The Wootens' arrival in the City of Angels had been on a balmy December evening with a swish of warm ocean air and a gold lamé moon, a plump crescent swinging in the sky like a carefree basket. The starstruck Lila Mae had yelped in delight when they spotted a vacancy sign on the Studio Plaza Courtyard, rundown motel units in San Fernando. The attendant had told Lila Mae yes, that was right, there was a movie studio a couple of miles away. Their mother turned to them and said, "See, kids . . . I told you!"

A few days later, Lila Mae got to talking to a waitress at Dupar's Coffee Shop who said, "San Fernando? You're lucky to be alive, lady!" Just that week, there had been the stabbing of a gorgeous aspiring actress the police called the Black Orchid. Far from scaring Lila Mae stiff, she couldn't hear enough details about the suitcase containing the young woman's decomposing body or the skid row men who'd been questioned in the grisly case.

As for their proximity to the Hollywood studios, the waitress told them the Studio Plaza Courtyard Motel was a couple of miles away, all right—a couple of dozen! But it didn't matter; the Wootens were already beguiled by the Disneyland leaflets and movie-star maps available in the motel lobby. They loved the giant palm trees that flanked the motel's driveway. They adored Stardust Melody, the desk girl with the platinum hair who was studying to be an actress and who let them take as many free peppermints as they liked from the small dish at the cash register. "You watch for me on the silver screen, now!" She winked at them with one big, bewitching eye.

During their cross-country trip, Rebecca had mourned from the backseat as the bluegrass melted into the waving grain of the Midwest and then became the cubic humps of Oklahoma sandstone, all the while vowing to hate California. But, the days became weeks, weeks became months, and eventually, and inevitably, the Bluegrass State was a ghostly memory. All too soon, the sassy, teenage Rebecca was like Eliza Doolittle, scraping away her Southern accent, switching her pageboy to a beehive, and shedding all her girlish Kentucky ways.

Transforming into a femme fatale, she rammed her entire foot in the turbulent California water and wrapped both arms around the blurry sixties. There were love beads and Woodstock and patchouli and darkened theaters showing obscure foreign films like *Last Year at Marienbad*. There were moments of madness, when at 3:00 A.M. she and her love du jour would jump into her red convertible Austin Healey and zoom to Joshua Tree. There, deep in the desert, under a topaz moon, they would sway to "Light My Fire" and "Black Magic Woman" with the golden stars flickering above them and the coyotes rustling in the bushes.

All the while—through the sixties and seventies and eighties—there were champagne toasts and yachts, midnight strolls in Paris, and south-of-the-border ruckuses at Hussong's Cantina. There had been dream houses and beaded Dior gowns, soirées at hilltop mansions and tempestuous affairs with lawyers and artists and European industrialists. In the midst of all that, there was even Prince Charming.

Yet now, after all those decades, she would get a whiff of Kentucky— some combination of sights and smells—and she would wrestle her wanderlust into some barely manageable anxiety. It was so Psychology 101, but Rebecca wanted to reverse it all, jumping right back to the sticky honeysuckled summers. She wanted to join Cleota McBride's sewing circle, sipping sweet tea with blueberry-haired matrons; she pined to snap half runner beans with her grandmother, putting them into the same wooden bowl Olive had used when Rebecca was a child.

Kentucky was also the ideal antidote for her middle-aged doldrums. In Blue Lick, she still felt like Miss America; in Los Angeles, she was the hunted—a woman over twenty-one (double plus) who, without major surgery, could hang onto the fantasy of youth for only so long. By jogging two dozen miles a week, slugging gallons of Evian water, and drowning herself in Parisian creams, she had managed to rescue her chin from suicide and slither into petite clothes. Still, she was on the cusp of overstaying her timeshare in La La Land.

Try as she might to quell the gravitational pull to Kentucky, everything urged her in that direction, even her mother's ancestral tales. The latter was something that irked her no end, particularly since she'd spent her childhood plugging her ears whenever Lila Mae started the "illustrious background" stories. Every time they chugged down Main Street, which was practically every day, there would be a sales pitch in which the featured attraction was one Adams or another, usually their great-great-great-grandfather, Thomas Breckinridge Adams. They endured magniloquent—and, Rebecca detected, inconsistent—ballads of the highfalutin patriarch. Adams was a handsome, dashing tycoon and pioneer Kentuckian who had constructed the railroads and banks, and erected government structures throughout the South.

Pointing to the buildings with a prideful, possessive finger, Lila Mae would say, "Kids, see that sign that says Adams and Miller? Well, that belonged to your ancestors . . . and that one with the big steeple? That was theirs, too!"

Often Rebecca, fluttering her eyes behind her *Modern Screen*, would snip, "Why's it such a big deal to *you? You're* not even an Adams!"

"Your grandmother's an Adams and that's what counts," Lila Mae would retort, staring Rebecca down in the rearview mirror. "Someday, when I'm dead and gone, you'll all be *very* sorry you didn't pay more attention to your heritage."

Even in California, Lila Mae promoted the family as long-suffering land barons who would stir from the cinders someday to claim their treasure. For the most part, the stories went in one of Rebecca's ears and out the other, and she'd sigh, "Sure, Mom. Blue Lick still belongs to the Adamses like Texas still belongs to Mexico."

But, one providential day—many decades later—during a visit to her grandmother, Rebecca and Olive spotted the FOR SALE sign on the old Adams & Miller Mercantile. The building was three crumbling stories of brick with arched pediments and eagle finials, all guarded by the vultures that darted in and out of the cracked windows. When Rebecca asked her grandmother why everyone was letting the town fall apart, Olive said, "They's blind men and they need ya to rough 'em up sum."

Rebecca reared back and said, "Me?" at the absurdity of the idea. Olive said, "Why not?" and told her to call Uncle Shorty's wife, Maybelle, a realtor who would show her the place. "It kills me to recommend her, but she's got the eggs-clusive on ever' property in town."

Since Olive was so insistent on Rebecca checking out the building, Rebecca didn't see any harm in just taking a peek.

"You won't be sorry!" Maybelle said. She assured her that the town was definitely on the upswing—a notion the woman justified by pointing to the added gas pump at the Marathon station and the newly opened Merva Jean's Five and Dime. As she hopped around in enthusiasm, Maybelle's beige corkscrew curls bounced like a dozen scampering golden retriever puppies. "You fix that Adams building up and I'll rent it out faster than a housefly shows up at a Fourth of July picnic!"

When Rebecca heard the ten thousand dollar asking price, she made the mistake of yipping, "Is that all?" In California, the same building would cost hundreds of thousands of dollars and didn't even exist.

"Oh, what a place this would be!" the wily realtor exclaimed. "Did ya see Olive's face? What she wouldn't give to have that building back in the Adams family."

Further inspiration came when Rebecca learned that her favorite photo of her great-grandmother, Beryl Polk Adams, had been taken in front of the Adams & Miller Mercantile building. A prim Beryl, wearing a white starched collar and a cameo, sat on a Victorian chair with braided tassels. Scattered around her, like delicate seashells, was a passel of young boys and one little girl—Olive. She had the mesmeric eyes of a prophetess and a mouth like two flower petals pressed together.

The Adams & Miller building was, as Olive put it, "The *center of all activity*. In my day, that's whar ever'thang come from—candy, grain, high-button shoes, you name it!"

During Rebecca's teenage days, the building was Klink's Drugs, the meeting place where she and her girlfriends would twirl around on the red-topped stools whipping their ponytails, flashing their opaline teeth, their french fries and milk shakes before them and their boyfriends flanking them. It was the spot where Rebecca would slip a nickel into the jukebox and play "Dungaree Doll" or "Rockin' Robin" and dream her dreams.

It was also at Klink's that she often avoided Clayton Dawes Wooten, her swaggering, perpetually snockered grandfather, and where Willadeen Foster's water broke, even though nobody knew the pimply, chubby fourteen-year-old was pregnant. Rebecca was the first to see the girl cup her two arms around the lump beneath her flowered shift; seemingly the only one who heard the girl's plaintiff yowl, "Papaw!" She was the only one who ran searching for Wilson Foster, the grandfather, an obdurate tobacco farmer with one bulging albescent eye, who was inside Klink's getting the girl an ice cream cone and who, rumor had it, was also the father of the surprise delivery.

With Olive prompting her and her own memories fueling her fantasies, Rebecca pressed her fingertips against the darkened window and stared past the cobwebs that were ruched like a theater curtain. It was all there, strung out like the props in a theatrical production—a paper skeleton pinned to the wall, the apothecary drawers labeled: Tincture Merthiolate, Zinc Peroxide. And across the ceramic floor were the dried leaves of a philodendron plant, gathered like petrified teardrops.

"I'm afraid it's a lost cause," Maybelle clucked. "If old man Prisby don't get a buyer, soon, then . . . here come the CASTLECO bulldozers. Such a derned shame . . . one of the crown jewels of Blue Lick, that Adams building is."

Rebecca knew Maybelle was a fancy operator, one who knew nothing about the glory days of Blue Lick Springs, but she had said the magic trio of words: bulldozer, crown jewel, and lost cause.

In some tantrum of sentimentality, Rebecca made a lowball offer, one that, to her utter shock, Maddy and George Glen Prisby, the owners, accepted right off the bat. This left her with the big—perhaps insurmountable—problem of breaking the news to David. Finally, Rebecca got her nerve when she and Carleen were in New Orleans at Ye Olde Absinthe House. The phone call got off to a shaky start, but by the end of it, David had stopped saying, "It will be an icy day in hell" and was asking, "What in God's name will you do with it?" She decided to break the news about the asbestos in another conversation.

Although Maybelle congratulated Rebecca on her successful bid for the fixer-upper, and Olive said, "Good fer you, honey!" after the blush of excitement had worn off, Rebecca realized that the property, as princely as it once had been, was much more of a tearer-downer.

As the contractor stripped the walls of loose plaster and exposed the planked floor, the vision of a big, old-fashioned general store began to blossom: a sun-tinted room with farmers in bib overalls, bins of horehound drops, gingham bonnets, and bolts of organdy. David said, "What is this, *The Waltons*? Nobody's worn a bonnet for decades!"

When Rebecca asked her daughter, Ava, who had an uncanny way of putting her finger on the heart of most matters, if she thought she was crazy, Ava replied, "You're not crazy, Mom, but there's *something* wrong with you!"

Shockingly, it was David who got the bright idea for the barbecue restaurant. Although it wasn't unusual for her husband, whose corporation had a thousand irons in the fire, to take on another business, Rebecca was awestruck as he began talking about T-shirts, mail-order sauces, and national chains. He also read an article stating that most successful restaurants were named after a person, some homespun type, working the griddle and fryer. When he suggested the name Miz Becky's, nothing could have stunned Rebecca more. Surely her husband didn't want his wife's face plastered all over mason jar labels like Orville Redenbacher and Paul Newman, particularly since she could hardly boil water and especially since nobody knew her from Adam. Lila Mae said, "Nobody knew Redenbacher either, but that didn't hold him back!"

Sometime after cracking the hump of the Miz Becky's remodeling, she noticed yet another building, this one a Flemish bond brick with turrets and carvings and beveled crystal windows. Her heart fishtailed and she muttered, "Oh, shit!" when at the tiptop, she spotted the original sign: ADAMS & SONS—1878.

This latest Adams building, once the site of her grandfather's banking business, was, once again, a crucial link in Olive's family history. "I got so many mem-rees of this place," she said, her eyes misting, then shifting to Rebecca. "It was the *center of all activity.*"

Rebecca figured she could give it a paint job and rent it out, but that was before she and Carleen stopped for coffee in a charming Napa Valley confectionery. By the time they finished their second double espresso, they had gotten carried away, hatching a plan for a tea or sweets shop, one they would decorate with panelled rosewood and English porcelain. They could make their own bourbon balls and place them in gold foil boxes. Rebecca said they could also sell crumpets and spiced punch and call the place Miss Lila Mae's Confectionery! This was something she knew would please her mother and a move she hoped would make it more difficult for David, who had a soft spot for Lila Mae, to veto. Lila Mae, who was all for the idea, said, "That homemade candy will sell like hotcakes!"

Her mother wasn't the only one who kept egging Rebecca on. Just when she wondered if Miss Lila Mae's was a passing fancy, Carleen would fan the flames. "Come on! Those Kentucky women will love a place like that." Forgetting her West Coast affiliations, as well as the five-hour plane commute to work, Carleen even carved a role for herself; she could serve cucumber sandwiches and Formosa oolong tea to the Blue Lick Springs ladies. "Oh, this will be so exciting!" she said.

Before Rebecca could blink, Olive was whipping together recipes and gathering ingredients. Plus, the *Blue Lick Springs Gazette* printed an article calling Rebecca a godsend, touting her work as a preservationist, and making it almost impossible to stop the runaway train of activity.

As for the bowling alley and barbershop, that's where her trail of logic ran cold. Olive had plans for the former, saying, "Fix it up good so's the young folk have sumthin' to do 'round this ole place . . . 'Stead of loiterin' down to the laundree-mat." So, now Rebecca was not only feeding the town great barbecue and delectable sweets, she was rescuing its lost youth, as well. As for the bowling alley, it was an exercise in Confucian logic compared to the barbershop.

David, she could tell, had very mixed emotions about Blue Lick Springs—thrilled that Rebecca had found something so fulfilling, yet nervous that a little chunk of her heart was drifting south. But, if David was uneasy now—and he still didn't even know the half of it—he was headed for either divorce court or total heart failure once he found out about Rosemont.

Chapter Five

Rebecca

JUNE 1999

Rosemont, a stately three-story Greek Revival home, was situated on hundreds of acres of wooded Kentucky pastures, and was built in the early nineteenth century by Thomas Breckinridge Adams Sr. Not only was it the undisputed gem of Blue Lick Springs, it was one of the grandest estates in the South, a property that would surpass all of Rebecca's other acquisitions, possibly break the bank, and maybe even wreck a marriage.

The legend of Rosemont had enlivened many a Kentucky supper table, provided marrow for park-bench gossips and timber for Lila Mae's own rendition of the story. Her particular specialty was Rose Abigail Adams, the original lady of the house. Rose was a patrician beauty who wore her raven hair plaited high on her head and ruled Rosemont's hallways with a loving, but firm, grip. Her doting, wealthy husband had encouraged her to fill the plantation with finery, something that accounted for the iron balconies from New Orleans and trompe l'oeil wallpaper from Paris. To fulfill her husband's wishes, there were shopping trips to New York where Rose and her sister, Dolly, commissioned parlor suites and bedsteads from Duncan Phyfe. In Boston, they purchased a mahogany Chippendale secretary; from London, came silken drapes trimmed with Italian passementerie. As for the Adams children, Lila Mae said they wore velvet breeches and satin frocks and looked just like Gainsborough's *Blue Boy* and *Pinkie!* In its heyday, Rosemont was the site of garden parties and political meetings attended by governors and presidents, as well as a frequent overnight stopover for Henry Clay and John Hunt Morgan.

"Rosemont's just throbbin' with Kentucky history and Southern glory!" Lila Mae used to enthuse, the exclamation points lined up like cheerleaders. "That circular staircase, that's what I'd like to see . . . and the Gilbert Stuart paintings, same as in the White House! There's a gilded ballroom with carved swans' heads, too!" Lila Mae would play up the house until it sounded more spectacular than the Palace of Versailles and more important than the Battle of Gettysburg. In short, no tour of the South was complete without a visit to the magnificent and historic estate.

Just when you were bug-eyed, slack-jawed, and begging for more, Lila Mae would pause for a sip of Coca-Cola, then add, "That's what they tell me, anyways." In other words, she had never actually been inside the place herself and the royal "they" who had supplied said decorative details and folklore were reduced to identities such as "this one or that one" and "one person or another." Lest you had a hankering to visit the place yourself, she'd say, "Oh, dear me. I, I wouldn't do that if I was you!" What she really meant was, "You'd have to be a fool to do so!" That's because Rosemont was haunted. Naturally, there was a story for that, too.

After generations of political and social prominence, all of Rosemont's gaiety and grandeur had come to a crashing halt when the Adams riches vanished. All it took was several years of foolhardy spending by James Butler Adams and his frivolous wife, Martha, capped off by one debauched weekend of riverboat gambling. One Adams or another made unsuccessful attempts at scraping together the money to salvage the house, but it and the contents were auctioned off to pay the creditors.

Waiting anxiously in the wings—pretty much like Rebecca was now—were Harrison Henry Montgomery and his wife, Eudora, who, according to Olive, "bought Rosemont fer a song!" Soon after, Rosemont's five thousand acres were chopped up, leaving the Adamses with a paltry four hundred acres and the Cottage, currently Olive's home. The original Rosemont had remained in the Montgomery family since the early 1900s, a quandary that obsessed Olive and Rebecca hoped to reverse.

One humid July afternoon, just months after Harrison and Eudora Montgomery took possession of the house, their only daughter, Minetta—dressed in her party ruffles—drowned in a well on the property. According to Lila Mae's sources, "The ink wasn't even dry on the deed when tragedy hit! On the poor girl's birthday, no less!" Nobody had ever mourned the death of a loved one like Harrison and Eudora Montgomery. The latter, swathed in black linen and mourning tulle, stood over the coffin, one black slippered foot in the grave, and keened, "Take me with you, Minetta!"

Three months later, a field hand was thrown from his quarter horse, breaking his neck. The next week, a housekeeper waxing the floor tripped on a scatter rug, toppling out of a third-floor window. There had been other casualties: the poisoned carcass of Dixie, the family's Labrador retriever; the death of Minetta's baby sister, Violet, who choked on a chicken bone . . . even the grass carp in the Montgomerys' pond had been electrocuted during a violent summer storm.

With each new Montgomery generation, the tragedies marched on. Rosemont's present owners were Hamilton Swinton Montgomery and his wife, Ramona, a woman of neurasthenic bent who rarely left the grounds and whose existence was confirmed by mere sightings. The Montgomerys were the same occupants who had lived there when Rebecca was growing up and they, too, were unable to escape the curse. Their young daughter, Babette, died of polio in an upstairs bedroom that was still referred to as "the sick girl's room."

Normally, Rebecca would question her mother's stories, revolving her eyes and grumbling, "Ha, I'll bet!" But, this time, her grandmother went along with the Rosemont fable, too. Instead of saying, "Well, now I think ya mighta gotten carried away sum, Lila Mae," Olive agreed, "That place is hexed, jinxed as shore as shootin'."

The Wootens had their own ideas about the cause of all the mysteries. Quite simply, the house was in mourning, voicing its protestations about the Montgomerys' takeover. Things would never be right until the house was returned to an Adams heir.

Because Olive's farm had once been part of the Rosemont plantation and mostly because of Lila Mae's seductive stories, their grandmother's big worry was that her grandchildren would wander onto the wrong property. "You mind yer own business. That ain't no place for you kids." Olive told them that Ole Man Montgomery was "out of his cotton-pickin' mind" and would shoot anybody on sight. And if Montgomery didn't get them, then Olive herself would. "I'll skin you kids alive if I hear tell of it."

One morning, after another ambulance visited Rosemont, Rebecca waited until Olive and Lila Mae were pickling cucumbers. When the coast was clear—that is, when they were in the basement gathering glass jars—she flew out the back door, ignoring Carleen, who shouted, "You're gonna git a lickin'!" and Billy Cooper, her younger brother, who yelped, "Mama, Mama! Becky Jean stold my binocalurs!"

Dashing across the alfalfa fields, curving through hackberry groves, Rebecca kept running and running, hoping something would sweep her in the right direction. When she reached the banks of Boone's Creek, she slithered through the waist-high cattails and pickerelweed, still not having the foggiest idea where she was headed.

As she skittered first one way, then another, all of Olive's warnings were exploding in her head: Minetta's ghost, wearing the fateful coral dress, would be pirouetting through the clover, flapping her tiny white hands, frightening away curiosity seekers. There would be coil-horned animals and wild-eyed men with arrows just to scare heedless children—foolish children, just like Olive's granddaughter—away.

From high and low came the breathing of unknown critters and the slithering of bellies across stone. Close by, there was a hissing sound. It was the exact opposite of what Rebecca'd always been told to do, but when she discovered two rattlesnakes at her feet, she screamed and started to run as fast as she could.

Out of breath and scared stiff, she was just about to give up, when suddenly, she heard muffled faraway sounds—a murmuring engine, the slam of a cellar door. With her heart pounding, she ran forward until she saw a trail of rusty fencing, one that seemed to separate Olive's property from the Montgomerys'.

Rebecca had halfway expected clarion trumpets to accompany her first sighting of Rosemont and Lila Mae's descriptions had prepared her for carriages, waistcoated gentlemen, and tinkling bourbon glasses. Here and there, twirling their umbrellas, would be the Colonial Dames of Blue Lick Springs, all gussied up in their organdy gowns and lace hats. They would eat tea cakes and sip their mango punch, "as sweet as French perfume."

Suddenly, through trees so colossal that they covered the ground with spidery shadows, Rebecca spotted a cobblestone path. Then a lamppost. She could hear her heart throbbing as she took one step, then another. As her eyes roamed the landscape, finally, there was Rosemont. It stood, like an old, blurry photograph, its majestic columns bursting through the tangled underbrush that enveloped it. At the entry were two empty Grecian urns. Here and there were corroded settees and garden statuary, overturned and scattered as if they were victims of a barroom scuffle.

Beyond it and all around was a scene so otherworldly that she stumbled backward in shock. Spread like lava around the grounds and continuing into the woods behind it were blankets of vinery . . . robust, dark green ropes that covered sheds and old cars and dead tree trunks and barns, stretching over the land like turbulent ocean waves. It was as if all the Montgomerys' sorrow had been a fertilizer for the foliage, as if the property had been smothered by the weight of its own misfortune.

In spite of the desolate scene, there were small beacons of life. Squatted on the back steps was an old black man, the limp wrists dangling between his legs like the helpless hands of a puppet; and a woman, thin as a gate post, with hair that hung like dirty twine. She swept her hand to her forehead almost in a salute, squinting at the green sky.

Hobbling along was a tall, crooked man with a beard that looked like twisted vines. "Henry! Ramona! A storm's comin'. Henry! Help Ramona gather her things." He had bulbous eyes and wild, black hair that flapped this way and that. "Hurry! Hurry! Into the basement!" The man scurried along, his leg thumping the ground in a syncopated tick-tock.

The black man uncoiled slowly, going inside his small hut and returning with a box that he held in front of him like a tray. Soon, he disappeared inside the house and began snapping shut windows and pulling drapes.

Above Rebecca was a yellow-green sky, a sky that seemed to be sucking all the life through one small hole. Suddenly, it turned charred black and bulged like the ripe belly of a pregnant woman. She had seen that before, clouds curling into tight balls then colliding into one deadly vacuum.

Somewhere came the sour pierce of neighing horses. She knew she had to go, but before leaving Rosemont, she looked over her shoulder and through the trees. As she did, Ramona Montgomery jerked upright and snapped her head to the side. She paused, and like an animal that senses the unseen crouched hunter, she listened to something that only she could hear. From so many dozens of yards away that it couldn't possibly be so, Rebecca was sure the woman behind the giant oaks had spotted her. Then Hamilton Montgomery grabbed her by the elbow. She lifted up slowly, putting her hands in the air like a mime feeling for a wall and Rebecca knew in her heart what nobody else in Blue Lick knew: Ramona Montgomery was blind.

As Rebecca dashed through the pastures, the trees spun like pinwheels, and she could hear Lila Mae calling after her, "Rebecca Jean Wooten! Where are you? Rebecccaaa Jeeean!" She could hear the frantic clanging of her grandmother's bronze dinner bell; she could visualize her mother, pacing the grounds, the one unruly swirl of hair tumbling over her brow.

When Lila Mae finally saw Rebecca, her arms swung like a windmill's and she hopped toward her, shrieking, "There are *funnel* clouds in the area. Do you hear me, young lady? *Funnel* clouds! I oughta tan your hide, so help me Hannah!" As they shooed Rebecca into the basement, her grandmother kept saying, "You shore picked a bad day to go gallivantin'!"

When they joined Carleen, Billy Cooper, and Baby Sister in the cellar, as they turned on the transistor, snacking on corn curls, drinking orange Kool-Aid, singing "Ain't That a Shame" and "Lollipop!" and waited for a tornado that touched down two miles away, they eventually got around to pumping Rebecca for information.

"Well," Lila Mae huffed, "I suppose the Queen of Sheba ain't gonna tell us what she was doin'. She'd rather worry us out of our skulls!" Rebecca kept saying it was no big deal, that she just got lost, "That's all!" but she couldn't have done justice to her adventure anyway. Like a dream that disintegrates in the telling, the moment was already darkening.

But, as she'd been soaring across the meadows, she wondered if those marble statues did spring to life at midnight. Maybe Minetta did roam the grounds sprinkling her bad fortune around her. Maybe the tarnish would turn gold, the shadows to sunlight as soon as the house was liberated.

Although that had been the first and last time Rebecca had actually seen Rosemont, the image was seared into her memory. And when she thought of it, which was often, it was, as Lila Mae usually said when she was describing something too good to be true, "just like something out of a movie."

Even though the house had been in the Montgomery family for all those years and the family had no intention of ever selling it, Rebecca had her heart set on it. So set that she had already purchased a crystal chandelier for the entry hall, as well as limestone statues. The former was something that David almost stumbled across when he was searching for his skis, and the latter, two cherubs entwined with laurel wreaths, had been designated for the garden, which Rebecca planned on getting back in shape just as soon as she owned the house.

There was only a molecule of evidence suggesting that Rebecca could *ever* get her hands on Rosemont. But Olive, who had years of desire under her belt, wouldn't let up. "Now Hamilton Montgomery don't need that house . . . with Ramona stuck up thar in the sick girl's room. Sumbody needs to do 'em a favor, git 'em outta there. I say ya give 'im an offer he cain't refuse. Heh, heh, we'll all be livin' in the lappa luxury then!"

Missing from these midnight dreamfests between grandmother and granddaughter were crucial details, such as how they could convince Hamilton Montgomery to actually sell Rosemont and who, exactly, would pay for it. Even with her fertile imagination, there was no successful angle of approach that Rebecca could come up with. There was a limit to how many dreams David would bankroll, and Rosemont would probably fall into the ever-expanding "over my dead body" category.

And even if she miraculously *did* cajole Hamilton Montgomery and sweet talk David, there was one more mountainous barrier at least— Reginald Peepers and his crew of spoilsports. She could turn cartwheels all the livelong day and the cold-hearted accountants would sit there with their eyes obsidian and beady, completely unmoved by her fervent urgings.

With all the plotting and scheming, Rebecca was treating the situation like some pressing matter, when no one had a gun to her head at all. In fact, it was quite the opposite. But something was definitely in the air, some big musical chairs extravaganza just waiting for the conductor's baton. And, she wanted to be stirring in the wings. Obviously, if the circumstances did change, there would be details to iron out—major ones—but there was no way around it: She just had to have Rosemont, come hell or high water.

Chapter Six

Carleen

MAY 1999

The only good thing about making the termite appointment when Carleen did was that Lila Mae was in town. Together, the women formulated a game plan, discussing all the things they would do if the jewel thief went haywire. The gardener had been told to stick around and Carleen's neighbor had the cell phone ready to call 911 if the ex-con got uppity. That was another thing. Carleen kept referring to Smitty as the ex-con, but she wasn't sure his run-ins with the law were all that far behind him. Someone told her he had been rounded up during the Emerald King Robbery a few years prior, something neither he or the warden had mentioned.

All morning Carleen warned herself, "This is it, you featherbrain. If you give that man one red cent," she slid the vacuum across her beige carpeting, "you'll have a tragic car accident. Cave in and you'll kill an elderly pedestrian . . . you spineless wonder, you!" She imagined the woman's horrified face, her body catapulting through the air, the sirens, the trial, the conviction, and finally, her life behind bars, the one she was doomed to lead if she succumbed to the pressure of the A-1 man and Nelson. Just to be on the safe side, she reviewed Dr. Broadman's advice: "*No* is just a word; just as simple to say as *yes*." She snapped off the vacuum, picked up her Starbucks and downed it like a whiskey shot.

Things got off to a real bang when the exterminators showed up in a neon-yellow van with a huge termite perched on top. The bug was almost the size of a Volkswagen Beetle with tentacles flapping in the breeze like unruly poppies. Then there was Smitty himself. When she'd met him at Vacaville, he was a gray ghost of a chap, and now he was ascoted and bejeweled. As he bounded up the walkway, Lila Mae peeked through the blinds and scowled. "That's like no pest-control man I've ever seen." Carleen could only imagine what her neighbors, some of whom were already milling around outside, were thinking.

Without even knocking, Smitty burst through the door like those strippers that pop out of birthday cakes. "There she is!" he exclaimed with outstretched arms, then turned to the younger man at his side. "Son, this is that nice lady I've been telling you about . . . she believed *everything* I told her!"

Smitty's son was a reed-thin man with several missing teeth and a hacking cough. He had a caved-in midsection as if he had been punched in the stomach and hadn't recovered. But he was dressed in his starched white uniform with a small black cap and carried a case of tools and equipment. He nodded politely, said, "Ma'am," then handed Carleen his A-1 Pest Control business card with his name: Leonard Arthur Slidell. Not that there was such a thing as a "violin type," but Carleen had a difficult time visualizing the man in an orchestra pit with a fiddle under his chin and sheet music before him.

Lila Mae was on the beige sofa with her ankles in a ladylike cross, giving the men her "I'm nobody's fool" look. That was over in no time flat, when Smitty bent down, kissed Lila Mae's hand and exclaimed, "This lovely lady can't be your mother!"

With that, Lila Mae craned her body toward the man and said, "Why, aren't you sweet, Mr. Smith!"

Carleen saw no reason to beat around the bush, so she told the men she was sorry to get them there under false pretenses, but she had *no intention* of having the house exterminated.

"Actually," she cleared her throat, "I just scheduled this to keep my husband off my back. I have serious concerns about the safety of the extermination process. No matter what you tell me, those sprays *can't* be healthy!" She was all ready with her next response but Lenny Slidell said, "I have to agree with you, ma'am."

In a calm, reassuring voice, he said, "Nobody wants to be exposed to dangerous substances." He promised Carleen that the chemicals A-1 used were perfectly safe, that their company—tops in its field!—had treated hundreds of thousands of homes over the decades they'd been in business without any problems whatsoever. "I could talk until I'm blue in the face, but 221 million satisfied customers tells you everything you need to know about A-1! This guarantee," he had slipped a gold-medallioned paper from its plastic sleeve and patted it like a baby, "tells you the rest."

Just about then, Smitty said, "Show 'em the brochures, son!" So, the man propped his knee up midair like a makeshift table and tried to balance his scrapbook on it. It was too much for Slidell to handle, so Lila Mae said, "Here, let me help you with that!" and cleared the coffee table for him.

Incidentally, as Slidell was talking he had apparently been taking tiny steps that nobody was aware of, because when he started his sales pitch, he had been near the front door. Somehow he had gone past the kitchen and now he was all the way in the living room. Carleen honestly didn't know how he'd managed to get that far.

After they got the book situated, Slidell turned the pages of illustrations and artist's renderings showing the fiendish termites at work. One pictured a family as they lounged unknowingly in a rumpus room while the termites, wearing bibs and using forks and knives, dined on their suburban house. "See," Slidell said, "they're makin' a joke out of it, but that's about the size of it." Yet another drawing showed a man who had fallen through an attic floor. Both of his legs came out the other side and were hanging through the living room ceiling. The stunned wife had her hands clapped to her face and seemed to be saying, "Oh, my! We'd better call A-1!"

"Now come on." Carleen guffawed, as they drank coffee. "These termites in your pamphlets are bigger than this German shepherd in the rumpus room drawing."

"Now, you can cut up all you like, Mrs. Carlyle," Slidell admonished, "but there's nothing'll get you like a termite."

"I do know a thing or two about termites and you are absolutely, positively, one-hundred-percent right!" Lila Mae batted her blue saucer eyes and said, "Gentlemen, you're not gonna believe this, but years ago, my husband's leg crashed right through a coffee table. We were serving refreshments on it one minute and the next, it couldn't even support a human foot! Yes, indeedy, termites can ruin just about anything they set their sights on." Lila Mae took a sip of coffee. "And they set their sights on *everything!*"

Smitty whipped his good eye toward Carleen to see if the story had registered. "You listen to your mother, now, she knows!"

"I believe you about the damage," Carleen said, giving her mother a thanks-for-nothing look. "But I've been through the extermination before, I had the same guarantees and in the end, it was a total disaster."

"That *is* true, Mr. Slidell. She had a horrible time of it!" Lila Mae, the dual advocate, leaned forward in inquisition. "Why do you think all of her houses were infested? It's almost as if the termites are picking on her!"

"Welllll," Slidell rubbed his jaw like an orangutan and said, "sometimes it's the building material. But one of the most common ways, believe it or not, is furniture."

When Carleen said, "Furniture?" Smitty rocked forward and said, "Mostly antiques. They get a foothold on one piece and you can't hardly stop them." That's all Nelson, who hated anything over fifteen minutes old, had to hear.

Although she still had no intention of going along with the men, the thing that threw Carleen for a loop—and sounded plausible, as well— was their claim that A-1 had just patented a nontoxic process containing Pantazine.

"With all due respect, ma'am," Slidell said, "you're behind the times! Nobody uses those chemicals anymore. They're illegal. Pantazine is brand, spanking new and it's an A-1 exclusive formula."

"It sounds great," Carleen retorted. "But I've heard all that pure as rainwater, one hundred percent guaranteed crap before." She could imagine Dr. Lorraine Broadman applauding wildly.

As if he had taken all he could take, Smitty jumped up and, like Tarzan beating his chest, roared, "Hell! If it's good enough for the White House, it's good enough for this place!"

Carleen wasn't thrilled with Smitty's outburst, but the idea that they could have something in common with the White House had Lila Mae bubbling and flitting and exclaiming, "Oh, my! The White House! What a calling card!" So, the two men didn't leave in a huff after all.

One thing led to another and, half an hour later, Carleen was working on her third cup of coffee and rolling her eyes at Lila Mae, who was trying to convince the men that Carleen's weekly pet peeves column "That Just Gets My Goat" (the one whose last topic had been soft-drink cups that don't fit the designated holders), should win the Pulitzer Prize. Nelson had already called twice just to make sure Carleen was going through with the extermination. There were brochures and charts propped all over the place and lipsticked coffee cups scattered here and there. Smitty, who was sprawled out on Nelson's Barcalounger and nursing a double French Roast, was spinning yarns about tea and crumpets in the Green Room. As for Lenny Slidell, Carleen didn't know where he had suddenly disappeared to. Actually, they had sort of forgotten all about him, until finally they heard a voice cry out, "I found them!" from the crawl space under the house. Seconds later, he came rushing in, shiny-faced, breathless and hollering, "Arthur, you won't believe the type they have!"

This was enough to rouse Smitty out of the lounge and for Carleen to yelp, "Type? There's more than one?"

"The most common is the North American variety. Then you've got your . . . Vietnamese." Smitty said "Vietnamese" in a way that told her they were the worst kind, as well as the ones her house probably had.

By now, everyone but Carleen had their spectacles out, taking turns staring at the oddity captured between Slidell's tweezers. Carleen figured it was a great time to let them know she wasn't falling for it, so she told them their contractor said the biggest problem was not termites. "He said we've got dry rot."

"Dry rot? Lookee here, Mrs. Carlyle." Slidell wiggled his fingers for her to take a look and held the magnifying glass over the bug. "I've

never seen dry rot with arms and legs and teeth, have you? This is *bad,
real bad.*"

"Besides, lady." Smitty slipped her a foxy smile. "You got something
else in mind? You're not gonna let your house collapse, are you?"

There was absolutely no denying that the men were two very slick
talkers. But, for every plausible statement they made, there were two
that were hogwash. Just the amount of time A-1 had been in business
was fishy. When Carleen stopped to think about it, twenty-five years was
actually measly. The *Yellow Pages* alone advertised two other established
pest control companies, one that had been in business since 1904. And
yet the men bragged about A-1 as if their firm, a *family-owned operation*
they kept repeating, had been around since Adam and Eve. Plus, their
business card had a sketch of a horse-drawn carriage and several distinguished men with beards, each one framed by a laurel wreath—
presumably a long line of Smiths—as if they were the founding fathers
of extermination. None of this jived with the information underneath
the drawing which said: A-1 EXTERMINATION, SINCE 1992. As far as the Pantazine claims, Carleen would have to look into those.

Still, there didn't seem to be much choice, especially since she and
Lila Mae were going to Chez Panisse for lunch and Carleen was beginning to think they'd be trapped there all day if she didn't take some action. But, if she *did* buckle all because of a lunch date, what about Cassie?
What kind of mother was she if she invited health hazards into their own
home? Though, if she *didn't* sign, what would she tell Nelson? He'd been
in such a rare good mood when she told him everything was on target.
But how far did she have to go to be a devoted wife? If he told her to
jump off the Brooklyn Bridge would she do it, for goodness sake? And
what good did it do her to tune in to Dr. Broadman every day if she was
going to turn around and do the exact opposite?

In the back of her mind, there was something else that nettled Carleen, and it was so ridiculously embarrassing that she couldn't believe it
was a factor in all this. She actually felt sorry for Lenny Slidell. Physically he had everything going against him; a shag of clay-red hair and bug
eyes. When he bent over to examine the termites, she could trace his
skeleton, like the spiked bones of a dinosaur in a museum display,

through his cotton uniform. And what about that horrible cough? It sounded like a dozen barking dogs.

But Slidell was no angel, either. Against Carleen's protests, he had wormed his way into the bedrooms, pointing his flashlights everywhere and burrowing into places like a groundhog. Plus, he spent a lot of time in the master bedroom even though Carleen told them as far as she knew there was no damage in there. Plus, a lot of other things.

On the other hand, he'd returned a sapphire ring that he'd found under a rug. Neither Carleen or Lila Mae recognized it and, for all they knew, it could have been glass, but Lila Mae gushed, "Why, thank you, sir!," making such a fuss that the shy man blushed. There was also the aborted musical career, something that broke Carleen's heart. She also didn't like the way his father bullied him around. As ridiculous as it was, she actually felt pity for the poor man who was supposed to be her op-ponent in the war to take control of her life. And there he was, along with two others who were urging her to sign up, looking like one of those Ethiopian orphans up for adoption.

It was the last thing Carleen had in mind when the men showed up (she really hoped to get them out of her hair for good), and it was against so many of her principles. But she felt so immobilzed that she author-ized them to go ahead and FedEx the termite to a special lab for analy-sis. And then, because everyone was pressing her to do so, Carleen signed the stupid paper for an "in-depth examination." She supposed Dr. Broadman, who'd *never* compromised, would consider her a wimp, but at least this was a justifiable *maybe*. Come to think of it, the "in-depth in-vestigation" was what Carleen thought Smitty and Slidell were sched-uled to be doing that day. She'd just be saying *yes* to the same thing twice! There was one minor victory, too: She had refused to give Smitty the signed contract he asked for or a down-payment check, which meant she could put a stop to all the nonsense at the other end.

One thing was certain: It hadn't helped Carleen's mission that Lila Mae was practically rooting for the visiting team. To think that before they arrived, her mother was the one who threatened to call the police if there was any foul play! At one point, Carleen even wondered if she was going to invite the men to Chez Panisse. Plus, after Smitty and

Slidell finally left, Lila Mae, who could make even a one-eyed, one-horned, flying purple people eater seem normal, had closed the door behind her and said breathlessly, "They were awfully nice, weren't they?"

Smitty and Slidell's fast talk was exactly what the spokesman at a meeting to ban Malathion and other toxic chemicals told his listeners to be on the lookout for when dealing with pest-control companies. A few days after the extermination appointment, Carleen had shown up, as she did every month, in a high school gymnasium in Palo Alto, to attend the Environmental Watchdogs Association meeting. She had taken her seat in the front row and waited for the speaker, a man named Deke Arnett, to mount the podium. Wall-sized, sepia-toned photographs of atrocities—scorched farmland, brooks babbling with chemicals—served as a constant reminder of global danger and the need for vigilance.

Without admitting anything and hoping to get feedback that squelched her worst fears, Carleen raised her hand during the question and answer session of the meeting. "An asthmatic friend of mine just signed a contract to have her house exterminated and the company swore this new chemical—something called Pantazine—is safe." Carleen batted her oval, sky-blue eyes, as clear and innocent as a windowpane. "I told her to be cautious, but she scheduled the extermination, anyway!"

"No offense, but that's just plain *stupid* . . ." Arnett shook his head and strolled back and forth. "Pantazine is one hundred percent poison! It remains potent for months! It's suicide! Let's face it. What *can* these companies say?" The man shrugged his bony shoulders. "*Of course* they're going to claim the chemicals are safe. They said the same thing about Chlordane five years ago." The small crowd buzzed in agreement.

Arnett halted in front of a gargantuan photograph of chemical burn and toxic poison victims. "Now, as we know, Chlordane has been banned. . . . In the meantime, have your friend cancel that appointment and we'll get her information on an alternative treatment that should be on the market fairly soon. The house isn't going to fall down overnight, now, is it?"

After the pep talk, Carleen was uplifted, buoyed by the camaraderie as well as the hardcore information on both Pantazine and Dr. Zollinger's Poplar Extract. The latter formula, she was told, was the result of a ten-year study on why termites don't infest poplar floors, something that sounded very legitimate and was more than enough ammunition to set Smitty and Slidell straight. She couldn't blame them for thinking she'd fall for all that 100 percent natural malarkey . . . most people probably did. And, she wouldn't be rude or anything, but the result would be the same: The exterminators could take their Pantazine and shove it! She would tell them that she'd signed the in-depth analysis contract under duress—if three against one wasn't duress, she didn't know what was—and notify them that the examination was off. If worse came to worst, they might have already sent the termite to the out-of-state laboratory and she'd have to pay the fifty dollars. But that was a small sacrifice.

She had it all set in her mind, this plan of hers. It swept her all the way across the Carcenas Bridge, right past Nordstrom and even up the hill toward Mount Olympus Park. It all shattered like a Waterford goblet when she saw Nelson's silhouette through the den window. All the strategy and resolve in the world could crumple in a battle of the wills with her pushy husband. He would wheedle, persist, and hound her, trying to make sure that the pest people showed up, spraying the very poison that she and her cohorts were trying so hard to prevent from being marketed. Oh, her fence-straddling just irritated her no end!

Just that morning she had read the story "I Fell off a Cliff and Clawed My Way Back to the Top . . . with a Broken Neck." Carleen had thought, "My gosh, what kind of a shrinking violet am I?" How could she ever expect to make anything of herself if she couldn't establish her ground with her own husband and a termite inspector?

Chapter Seven

Irene

MAY 1999

To keep the wolves and ex-husbands at bay, Irene put her red tufted barstools and plaid hide-a-bed into storage, packed her seasonal clothing—an old red car coat and mittens, one summer suit, a dozen pairs of extra large shorts, plus her *Cats* album (autographed by Deuteronomy)—and moved to the Cottage, a white farmhouse in Blue Lick Springs, Kentucky, to stay with her ninety-five-year-old grandmother, Olive.

Irene was already thinking, "Oh, brother," when she stepped off the Greyhound bus at the Blue Lick terminal. Obviously, her memory of Kentucky, a place she hadn't visited for two decades, had accented the positive and eliminated the negative.

Irene wondered, as she took in the old-fashioned sights, if Blue Lick had been informed of the Civil War. Right off the bat, she saw a rusty car slapped with Bondo, and topped with a Confederate flag aerial. She passed a shack with an old black woman with a maroon bandanna coiled around her head. She was squatting on a stone step, her gnarled legs wrapped in brown hose so stiff they looked like grocery bags. Gathered around her, feathers flying, beaks popping, were black-bodied, red-snouted roosters. A girl with braids dotting her head like flowers in a garden was beating a threadbare oriental rug.

Overhead was a sky of pink flower blossoms, and a high, hot sun that struck Irene on the back of her neck like a cape. She blew air into her own face, her feet sweeping along, as she walked toward the spot where she was to meet her ride.

The Cottage, once part of the Rosemont plantation, sat on Honeysuckle Way, a country road lined with sycamore groves and junipers. Down a long dirt driveway, situated in a halo of sunlight and fringed with overgrown shrubbery, was Olive's clapboard home. Wrapped around the house was a wide veranda with swings and terra-cotta flower pots. Here and there, nestled on knolls and in valleys, were tobacco barns and milk sheds, corroded tractors and wheelbarrows. All of it had an unmade, rumpled-bed appearance, but it was, as Rebecca might have put it, an icon of Rockwellian splendor.

In Olive's garden, a hodgepodge of vegetables and waist-high weeds, was a middle-aged man leaning against a hoe. Bare-chested and muscular, he looked nothing like a typical farmhand. He was wearing blue jeans and black work boots, and his shirt was untucked at the back of his waist hanging like a horsetail. Both arms were tattooed with snakes, dice, hearts, arrows, and women's names, seemingly a graveyard of past loves and bad habits. He slammed his hand over a bug that pestered him, then threw Irene a dark, piercing frown as if she'd brought the insect with her.

Two peacocks, settled on the roof of Olive's old Buick, signaled Irene's arrival with their startling, plaintive mewing. "Jesus!" Irene muttered, jumping back in surprise. Already, she could feel the skin beneath her cotton blouse percolating in the heat, a heat so intense that she gasped for air, sucking in a rich, nauseating mixture of honeysuckle and manure, but some alien feeling of contentment, as temporary as it might be, held her hand.

Lila Mae had managed to convince Irene that her move to Kentucky would extend her grandmother's lifespan as well as bring the entire town to the brink of euphoric frenzy but, as she stood on the porch, there was no sign of brass bands and cheering crowds or, for that matter, Olive. Rattling the screen door brought no response at all. After hollering, "Helloooo, anybody home?" through the crackle of *Judge Judy* and a clanging grandfather clock, Irene heard a weak voice cry, "Help," as if it belonged to someone not used to asking for it.

Beyond the blackened screen Irene could see a china cabinet and a horsehair davenport. Against one wall was a walnut piano dressed with two silver candlesticks and a music book titled *How to Play the Piano Overnight*. Hanging on the opposite wall was Olive's membership certificate in the Daughters of the American Revolution. Next to it was a plaque saying: GIVE THE DEVIL AN INCH AND HE'LL BE YOUR RULER.

Finally, in a shadowy corner, she noticed an upholstered chair turned so far backward that it was almost upside down and two small, slippered feet kicking in the air. "Grandma?" Irene dropped her tapestry carpetbag and rushed inside the parlor. "What's going on?"

"Somebody get me outta this G.D. thing!" Olive, sweaty and agitated, her face as red as poinsettia petals, gestured to a remote control at her side. As Irene struggled, pressing buttons and pulling levers, the chair jutted up and down and side to side. Eventually, Irene must have pressed the right one because the tiny, fragile woman began to shimmy and slither her way back to normal.

"Dee-luxe, my foot! Ya gotta be Who-deeni to git loose!" Olive snorted, giving the chair a kick and patting her mussed clothing into place. She was wearing a lightweight tan suit with a silk scarf slipped over her neck like a lariat. Around her wrist was a petite gold watch, and two disk earrings perched on her jawbone like bronze battle shields. "It's just a big ole dinosaur with a complicated control panel and a thick instruction booklet. It's that she devil's doin'. Maybelle picked it out. I'm pretty sure she did."

According to Olive, the therapeutic chair, one that went backward and forward and did all sorts of unnecessary acrobatic tricks, had been advertised on television and in magazines by Annette Funicello, and had been bought *with* Olive's money but *without* her consent. Not only didn't the chair live up to its hype, Olive swore it was actually a trap designed to keep her in one spot. She threatened to get rid of the stupid thing, and told Irene to call the Salvation Army.

"I need that thing lak I need me another hole in my head. Why, them two wuz swayed by a slick advertisement and that Mousketeer a-sellin' it! They's just lak kids, Irene. Shorty never has growed up and him almost seventy year old! Stick around, you'll see!"

Just when Irene supposed that was all the greeting she was going to get, Olive tossed up her speckled hands in exclamation, and studied her granddaughter with eyes which were the blue of a faded Kentucky sky. "Well, I beg yer pardon!" she said. "Is that really you, Baby Sister? I didn't mean to git off on the wrong foot lak that." She instructed Irene to get her back to her regular chair where she belonged.

The regular chair was Olive's beloved Queen Anne—pink velveteen and feathered with Siamese cat hair and needlepoint pillows. It sat in a sunny nook of the parlor, within striking range of her rabbit-eared Magnavox television set. At her feet was a box of Russell Stover chocolates.

Although Olive kept apologizing for not giving Irene a twenty-one-gun salute, it didn't mean she had the chair incident out of her system. "Now you seen it with yer own two eyes, didn't ya?" she asked, as if priming her granddaughter for a court appearance. "Yer a witness to me a gettin' stuck lak that, ain't ya? You tell them two what they put me through."

The "them two" to which Olive kept referring were her son Curtis "Shorty" Wooten and his second wife, Maybelle. Since the couple lived on the grounds of the farm, they were in the picture on a day-to-day basis, something that prompted warnings from Olive, particularly about her daughter-in-law. Right away, she told Irene to hold on to her pocketbook. "Maybelle'll do ya lak ever'one else, if she cain't sell ya real-estate land, she'll sell ya them Avon products of hers. Calls it a makeover or sum such."

Even more irritating, the she devil was of the wrong political persuasion, a Democrat who supported Bessie Belle Thornton, an Afro-American councilwoman seeking re-election. The candidate was built like the Alamo—big and broad—and depicted herself as a mover and a shaker. Her campaign slogan was "Let's get *oooonnn* with it . . . I got places to go and things to do!"

Irene was instructed to wait for the commercial break in *Judge Judy* and she could see the political advertisement with her own eyes. When it came on, Olive's left hand hooked the air like a pitcher in warm-up exercises and she said, "Take a look at that *two-ton biddy*, will ya? She's a mover and shaker, all right! 'Let's get *ooonnnn* with it,' " Olive mimicked the councilwoman's drawn-out, exaggerated way of talking. " 'I got places to go and things to dooo.' Ha!" she sniffed sarcastically, "We already give ya a chance, ole Bessie, and ya made a messa thangs! Maybelle thinks she's tops, though, . . . you ask her yerself!"

The only reason Maybelle liked Thornton, Olive claimed, was because the woman had bought two pieces of property from her. The main reason Olive didn't, Irene suspected, was that Bessie Belle was the daughter of Ben Carter Thornton, a judge who had ruled against Olive when she protested the demolition of Blue Lick's historical train station.

If the endorsement of Bessie Belle wasn't enough to hold against her daughter-in-law, Olive had more ammunition. "Maybelle don't even drink Co-Colas like a normal person," she informed Irene. "Huh! She's gotta have herself Pepsi!"

Drinking Pepsi, above all else, was a breach of religion to a family who drank Coke like tap water and treated it as a peace pipe. After a dog-eat-dog battle, it was never "I'm sorry," just, "You want a Coke?" Rebecca had joked once that if she were stranded on a desert island, she needed three things: Coca-Cola, lipstick, and *Gone with the Wind*. Lila Mae and Carleen had both said, "Me too!" When Irene gave them a funny look, they said, "It's a Southern thing, I guess!"

As for Shorty, a retired electrician and the runt of Olive's litter, he was like a pit bull on amphetamines: a feisty nervous wreck of a fellow whose Vesuvian temper could elevate any topic to emergency status. He had recently become a deputy sheriff, a position held by at least half of the voting-age men in Blue Lick, but Olive claimed her son was "all puffed up like he's the guv'ner!"

When Irene asked Olive if her uncle's tantrums were as bad as what she'd heard, she said, "I'd say so. Shorty's gotta personality lak a cheap hair dryer—two settings: hot and cold." She cocked her head toward the floor as if depositing the words on the ground and huffed, "That little shrimp!"

Anxious to give her granddaughter the grand tour, as well as point out the foibles of the house, Olive shuffled from room to room, instructing Irene to limit her showers to avoid flooding the bathroom and warning her about a loose floorboard. Both of those things could have been repaired if only Shorty, the procrastinator, would get with it.

When Irene noticed that Olive had disappeared into the parlor seconds before the kitchen light came on, Olive pinched her brows together and said, "That's another thang . . . the electrical system is all fouled up."

There was no use for Irene to go into her room at night until she was good and ready for bed, Olive advised her. "Ya see, ya cain't even turn off yer own light." The switch controlling that was in Olive's bedroom. Her grandmother's controls were in Irene's room. You had to go all the way into the laundry room to turn on the dining room lights and so on. Shorty, who had done the remodeling job sans the normal inspections and permits, said the paperwork was "just a gimmick, something to waste ever'body's time and money."

"Yessireeebob! That's Shorty's system fer ya," Olive said. "He'll have ya runnin' all over tarnation. And he calls hisself an electrician."

"That could be dangerous, couldn't it?" Irene asked.

"WHY SHORE IT'S DANGEROUS!" Olive let out a lung-shuddering yelp. "It's a wonder we ain't been burnt to a crisp, with them wires goin' ever' which way."

While Olive ranted and raved about Shorty and Maybelle, and the therapeutic chair, there wasn't a word about the trouble brewing with her own property. Lila Mae had told Irene that a developer was gobbling up everything like Pac Man, and he was determined to purchase her grandmother's farm. And Rebecca had informed her that she might have to get to the bottom of a few things. Knowing her sister, she was planning on bonfires and stampedes and any skirmish that included the phrase "aiding and abetting." But just across the street Irene had seen a COMING SOON sign for Honeysuckle Groves, a housing development, and another billboard for the new industrial complex, so something was definitely afoot. So far, there was no word from Olive.

Just as they did each night, the shrimp and the she devil showed up around dinner time, first Maybelle, who waltzed into the room like Ginger Rogers, trilling, "Yoo-hoo . . . Avon calling!," then Shorty, who was wearing oven mitts and carrying a covered casserole, behind her. Shorty was quick and narrow and pointed like a fox with darting eyes and hair that was slicked back and curled over his small, flat ears. On his face was a shiny gleam, one which Irene would begin to avoid in the coming weeks.

He kicked the screen door shut with his foot, all the while hollering, "Now that just BURNS ME UP! WE DON'T NEED COMMUNISTS BRINGIN' THE COUNTRY DOWN! THIS'LL DO THE JOB FOR 'EM!"

Maybelle, who had the air of a fancy bird, said, "Don't mind him, he's been blowing his stack for hours." She was in head-to-toe gingham with a kerchief reining in her blond-petaled hairdo. Around her neck was an Aztec sun pendant that fell against her chest like a phys-ed teacher's whistle. She presented her beige hand like a princess, and said, "Maybelle Mouser-Wooten." Then she paused for a theatrical moment before adding, "The Mousers of Egypt."

"They's from Egypt all right . . ." Olive told Irene. "Egypt, *Kentucky!* Oh, she'll tell ya that, like her kin wuz from some exotic lo-kay-shun, but don't ya believe it!" Olive said the Mousers were "a bunch of no-bodies!" who sold discount women's hosiery, used lawn-mower parts, and other useless odds and ends. "They'll peddle anythin' they can git their grubby paws on . . . then they sell 'em from the hood of a car, no less! Maybelle acts lak she's the Queen of Siam, though, don't she?"

Olive said all this in a stage whisper, one which Irene was sure Maybelle could hear and one which caused the woman to draw her mouth into a prissy button.

Irene had been dreading their first dinner together, thinking she'd have to fill in huge blanks—more than blanks really—entire epochs, with colorful tales of the California Wootens. In other words, she would have to lie like a rug. Except for a few minor bits of information, she hardly opened her mouth. The combustible trio was in a perpetual state of spark-flying debate.

They had barely said "Amen," when, like a music box whose lid was suddenly opened mid-tune, Shorty yelped, "I THOUGHT I'D SEEN IT ALL!" This was accompanied by bulging veins, several emphatic thumps to the table and gripes from Maybelle who said Irene didn't want to hear all that carrying on her first night there. Olive said that might be, but she also couldn't blame Shorty since she knew why he was all stirred up.

"Is it that feller from Alabama? The killer who got aholt of them pretty Dairy Queen waitresses? They got his records mixed up or sum such."

"That's the SOB, all right!" Shorty confirmed. "They let *him* out so now *he's* all footloose and fancy free, *then* they put Davis Lee Durwood, a fine, upstanding church-going man, in the clinker, ALL ON AC-COUNTA SOME RAT HE KILLED!"

"Free as a bird on accounta a paperwork glitch," said Olive, shaking her head. "Mercy, mercy me."

"YA SEE, IT'S ALWAYS THE TECHNICALITIES THAT GITS YA!" With the way Shorty's colorless eyes were popping and batting, Irene figured Durwood was a childhood friend. He was actually a man they'd read about in the *Enquirer*.

"They put someone in *jail* for killing a *rat?*" an incredulous Irene asked.

"Curtis ain't tellin' the whole story," Olive said. "See, the rat turned out to be endangered or sum such."

"Now that scares me, it does." Maybelle frowned and flipped her high-heeled sandal up and down. "How would a person know one rat from the other?"

"A rat shoots across MY livin' room floor—*any* rat—and I don't care if it's from *Jupiter*—I'm gonna *kill* it!" Shorty stamped his foot on the word "kill" and added, "AND I AIN'T SPENDIN' NO TIME IN JAIL FER IT NEITHER!" His voice was scaling all the octaves, everything from Callas to Pavarotti as he threatened to launch national letter writing campaigns. "You tell them MONGOLOID IDIOTS that Shorty Wooten will be contactin' 'em! You tell 'em that!"

"You be careful, Curtis." Olive waggled her knotty finger at him. "One little slipup and we'll be visitin' ya in the slammer. It's the real crooks who git by with murder." Olive's little beagle eyes flashed him a deadpan warning. "You'll have the Mongoloids after ya, too!"

The food was getting ice cold, Shorty was hollering, "THEY DON'T SCARE ME NONE," and Maybelle, trying to restore calm, and desperate to make a sale, was telling Irene her eyes needed to be "brought out some," and Love That Aqua was just the mascara color to do it. Olive had switched on the Magnavox and told everybody to shut up, it was time for *Hollywood Squares*. After all the flying dander, Irene wasn't sure Olive's tactic would work, but in no time, everybody had forgotten about the exotic rat and was haggling over what Nevada meant in Spanish and guessing how Thomas Edison proposed to his wife. Shorty was feeling like a million bucks because he knew that the Nash Rambler was the first American car with seat belts and Olive was thrilled because Maybelle got everything wrong, but Whoopi Goldberg didn't. "Boy, that Hoop-ee," Olive chuckled, pointing her fork toward the screen and chiding her daughter-in-law, "she knows all them answers, don't she?"

After the bonus round, there was a commercial break and more political advertisements, one for Thornton and another one for her opponent, Denny Spicer. No one had to ask Olive who she was for, but she had some unfinished business with Irene. Her grandmother drew her eyes together in a threat and asked, "You wuddn't vote for the likes of Bessie Belle Thornton, would ya, Baby Sister? Maybelle says she's all fer her, ain't ya?"

Out of the corner of her eye, Irene kept spying the Haviland platters on the sideboard—a cherry pie, caramel tarts, and a big multilayered white cake—thinking, *Let's get* ooonnn *with it!* Something told her that her room and board and sweet tooth were at stake, so she agreed with Olive and told her she didn't think Bessie Belle Thornton was fit for office either.

After a few days, Irene had eaten more home-cooked food than the average American does in six months. Every meal was an informal, but sit-down, affair with whole roasted chickens and cutlets of veal, ears of corn, field greens in vinegar, and pitchers of lemonade or tea. As for desserts, there were banana cream pies and lemon cakes and fudge brownies. Throughout the house, there were small silver bowls of marzipan and toffee. But the bewildering issue for Irene was the food itself. Basically, from whence did it all come? One look in Olive's refrigerator would send any hungry person running for a smorgasbord. On each shelf were bottled pickles and juices and dark cane syrups. Her cabinets and counters contained green glass jars and crocks; the drawers held coupons smudged with cake frosting and stray Cheerios. There was a cruet filled with lard and canisters of brandied pears. But you could never open up the Frigidaire door and eat something on the spot. When Irene told her grandmother, "You don't have anything in the refrigerator to eat, just ingredients," Olive stared blankly and said, "What else is they?"

From this assortment of goods came magical, mouthwatering banquets. Olive would stand at the stove while stirring pinto beans or dumplings. She would dig into a fossilized paper bag and pull out a fistful of flour, rolling it across waxed paper. Her nimble hands, coated like two white gloves, would knead and cut the biscuit dough into perfect circles. Cabbage, carrots, and kale would be plucked from the garden and dissected, rolled in butter or cradled between layers of vegetable casseroles. Wrinkled, goosefleshed pieces of yellow chicken would go into the black cast-iron skillet, bubbling with lard, and transform into golden brown nuggets. Olive did all this with an odd, antiquated assortment of kitchen aids: jar openers resembling ice picks, spoons and ladles crudely fashioned from tiger maple, and potato mashers that seemed to have been made from auto parts. Olive would test the cornbread by sticking its center with a broom tendril.

"You watch what I'm doin'." She would blow the silver hair from her brow and wink at Irene, the little sunbeams around her eyes crinkling. "Learn ya sumthin'!" Then she'd slap her dusty hands against her apron and move to the next course.

Near the butler's pantry was a laboratory with shelves and drawers and glass cabinets. Here and there were a mortar and pestle, and bottles with leaves and twisted bark and ancient mushrooms and ginseng. One container marked *belladonna* stored the bell-shaped, flowered herb, and even had a skull and crossbones warning on it.

When Irene asked her about it, Olive said, "This is where I do my doctorin'. I don't believe in none of that modern stuff."

"You don't?" Irene said, looking around at all the cubbyholes. "For anything?"

"Doctors . . . whadda they know, enyways? First they git ya in their trap, then they finally come in the room to see ya, and says, 'Ummmmm, whadda we got here?' When ya leave you've got ya sum expensive pills and another appointment. It's all a racket!"

Olive hadn't visited any doctor in decades, relying instead on her home remedies—epsom salts, herbal teas, and brown gooey tonics all made in her kitchen. She didn't believe in pills, either. After one or two, she'd add the bottle to the archives of prescriptions in her bathroom, along with her trusty Lydia E. Pinkham tablets.

"How ya gonna argue with a ninety-five-year-old?" Shorty griped. "You ain't got no position!"

Last, but not least, there was the "top secret" operation that kept Olive in motion. With the gurgling vats of fruit and chocolate on the burner, and her apron spotted with buttercream icing like an artist's palette, Olive experimented with one recipe after another. In the butler's pantry was a pie safe, a painted wooden cabinet with perforated tin insets, which is where she stored the sugary goodies: Run for the Roses pies, bourbon balls, five-layer coconut cakes.

Though the enterprise was still on the drawing board, Irene, as well as everybody else in Blue Lick, knew the confections were for Rebecca's candy shop. Still, Olive would lift her eyebrows in defiance, lick her chocolate-coated fingertips, and declare to Irene that her lips were sealed about the mystery business.

In the evening, right after supper, was the pilgrimage to the veranda. Taking a nip of apple wine, Olive would crane her neck, gaping into an orange-streaked sky. The eyes that had seen thousands of sunsets would study the paths and gullies that etched through her property, with the wonderment of a child. She was still enthralled by the brown cottontail bunnies that scurried through her crepe myrtle, and every time she spotted a firefly, she'd say, "Oh look! A lightning bug!"

By this time, the wine had kicked in and Olive would start singing something snappy like "Dixie" or "Red Red Robin," lashing her arms like Lawrence Welk. In a voice like dying sunshine, Olive would almost always end the evening singing "His Eye Is on the Sparrow."

Before they turned in for the evening, there were cookies or cheese and crackers and other bedtime snacks. With the help of a dozen Dexatrim per day, Irene had finally lost three pounds and was struggling to keep it off. Since food was the main attraction in Olive's house, and there were calories in the Kentucky air, with Irene's zero resistance this was not going to be easy. Maybe none of it would be.

To get Irene to warm up to the relocation, Lila Mae had presented Kentucky as her daughter's salvation. Then, like a burdensome suitcase handed over just seconds before a train departure, Lila Mae crafted a pessimistic picture after Irene bought her bus ticket. She was "gravely concerned" that Irene would never find a job unless she wanted to scrub toilets or pump gas. What Lila Mae really meant was she wouldn't get work unless Lila Mae herself used her connections. That's when she broke the news that she'd already set something up with Silkes's Funeral Parlor. The owner, Dan Silkes, was waiting for Irene's call.

"A funeral parlor?" Irene shrieked. "Forget it!"

"Well, beggars can't be choosers, Irene Gaye," said Lila Mae, with her mother-knows-best voice. "You've got a lot of, of stuff to deal with, you know what I mean."

"You mean the sex, drugs, and rock and roll?" Irene blurted out. "Is that what you mean, Mom?"

"Well, I swanee, you don't have to put it like that!"

Irene loved to scare the liver out of Lila Mae, so she told her mother she was fine, that she was down to a gram of cocaine and a pint of whiskey a day. "I'm trying to cut down!"

"Irene!" Lila Mae panted. "If you're trying to give me a heart attack, you're doing a good job, so help me Hannah!" Irene could imagine her mother's troubled eyes big as manhole covers—just the type of anxiety she had hoped to create.

It didn't take a genius or Lila Mae's sermons to realize that Irene wasn't exactly the ideal candidate for employment. Her red-and-purple hair, unusual enough for Los Angeles, was outrageous in Blue Lick. Even Olive, who had been warned about her granddaughter's unorthodox looks, had slid her eyes up and down Irene and said, "Well, good gravy! Yer gonna tone that down sum, ain't ya?"

If she got really desperate, Irene could always seek waitress work at Miz Becky's BBQ Shack, a trade she didn't think she had ever been cut out for, even though she'd spent one third of her adult life doing it. With all the weight she had gained, simply supporting her own body was exhausting. Restaurant hours were long, plus, what with her carpal tunnel situation, how did she know she could even hang on to a tray of food? Besides all that, who wanted to work for a slave-driver relative?

Once, when she'd been desperate for money, Irene ran errands for Rebecca during the Christmas holidays, but she couldn't keep up the exhausting pace and quit after her first paycheck. Rebecca was possessed of such ferocious energy and fierce determination that she could grind them all into the ground.

"Honey!" Lila Mae would preach. "You'd better take care of yourself. Get you some rest." But Rebecca would retort, "We'll all have plenty of time to sleep when we're in our coffins!"

But it was unfair to single out Rebecca for blame. Exhaustion was the leitmotif in Irene's life. The source of this lethargy and her health problems was no mystery—it was her seesawing weight. When she was existing on Tic Tacs, Diet Coke, and amphetamines, she was a mere splinter and her family used to practically cram food down her throat. But now, with her depression, there seemed to be a shuttle filling some city dump–sized hole in her body and no matter how much and what she shoveled—jelly beans, Popeyes fried chicken, mashed potatoes, Sara Lee cheesecakes—anything and everything, really, there was no saturation point. With the scales tipping one-hundred-eighty pounds, there was no way around it: The five-foot-four Irene was a big old woolly mammoth, one of those behemoths on display at the La Brea Tar Pits.

Often, with her belly full and the clock ticking midnight, she would vow to make a clean start the next day. But some labyrinthine psychology (or the fragrance of cinnamon buns) would intervene and her willpower would fall prey to her urges.

In her efforts to lose weight, there was nothing she hadn't experimented with—Redux, Dexatrim, Weight Watchers, Fen-Phen, and liquid diets. She'd even tried enrolling in an aerobics class, but the routines were so choreographed that she felt like a stumblebum. She was sure the other participants had been faxed instructions for the steps.

So now, when her sweet tooth flared up, which was constantly, Irene tried new approaches: stubbing out her cigarette on half-eaten pies or chewing the candy and pastries but spitting them out before swallowing. "What's the matter?" Carleen joked. "Don't you even have the guts to be a bulimic?"

Rebecca, the expert on everything—according to Rebecca, anyway—loved to give Irene tips. "Do you know what your problem is, Irene? You fail to see the connection between the candy bar you're eating right now and the five pounds you gain every week." As much as Irene resented her words, at least she was honest, none of that "you're not fat, just pleasingly plump" bullshit.

Irene needed to lose practically as much as Rebecca or Carleen weighed, both of them being gracile and streamlined, built for speed and efficiency and admiring looks from strangers. Their curves were in all the right places and no matter what they ate, they stayed that way. Even though they were both many years older than Irene, they looked ten years younger and reminded Irene of those delicate ballerinas on the tops of music boxes. It was sickening, just sickening.

Whenever she went to a concert or sporting event, she'd notice jolly-faced women twice her size, licking ice cream cones, their eyes sparkling with life. Irene always wondered what in the hell these tubs had to be so happy about and why, if they were really as miserable as Irene, they just didn't cut out the crap and growl at the world. She wondered how the blubbery Bessie Belle Thornton held her head up. Yet there she was running for re-election for an important political office and Irene was just simply . . . running.

Yes, the hole Irene had created for herself went all the way to China and she had to crawl out of it one inch, one pound, one less Nestle's Crunch at a time.

Underneath all the tangled feelings—the trepidation, the stranger-in-a-strange-land feeling—Irene was relieved to be in Kentucky. How lucky she was to be there with a gust of summer perfume in the air and the chirruping of the frogs from some mysterious ravine and Darrell hundreds of miles away. How fortunate that the only inconvenience was the mixed-up electrical system and the evening gripe sessions.

It would take Irene a few days to get her bearings, then she would

go through the motions of looking for gainful employment. Otherwise, they'd be calling her a no good, lazy slob behind her back. There
were also her finances to take into consideration, which would go
from bad to worse to triple impossible. Bankruptcy, Irene thought, the
great motivator.

And then there were those darn church signs, haunting and taunting
her. The latest one, the slogan she spotted at the Living Hope Baptist
Church, took the prize so far. It said: GOD FEEDS THE BIRDS BUT HE
DOESN'T THROW FOOD INTO THEIR NEST.

Chapter Eight

Rebecca

JUNE 1999

As if things weren't bad enough, they couldn't get Sheriff Burkle on the line right away. They got Curtis Wooten instead. This was somewhat bad news since Uncle Shorty had a county-wide reputation as an exaggerator as well as a top-notch blabbermouth. Not that it had anything to do with the stickup, but his wife, Maybelle, was the realtor handling Rebecca's purchases and she couldn't keep a secret either. Unfortunately, the barber pole and another shipment of furniture for Rosemont had just arrived at Olive's farm and Uncle Shorty would be dying to give Rebecca the latest delivery details. If he had any second-hand real estate information from Maybelle, he'd probably blab about that, too.

So, Rebecca knew she was in for it when Shorty had answered the phone and said, "Deputy Shuruff Wooten here." They kept asking for Jimmy Buzz to pick up the line, but just as Rebecca feared, Shorty belly flopped right into Dante's Inferno. "Ooooeeeee! This ole town's hotter than them three-alarm ribs Miz Becky's serves!" Just to make sure they were in on things, Shorty stuck the phone receiver in the air to soak up all the background noises—a caterwauling infant, a crackly police radio—all fused with a jukebox playing Tammy Wynette's "Stand by Your Man."

"Yep, ain't nobody seen the likes o' this much commotion since Ruthie Lee Horner's wheelchair went haywire in the Walmark! Ever'-body's just all tore up!"

"Is this guy for real or is this the Hee Haw Channel?" Little Peep switched knowing looks with his associates. "Yeah," one of them sniped, "is it live or Memorex? Ha-ha."

"I can assure you it's live . . . very live!" Rebecca threw the men a dirty look. Judging from Shorty's anecdotes, things weren't too bad, or he wouldn't have been discussing the Horner wheelchair fiasco.

Rebecca knew it was too good to be true that her uncle would hand over the phone without piping up about something or other, and she was right. "You know that developer, the one who's been buyin' property around here, Mr. CASTLECO?" Shorty asked. "Well, one of his people come into Miz Becky's and that new building you bought, he told us, he said—"

"Uh, Shorty, could we discuss this later?" Given the choice, Rebecca actually preferred to talk about the robbery than to take her chances with the unpredictable uncle.

"Yes, Deputy Wooten, we need to speed up the tempo on this, so could you get Sheriff Burkle for us? This is a matter of utmost importance!" Little Peep gave his head a self-important nod, as if to say, "Let's show 'em who's boss."

Rebecca's hopes were high that the sheriff, who was as different from Shorty as Laurel was from Hardy, would return the train to the track. Sheriff Burkle was level-headed and unflappable, and she was thrilled when he finally picked up the extension, giving them a lanky, friendly, Texas Ranger of a hello.

"So, how y'all tonight?" Rebecca could picture the man with his big bear hug of a smile, his two front teeth rimmed in gold like twin picture frames. "Y'all doin' okay?"

"Huh, you tell *us* how we're doing." Little Peep made sarcastic half moons of his eyes and huffed. "You're the man with all the information!" On a yellow legal tablet, Peepers wrote the words "BBQ Incident" and underlined them three times.

"Hi, Jimmy, we're all here on the speaker phone, the accountants, too. What's going on?" David couldn't bring himself to call him Jimmy Buzz anymore than Shorty Wooten knew the correct pronunciation of Wal-Mart. "What happened?"

"Jimmy Buzz, is everything under control, is everything okay?" Rebecca leaned forward, squirming and twitching uncomfortably in her seat.

"Yes, Mr. Burkle, why don't you tell us aaa-lll about it." Peepers had stretched way back in his chair and brayed in a condescending, big-shot voice.

"Weeeellll, now . . . let's see, sir." Burkle, who nursed the thought like a sweet lozenge, let his response putt-putt-putt around his brain. Finally he said, "I, I don't rightly know how to put this."

"Great, just great." Little Peep threw his hands in the air, and hit the table with a noisy clunk. "We got Dumb and Dumber in one police headquarters."

Rebecca, who felt protective of the man, told Jimmy Buzz to simply start at the beginning. "Just take your time."

"Well, first off, I had to butter up the customers. I had the Daughters of the American Revolution ladies, they were havin' a get-together, then besides them, there was—Ollie Reed Herman, Whitie Whiteman, and Icie Smith—they was here at the time; Icie's that kook who wears the crazy Civil War cap, she was married to the fellow who—"

"Mr. Burkle." Peepers, straining to keep cool, shut his eyes and pumped his two palms toward the floor like he was dribbling basketballs. "Let me cut to the proverbial chase, if I might. Were there any disgruntled employees or customers, any injuries, any possible liability claims, any—?"

"With all due respect there, Mr. Peep," Burkle interrupted. "Why would anyone get sued? Fer what?"

"You had a robbery, didn't you, Sheriff? It's 1999, isn't it?" Little Peep declared. "It's always the owner's fault! A burglar breaks into your house, suffers a concussion, gets mangled by Rover—it's lawsuit city!"

"Well, you won't have none of that this time, I'll grant you that! We've got ourselves a group of fine, cooperative folks. Besides, Deputy Wooten give ever'body free cobbler."

"C-c-cobbler?" The word bubbled out of Little Peep's mouth.

"You know, somethin' to make their nerves right." Offering free dessert was the policy they'd decided on to calm down the customers when a waitress spilled food or gave slow service. But nobody had considered what appeasement, if such a thing was even possible, they'd offer in the case of a robbery.

"Are you joking? There are dunces who would settle for pie? No way!" With that, Little Peep began chanting, "LAWSUIT, LAWSUIT, LAWSUIT!" like a berserk cuckoo clock.

Normally, Rebecca would have hopped up and said, "Now listen here, you midget!" then indoctrinated him on the virtues of rural Kentucky, a sojourn to the fabulous, crime-free fifties. What a laugh that was turning out to be.

"Can you give me anything . . . anything at all, Mr. Burkle?" Peep's hands were pressed together as if in prayer.

"Wa-e-ll." Burkle took a long warm-up breath. "Let's just say, we give them crooks somethin' to think about, a little farewell soo-veneer, by cracky."

"Oh, so there were some injuries?" With the situation looking so promising, Little Peep began to wiggle and pant and fidget.

"Oh, you might find a bruise or scrape or some such . . . nothin' to speak of," said Burkle.

"Nothing to speak of? Don't you think it's time we got to the bottom of this, Sheriff?" Peep gave him a fake weary tone, like a vagabond who had been traveling down a long road. "Aren't you tired of this cat-and-mouse game?"

Burkle still wouldn't cough up anything and they might have been there all night if Shorty hadn't let it slip that Letty Bookbinder, a DAR bigwig, was involved. After that Burkle had to admit that, yes, Bookbinder had stopped the skinny thief in his tracks and Burkle had handled the heavyset one. Another woman named Doreen Sutcliffe, who happened to be in town for the gourd festival, had also pitched in.

"Ole Letty, she's a corker!" Burkle chuckled. "Yep, she pinned one feller's arms behind his back and Doreen Sutcliffe crowned him with a copper kettle. That ole boy was out flat! My guy wasn't feeling like no ballet dancer neither; I took cer of his toes!"

"This is all very charming," Little Peep snapped. "And I have no doubt that Ms. Bookbinder deserves a bronze statue in the town square, and yes, it was a lucky break that this Sutcliffe woman was in town . . . but you're not giving me much, Mr. Burkle, YOU REALLY AREN'T!" Peep's eyes were orbicular and belligerent and his hands pretended to strangle Jimmy Buzz.

"Wa-ell, I might not be, but there's more to this than meets the eye." Now it was Burkle's chance to flare up. "I GOTTA GIT IT STRAIGHT IN MY HAY-ED FIRST!"

Composing himself, Little Peep took several deep breaths as he tick-tocked his pen back and forth against the desk. "Perhaps you should review your police notes, maybe they'll refresh your memory."

"Police notes? Let me ask you somethin', Mr. Peepers. You ever been on a crime scene, sir?"

"No. Have you, Sheriff Burkle?" Little Peep, quite tickled with himself, slapped hands with Phil Bustamante, who said, "Touché, Reggie!"

"Ya see, we got ourselves a crime in progress here, Mr. Peepers. Now you can horse around all you want with this pro-ceed-drill bullcrap, but let me tell you somethin': We got haywire citizens, we got folks from Harlan and Bullitt counties who showed up pokin' their noses where they don't belong. We got half a dozen Daughters raisin' Cain. Then there's Bobby Red Bobblett and Switch Banfield, over here from Little Fork, they's here with their ambulance equipment. Then there's that little gal who works for the Gazette, she brung her tape recorder and some curly-headed feller I ain't never seen before with a camera snappin' up a storm. In other words, I got my hands full and I ain't got time to be takin' no notes! Now you ask any seasoned law enforcement officer and they're gonna tell you the same thing, boy. Notes, this ain't no elementary school!"

"Good for you." Little Peep clapped like a circus seal. "You can string a few words together!"

"You'd better get to the bottom of this." David pitched Rebecca an exasperated look. Normally he would have taken the bull by the horns, but there was a tacit understanding that Kentucky was Rebecca's bailiwick.

Rebecca said, "Could you stop beating around the bush, Jim Buzz? You have us very nervous." That's when he mentioned a third culprit, some shadowy figure who was in the getaway car, something that was news to all of them.

By now, Peep had a stack of smoke shooting out of his head. "You are trying my patience, Burkle! You really are!" He dropped forward, putting both arms on David's desk as if he were doing a pushup, and shouted into the speaker phone, "For God's sake, man! My clients need to know—did anyone get SHOT? That's what I'm getting at!"

"Now what do you think? This here is Kentucky, Mr. Peep!" Burkle exploded. "Of *course* someone got shot!"

"Shot? Wha-what do you mean, shot?" Now that he had gotten more information than he'd bargained for, Peep grabbed his chair, his neck veins glowing. "B-but, a minute ago, you were talking cuts and bruises and cobbler. Now you tell me there was gunfire? Y-you can't mean that." His voice was low and controlled like a casket salesman.

"Ha-llfire, man, who do you think yer dealin' with? You cain't just twiddle your thumbs when ya got hoods in front of ya, ya git my drift? All them questions about how ever'one wuz doin', why I thought you wuz talkin' 'bout the customers, the townsfolk, how they wuz doin'. That's who's impordant. The robbers, if you're a-talkin' 'bout them, sure they got roughed up some. I plugged 'em myself!"

"Roughed up? Frankly, it's a little more than 'roughed up' if there was gunfire! Wouldn't you say? Jesus!" Little Peep tugged his bow tie. "So, are you going to tell me how bad it is or do I have to drag it out of you syllable by syllable?"

"Well, one ole boy's a goner'."

"Goner?" Little Peep cocked one Dumbo ear. "What do you mean 'goner'?"

"Wa-ell sir, we're talkin' chalk outlines, white sheets, and funeral parlor coffins, that's what we're talkin'!"

"My God, a fatality? You don't mean it, man!" Little Peep delivered the line dramatically, like an actor in a Noel Coward play. "Why in the name of God didn't you tell us?"

Rebecca told him it was no time for jokes. "Jimmy Buzz, now cut the comedy and tell us what went on."

"I done told ya, Miss Becky. I had to do away with one of the SOBs!"

"Are you saying that someone was really killed? Oh, God!" Rebecca was numb, collapsing deeper into her red cashmere cardigan, trying to smother the chill that was settling in her bones. She heard the words, but she didn't want to believe the information. She had been hoping that, as sadistic as it might have been, Burkle was simply getting back at Little Peep.

"Do you know who it was?" David asked. His hair had a mad-scientist tousle to it and his tie was loosened as if to accommodate his growing anxiety. With their luck it was probably the minister, mayor, or county judge who'd been hit or worse, one of the Daughters of the American Revolution! Oh, Olive would clobber her when it got out that the Kentucky Daughters were involved.

"It's one of the fellows from that rough bunch. There's a group of folks who got a glimpse at the others, just to see if anything rung any bells. Don't worry, we'll round 'em up, yes we will. They won't get far!"

"So, the other two actually *got away* then?" David asked. The way Sheriff Burkle had been building up the role of the Bookbinder and Sutcliffe women, Rebecca had assumed the other two suspects were bound in duct tape and handcuffs. But, on top of the dead body, apparently, there were two robbers on the lam.

"This is bad news, tragic news indeed!" Little Peep, now fully recovered, was doing his best to look sad, but dotted across his face, like medals on an officer's uniform, were ornaments of victory—a tiny smirk, an arched eyebrow, a curved upper lip. "There will be statements and police reports and just all types of red tape! There isn't enough cobbler on the planet to keep this situation quiet."

"Listen, this here is cause for celebration. So just stop all the boohooing." Burkle said the dead body belonged to Eddie Ray Youngblood. "He's a mean-to-the-bone crook, a murderous galoot who's been afoul of the law since he wuz a boy. He come in here all likkered up, ready to shoot the place down. Don't you go feelin' sorry for that boy, I mean it now!"

The name Youngblood was one Rebecca, as well as most Kentuckians, knew well. Growing up, any time one of her children was on the verge of disgrace, Lila Mae would swat their behind and say, "Good Lordy! People'll think you're a Youngblood!"

For obvious reasons, it was fortunate that the victim hadn't been one of Blue Lick's beloved citizens—in fact, many people would see a dead Youngblood as a plus—but Rebecca wasn't exactly celebrating like Jimmy Buzz. She felt responsible, just knowing their place of business hosted a tragedy of that magnitude. She was also irked at herself for having been so nonchalant, doing everything in her power not to call Burkle right away, even picking fights with everyone.

She could only imagine what it would take to physically erase the evidence: a tribe of women on hands and knees, scrub brushes and lye soap in hand; a customer base, flimsy enough to begin with, that would have to be restored; and tighter security measures in a community where front doors remained unlocked and banks still honored counter checks. There would be donations to make, flowers to send, sympathy notes to write. She was sick, simply sick with a concoction of emotions. "Jimmy, this is all we need—a fatality. What can we do?"

"One thing you're *not* going to do is send posies and love notes to the victim's family. You start that pen pal crap and you're implicated in the guilt." That was Little Peep talking. "Don't put anything in writing, even a sympathy card." He stopped for a moment then made his triumphant announcement. "Just prepare to get the pants sued off you!"

"Great!" David expelled the word in one neat, disgusted syllable and took a sip of water.

"That's just tough toenails!" Burkle replied. "You step on somebody in these parts and you git what you git."

"I'm just telling you how the world works, I don't care if it's the Kentucky sticks or the moon. This is one hell of a catastrophe!" Peep countered.

Sheriff Burkle couldn't have known that his descriptions of street gangs in Blue Lick Springs were more shovelfuls of dirt on a double grave: his own and Miz Becky's. How could he realize that with every utterance of the savage details, Little Peep, whose chest was plumped up like Napoleon's, and his plan to close the restaurant, became more palatable. Jimmy Buzz was not only jeopardizing his own job, but the fate of Gladys's Famous Red Velvet Cake made from his mother's prized recipe. Even Rebecca's grandmother had relinquished her secrets for Miss

Olive's sour-cherry pie. It was the end of a dream for so many good people. But, if there was ever a legitimate reason to shut down operations, this was it.

As if the news about the shooting wasn't enough, Shorty, back in the picture, blurted out, "I might as well leave things on a high note. Rebecca, them bowlin' pins finally come in. So's, we'll get that alley open by July fourth, or my name ain't Curtis Allan Wooten! That old boy is takin' his good, sweet time restorin' them barber poles, though!"

When nobody said *boo*, Shorty said, "Say, I didn't let no cat outta the bag, I hope."

In light of the dead body and missing crooks, Rebecca was sort of off the hook, at least temporarily, but she knew Little Peep heard Shorty's bowling alley comment because he narrowed his eyes and muttered, "I hope that's not what I think it is."

When Rebecca happened to glance at David, he said, "What's this about a bowling alley and barber pole?" He didn't say it out loud, but that's what his eyes were telling her he meant. The good news—and only an optimistic moron would call it that—was that Shorty didn't mention the candy store or the antiques she'd bought for Rosemont.

David was no stupe, and he certainly knew how Rebecca operated, so it was a fatal mistake for her to think that she wouldn't be interrogated later . . . one more inquest to add to the vicious cycle. The remedy for that would have been to simply stop buying more property, something she kept vowing to do. But she would get a bucking bronco of an idea and no matter how hard she tried to lasso it into submission, before she knew it, she was the proud owner of another building.

More than once David had told Rebecca it was the underhandedness he hated more than the actual money spent. "Why don't you just *tell* me?" he always begged, indicating that her tactics, not economics, were the real source of his irritation.

Once, when he had convinced Rebecca to be up-front with him, she broached the subject of Kentucky property, but David had said, "Oh, no, you don't." Since honesty was not the best policy, what else could an obsessed, determined person do *but* sneak around?

Besides, there were already so many lost souls—buildings whose brick and mortar remains had been swept into trucks and taken, one load at a time, to the city dump. There had been architectural master-pieces knocked down for the sake of another parking lot. Someday they would all be sorry, even the Little Peeps of the world who thought progress was a good idea.

Obviously, she had to admit that three new businesses were lunacy. She'd known it while she was slipping cash payments to the owners, and collecting antiques. But Rebecca continued to hope against hope that the moment of truth would never occur.

If David and Little Peep knew the whole story, they'd flip. Rainy-day funds and nest eggs had been used for down payments on buildings or to cover checks to renovators. David was accustomed to large checks writ-ten to her family, so Rebecca got them in on it. She switched checks with her mother, so it looked like a large sum had been for Lila Mae, not Bai-ley Tucker, the owner of the bowling alley and confectionery property. First she gave her mother a check to deposit, then she had her mother write the down payment to Tucker.

"Dear me," Lila Mae had fretted. "I'm not sure how this works, but you know what you're doing, honey!" With the thousands that had been dumped into Lila Mae's account, David probably thought her mother was hooked on morphine or something.

Rebecca tried the same technique with Carleen until her attorney husband got wind of it and called Rebecca to say "What kind of a hoax are you trying to pull now?" She had even sold jewelry to a friend, rob-bing Peter to pay Paul. And here she was married to a millionaire, mak-ing her financial shenanigans all the more absurd!

Shorty, the big mouth, wasn't finished yet. Just when they were about to hang up, he said, "I tried to tell ya before about that CASTLECO developer. He sent some feller in here to ask if the owners wanted to sell Miz Becky's. Maybelle tells me they're scoopin' up every-thing in sight!"

Shorty's bad news stung the atmosphere like pelts of hail: CASTLECO had been buying acreages and parcels in different names, piecing together house after house and farm after farm. They were, as Shorty had sug-gested, determined to buy every shred of real estate in Blue Lick.

"Is this *the Horace* Castle? Well, now, this *is* a high note!" Little Peep arched his chest and pulled each shirtsleeve. "Just send CASTLECO our way; tell 'em to get out their checkbooks."

"Wait a minute! Are you talking about the barbecue *restaurant* or the Adams *building?* I'm *not* selling that property!" Rebecca set her smoldering green eyes on Little Peep; then added her standard line. "Over my dead body!"

Peep raised both eyebrows and muttered, "Well, we've already got one of those, haven't we?"

When she caught David's eye to see which way the wind in his universe was blowing, he told her to calm down, they'd discuss it all later. Lucky for Rebecca, David wasn't a reactionary; instead, he would slice right through the claptrap, always making a sound decision based on facts, not emotions. In this particular case, that might not turn out to be a good thing.

David, already cobbling together a solution, said, "You should probably hop on a plane, just to make sure everything's all right, don't you think so, honey?" Normally, David and Ava tried to discourage Rebecca from visiting Kentucky since she had a tendency to go for three days and disappear for three weeks, returning with a pocketful of secret deeds. But it was obvious that someone needed to keep tabs on the situation. The best thing about David's suggestion was that he'd called her "honey."

Jumping on the bandwagon, Little Peep nodded vigorously and said, "It would behoove us to have someone in Kentucky," tying the trip to the shutdown of all out-of-state enterprises. "Yes, there's still time to get out while the getting's good!" Peep said maybe he and Phil Bustamante should accompany Rebecca on the trip, that, between the three of them, they could get more accomplished, and David thought it was an excellent idea.

Great, just great, Rebecca was thinking. Although she managed to keep a wax-doll smile on her face, she could think of nothing worse than to be trapped with those two.

Through the window, she could see the early traces of a creamy moon, and the vast blue-black sky glittered with stars. She imagined it stretching across California and the entire west, getting darker and moodier as it moved through Alabama, Mississippi, and Tennessee until it reached all the way to Kentucky. In moments, Rebecca and David would drive to their home at the beach. All along Pacific Coast Highway, under a blinding full moon, they would pass beachcombers and fringed hitchhikers thumbing rides to Montecito. They would stop at Giorgio's for linguine carbonara and Merlot and all would be fine and dandy. It seemed surrealistic that, halfway across the country, the feathers were being plucked out of her dream.

Maybe she had all this coming to her. Riding around on a high horse of conceit, she had magnified the importance of her measly role in Blue Lick's renaissance to an unrealistic height. How imbecilic it was of Rebecca to believe that she could add some polish to a few buildings and protect the town from the ailments of the modern world and also rescue Rosemont!

When the dust settled and everything had been sorted through, perhaps the biggest impediment was not David or Little Peep at all, but CASTLECO. She couldn't stand the sound of their name. CASTLECO this, CASTLECO that. Who were these people anyway? Why, after years of apathy and neglect, had Blue Lick Springs suddenly caught a big developer's fancy?

Months before, her grandmother had warned her the bulldozers were coming, men in silk suits and hardhats. Olive had spotted them across the street from her land, the development plans rolled into blueprints, clipboards at their chests.

"They show up pointin' their fingers, turnin' it all topsy-turvy! They'll bulldoze three-hundred-year-old trees, then here comes a landscaper a few months later with sum spindly ole things in a five-gallon container." Olive, licking the pink whisker of spirits from her mouth, would stamp the table with her snifter of apple wine. "They won't rest till they've turned ever'thang into asphalt. Out with the old, in with the new! Any day now they'll be a-comin' fer me, I reckon."

In the past, Rebecca had locked eyes with Uncle Shorty or Lila Mae or one relative or another, hiding their knowing grins from the ever eagle-eyed Olive who would be on the lookout for such subtle communciation of cynicism.

"Just let the woman holler her ole scorched lungs out." Shorty would wait until Olive's back was turned and the rumble of her television set drowned out his mutterings. "I don't know where she gets them crazy notions." Maybelle would rattle her bouncy curls at her mother-in-law's capricious beliefs. "It ain't all that bad!"

Even when her grandmother told her about the changes that would be "Blue Lick's ruination," Rebecca believed the comment to be just another string of syllables to congest the air in dinner conversation.

Yes, the robbery was a monster with several different heads, much more than the crime itself: It also meant the death of her dream to reinvent her hometown, and her grandmother's disappointment, the grandmother who was depending on her to keep the torch blazing and the real-estate purchases coming.

But time was Rebecca's enemy. While she took toddler steps to return Blue Lick to its nineteenth-century glory, the developer was storming the city the way Sherman annihilated Atlanta. Unfortunately, she had to speed up the tempo, turning what she had hoped to be a leisurely process into a game plan with winged feet, one propelled by an all-star cast. She'd have to be Delilah and Mata Hari and Mother Teresa all in one.

Worst, she had to accomplish it all, whatever the *all* turned out to be, without the benefit of feedback from David, the one person whom she trusted, and on the sly, safe from the person whom she loathed, Reginald C. Peepers Jr.

Yes, Rebecca had a horrible feeling it was all going down the drain, swift as a barrel tumbling down Niagara Falls.

Chapter Nine

Rebecca

June 1999

It should have been no surprise that Rebecca's Blue Lick Springs enterprises were turning out to be more trouble than she bargained for, or that she had to resort to chicanery to keep it all afloat. She already had an eighty-two-page list of things to do, a document that was supposed to help her juggle all those hundreds of details necessary to keep her family's lifestyle from unraveling, but it was actually one that got longer with each passing day.

Instead of making a dent in the escalating mess, she was researching period architecture and rallying to save threatened farmland. Rather than flying to New York to discuss her documentary project, she had ended up in Blue Lick Springs for the final sampling of red velvet cake. And, when she was supposed to accompany David on a corporate retreat, she was in Bowling Green hunting for antique leaded windows for the confectionery. She even missed a deadline for the first draft of a book on historical Southern gardens she was cowriting with a friend whose phone calls she'd probably have to start dodging.

It seemed way too simple to pin her problems of overcommitment on computers, but Rebecca continued to blame them for the dilemma she was in, anyway. "Computers?" David gave her his straitjacket look.

"They should make things *easier*. You must be doing something wrong."

Of course, she couldn't accuse computers of creating the entire debacle, but she'd been doing just fine with her hand-written lists since she was a little girl, entries as simple as: "Do arithmetic homework" and "Feed goldfish" on a sheet of pastel notebook paper. But she'd let her friends convince her that the only way to be super-duper organized was with a laptop. "I can't believe *you*, Miss Organization, aren't computerized," they'd exclaim. So, after fifteen years, she finally succumbed.

In the beginning, she made a very basic, general list of things to do. What a wonderful feeling to trap all the ideas and tasks on one screen! How tidy it seemed to have an eagle's view of everything that needed to be accomplished! How easy it would be to actually accomplish it all! Each day she would wake up like Lady Macbeth, tackling first the cut-and-dried matters such as "Take clothes to the cleaners" or "Pick up Ava's prescription." With one finger on the computer's delete key, she would shout, "Off, off, damned list!"

Seduced by the feeling of achievement and the sheer exhiliration of moving volumes of text from one spot to another, she spent hours pruning, shearing, and rearranging information. As the list grew, it begat more lists. Those hatched sublists with even more topics. Soon enough she discovered items such as "African safari" next to "Take dog to vet." Thus, she created a list of everyday chores and another separate section for trips. It wasn't long before she realized how nonsensical it was to put African safari, which was actually more of a vacation, in the same category as "Brunch in Santa Barbara." So, she created categories of trips. This led to more divisions: tropical, historical, cultural, educational.

Before long she had head-spinning columns of restaurants to visit, birthday gifts to buy, movies to see, books to read, articles to write, letters to send, a room-by-room list of remodeling tasks, a disaster page with earthquake information in case she happened to be in California, and tornado instructions for the times she was in Kentucky. There were calendars of appointments, lists of hiking trails, and names of the top doctors to call in case anyone she knew ever needed an organ transplant. There were catchy titles for novels she hadn't yet written and even a list with the names of songs to use if one of the books ever got published, then made into a movie, and Rebecca had some say-so in the music selections. It was a process that pretty much assured her no spare time and would only work if she lived to be as old as Methuselah.

Knowing how Rebecca operated, it wasn't surprising that she had become a human *Yellow Pages* for her family and friends. They would call for the name of a top-notch plumber or reliable electrician. Since she had great connections, they would ask her to get them a reservation in a fully booked hotel or the best table at a popular restaurant. The idea that Rebecca, who thrived on challenges, could do a favor, gain a cross-off, and win a best-friend award, was actually appealing. No matter how many issues she solved or favors she did, the tasks were cats with nine lives, landing right back in Rebecca's lap. Many of them had but one solution: money. It was the stone with which she killed so many birds.

Oh, how she would love to grant everyone's wishes in the true spirit of charity, to smile seraphically, and gently pat their needy head and say, "Yes, my child" like some saintly Mother Superior. Unfortunately, she usually felt like she was fiddling while Rome burned, gritting her teeth and huffing and puffing as their woeful tales unfolded. Her heart would pound, her lungs would rise and fall in hyperventilation as she would simply want to shout, "How much? Just tell me how much!"

What Rebecca really hated was the way everybody in her family from Lila Mae to Baby Sister would always chastise her for moving so fast, for taking on too much, as if they—most of them total flops—had some secret formula for success.

"Slow down, you're going to kill yourself!" they would shriek in one breath, then turn around and ask for a favor that added to the burden they insisted she should lighten.

The current thorn in her side was Lila Mae's seventy-fifth birthday party. Rebecca shouldn't have been surprised that the event was gobbling up days and days of her time and becoming a test of her organizational fortitude and filial devotion.

In spite of Lila Mae's insistence on keeping things simple, there were four hundred names on her guest list, all decorated with asterisks and anecdotes, and most of which didn't include phone numbers or addresses. The names had also fallen into two groups: people who couldn't attend because they were dead, and friends who might be alive but were nowhere to be found.

Among the missing were Lila Mae's best friends from childhood—twin girls named Lula and Lurlene, although she thought Lula had passed away. There was a darling waitress with flaming orange hair who worked at a roadside cafe between Bullhead City, Arizona, and Oatman, California, and the plumber in Sparks, Nevada, whose parakeet she'd saved from a burning house. At the top of her list was Benny Feather-horse, but when his name came up, she'd sigh, and moan, "I suppose he's in the state pen, though."

In spite of Lila Mae's unlikely and difficult choices, she still left you with the same loud and clear message: It just wouldn't be a party without the missing twin or the parakeet man.

While tracking people down, there were the inevitable conversations about a fourth cousin, generally somebody Rebecca had never laid eyes on, who was dying of a horrible disease, so Lila Mae would say, "you *should* call Victor. It would do him a world of good." Realizing what she was asking, Lila Mae would add, "Just whenever you get a chance. I know you're busy." Of course, the man was dying and his days were numbered.

As much as Rebecca griped about the birthday party, it was actually the perfect project—one with a clear-cut beginning, middle, and end, one with add-ons and cross-offs, minor setbacks and major victories. The day after the event, it would be out of her hair and off her list of things to do, at least until the next year. It was more than she could say for the rest.

The last category—a confounding and slippery slope—was problems Rebecca knew she couldn't solve but always tried to anyway, the items that packed a punch larger than the number of alphabet letters they used. One such issue was Carleen. Often her sister would joke that she still didn't know what she wanted to be when she grew up. But Rebecca knew Carleen's jest camouflaged deep sadness. Sometimes Rebecca wanted to wrap Carleen in baby blankets and whisk her away to some wonderland with pastel skies and gumdrop trees; other times she wanted to bully her into taking charge of her own production.

More and more often, she just wanted to blurt out what Carleen's real problem was—her husband, Nelson. Not only did he make it clear that Carleen was second rate, ruffling her newly arranged hairdo with his bully hand and humiliating his rattlebrained wife if she wasn't au courant on the Middle East, Rebecca also had doubts about Nelson's faithfulness. The suspicions weren't based on anything concrete; there were no eyewitness reports or steamy Polaroids, just an inkling that haunted her. Occasionally, Rebecca would comment on Nelson's mysterious whereabouts to Carleen, saying, "Maybe he's having an affair. Is that possible?" But all Carleen said was, "Nelson?"

But in deep, dark, secret conversations, Carleen admitted that Nelson's late nights had disturbed her. When she got the nerve to question him, Nelson had been indignant, blaming his erratic schedule on his demanding career.

Once she confessed that she had dreams—pleasant ones—that Nelson died in a car crash! "I wasn't really glad he was dead," Carleen said. "I just feel so trapped. Obviously, it's not the perfect marriage."

"I know all about the perfect marriage," Rebecca joked. "I've had three of them!"

On an up note, Carleen was the only family member Rebecca could count on for unwavering support, the one who knew the breadth—and irrationality—of her vision and the exact names of all the dancing skeletons. "You see the barber pole and open a barbershop," she said. "We visit an ice cream parlor and you design a confectionery. Stay away from red-flocked wallpaper and Victorian couches, otherwise I can see it now: Miss Rebecca's Bordello!"

More and more often, Carleen would remark, "It's one of those days. I'm three loads of laundry and two mopped floors away from skipping town. Maybe I could run that candy shop or the bowling alley. Wouldn't it be funny, Rebecca, if we all moved back to Kentucky?" Even though Rebecca had these same visions, the thought teetered somewhere between a craving and panic.

But, of all the heartaches and family problems put together, nothing compared with the burden of her missing and vagabond brother, Billy Cooper. He was not simply an issue on a list, but an entire project, one that touched so many buttons: fury and desperation, determination and hopelessness. The never-ending problem with Billy Cooper was always buried under some low tide of consciousness. But even a fairy god-mother's wand seemed incapable of embracing her brother. Like the swallows returning to Capistrano, Rebecca's thoughts always drifted to Billy Cooper.

Even with so much evidence to the contrary, in Rebecca's head was a picture of blissful arcadia. When all of Lila Mae's wishes had come true and they had located the flame-haired waitress, and when Carleen was on top of the world, and when Irene—svelte, coiffed, and sans her cache of pharmaceuticals and husband number five—had a flourishing career; when Billy Cooper had a roof over his head and grain in his belly, and when Ava was all grown up, well-adjusted, and dating some clean-cut Harvard premed student; when Olive's farm was flower-bedded and picket-fenced and safe from the claws of Horace Castle, and when Rose-mont was back in Adams hands where it should have been all along, then the pages of her list would float out of her life like tattered lace. Then, and only then, would Rebecca feel her work was, at long last, done.

Chapter Ten

Carleen

JULY 1999

Every time the subject of Carleen's career came up, she got a bad case of vertigo or whatever the name of it is when you feel dizzy and confused and topsy-turvy. For a fleeting moment in time, when Carleen was pursuing her show-biz dreams, she worked as an extra on *Mayfair Memorial Hospital*. On Thursdays, her work day, she waltzed on clouds, flitting across the set of the make-believe world, dodging cameras, and trading smiles with her fellow cast members, especially Connor Stevens, the tall, dark, and handsome actor who played Dr. Ashton. And even though she had been much too old to ever make anything wildly successful of her aspirations, she had still felt like Bette Davis when the assistant director had complimented her on the Siamese twin scene.

Nelson had never even known about the *Mayfair Memorial* job; he certainly didn't know that those eight hours on the set had been the happiest of her entire life. There had been some close calls—a phone message from the production secretary and an outdoor scene shot in front of Nelson's office building in downtown San Francisco. In the end, the cloak-and-dagger antics had been so much pressure that it was actually a relief when she went back to her column, "That Just Gets My Goat," the job she seemed doomed to have until her dying day.

On a daily basis, her column was manageable, even enjoyable. The nature of it—driving through the quaint, rural roads of the Bay Area looking for anything that rubbed her the wrong way—was wonderfully stress free. No car phones, faxes, beepers, doorbells. And most of the time nobody knew exactly where she was. She had freedom! She could cater to her urges, swinging to the roadside when she spotted an antique shop or stopping for triple ice cream cones at Von Almann's Country Store. Sometimes she would even cruise the streets of Berkeley, hoping to get a glimpse of Billy Cooper.

Out in the wide open spaces, she would pop in a CD, blast the speakers, and howl like a lovesick coyote. "Don't cry for me Argenteeeeeena!" Lifting her palms in the air like Eva Peron, she could sing to the throngs of adoring Argentinians. Then with a flick of her CD player, she was Tevya from *Fiddler on the Roof*: "If I were a rich man!" Each note seemed to come from some foreign place in her, a spot that flushed out all her frustrations and heartaches. How exhilirated she felt, how free of her troubles! Often, when Cassie was out of school for a holiday, she would tag along with her mom and they'd stop for hamburgers and Coke floats or buy fresh pears from Napa Valley orchards.

Still, as thrilled as Carleen was roaming the hills and dales of the wine country and the town squares of Sonoma and Petaluma, when everything was said and done, she was still the lowly, unpaid Goat Lady of Chesterfield Bay.

In a murky trench of Carleen's brain was the notion that this wasn't her "real" life, and that someday she would wake up to a recorded message saying: This was a test . . . This was only a test . . . Please stay tuned . . . What relief she'd experience, knowing that all the kinks had been ironed out, paving the way for a glorious second chance.

Time, though, seemed to be running out. Whenever Carleen filed a tax return or renewed her driver's license, she realized another year had gone by with little to show for it. "Time flies when you're having fun!" Lila Mae would often sing. Now time was just flying, period.

The only thing that was halfway cooperating in this beat-the-clock gallop was her looks. Whenever Carleen studied the mirror, she thanked God they were putting up a middleweight championship fight. At one point she worried that her delicate features, the ones which a young, in-fatuated Nelson poetically said were "as precise and finely wrought as an English teacup" wouldn't hold up. But when the light was dreamy and mellow and Carleen had had a good night's sleep, her face—a delicate oval with chiseled cheekbones and sapphire eyes—was luminescent. Her butterscotch hair was still soft and shiny and meandered around her face in shoulder-length wisps. Still, Carleen feared, it was a face one would recognize, but not necessarily remember.

Then, other days, Carleen felt like the ugliest beast in the jungle. Whenever she looked in chain-store mirrors, she was confronted by the furrows that a *Harper's Bazaar* article called "marionette" lines. A sidebar of helpful tips would suggest ointments and Chinese herbs; echinacea, ginkgo biloba, Saint John's Wort; everything to handle her middle-aged beauty needs and physical conditions. Even with all that, Carleen never felt one hundred percent.

With each visit to a doctor the number of minor problems grew. At last count there were twenty-eight itises—conjunctivitis, arthritis, bur-sitis; half that many syndromes—carpal tunnel, chronic fatigue, and lazy leg. Now the doctor had switched to disorders—fibromyalgia, torticol-lis, ganglia—even some oddball condition pertaining to her magnetic field. Whenever she wore a wristwatch it stopped, plus, every time she was around a cash register it would go haywire. Just when she finally got to the front of the market line, the checker would suddenly say, "For goodness sake" or "Well, gee whiz" like she was stumped. Finally, she would pick up their microphone and say, "I need a manager on seven!"

It was almost impossible to keep step with the ailments, let alone the cures. Sometimes, the remedy for one condition was often the thing to avoid for another. For a time she was eating garlic, which had been touted as an aid to relieve sinusitus until she learned that spicy food, gar-lic in particular, magnified her rosacea, a sensitive skin condition that her dermatologist said she was developing. What good did it do her if her ship came in and she looked like the wreck of the Hesperus?

There was the crux of the matter. So far, there was no sign of a vessel of any sort, let alone a ship. At one point, Carleen believed that her weekly column could be her salvation, and initially, it had all the earmarks of an overnight success story. It began, simply enough, when Carleen wrote an editorial proposing a ban on leaf-blower use by gardeners in the area. Fed up with the blast of noise coming from one yard or another, Carleen finally sat down with a pen and paper to air her complaint.

"If you have ever watched a gardener—noisy, smelly machine strapped to his back—chase one solitary leaf down a driveway rather than stoop down to pick it up; if you've ever keeled over after inhaling the poisonous fumes billowing from your petunia patch, then you know how utterly idiotic it is for Chesterfield Bay to continue the use of this obnoxious, unhealthy equipment."

Before she mailed the letter, Nelson reviewed it, something she hoped would trigger a proud-as-a-peacock reaction. "Honey!" He would jump up. "What a great writer!" When Nelson handed it back to her, all that remained were a few fundamental observations drowning in the quicksand of her husband's voluminous margin notes. In spite of his dictate to "ax all the run-on sentences and hokey expressions such as 'keeled over,' " Carleen, for once in her life, totally ignored him. A few weeks later she learned that it was her plain-speaking style that won the community over. "Trumanesque" was how one letter to the editor described it, and a local appliance repairman wrote, "It's about time someone spoke up about those darned leaf blowers!" A week after the letter was printed, the Chesterfield Bay Association voted unanimously to ban the offensive equipment.

A month later she had been jogging along Wallace Lagoon when a biker veered out of the special path and nearly plowed her down. When the cyclist sideswiped another couple, then crashed into a eucalyptus tree, inspiration struck, and Carleen could hardly wait to grab her notebook.

"I suppose they think they're big shots," she wrote, "whizzing by at ninety miles an hour scaring the living daylights out of the elderly and small children and clobbering everything else in their path."

Once again, Nelson lectured her. "Too many clichés. That homespun style might have worked once but don't push your luck."

But when the mayor's daughter was injured by some daredevil on two wheels, Carleen's editorial was hailed as insightful and motivational. People began to stop her in Staley's Market and flag her down at the ice-skating rink just to tell her how much they appreciated her efforts to make some necessary changes in their community.

Her crowning achievement was the open letter she penned to the chairman of the board of McDonald's, complaining about the unfriendly service at Chesterfield Bay's local franchise.

"Why all the happy-face signs and *Thank you for visiting!* banners if the employees actually waiting on the customers are zombies?" she wrote. "We certainly don't expect ticker tape and confetti. Nor do we anticipate the clean-cut, friendly teenagers and nimble octagenarians depicted in the restaurant's television commercials. We do expect—and think the customer deserves—a plain old, ordinary smile, even if it's as plastic as the AstroTurf on the restaurant's playground."

Almost immediately she received a letter from Edgar Manning, the head of McDonald's marketing department, and Joshua Beaton, the chairman of Beaton, Richardson and Bardwell, the advertising agency that handled the restaurant's account. They thanked her for bringing the situation to their attention and treated the entire town to free coupons. Nelson was miffed by all the hubbub and visibly jealous when Carleen's photograph appeared on the front page of the newspaper.

Thrilled with her newfound rank, in her spare time Carleen began to write gripe letter after gripe letter about all the things, petty and major, that drove her crazy.

Soon, Roddy Berlin, the editor-in-chief of the *Chesterfield Bay Sun*, approached her armed with praise and propositions, asking Carleen if she would compose weekly editorials. "We think you're just terrific!" the effeminate, dimpled Berlin gushed. Carleen, buoyant with confidence, was thrilled to join their little team.

Before Carleen got too worked up, Berlin added, "We can't pay you anything, at least for now." But Carleen was so thrilled that she said, "Please! I don't expect a penny!" All she cared about was having her very own newspaper column! She celebrated by calling Rebecca, who squealed in delight, and suggested a telephone martini. They clicked their glasses to the plastic receiver and her sister said, "Here's to great things!"

The plan, incubated by Rebecca, had been for Carleen to create a following in her tiny town, then expand her base of newspapers. As a sideline, she could appear at regional activities—parades and sporting goods store openings—slowly developing a local celebrity status. Maybe then the *People* or *Us Weekly* scouts would discover her.

Although the column did give Carleen a creative outlet and sense of importance (it still amazed her when she was accosted by fans at supermarkets and Little League games), the swift progression of events had stopped dead in its tracks.

Visions of being the next Ann Landers or Dear Abby quickly vanished when she received form letter after form letter in reply to her syndication queries. "We are sorry but" or "Your inquiry of January 19 has been forwarded to me. Unfortunately . . ."

To add insult to injury, it had been over ten years and Roddy Berlin still hadn't offered her a cent for her column. Once she had stomped into his office, ready to quit if they didn't pay her one hundred dollars per month for expenses. Surely, all her family and friends coached her, "there is a skimpy amount like that available. After all, it's their most popular feature."

But Berlin shook his balding head and moaned, "I'm stretched so thin they're liable to close down the whole shebang." By the time he finished, Carleen was more concerned about Roddy Berlin, a sixty-four-year-old newspaper veteran with a diabetic mother and no other place to go, than she was about a paltry sum that wouldn't even cover her gasoline expenses.

No sympathy was to be had from Rebecca when Carleen reported the results. "You gave your services away for nothing for so long, they take you for granted," she scolded. "Promise me you'll do something about that."

Tired of being double-dared by Rebecca and sick of hearing Lila Mae tweet, "Rome wasn't built in a day!," Carleen kept swearing that she'd make some headway.

Someday, Carleen often thought to herself, she'd open the mail and there The Letter would be—a neatly typed paragraph on engraved gold letterhead. "Yes, Ms. Carlyle, we are anxious to pursue negotiations with you" or "Please call us at your earliest convenience regarding 'That Just Gets My Goat'!"

Meetings would take place in restaurants with crystal chandeliers and waiters who would bow and say, "Just as you wish, madame!" After the French wine and crepe suzettes, they would whisk her back to corporate headquarters to meet the boss, a man named J.T. or J.R. Perhaps, too, there would be a whiff of flirtation between her and the chairman of the board. There would be celebratory announcements that Carleen Carlyle would soon be writing for the *San Francisco Examiner*.

Then, having established herself as a known newspaper columnist, offers for television shows and books would pour in. At one time, she had actually tinkered around with her gripe letters, combing her files to assemble a collection of her work. Rebecca even came up with a catchy title, *Poison Pen Letters to President Reagan and Other People in Charge of the World*. But the project was much more complicated than Carleen had guessed and by the time she got around to writing a book proposal, Ronald Reagan was out and George Bush was in. Since then, the country had gone through wars, scandals, and overthrows of governments, not to mention more presidential terms.

As far-fetched as it seemed, she even thought about a stand-up comedy act incorporating her pet peeves. Pages of notes and jokes and anecdotes, even entire scenes were scribbled on yellow tablets and pressed between her shiny, slick bureau drawer paper, like the chrysanthemums she'd preserved from her grandfather's casket.

But, when everything was said and done, more than a decade had gone by and "That Just Gets My Goat" was what it had always been: a collection of semiclever gripes that the commonfolk could relate to, ones which appeared each Sunday in a rinky-dink newspaper with a circulation of 1,200 in a town that didn't appear on ninety percent of the area's maps.

In other words, she was a medium-sized fish in a minuscule pond. She had also begun to notice something else: Since complaints were her business, they were wrapping themselves around her, strangling her sunny outlook. There was no denying that her personality was changing for the worse. Yes, the zany, happy-go-lucky, free-spirited Carleen of old had turned into a curmudgeon.

As for her precious celebrity status furnished by the column, lately it was a noose around her neck, one which made it virtually impossible for her to leave the house in curlers, without makeup, or in a bad mood.

The tide was beginning to change with her popularity, too. In the past year, she had written a dozen nasty columns on bad service in which McDonald's always figured prominently. Roddy Berlin had just received another letter from Joshua Beaton, the McDonald's advertising executive who had sent the free coupons. Now Beaton wanted to meet with the officials of Chesterfield Bay. "The folks at McDonald's are *very* concerned about image and good service," the executive had written. He also wanted to do a public relations article, showing that a bigwig from the company cared enough to personally visit Chesterfield Bay.

To Carleen, it was the very reaction she'd hoped to trigger with her column and she was saying things like, "Well, that's more like it!" But Berlin set her straight. In an off-the-record phone call he'd had with the agitated executives, they basically told Berlin enough was enough. "In other words, Carleen," Berlin said, "lay off! or get laid off!"

So, in addition to all the other things she had to dread, Carleen could add "meeting with stuffy Madison Avenue advertising types" to her list. She could see it all now—a long, drawn-out event with a bunch of pinstriped suits in which she would have to smile and charm and backpedal and apologize all to satisfy a newspaper whose payroll she wasn't even on.

Chapter Eleven

Irene

JUNE 1999

After all Irene had gone through to get some peace and quiet, the idyllic lifestyle everybody in Kentucky had played up was horse-feathers. Irene had hardly gotten her bearings when there was a robbery and fatal shooting at her sister's barbecue restaurant, an event that resulted in escaped criminals, a getaway car, disappearances into the wild blue yonder, and other expressions usually heard on *America's Most Wanted*. It also spawned wagging tongues and much speculation that it was more than a simple robbery.

The dead man was a fifty-year-old lifetime misfit named Eddie Ray Youngblood. In California, Irene was used to people being defined by their jobs or their cars, so a last name was meaningless, but even she was all too familiar with the Youngblood name.

The biggest concentration of the unruly Youngblood tribe—there were seemingly dozens of them spread across several counties—consisted of a slew of second and third cousins living in chicken coop boxes in a shantytown near Boone's Creek. In spite of their slovenly trappings and bad reputations, the Youngbloods were known as slick operators, as shrewd as card sharps and as swift as pickpockets.

"No man's land's what they call it!" Olive screwed up her face in distaste. "I wuddn't step foot over thar fer a million-dollar bill!" And then, as if Irene might be tempted to hang out with the repugnant crew, she added, "And you shouldn't neither."

True to the Youngblood tendencies, Eddie Ray wasn't the only miscreant in his branch of the family. There was Butch, an older brother, also an ex-con with a drug addiction, who was, according to Olive, "ever bit as rotten as his dead younger brother." Nobody thought much of their older sister, Cookie, either. As a pregnant teenager, she had taken off years before, searching for the bright-lights-big-city, and hadn't even returned for the funeral when her parents were killed in a car accident.

As unmanageable as the two brothers had always been, the situation had gone from bad to worse after their parents' death. Eddie Ray and Butch had fought tooth and nail about everything from their parents' burial to the sale of the family home. The house was only a small sharecropper's cottage, but it was on one hundred acres of valuable farmland, an opportunity Butch couldn't pass by. Eddie Ray had turned sentimental and was blocking the sale, a turn of events that had caused hostility and internal warfare.

None of this would have had a thing to do with Olive and Shorty, if it hadn't been for the Mishap—Eddie Ray Youngblood's death—at Miz Becky's. With the fresh scent of tragedy hanging in the humid pink dawn and a pot of hot coffee to spike their imagination, Shorty and Maybelle paced the living room floor. "Lordy, lordy, what a tragedy. We shoulda seen it comin' all right," they lamented, hanging their heads in puzzlement and offering creative possibilities to the who, what, when, where, and why of the distressing situation. Olive was in on it too, sitting in her rose chair, swathed in a poplin robe, looking like a wilted angel.

"Thar parents' car wreck just tore the poor boy up," a sniffling Olive offered the first account of the crime. "I'd say Eddie Ray snapped when he saw they wuzn't no way to fight his brother fer that farm. He figgered it wuz time to move on, git Butch outta his hair, maybe even git outta Blue Lick, buy him a little place in another town. So, he, he took aholt of his shotgun, drove to Miz Becky's fer sum gitaway cash. Then sumwhars along the line, what happened jest happened." Olive lifted a shaky coffee cup to her lips, took one small sip, and sat back. "Either that . . . or sumthin' else."

"So, you think the robbery was motivated by a family feud, Grandma?" Irene leaned forward and quizzed. "If that's the way it happened, then who were the other two robbers with Eddie Ray? What would they have had to do with the beef between Eddie and his brother? It, it just seems like it was all planned."

"Oh, it wuz planned, all right!" Olive, irritated with the line of logical questions, jerked her head toward Irene. "I never said it wuzn't, and I don't know ever'thang, neither! You wuz thar right afterwards . . . What do you think Curtis?"

Shorty, himself a deputy sheriff, was anxious to fill in the blanks. "Now, Sheriff Burkle's a fine man, but I think everybody's got their wires crossed. Eddie Ray no more tried to stick that place up than I did!" According to Shorty it was really Butch Youngblood who had barged in to Miz Becky's. "If I live to be a hundred, you can't convince me that Eddie Ray held up that rest-rent. He was a nice guy when he wuzn't drinkin'."

"Eddie Ray had his problems," Maybelle placed a painted metallic nail to her lip and replied. "But Butch's the one I'd a thought of first, too. You're on to somethin', Curtis Wooten!"

Buoyed by his wife's vote of confidence, Shorty strutted around the room. "What a setup Butch has goin' for hisself. He must be gettin' a big kick outta this! Eddie Ray, his dead brother, gettin' all the blame for the robb-ree."

Olive was in her Queen Anne chair, slipping small wafers into her mouth, and moving her eyes from left to right, as if considering one side of the debate, then the other. In a turnabout, she scooted upright and seconded Shorty and Maybelle's motion. "Yessireebob! That sounds right to me. It wuzn't Eddie Ray, after all, it wuz Butch did it! He's the type all right!"

"Wait a minute," Irene said. "According to the reports, Butch wasn't even in town. Someone claimed he had to rush back from a Billy Ray Cyrus concert in Branson, Missouri."

"Missoura, my foot!" Olive snapped. "Why, Butch Youngblood wuddn't walk 'cross the street fer Billy Ray Cyrus. See, them thieves had kerchiefs or sum such over their heads. Now how'd the po-leece know one Youngblood from another?"

"That's right! For all anyone knows," Maybelle said, twirling her Aztec medallion, "maybe Eddie Ray wasn't even *at* Miz Becky's! It coulda been *all* Butch."

"Obviously, Eddie Ray was there," Irene said, in a I-hate-to-burst-your-bubble tone. "After all, that's where he was killed. Plus, if he wasn't there to rob it, what was he doing there? Eating barbecued chicken?"

"You got a point there." Shorty tickled his chin in thought.

"Well, silly ole me." A brooding Maybelle slunk back in her chair, crossed her arms and then, as if trying to stump everyone, said, "What about this getaway car you hear so much about? I wonder what happened to that."

"It . . . got away!" Olive let out a proud cackle. "But that don't mean it's in Salt Lake City, Utah, neither. It cudda 'got away' a few blocks from here."

"Gettin' by with murder," Maybelle mused as if she'd just coined a new phrase.

"I'll call Butch a killer to his face, too!" Olive clamped her bony hand over the arms of her chair and lifted up. "I will, I ain't scerred of that little pipsqueak."

"That crazy Butch better not show his face around here agin," Maybelle warned. "He tangles with the Wootens, he'll be sorry!" Since she had only been a Wooten for a few years, she seemed overly possessive of their hotheaded tendencies.

"That's just great!" said Irene. "Do you *really* think Butch Youngblood would come *here?*"

"Why shore," Shorty chimed in. "Why wouldn't he? We've known him since he wuz born. He does our yard work, that is, when he bothers to show up."

Oh my gosh, Irene wondered, was Butch the guy she'd seen weeding the garden on the day she arrived, one of the black-sheep Youngbloods? There they were, stuck a half mile from the road, buried in shrubbery and shielded by thin screen windows and a front door nobody ever bothered to lock. And a criminal on the loose who knew every gorge and ravine on the property!

"Shouldn't we *do* something?" Irene's eyes had an are-we-all-going-to-die look of panic. "We have to protect ourselves, don't we?" Looking around, it seemed she was the only nervous wreck in a room of paper warmongers.

"Shorty'll stand up to Butch or eny Youngblood, don't you worry none!" Olive punched her fists and nodded to her son. "He may be small, but he can handle hisself in a fight, yes he can! And I still got my stinger, yes I do!"

With the sun already risen, Irene, and it seemed Shorty and Maybelle, too—were willing to drop the muddled situation—Butch was the culprit, Eddie Ray wasn't, there was a Mr. X who got off scot-free and that was the end of that. In fact, Maybelle was picking up her empty Pepsi cans and Shorty was headed for the front door. But before the cement cured, Olive, like a theatrical director whose cast thinks they're finished for the day, stopped them in their tracks for one more take.

"You don't reckon that developer, that Castle feller, is behind this, do ya?" said Olive, her head bent in thought. "Them developers'll stop at nothin', ya know. It wuddn't surprise me none if thar tryin' to scer yer sister into sellin' Miz Becky's. I have it on good authority that they want her place and she ain't sellin'. Ever'time they meet with resistance, they's trouble. Same thang happened to Ole Man Rochester. He told Castle to go fly a kite, and the next day someone shot the winders right outta his place of business."

"You're kidding," Irene yelped. "What happened?"

"They's a big ole CASTLECO sign on the building right now. Yessireebob! I say Castle sturs things up, then gits ya to sell fer a low price. And sumbody's doin' his dirty work fer him. See, he coulda put them Youngblood boys up to this robb-ree and they's jest stupid enough to go along with it. I seen somethin' jest lak it on the television set onct."

"But wait, if that's the way it happened, Grandma, would two brothers, who you said were fighting, unite for a robbery?" asked Irene. "And you said something about not knowing one Youngblood from another, but one was skinny and the other one was stocky, so wouldn't that—"

"All I know," said Olive decisively, "is the devil's got his paw prints all over Butch and Eddie Ray Youngblood, so thar's no tellin' what wint on. This is bad fer this town . . . What a reputation we'll have."

All this amateur-hour sleuthing was done in between requests such as, "Curtis, pass that caramel corn, would ya?" and "Maybelle, git me another glass of wine, please." Irene had gulped it all up, mouth agape, eyes agog, and brain tuned to some channel of permanent fright.

As unlikely as it might appear, Olive did seem to be on to something. Even though it may not have been connected to the robbery, maybe the developer *was* intimidating people; maybe the Youngblood men *were* behind the BB-gunned windows and fires. Maybe both Youngblood brothers were there to rob Miz Becky's together—hired hands for Horace Castle—just to shake up the town. If that were the case, then why the long song and dance Olive had gone through to describe the brothers' rift? It was odd, too, that at the end of it all, Shorty said very casually, "Don't get yerself too worked, we was just passin' time!" In any case, dozens of possibilities and loose ends were doing a lively jig, thumbing their noses at neatly packaged conclusions.

One thing was perfectly clear, anyway: At the rate things were going, Blue Lick Springs would have a worse crime rate than New York City. It wasn't exactly what Irene had bargained for when she set out for broader, safer horizons.

The good news was that, despite her unusual big-city looks and without having to resort to the funeral parlor, Irene landed a position as a medical claims adjuster to Buddy McCracken, the manager for Bohannon Insurance Group in nearby Oddville. After exhausting all the possibilities presented by her grandmother and Uncle Shorty, Irene had spotted the help-wanted ad tacked on the bulletin board of the Piggly Wiggly. Olive wasn't sure she'd "ever heared tell of anyone by the name McCracken," which was supposed to be a warning.

The company headquarters was a stucco rectangle situated down a sinewy gravel road, and arched between Hub Cap Heaven and Arlen's Appliance Repair. As for her boss's office, there wasn't a high-tech device to be found. Instead, there were crooked stacks of dog-eared file folders, and Kiwanis Club plaques. In the center of the disorganization sitting in a chair beneath a mounted blue fish, was McCracken himself, a barrel of a man with a gap-toothed grin and bluish-black skin. In his pastel suits, he resembled a Las Vegas master of ceremonies, but he had twinkly eyes the color of strong, sweet coffee and the cuddly disposition of a Saint Bernard dog.

On her first day, McCracken handed Irene a document and said, "Put this in a vanilla envelope and send it off to Jeanine Pillsbury, would ya, honey?" The next day he told Irene to call his wife, Ruby Pearl, and tell her he had to leave early "on account of a fooneral." Then, in a conversation about Irene's Kentucky roots, McCracken mentioned that his own ancestors had "come over on the Maytag!" It was all Irene could do to keep a straight face. Plus there was the "honey" business, a crack which would have landed a Los Angeles businessman in labor arbitration.

McCracken told Irene that until recently his branch of Bohannon had been a one-man show, but lately he had been flooded with claims. "We got more accidents than Chicago, Illinoise!" he lamented, "and there isn't a normal one in the bunch." One by one, he flipped through the charts: "Jay Beeker, Jr., whooplash, says a bumper car at the State Fair went haywire; Edna Earl Davenport was plowed down by a grocery cart and has soft tiss-soo damage; Warren Jerome Stevens swallowed a golf ball." Every one of them was a patient of Dr. Roy K. Hand, an Arkansas transplant, who'd recently opened a practice in Blue Lick.

Beyond the illegitimate personal injury issues, there were also abundant property damage claims. "Nobody can figure it out—overturned garbage cans, buildings spray painted, even windows blowed out!" Mc-Cracken showed Irene the 1997 comparison charts and gazed at her as if she were one of those television show angels who hopped from hamlet to hamlet performing miracles. "There's something behind this and nobody can tell me different." McCracken stamped his palm down as if it was an official seal.

Irene listened dutifully, putting whatever vague twos and twos she had together, formulating a logical brew from Rebecca's speeches and Olive's parlor games. There was certainly a three-ring circus of activity; no one would deny that.

Before McCracken had even said, "you're hired," she'd been staring at the royal-blue fish with the sword sticking out of its forehead, thinking if, by chance, she *did* get the position, she couldn't wait to call her mother, the mother who predicted "There's no way on God's green earth that you'll get a job in rural Kentucky with purple hair." Then she would have a jelly doughnut to celebrate. If she didn't get hired, she'd eat two just to drown her sorrows.

By the time McCracken said, "Well, Ms. Wooten, I think you might work out very nicely," Irene had already anticipated her fleeting golden moment with Lila Mae. Her mother would toss up one strand of ticker tape, say, "Oh, that's great, honey!" then dole out advice about *keeping* the job . . . which is "certainly a lot harder than *finding* one."

After that, there would be fifteen minutes of grilling and pumping and questions that Lila Mae had already asked her one hundred times. "But you are enjoying it, aren't you? Didn't I tell you Kentucky is beautiful? Aren't you glad I made you move?" There would be no getting off the phone unless Irene gave her mother concrete evidence that she was the empress of great decisions. "Yes, mom, you were right!" Irene would tell her. "It was just what the doctor ordered!"

Irene knew how ridiculous it was that she spent half her time scoffing at Lila Mae's advice and the other half bending over backward to prove she'd followed it. But Lila Mae had her children, particularly Irene, right where she wanted them—worker bees all, furnishing frankincense and myrrh and bundles of praise, all treasure for their ravenous queen.

Surprisingly, the first few days in Kentucky had been nirvana. She had roamed the property, dipping a metal scoop into well water, clipping the dandelions and crepe myrtles for her grandmother. She splashed her plump, white foot in the mossy pond water, and even smashed her face right into the sweet Kentucky bluegrass. Near sunset, she had jumped atop Daisy, Olive's old quarter horse, not because she was fond of horseback riding, but just because she wanted to rub up against Kentucky, and clopped along the crest of the hill on her grandmother's farm. She had watched the sunset, a big bloodshot roundel, drop behind the banks of limestone. But collecting in the southwest sky, like a secret signal to

Irene, were magenta storm clouds and thunder like thousands of warpath drums.

Now, at night, when the yellow Kentucky moon was high in the sky, Irene would retreat to her bedroom with nothing but a swamp cooler to cut the stupefying heat. Through the plaster wall, she would hear the grandmother noises: shuffling slippers, the clicking metal walker and toilets flushing. Above it all was the joyous singing: "I sing because I'm happy. I sing because I'm free. For his eye is on the sparrow and I know he's watchin' meeeee." After that came the plop of Olive's false teeth as she deposited them in the ceramic cup.

It was those evenings, after Irene and Olive had tapped on the wall—their signal to turn off one another's lights—that Irene would move carefully around, avoiding the noisy floorboards, finally slipping into her canopy bed. Staring at the swirled ceiling, waiting for the soft buzz of her grandmother's slumber, Irene's heart was filled with longing and her head with rebuttals to the argument that she had to leave California.

The night she arrived in Blue Lick, she had opened her leather suitcase and discovered a simple black Bible on her stack of blouses. Slipped inside was a note from her mother, something that staggered her. Lila Mae had a lot of ways to drive them all crazy, but her religious zeal wasn't one of them. Nonetheless, Irene opened the folded paper— monogrammed LMW and smelling of Arpege—and read: Remember, Irene: Jesus died for your sins. All My Love, Mom. "What in the hell is that woman trying to pull?" Irene had grunted to herself. Although she crumpled up her mother's note, she couldn't bring herself to get rid of the Bible, so Irene had left it on her bedside table, something she knew would also win brownie points with Olive.

Later, as the days rolled by and she found herself strangely drawn to the Book, she played a little game with the Holy Ghost, a sort of advice roulette, opening the Bible randomly, asking God, if he didn't have anything better to do at that particular moment, to lead her to a significant passage and she would interpret it as a message. The first quote that caught her eye was pleasant enough, but benign: "Blessed are the pure in heart; for they shall see God." Trying again, she turned to: "Fear not therefore; ye are of more value than many sparrows." Another said: "Woe unto you also, ye lawyers!"

The attorney passages could have related to Goldfarb, something that seemed fateful but was neither here nor there, and the reference to sparrows, the major theme of Olive's musical repertoire, surprised her. But that didn't mean some divine guiding hand had meant for her to see it.

Irene tried to make heads or tails of the information, but after giving it her all, she really didn't understand what people saw in it. Why in the world should she care about the Babylonians and Philistines, Bathshebas and Nicodemuses, and where were spots such as Capernaum and Zabulon, if they even still existed? And what the hell was all this verily verily stuff? There were some real whoppers in there, too—burning bushes and Jonah and the Whale! When she tried to mutter a few feeble offerings of prayer, she felt foolish asking as she did, for the God of Small Waistlines to make Dexatrim work miracles while she was still eating Olive's cakes and meringues and country hams.

Yet, often Irene wondered if there was someone upstairs, some giant puppeteer in the sky plucking all the planet's strings. She wondered if the silhouette of pink angels that flickered against her bedroom wall were the same angels that Lila Mae assured her were protecting her when she was a wee girl afraid of the dark? Maybe her mind was playing games, maybe it wasn't Olive she heard through the bedroom wall. Maybe it was the angels who were singing: "I sing because I'm happy, I sing because I'm free. For his eye is on the sparrow . . ."

After her grandmother had snapped off her bedroom light, Irene would listen to her *Cats* album. It wasn't possible to play it at its absolute capacity, but she would listen to the lyrics again and again, singing along with Grizabella's song. "Mem'ry, all alone in the moonlight . . ." Although she had seen the play ten times and must have heard the tune hundreds—she played the album every day of her life—it never failed to destroy her, scraping some part inside that had no name. It would infuriate Irene when the phone rang and she'd even been known to scream "Shut up!" if friends refused to treat the music with the reverence it deserved. She loved the part when Grizabella hit all the high notes. "Mem'ry. All alone in the moonlight . . . I was beautiful then . . . Let the memory live again." The ancient cat would reach into the bowels of her loneliness and sing her soul out, straight into the heavens and into some deep, dark inexplicable wound in Irene.

Often Irene would stare at the mystical sky and metallic stars, reviewing all the reels of her life. She tried to snuff out the feeling of unease, sweeping it into a little cave of her consciousness. But it was a permanent visitor, one that continued to rap on her door: Irene was haunted by the notion that her decision to come to Kentucky had been a hasty one.

Now that the object of her angst was twenty-five-hundred miles away, she began romanticizing the City of Angels. More and more frequently, Irene would crave a double latte at Starbucks or fried plaintain and huevos rancheros in an Olvera Street cafe. There were days when she longed to touch the brindled trunk of a palm tree or to promenade the rickety planks of the Santa Monica Pier, chowing down seafood and Dos Equis at Rider's Oyster Bar while watching the red Pacific Ocean sun shift across the canyons of Pacific Palisades.

She'd even begun to wonder if it had been all that bad. Couldn't she have simply taken a small vacation, visited Carleen in San Francisco, stayed at Rebecca's beach house, instead of leaving lock, stock, and barrel?

And anyway, moving might not have solved the problem that it set out to eliminate, since she had already received hang-ups on her grandmother's phone. Olive said not to worry, that she got them all the time, too. "It's them doggone Sprint people wantin' me to change service!"

But Irene could read those few seconds of silence; she could feel Darrell's fire-hot fingertips curling around her throat. What if it were Darrell? What would happen if he had already traced her to Kentucky?

Through the window, a rusty moon threw a vermeil sheen on the land. There was the hoot of an owl and the sizzling and rattling of cicadas, as if something mysterious was being stirred up.

Chapter Twelve

Rebecca

JUNE 1999

There wasn't a soul in the world who could have convinced Rebecca, even if they had sworn on a stack of Bibles, that a few days after the unpleasant powwow in David's office, she would end up at the Heart of Fire Pentecostal Church doing the Virginia Reel with Little Peep on one side of her, Phil Bustamante on the other, while Dolores Peepers hovered around the bandstand trying to find out if Reverend Mooney Stagg—the fiddler—knew how to play "Ghost Riders in the Sky."

It was flabbergasting enough to Rebecca that she had Little Peep and Bustie tagging along to Kentucky, but when Peep's secretary called to say that Mrs. Peepers would be accompanying them, Rebecca didn't know what she was in for.

Far from being the obedient wife of a penny-pinching accountant, Dolores, Little Peep's other three-quarters, was a porcine, fire-snorting dragon, one who was usually bedecked like a newlywed's car with brooches and jeweled bracelets. She was also a bully who pushed her husband around like a driveway pebble.

Once, Rebecca had been in Peep's offices when the woman thundered through the building, her hips swishing like a janitor's mop and her baroque pearls swinging like a 1920s flapper's. "Where the hell is the little bastard?" her voice boomed through the hallways. "Damned son of a bitch, never around when you need him." Rebecca assumed the woman was another dissatisfied client, so she was shocked to learn that the ermine-clad hellion was none other than Dolores Peepers, or as everyone called her "Big Dee."

The reason Big Dee insisted on tagging along to Kentucky was that she was homesick for the South. Dolores Hicks Peepers, a beautiful debutante from Nashville, Tennessee, was the only child of a fifth-generation banker whose plantation, Heaven Hill, was a gathering place for the Southern elite. Miss Hicks had grown up in a world of cotillion, ice-cream-colored ball gowns and a lawn sprinkled with blue-blooded gentlemen. Even after years in East Coast boarding schools and then California, her Tennessee tentacles had a stranglehold on her. When Big Dee learned of her husband's Kentucky business trip, she demanded to go with him.

Rebecca found all this out on the plane trip when she and Dolores got buddy-buddy. Through some stroke of good fortune for Rebecca, they all couldn't get seats on the same plane so they had to take two different flights: Rebecca and Dolores on one and Little Peep and Bustamante on another.

Every time Rebecca had bumped into the woman she'd been dressed in emeralds and chinchilla, so she didn't know what garb she'd turn up in. This time Dolores was in melon the color of Georgia clay: melon pedal pushers and blouse, plus an orange turban with a jeweled clip that made her look like a maharani.

After the first Bloody Mary, Dolores lit into her life story and by the third, she began divulging more intimate details than Rebecca ever wanted to hear. According to Dolores, she had been a "raving beauty" with golden locks, an eighteen-inch waist, and, since the Hickses were ancestors of Andrew Jackson, a pedigree to end all pedigrees. She had also been a sucker for Little Peep, who was supposedly a real ladies' man. Luckily, Rebecca managed to keep from saying, "Is this the same Reginald Peepers?"

In the intervening years—almost two decades of misery and

melancholia—Miss Dolores had left her beloved Tennessee as a curvaceous belle and slowly transformed into big, brash, unhappy Dee. She had found solace for the heartbreak of her disappointing childless marriage in the fried chicken dinners that she rushed back to Heaven Hill to consume with her still-doting parents, Sally Settle Hicks and Lyman Crittenden Hicks III. Underneath it all, was the suspicion that Little Peep had married her solely for her multimillions, and Big Dee's disdain for Los Angeles. To put it mildly, she was miserable being so far away from Heaven Hill.

Irene picked up the two women at the Louisville Airport in Olive's twenty-year-old Buick Skylark. Rebecca had been thrilled to see that Irene was a few pounds thinner and that her addiction to Dexatrim and Ernest and Julio was seemingly under control, but Baby Sister still had the warrior spikes and scowl and the discomfort of someone who was a Martian in her own skin. Her taste in clothes hadn't changed either; she was a fright in espadrilles and tomato-red stretch pants that barely covered her kangaroo pouch. Instead of saying hello or hugging Rebecca, she greeted them by grunting, "Where do you want me to put these suitcases?"

But she could tell Irene was relieved to see Dolores Peepers, who had at least twenty pounds on Irene. When Rebecca had told her she would be with a friend, Irene said, "If it's some glamorous stick with gigantic boobs, get someone else to drive you."

The threesome rode to Blue Lick Springs under puffy apricot clouds and over geometric bridges that looked like metal lace. Big Dee bubbled with excitement, remarking about every detail, "Oh, what gorgeous willows!" or "Quick, look at that old plantation house!" Everything reminded her of Tennessee: the red barns with bouquets of tobacco, the brick houses with lawn flamingos, and the Wild Bill's Fireworks stand, decorated with explosives and swaddled in American-flag bunting.

As they approached Blue Lick, everywhere Rebecca looked there were CASTLECO signs, signs that hadn't been there a few weeks before. They were plastered on ramshackle buildings and on stakes in the ground where fresh dirt was being pushed into pyramids. Another

CASTLECO billboard sat in a field of waving grass; this one had an engraving of a building with minarets and moats and a sign saying: A MAN'S HOME IS HIS CASTLE! CASTLECO—WE'VE BEEN MAKING FAMILIES FEEL LIKE ROYALTY FOR OVER 75 YEARS!

When Rebecca spotted: HONEYSUCKLE GROVES—COMPLETION DATE, FALL 2000, the little beasts inside her started jiggling their instruments—a full John Philip Sousa marching band of tubas and kettle drums. "Oh," she snapped, "those people just make me sick!"

Big Dee fumbled through her purse for her glasses and stared at the sign as if her eyes were deceiving her. "Well, will wonders never cease? Horace Castle's come to Blue Lick!"

"Do you know him?" Rebecca asked.

"Who doesn't? He's the biggest developer in the South. He's storming his way through it, state by state."

Irene, with fresh scuttlebutt, said, "Castle is coming to Blue Lick in the next few days to close another *big deal*."

The development company had stepped up their purchases, rezoning the entire town, bulldozing huge black oak trees, and relocating graves at the Elmwood Cemetery.

"Moving *graves?*" Rebecca growled. "Now that's low!"

Big Dee said CASTLECO was trying to ruin her hometown, too, but that Daddy's fixing their wagon! The developer had invaded Nashville like a swarm of locusts, but their plans to build an outlet mall and four skyscrapers one mile from Heaven Hill had been thwarted by Lyman Hicks. "Horace Castle was furious. He's not used to rejection, so he just keeps plugging away. Now he's trying to build an amusement park on the same property! I'm surprised he's in this neck of the woods, though."

"I'm surprised that he's still spending money like a drunken sailor," Rebecca said. "David found an article in *Business Week* that called Castle's company a 'crumbling empire.' It's in my purse." Irene wasn't interested, but Big Dee was all ears, so Rebecca began to quote the magazine:

> As the demand for housing clashes with urban sprawl and the trend is toward big-city rehabilitation, is the country facing urban crawl? If so, what is the fate of Horace Castle, the un-

rivaled king of the housing development? Is his fast-growing empire grinding to a halt?

"There is no slowdown of any variety," said Joe Lee Buttons, CASTLECO's Director of Operations. "Mr. Castle is simply concentrating his efforts in fewer spots, consolidating his interests rather than cutting them back. I can assure you, CASTLECO is solvent."

"Ha!" Big Dee cracked. "What else is he going to say? Horace Castle is flat broke?"

"They all lie," Rebecca agreed. "David read the article and said it doesn't sound good. There's also a lawsuit against the Appleblossom Country Club, which Castle owns. An Afro-American family claims they were refused membership. David said it's the trickle-down effect, just another problem to deflect your focus and taint public opinion."

"It doesn't surprise me that Castle's overextended," said Big Dee, "and it doesn't surprise me that he keeps spending!"

"How is your father stopping him?" Rebecca asked. "Unfortunately, Castle already has a real foothold in Blue Lick."

"He's fighting him tooth and nail. Reggie has been going through this with Daddy. Ask him to give you some pointers."

"To be honest, the only pointers your husband gives me point in the other direction," Rebecca, stopping short of character assassination, said. "He wants me to *sell* everything."

"Huh, that sounds like Reggie." Big Dee crossed her plump arms like a Buddha. "He has this same argument with Daddy. Reggie's big on 'liquid' assets, but Daddy keeps telling him, 'Boy, the kinda liquid you're talkin' about can slip right down the drain!' Daddy believes there's nothing like property. He says, 'Land, they're not makin' any more of it.' " As the woman presented the case against her own husband, Rebecca wondered why Little Peep didn't see things in the same logical way.

By the time they got to Blue Lick, Big Dee was hungry, so they stopped by Miz Becky's, only the place was jam-packed and they couldn't get a seat. This was partially because business had really picked up since the robbery, but mostly because to guarantee that the restaurant was mobbed when Little Peep got there, Rebecca had slipped Jimmy Buzz cash—some $2,500—to distribute to the townspeople.

Standing in the doorway, carefully avoiding the spot where the mishap had occurred, Rebecca's pride of ownership was in full blossom—the fragrance of piquant sauces and hot cornbread, and the three-layered cakes and lemon tarts decorating the glass containers gave her a thrill. All around were baskets and crocks of fresh zinnias and bachelor buttons.

Big Dee, swinging her head from side to side, exclaimed, "You've got yourself a nice little business here!"

"Why don't you tell your husband how great it is?" Rebecca suggested. "This is the place he's here to close down."

"Hell, he wouldn't know a good thing if you painted him a picture," Dee confided. "What smart businessman wouldn't love it? Look at the crowd!"

"Yeah, business has tripled since the robbery, hasn't it, Rebecca? I wonder why." Irene, who had no business taking the high road but usually took it anyway, loved to chide Rebecca for anything that wasn't aboveboard. Too bad Irene didn't practice what she preached.

They ate chicken and cole slaw and chocolate cake, washing it down with crisp bottles of Budweiser. Irene and Big Dee got seconds of everything, all the while discussing diets. Big Dee gnawed on a buffalo wing and said the only thing that ever worked for her was the liquid diet and Irene said she preferred the Knott System, "Knott dieting!" Both women threw back their heads in laughter like whinnying horses.

The one thing Rebecca prayed to avoid was an encounter with Uncle Shorty's wife, Maybelle, but they weren't at Miz Becky's for too long when the pasty-faced woman turned up. With her head studded with curlers, fluorescent yellow ones the color of a caution sign, and wearing a dress and boots to match, she was hard to miss. She was also carrying her real-estate listing book. Although she had been warned to keep her trap shut if they bumped into one another, Maybelle's idea of discretion was a conversation peppered with initials instead of full names, accompanied by arched brows and knowing gestures, and, if all else failed, a cupped hand and the caveat-filled preamble, "I shouldn't be telling you this, but . . ."

Hardly saying two words to Rebecca and Irene, she held out her white-gloved hand to Big Dee and said, "Pleased to make your acquaintance. Maybelle Mouser-Wooten—the Mousers of Egypt."

Like an Olympic relay runner, she snatched the conversation midstream and in no time she had sideswiped, if not delivered a frontal assault on, all the taboo topics. There was *more* property for sale on Main Street, she told Rebecca, property that wouldn't last, property that "you know who will want." Plus, there were problems, *big* problems, with the recent delivery of antiques. And, of course, there was the Mishap.

Rebecca, who felt like crowning the woman, said, "Mrs. Peepers isn't interested in all this," and kicked Maybelle's ankle under the table. Although she flinched and said, "*Ouch!*" at least she changed her tune slightly.

"The point being," Maybelle snipped at Rebecca, "we've got more activity in this little ole town than Carter's got pills! I just want to make sure our honored guest gets the red-carpet treatment. Have you seen anything, ma'am, *anything at all?*"

Big Dee had been plucking her pearl choker like a banjo player strums his instrument and sizing up Maybelle with a jaundiced eye. She rolled out her lower lip, set her eyes in a glower and pouted, "Not a thing. I haven't seen a damned thing."

"Well, we're gonna fix that right now!" Maybelle clapped her hands like a child deciding which birthday gift to open next. Big Dee couldn't have been more excited when Maybelle decided they should take a lay-of-the-land tour.

As they bobbed along Main Street, birdsong serenaded from treetops and church bells pealed. The sun shot crystal beams of light onto the stone and brick facades as merchants draped Fourth of July ornaments over cornices and transoms. Young children bought Fudgsicles from an ice cream truck, and Pappy Bagler, chortling past the star-spangled windows of the shops like a parade's grand marshal, waved to them from his electric lawn mower. A woman walking a cocker spaniel breezed past Big Dee and said, "Hi, hon!" as if they'd known each other their entire lives.

"How nice everyone is, just like Tennessee!" Dolores chirped. She threw her big orange face to the sky, a happy sky filled with sudsy lavender clouds. She breathed in the floral humidity, her bosom heaving in ecstasy. When she said, "Ahhhh, there's nothing like the South," Irene, who had a grudge against all things Southern, cracked, "There's nothing like it, all right, especially since it's Murder Central. I guess you know about the big Youngblood killing—Eddie Ray is dead! Goners!"

"Oh, how awful!" Big Dee made a robotic exclamation while sorting through her cosmetics case.

"Grandma says there's something fishy. She even told that to the *Gazette!*"

"That sounds like her!" Rebecca chuckled, not wanting to play up the situation, since she was still trying to promote Blue Lick as a good spot to invest your money. But, as they ambled through the town, an undertow of anxiety and sadness tugged at her. Regardless of how incorrect it was to mourn a Youngblood, Eddie Ray was a boy with whom Rebecca used to play blindman's bluff, a boy whose mother had given Rebecca and Carleen Tonette permanents for two dollars each and fed them pimento cheese sandwiches while his father had repaired their bicycles and whistled, "On top of Old Smoky, all covered with snow."

Big Dee, unaffected by news of the crime, twittered like a magpie. As they charged through the streets, canvassing first one side, then the other, she asked question after question about the vacant buildings they passed. Maybelle answered Dee with a coy twist of her mouth. "Weeell, this one is going to be a sweets shop and that one across the street is a bowling alley. They say it's going to be open by July Fourth . . . but *you* tell *me.*"

When Big Dee asked her exactly who owned the buildings, Maybelle said slyly, "I know, but I been sworn to secrecy."

"It's not CASTLECO, is it?" Big Dee asked. She was thrilled when Maybelle replied, "Good gracious, no!"

Rebecca was already in a bad mood, but as they turned the corner at Cherry Hill Lane, she noticed some commotion on the knoll. Beyond the sugar maple trees was Cherokee Mills, balancing on a promontory, a beautiful, monstrous finial that capped Blue Lick. Currently, it was surrounded by cranes and bulldozers, its dignity being diminished with each crashing blow of the wrecking ball, with every steeple and pilaster that spilled to the ground in dusty humps.

While Irene gave the scene a desultory glance and asked how much longer the tour was going to take, Rebecca's heart throbbed in agony. "Wh-when did all this happen?" One hand rested on her hip as she hopped around. "I was just here last month." She wanted to wring the necks of the hard-hatted men studying blueprints and slurping Coca-Colas. She wanted to scream *Stop!* to the construction crew operating the cranes and sorting the fallen bricks into stacks.

Maybelle told them CASTLECO was going to raze the mill and build an aluminum storage facility. "That's all the rage, they say, them storage units!" The lamebrain seemed thrilled to be up to date on this trend and even happier to live in the city that was about to participate in it.

"Oh, yeah." Rebecca began an Indian war leap. "Just what Blue Lick Springs needs—one-hundred-thousand square feet of storage space! No wonder Castle's empire is crumbling, spending money on stupid stuff like that. This makes me sick!"

"You and me both." Big Dee moved her head back and forth. "They pave paradise to put up a parking lot."

"Well," Irene sighed and shrugged her shoulders. "You can't stop progress. We'd all still be in covered wagons if we didn't move forward."

"That's true!" Maybelle trilled, bobbing her head like a high-octane toy, calculating how many real estate commission checks she could garner from such progress.

"Knocking down a piece of beautiful architecture that's been there since 1860 and putting up an aluminum barn is progress? Not in my book! And in L.A., we might as well be in covered wagons," Rebecca snapped, her arms peddling, her feet pacing in abstract spirals. "We can only drive about two miles an hour. That's what happens when you build more and more and more! Developers would pave over the Grand Canyon if they thought they could make ten cents. Progress, my foot!"

Irene, who had heard Rebecca's broken-record speech umpteen times, merely yawned and glanced at her wristwatch.

"This man has literally ruined all of Atlanta and parts of Savannah and Charleston," Big Dee added. "He's still not through with Nashville and I hear he's exploring Memphis and Natchez, Mississippi. He's even taking antebellum homes to create country clubs. He uses the house for a fancy clubhouse, then turns the acreage into a golf course and condominiums."

"If that's how he operates," Maybelle piped up, "then sure as shootin' he'll be after Rosemont." The word suspended in the air like one single musical note, holding its own for a moment before being joined by an entire orchestration of dramatic details: It was a grand antebellum with a ballroom and formal gardens and gilded music rooms! There were carved bookcases and moldings and fancy staircases! Maybelle went on and on, capping it off by gushing, "Why, it's the pride and joy of the whole state!"

Until that day, Big Dee hadn't known the name of Rosemont from the man in the moon, but nobody was surprised that her eyes popped and so did the questions. "A house like that here in Blue Lick? Property around here can't be that expensive, is it? Does it have columns? Oh, I hope it has columns!"

"Columns?" Maybelle reared back. "Galore, I tell you!" She said even though they couldn't get inside Rosemont, she'd be happy to drive Dee by the house. "So you can see for yourself."

Rebecca finally delivered the bad news. "Maybelle, you forgot to tell her it isn't for sale."

With the attitude of someone who thinks everything's for sale for a price, Big Dee said, "Surely, there's some way to get it."

There wasn't much to see from the street except Rosemont's overgrown boxwoods and the oxidized iron gates with the pineapple ornaments. And pineapples, the welcome symbol, were definitely out of place situated as they were on top of these crooked, decomposing gateposts. Slave walls, low limestone fences laid by hand on the property, slanted this way and that and lined the road. Even the land itself seemed swallowed up by the tall yellow grass and sticker bushes that grew in monstrous tufts.

Rebecca made sure they didn't get any farther than the gate, but Dolores snapped photo after photo, asking too many questions for Rebecca's taste. "What do you suppose they'd take for it? Somebody ought to buy this place before Castle gets it or it falls to the ground. You'd think the owner'd prefer to sell it to someone who would preserve it, wouldn't you?"

As Irene tooted the horn and said, "What's going on?" Big Dee continued to tramp through the grass, poking her nose through tree branches and shrubs. And even though Rebecca knew it was impossible to see the house, which sat half a mile off the road, she stretched her neck through the oleanders anyway. Just knowing that the fabled home was beyond those cypress trees—the obelisk-shaped fortresses that protected the property from the curious eyes of the world—made her tremble with anxiety.

When they arrived at her grandmother's cottage, Olive was dozing in the loathed therapeutic chair, her head tilted back, her mouth wide open in a husky snore. All around her was telltale evidence: a banana peel, her hearing aids, and the chair's instruction booklet. When Maybelle spied the scene, she grunted, "Well, caught her red-handed!" She grabbed Olive's arm and shook it like a rag doll and said, "Wake up, sleepyhead."

Agitated by the surprise attack, Olive quivered to life like a startled bird and snapped, "Well, scer the liver outta me, why don't ya!"

While Rebecca was getting Olive situated on the porch, puffing up her calico pillows and fetching her petit-point footstool, Maybelle introduced Dolores. "Mrs. Dee is from Tennessee, ain't ya, sweetie?"

Olive, her eyes set on Big Dee's orange headdress, was hard-pressed to flatter a rival state. "Well," she said, "Tennessee's okay, I reckon." Seeing that Maybelle had plunked down a bottle of homemade apple wine and a near-empty box of Russell Stover candy, she barked, "Maybelle! Go git the good stuff. You know what I'm talkin' 'bout." Pestered by a wasp doing figure eights around her head, Olive crisscrossed her arms in the air like the swords of two dueling pirates, then turned to Big Dee and said, "That stupid idiot embarrasses me to tears."

Maybelle was back in no time standing over Big Dee with the incriminating mint-julep clusters and chocolate bonbons. She switched the tray from right to left as if enticing a toddler. "I got sumthin' homemade you're gonna love! Ummmmm, yummeeeee."

Big Dee's head moved back and forth like a tennis match spectator and she even reached out her hand a couple of times but missed. Olive said, "Fer cryin' out loud, Maybelle. Set them thangs down. I wouldn't mind havin' one myself."

Big Dee extracted her gold-rimmed spectacles, assessing the candy over the top of her lenses, as if she were a picky eater; she said, "My! My! These are heavenly!" Then she single-handedly ate the entire batch of bourbon balls.

Sitting in the peach-gold light on a fan-shaped wicker chair, framed by a trellis of wisteria, Big Dee looked like Her Royal Highness. As she devoured nugget after nugget, and sipped wine out of a globe-shaped glass, all her cares seemed to melt in the humidity. All the while she had a one-track mind—Rosemont. Every few minutes, she would crane her ostrich neck and ask, "Now where are we in relation to that plantation we just saw?"

Rebecca told her it was over that way, but she had to keep reminding the woman that it wasn't actually for sale. "Rosemont has been in the Montgomery family for years."

"That's a long sad story fer ya!" said Olive. "All this was Adams land onct, Mrs. Dee. This house I'm livin' in? At one time this belonged to Rosemont. Yip, the Montgomerys shoulda never owned the place. Rosement has 'Adams' written allll over it."

"I'd really give my eyeteeth to get in there," said Big Dee.

"Nobody's set sight on Rosemont fer years and if I wuz you, I'd keep it that way. I hope ya wuz careful when ya wint over thar. See, my sources tell me that Hamilton Montgomery jest chased someone off his land. They wuz tryin' to break in, they say. Now that ain't the first time the ole fool clipped sumone! Enybody knows Hamilton, knows better than to trespass on Rosemont."

"Grandma," Rebecca asked, "what do you mean by clipped?"

"You know derned well what I'm talkin' 'bout," Olive said. "It means sumone's walkin' 'round with a BB in thar backside!"

"Grandma! Hamilton Montgomery shot someone?" For Big Dee's benefit, Rebecca giggled, stuck with the unenviable task of making the shooting, the second one mentioned, sound like it was all in good fun.

"Yip, curiosity kilt the cat. See, ever'body and their uncle wants the scoop on Rosemont, my place, too, I reckon." Olive took the wine with her shaky, speckled hand, pouring herself and Big Dee another round. Suddenly, her bewildered eyes were two lanterns lighting the path through her thoughts. "Fer onct I don't blame Hamilton for runnin' whoever it wuz off. They's too much commotion 'round this town. It's hectic! They's no privacy anymore! I'd say that CASTLECO feller is behind all this. See, sum people'll sell to Castle the regular way and sum don't. And when ya don't, ya wake up one day and yer front winder's gone or they's red paint all over yer belongin's . . . They git ya to thinkin' the property's more trouble than it's worth and pretty soon ole Castle's gotcha where he wants ya." Turning to Rebecca, she said, "You better watch it. They're after that barbecue rest-rent. Now I ain't got all the answers, but ya cain't tell me thar's no connection between all these shattered winders and robb-rees, and what all."

"Castle's trying to fix the city up," Maybelle said. "Why would they do that? Maybe it's a coincidence."

Olive said it wasn't any coincidence that Raydeen Harper refused CASTLECO's offer until someone shot her business sign. And what about poor Eddie Ray Youngblood who'd told the CASTLECO developers where to go and now he was dead and gone, but Butch, the brother who'd sell his own mother, was still alive?

Olive stretched forward as if about to tell a ghost story. "See, I have it on good authority that Butch Youngblood wuz all fer sellin' their parents' house to Mr. Castle and Eddie Ray said he'd see 'em all *dead* before he stood fer that. So, the way I see it, Castle and Butch went after Eddie Ray first. Instead of doin' him in themselves, they talk him into doin' sumthin' they know'll git him kilt! Ya know, fix it up so Sheriff Burkle shoots Eddie Ray. Then they got clean hands. At the same time they stur up all that trouble at Miz Becky's to git ya upset . . . see, kill two birds with one stone!" Olive gave her head one decisive nod, plopped back in the chair, then froze like a sphinx.

"That's an awful lot of trouble to go to and a lot of risk," Rebecca said, "especially in such a public place. That would also mean the other robber was definitely Butch . . . seems far-fetched."

"You lost me," Maybelle jeered. "Kill his own brother for a piece of property?"

"I heared tell of it before, ain't you?" Olive said. "That's what they done in the Civil War. Brother against brother. You turn on Oh-fray Winfree . . . you'll see it today, too!"

"I'm with Rebecca. They could have taken Eddie Ray out in the woods and shot him or poisoned his beer or run him down with a tractor; there's a million ways!" rattled Maybelle, whose creative fixes elicited a few raised eyebrows. "Anyway, what's that robbery got to do with Rosemont and your place? We've gone over this a hundred times and the story keeps getting wilder and wilder. You've been watchin' too many of those soap operas."

"Just put two and two together," injected Big Dee. "If trouble and Horace Castle are in the same town, the math is right there."

"I don't know anything about what happened at the robbery," said Rebecca. "But I *do* know that ever since CASTLECO came to Blue Lick everything's haywire. All of a sudden, there are new buildings where old buildings used to be, old buildings that aren't there at *all*. We just saw what they did to Cherokee Mills and it's criminal. And now I understand they're going to build wall-to-wall houses? And strip malls? And industrial parks? And accidents and vandalism and who knows what else? Why are they picking on this town?"

"He's ruined every other place," Big Dee said. "He's running out of options."

"They see po-tin-shull," Maybelle had suddenly chimed in, more than chimed in, actually. She seemed to be waving a *Yeah, CASTLECO* sign. She spritzed herself with gardenia cologne, then unwound one of her curlers. "People need a place to live. Everybody has a right to that. They need to shop and work."

"Potential? They see dollar signs, is what they see," Rebecca said. "They're like stalkers, determined to stay in the picture whether you want them there or not. Let them go redevelop some junkyard. Why tamper with paradise?"

"Castle'll get what they want by hook or crook!" said a gleeful Maybelle. "That's what Joe Lee Buttons says, says they've got some master plan for the city. He tells me they're all set."

"Joe Lee Buttons?" Olive frowned. "He's that Negra fella, ain't he? A big ole galoot of a guy, a fancy-pants with gold rings on ever' finger and silk kerchiefs and what all."

"Buttons was quoted in that article on Horace Castle, wasn't he?" Big Dee added. "He was the director of something."

"He's the man in charge all right!" Maybelle crowed. "He used to work for the city, but he's with Castle now. They're gonna get whatever they got their sights on. Why not get ya a good price for yer property while you still can?" Maybelle removed the rollers, leaving spool-shaped curls across her head. "You don't wanna outsmart yerself and be left out in the cold, ain't that right, Mother Wooten?"

"You're not in the cold at all, if you don't want to sell." Rebecca's blood was spuming in anger at the escalating debate. And what about the way Maybelle was zigzagging on a dime? First, she was gung-ho about Rebecca's restoration work, and now this let-it-go-all-to-hell attitude. Besides, what was this "Mother Wooten" crap?

"I'd lak to see 'em try!" Olive pushed forward, as if readying for battle. "They mighta tricked Raydeen Harper and Iola and Esther and them, they mighta even kilt Eddie Ray, but I ain't signin' nothin'!"

"Don't worry, Grandma. You don't have to." Rebecca gave Olive a reassurance pat. "They can be interested all they like, but they can't make you sell."

"There ain't nothin' we can do about the situation, girl. Ask Shorty!" Maybelle folded her napkin into a small, precise square, as if her handiwork were about to be judged in a contest. "Now that's the way the ball's bouncin', God damn it!"

"Now I won't have that kinda talk, Maybelle." Olive directed two buggy eyes on her. "We have a guest, and even if we didn't, I don't want ya takin' the Lord's name in vain." She shook her head, grunted three times and muttered, "They're gonna build houses till they're runnin' outta our ears! This jest stinks to high heaven."

"Don't worry, Grandma," Rebecca said. "We'll get to the bottom of this. We're a loooong way from losing this farm." Initially, Rebecca thought Maybelle and her grandmother were on a tangent, hammering gossip and innuendo into the gospel truth. But something was actually astir and it was she who had stepped into a midstream picture.

"Even if something's in the pipeline, you can fight this," Big Dee said. "There are support groups and attorneys that specialize in it. I have access to the names, too."

"Hellfire!" Maybelle snorted sarcastically. "Around these parts, attorneys are as useful as a nun in a whorehouse!"

"Well, good gravy!" Olive wrinkled her face. "You know better than that. But she's right 'bout this hook or crook business. Sum say it's a figger of speech, but then how do ya explain all these robb-rees and what all?"

Irene, obviously still vexed by the dangling possibilities, said, "Grandma, can I ask you something? You think that at least two of the robbers were the Youngblood brothers and they were going to Miz Becky's to terrorize the place on behalf of Horace Castle? But you made it sound like Eddie Ray was killed because of his property squabbles with Butch. Then you said they got the sheriff to do the dirty work, so—"

"And another thing," added Rebecca, "if Castle and Butch did set up the robbery to get Eddie killed, then how could they be sure Jimmy Buzz would shoot Eddie and not someone else?"

You could tell Olive was stumped from the deep groove that had suddenly appeared in the center of her forehead. "Oh, they's details to be ironed out, I'll grant ya that . . . and summa that stuff I tole ya wuz jest side stories . . . but, if Butch wuz thar at the rest-rent, and I still say he wuz, then ya kin bet yer bottom dollar it wuz Butch that wanted Eddie Ray kilt, not the shuruff." She picked up her wineglass, took a sip, and said, "Besides, they's thangs nobody knows . . . lots of thangs . . ."

When Maybelle snickered and said, "That reminds me, you never told us who this so-called good authority was," Olive looked straight ahead like a hostile witness on the stand and said, "Yer forgettin' that Butch does werk fer me and I ain't as deaf as sum think. I gotta good mind to call the bunko squad on that Castle bunch. You watch, I'll do it, too."

Since they were anxious to switch subjects, Rebecca bought Skin So Soft for herself and Big Dee ended up with Orange Swirl lipstick which was the color Maybelle said almost matched her turban. As a last resort, Olive told Maybelle to "go in the parlor and play somethin' on the pee-ana." When Maybelle disappeared, Olive said, "She ain't the sharpest knife in the drawer, is she?"

In the background, with a flaming sunset and a whiffet of humid air jangling the trees, Maybelle pounded out "Heart and Soul," then "Summertime." By the time she got to "That Lucky Old Sun," she was over her head. The only good thing that came out of it was that Big Dee asked Maybelle if she knew "Tennessee Waltz," which she didn't, but she tried it anyway.

Big Dee tapped her big bulb of a foot, and studied the grazing horses and the black oak trees. She opened her nostrils, taking in the aroma of honeysuckle and bluegrass. "I just love this place! If I didn't know better, I'd think I was in Tennessee. What a shame it would be to lose all this." Turning to Olive, she added, "Don't worry, Mrs. Wooten. If you need help with CASTLECO, you let me know. My daddy's going through this and he just keeps telling those builders where they can shove it!"

"We'll sic 'em, won't we?" Olive's dim eyes perked up, and she gave her cane the customary poke. "I still got my stinger!"

Maybelle managed an anemic smile as she stood behind her mother-in-law's chair. Rebecca could tell by the way Maybelle was acting that it was all the same to her if she and Shorty lived across the street from a pasture as green as the English Cotswolds or a toxic nuclear waste dump.

It was too good to be true that Big Dee had never gotten to the bottom of the homemade candy. Every time the subject had come up, and between Irene and Olive, who had both been throwing hints about new enterprises and recipes, it had come up all afternoon, Rebecca had been on pins and needles. Big Dee had been plenty friendly, but that didn't mean she could be counted on to hoodwink Little Peep if she had inside information her husband pumped her for.

As they were leaving, Rebecca knew something was brewing by the gremlin smile on Olive's face. She tugged on Big Dee's arm and told her one more thing. "Now ya heard me mention our big operation, but I guess yer still in the dark, ain't ya?" This is exactly the way Rebecca wanted to keep it, but Olive had her mind set. "I wuzn't so sure at first,

Mrs. Dee, but ya ain't bad for a gal from Tennessee. Yer in the inner circle now."

They all followed Olive down the hallway and stood at the kitchen with its copper kettles and mason jars of brandied fruit. Big Dee rested both hands on her hips, and as her eyes roamed each shelf of divinity and pecan squares and peanut brittle, said, "My goodness, looks like you've been keeping yourself busy."

"Who do ya think done all this, Mrs. Dee, all that candy ya been eatin'?" Olive swept her arm across the room. "Baby Sister here and me. We got stuff galore . . . even workin' on sugar-free chocolate . . . See, I been showin' her the ropes . . . yep, Baby Sister's a real whiz."

"It's mostly you, Grandma." Irene beamed.

"Well, it's really the whole derned bunch of us," Olive said. "It takes elbow grease and a sizable sum of money to keep this goin'." Olive pointed her cane at the inventory and blurted out, "Ya see, Dee . . . ya see these samples? We wuz usin' ya fer a guinea pig. This is all for Rebecca's candy store, calls it Miss Lila Mae's."

"A candy store?" Dee tucked her chin to her chest with an indignant jerk, rested both hands on her hips and fumed, "Reggie didn't say a word about a candy store!"

Registering Rebecca's dirty look, Olive gave her a devilish smirk and said, "Well, ya ain't gonna keep it a secret ferever!"

Up the road when they reached the COMING SOON—HONEYSUCKLE GROVE SUBDIVISION sign, Big Dee hit the steering wheel, making Irene swerve to the roadside. She hollered "Stop!" After all the alcohol, Rebecca figured she was sick to her stomach, but she slammed the car door and marched through a pasture. When she reached the CASTLECO sign, she ripped it right out of the ground! Big Dee stood, a garden of weeds engulfing her ankles, a plastic glass of wine in one hand, and the CASTLECO sign in the other. Suddenly, she hurled the sign to the ground, hoisted the wineglass up like a torch, and stomped out a little Irish jig on the metal sign. "That'll show 'em!"

Why they all started whooping like they'd just won the lottery, and why they didn't put the kibosh on Big Dee's idea that they buy some spray paint and go to town on the remaining signs, Rebecca didn't know.

She also wasn't sure they should go back to Rosemont at midnight with flashlights to see what they could see. But the mere possibility of aggression buoyed their mood, and after that, they were in a fighting spirit. Even Baby Sister.

By the time Little Peep and Bustie arrived in Blue Lick Springs, Big Dee had combed every nook and cranny of the town. In the process, she had fallen in love with Miz Becky's smoked sausage and bourbon cheesecake; decided that something should definitely be done about CASTLECO; made a standing offer on Rosemont; and was thinking about putting a down payment on an adorable building at the end of Main Street. "My daddy set me up with a trust fund and it will be a cold day in hell when my husband gets his hands on it! Besides, these buildings cost less than a shopping spree to Neiman Marcus."

What with Big Dee being so sentimental about Kentucky, Rebecca was beginning to think she could completely win the woman over. There was no reason to believe that Little Peep would change his tune about closing the restaurant, but it couldn't hurt to have his domineering, wealthy Southern wife on her team.

The two men showed up wearing rumpled suits and toting their accountants' ledgers. They were also in foul moods which got worse when they discovered what a gay old time the women had had. When Little Peep saw his wife's turban he said, "For God's sake, Dee, what kind of a getup is that? You're in Hicksville!" To butter him up, Big Dee gave him a little peck on the cheek, but he snapped his head back and said, "You've been drinking, haven't you?" Then he started fanning the air in front of him.

As for Little Peep, he was dressed in a blue-and-white-striped seersucker suit and straw hat like an Iowa delegate to a presidential convention. His sidekick, Phil Bustamante, was sparkling like a Las Vegas casino billboard. He had on a green sharkskin suit and white patent loafers with brass buckles.

Little Peep's response to Blue Lick was the exact opposite of his wife's. Everything about the place repelled him. He turned up his nose when they passed a rundown shack with purple velvet car seats for lawn furniture. He said, "Get a load of that," when they spotted a hand-painted revival sign that said: LET THE BLOOD OF THE LAMB WARSH AWAY YER SINS. He started counting church steeples after they passed their third chapel in less than a mile and he turned to the backseat and looked at Bustie with bored, dead eyes when he read yet another sign saying: BE AN ORGAN DONOR; GIVE YOUR HEART TO JESUS.

The last straw was when Peep heard they'd have to go to the Heart of Fire Pentecostal Church to attend a fund-raiser for Eddie Ray Young-blood. Since the boy had met his maker in Rebecca's place of business, Olive said it would look "bad, real bad" if she didn't show up. Rebecca was afraid the Youngblood clan would throw rotten tomatoes at her, but Olive said, "That might be, but I'm tellin' ya, yer name'll be *mud* if ya don't go."

Peep, who scoffed at the dynamics of small-town America, had said, "Phil and I are here on business. I don't have time for any socializing. Pentecostal church!" He cleared his throat with a little harrumph and tugged on his coattail.

"Oh, come on Reggie," Big Dee griped. "Besides, that sheriff you have to meet is performing at the services."

"Performing?" Little Peep bugged his eyes. "What kind of a perfor-mance are we talking about? Is this a cooking demonstration or a Wild West show?"

When Rebecca told him it was neither, that Jimmy Buzz was the washtub player for the Kornkob Mountain Pickers, Little Peep threw his head back and said sarcastically, "Uh! He's got a gun on one hip, baby back ribs on the other, and now you tell me about a washtub? This is ut-terly preposterous!"

Big Dee jerked him aside and told him something that made him change his tune. When Peep spun around he had a hangdog look, but at least he said, "Okay, okay. We'll go to the God-damned Heart of Fire Pentecostal Church."

In the meantime, Bustamante, acting nothing like Little Peep's dour yes-man, had been watching the parade of young, suntanned girls in their flowered summer dresses along Main Street, saying, "Hello, doll!" whenever one struck his fancy. His shirt was pulled open to display a furry chest and a glistening diamond pendant. When, after a few minutes, one or two of them gave him the eye, Mr. Don Juan took a drag off his Tiparillo, blew out the smoke, and said, "Say, this isn't such a bad place, Reggie!"

Chapter Thirteen

Carleen

JUNE 1999

Usually when Lila Mae called Carleen all out of breath and flustered, it meant someone had kicked the bucket. "Oh, honey!" she'd say. "I'm so glad I reached you. Guess who was decapitated?" or "I'm just beside myself, Hiram Stucker dropped dead of sugar diabetes at Grauman's Chinese Theater!" Then she would try to get you just as worked up as she was, even though it was someone you'd never met and she hadn't seen for three decades.

So, you could have knocked Carleen over with a feather when she learned that Lila Mae had driven a neighbor who did extra work to a television studio in Burbank. The friend told her she might as well stick around, so Lila Mae sat all day as the director did take after take of several commercials. While she was there, a man approached her out of the blue, told her they were short on people, and asked her if she would mind being in one of the scenes.

"I didn't need any experience, he told me, even though I mentioned that I had come very close to being in showbiz at one time." The man said that was the least of his concerns and either she wanted to do it or she didn't. Lila Mae said they stuck her in a trench coat and told her to stand with a group of innocent bystanders who had just witnessed a carjacking.

"I had the time of my life!" she exclaimed. "I met all the stars and everyone was so sweet to me when they found out my son-in-law runs a big corporation with television networks, a movie studio, and everything! The casting director said I was *very* believable and he has other work for me. There's a Burger King commercial next week and one for Geritol, too. They'll shoot that in Cabo San Lucas, Mexico!"

"That sounds great, Mom." Carleen's voice dropped like a stone to the bottom of a pond.

"It's all about networking!" said Lila Mae, doling out her Dale Carnegie advice on *How to Win Friends and Influence People.* She must have realized Carleen wasn't herself because she said, "Honey? You sound down in the dumps. Maybe they'd let you do the Pontiac commercial with me. Couldn't we have fun?"

"No thanks, Mom. I think my television days are over. But I'm glad for you." In the background, Carleen heard the familiar racket signaling that the director was ready for his next take.

"Well, I've got to dash! I've got a million things to do before I leave. I'll try to call, but I hear horror stories about the phone service in Mexico," Lila Mae tweetled like a euphoric bird. "So I can't promise anything! Bye!"

The one-minute conversation was a far cry from the marathon phone sessions of old and the sound of the dial tone replacing her mother's happy lilt left Carleen feeling dejected, sad, even abandoned. She knew she was being a big baby and she really was happy for Lila Mae, but she was green with envy. How unbelievable that her seventy-four-year-old mother had lined up two glamorous jobs, and there Carleen was writing a column about hard-to-open medicine bottles and hoping Dr. Zollinger's Poplar Extract was everything the Environmental Watchdogs said it would be.

Now what was Carleen supposed to do? When she took an inventory of her family and friends, there were plenty of warm bodies on her list and she could always count on Rebecca in an emergency. But, in the end, Lila Mae was the only person who would listen to Carleen without proselytizing, the only soul who would treat her innane details with earth-shattering reverence, and the only one who was available 24/7.

With this new turn of events, Carleen felt like she was drifting farther and farther in turbulent water until she could no longer see the shore.

Growing up, Carleen had been the proverbial middle child, marooned between the glory of Rebecca's every move and the nihilistic, demanding Irene. Big Sister and Baby Sister. Both of them sucked the marrow of Lila Mae's spirit, leaving emotional leftovers for Carleen. Billy Cooper, Lila Mae's bouncing baby boy, didn't count because he was a boy and boys weren't supposed to be attached to their mother's apron strings.

Rebecca had a three-ring circus of a life and Irene had lived in a netherworld of drugs and debauchery. Billy Cooper was a satellite, floating in some tottery mysterious atmosphere, sending them only intermittent SOS signals. Through process of elimination, Lila Mae's maternal attention had no place to roost except with her middle girl.

So, for years, Carleen had an exclusive on her mother; she was, as Lila Mae trilled, "Number one on the hit parade!" Several times a day they would call one another, trading beef stroganoff recipes and fashion tips. They would synchronize their television shows, watching *I Love Lucy* reruns and the Miss America pageant together, always zeroing in on the same thing. "I don't know how Miss Rhode Island got so far, do you?," they'd complain in unison. And Lila Mae had a way of making Carleen feel like a million bucks, telling her how utterly *fantastic* she still looked and how brilliant her latest column was—the one about the two octogenarians who were jailed when they brought their own popcorn into the Cineplex in Little Bucket, Arkansas.

It didn't take a genius to figure out why Carleen craved her mother's self-esteem sessions and clung so desperately to her cloying accolades. It was Nelson. He was the mirror opposite of Lila Mae, making it plain that nothing Carleen did stacked up. He hated the way she made the bed, criticized the furniture arrangement, and gave her advice on which dishwashing liquid to use! She couldn't even leave the house without him barking, "You're not wearing that, are you?" He was sadistic, too, using his vocabulary like a saber to slice Carleen to bits, intentionally unearthing some esoteric word just to keep her glued to the dictionary and feeling like a nitwit.

Carleen's confidence certainly wasn't boosted by the fact that her persnickety husband was surrounded by brilliant female attorneys with whom she was forced to rub elbows. Time and again, Carleen had to loiter on the outskirts of conversations about Darwinism or Byzantine Empire architecture, offering such mundane responses as, "How interesting," or "Gee, I never thought of it that way." She also didn't know a Grand Guignol from Grand Central Station or Frederick Nietszche from Fred Astaire.

The women had beauty-queen looks as well: sizzling eyes and curves that meandered like country roads, plus they turned out perfect Grand Marnier souffles at their exquisite dinner parties, parties that Carleen abhored. Always there was the dreaded question, "And what do you do?"

"So, tell everybody you're a writer, for God's sake," Nelson would gripe. "You do have a column."

"One stupid pet peeve column doesn't make me a *real* writer!" she'd retort. "Norman Mailer and Tom Wolfe are writers!"

"All right, you win." Nelson would throw up his hands in mock indignation. "Tell them you're a nobody, then."

In Nelson's book, the women in his firm were goddesses. They were hardworking, charming, brilliant, and the backbone of Brown, Carlyle and Whittingham's operation. She'd overheard him say that he wouldn't take five men for one female.

As the managing partner, Nelson showered them with high salaries and perks, making sure they didn't defect to a competing firm. Just that week, he had Carleen drive to the wholesale jewelry district in Oakland, not exactly the garden spot of California, to pick up a gold wristwatch for an associate's birthday. The week before that, it was Louis Vuitton wallets and Gucci briefcases for two colleagues who had just won an important class-action suit.

When Carleen complained to Rebecca about her searches for these luxury items, Rebecca said, "Does that seem odd to you?" Carleen asked Rebecca what she was getting at, but her sister said, "Oh, nothing. It just seems extravagant," as if there was more to it than Nelson's proprietary business interest in the women.

Carleen had to admit her sister had planted a nodule of doubt. Yes, there were the late nights and out-of-town meetings and the business calls from a host of other nameless women, plus the whiff of some exotic female musk that she could hardly admit to herself, let alone to Rebecca. But, Carleen would do what she usually did: dump the suspicion into a musty grotto of her brain, and life would go crawling along.

For all Nelson's lavishness with his associates, he was a true cheapskate with Carleen. When he recently asked her for some Mother's Day gift ideas, she gave him a list of modest requests, nothing over seventy-five dollars. Admittedly, she was hoping for something extragavant, a Prada handbag like the one he'd bought for his assistant would have been nice. When Carleen opened the garden tools, ones on sale at Brookstone, she pasted on a fake crescent smile and said, "Oh, thanks." Nelson hadn't even removed the sale stickers that were in wild neon colors and all slapped on top of one another. The tools had gone from $32.95 to $24.95, then from $16.95 to $7.50 before they hit rock bottom at $3.99.

When Nelson turned his back, Carleen lumbered around like the bride of Frankenstein and pretended to attack him with the spade. Although it made Cassie giggle, Carleen actually felt like sliding the small rake across Nelson's scalp until blood oozed from his head. Then she'd take the cleats from the aerator shoes and clobber him senseless. She was already picking out his cheap coffin, plotting her defense, lobbying for a presidential pardon when Nelson told her that instead of brunch at the Mayflower House, her favorite inn, he and Cassie decided to surprise her with breakfast in bed. Then he asked her to please go back upstairs and wait for her treat.

For her daughter's sake Carleen went along, jumping into her already made-up bed. Downstairs she could hear metal scraping, teakettles screeching, even dishes cracking. When a dozen eggs had been squandered in a failed attempt to make eggs Benedict, long after she'd watched *The Andy Griffith Show* rerun and perused every last *Enquirer*, clipping the article about the woman who sold her kidney to buy a canopy bed for her spoiled teenage girl, Nelson tramped upstairs to break the news.

"You better take over. We goofed up." Nelson and Cassie didn't even keep her company in the kitchen, a kitchen loaded with filthy pots and gooey pans. Instead, he laughed off their incompetence by tugging their daughter and saying, "Let's get out of your mother's way, Cass."

So, while her husband and daughter lollygagged in front of the television set, chuckling in delight as they watched *Home Alone*, Carleen assembled the chips of her Mother's Day breakfast. When she compared this casual treatment to the trouble she had gone through for Nelson's law firm, a murderous rage enveloped her.

What she wouldn't give to tell the Jordan Lampleys and Anna Traminskys of the world, all first in their class at Yale or Harvard law schools, all about the magic show inside her. Carleen Carlyle would soon dazzle them all, absolutely blind them with fairy dust. Ah, then the shoe would be on the other foot! There they would be stewing on the sidelines, humped over their boring legal books, paralyzed in utter shock at how they had underestimated her.

So far, strewn along this crooked primrose path leading to the new, improved, totally fabulous Carleen were new leafs, new beginnings, and new chapters. More than once, she had pledged to live life to the fullest, chanting to herself, "Today is the first day of the rest of my life!" Encouraged by Dr. Broadman and the legions of self-help books, she decided to take charge! Enjoy life! What a pleasant, purging thought when left by itself, free from the shackles of yesterday's faults and tomorrow's inevitable failures.

There had also been butterfingered stabs at ennobling their lifestyle. She enhanced her dinner tables with candles and fresh peonies. She tore herself away from *Baywatch* and listened to *La Traviata* and *La Bohème*. Instead of her Diet Cokes and guacamole, Carleen prepared English tea, watercress sandwiches, and pecan scones, which she served with Fortnum & Mason marmalade. This is how it should always be, she thought, as she lifted the majolica teapot and poured the golden liquid into her teacup. What a marvelous feeling as she dipped the filigreed spoon into the orange jam. How civilized she felt when she patted her mouth with a Madeira lace napkin and looked out the picture window to survey all that was hers: the quarter acre of dichondra, the latticed arbor with the climbing lilac, the lamppost with the swinging sign that said THE CARLYLES.

Two days later, the tea tradition was interrupted when her neighbor Anita Roundtree's wheelchair went on the blink at Nordstrom. The wheels had locked right in the middle of their revolving door and three surly teenagers, who would shoot you if they had half a chance, didn't lift a finger to help. It seemed insensitive to ask Roundtree what she was doing in a revolving door in the first place. Carleen just told her, "Of course I'll pick you up, you poor, poor thing!"

A stalled car on the Bay Bridge backed up traffic so when Carleen and Roundtree got home, it was 6:30 P.M. and she didn't see any harm in skipping tea just once. The next day was hot lunch Friday at Rossmore Hall, and Della Hedger reminded her it was lemon meringue day! Not only did Carleen have to ladle mush, she was supposed to bake ten of her famous pies.

There was nothing to suggest that Cassie would fall apart if her mother wasn't at Rossmore to serve up meatloaf. In fact, the teenage Cassie even begged her to stop. "Mom, pleeease! I'm not a baby any- more!" But Della Hedger had Carleen's number, and as long as she kept exclaiming, "Mrs. Carlyle, you're an angel!," Carleen was ensnared. She wanted to scream, "Let me go!"

In the end, the whole tea ritual, like so many of Carleen's resolutions and plans, got lost in the shuffle of all those inane, indescribable details that, rolled all together, became the substance of her days and the bane of her existence.

The traditional and age-old excuse for Carleen's pickle was also the motto bolted to their family tree. It was an all-encompassing scapegoat called the Wooten Luck. The bad fortune was perpetuated by some anonymous spoilsports who had one goal: to prevent the Wootens from claiming their fair share.

Once, during a power outage, her father blew his stack when it in- terrupted *The Honeymooners.* "Well, Jesus H. Christ!" he hollered. "It just had to happen tonight of all nights. If this isn't *typical!*" When Rebecca and Carleen looked up and down the pitch-dark street, they said, "But, Daddy, it's not just *us!*" Their father gawked at them as if they were art- less fools. "The hell it isn't. It's part of the conspiracy to ruin our lives and don't you forget it!"

But Carleen certainly didn't have to journey far from home to produce punctures in the Wooten Luck theory. Rebecca had challenged the ridiculous doctrine to a duel.

For years, Carleen watched from her perch as class clown, while Rebecca, a cheerleader and straight-A student, was the apple of her teachers' eyes. Year after year, Carleen's teachers would ask, "You're not Rebecca Jean Wooten's sister, are you?" sliding their hands together gleefully. When, at the end of one semester her English teacher handed Carleen a report card with an F on it, she said, "I had such high hopes for you, Carleen Raye Wooten."

Rebecca had written articles, produced documentaries, restored historical buildings, and founded two charity organizations. Although she claimed to be all thumbs with a camera, on a whim, she entered an amateur photography contest and won first prize—a trip to the Fiji Islands, which she didn't have time to take, and $5,000, which she didn't even need. If Rebecca picked up a violin, Carleen figured she'd be playing Carnegie Hall in a year.

And yet, during her three-martini, forty-fifth-birthday lunch, Rebecca, her cloudy green eyes staring at the restaurant's pastoral mural, had told Carleen that sometimes she felt like a "complete, total failure. There's so much more I want to do." It couldn't have shocked Carleen more if she learned that the earth was flat after all. If you're a failure, Carleen mused, what am I?

How well Carleen remembered her big sister's dreams: Lila Mae behind the car wheel hollering, Carleen flipping through her Katy Keene comic books, Billy Cooper driving them crazy with his dart gun, while Rebecca stood outside a fancy plantation. Her eyes would scan the gardens, her chest bellowing as if she were inhaling some fragrant vapors and trapping them for a rainy day.

Carleen shared those same desires, but she would never outshine her sister, or claim them for her own. So she waited in the dark, silent wings for Rebecca's hand-me-down dreams.

In Carleen's own fantasy, she was a writer, a stand-up comedienne, even the high priestess of Lemon Meringue Pies! These secret desires began to strangle her, leaping around inside her like some free-spirited, rambunctious child, hammering its fists against the borders of its prison.

What in the world would Nelson—or anybody, for that matter— think if he knew Carleen longed to move back to Blue Lick Springs, that she had an irresistible hankering to manage Rebecca's confectionery, or set bowling pins at the new bowling alley? Was it crazy that Carleen had considered packing enough clothes so that when she was in Kentucky for her mother's birthday, she could just stay there forever? She'd even begun a subtle campaign to woo Cassie with rosy descriptions of small-town America: homecoming games and tractor pulls and lakeside picnics. Cassie moaned and said, "No way, José!"

Carleen knew her daydreams were schizophrenic—one day fantasizing about rural Kentucky and chocolate bonbons and the next, klieg lights and greasepaint, but she was desperate for some form of self-expression, anything to fill in those blanks in her soul. Maybe it was Nelson; maybe she just needed to get away from her husband.

All Carleen's desires were cinched together by a membrane of slim hope, a Scarlett O'Hara of an idea that "tomorrow is another day." But way too many tomorrows had faded into the scrapbook of yesterdays.

Whenever she watched her favorite soap opera, Carleen was struck by the relevance to her own situation. As the credits rolled, the announcer's deep, somber voice said: *Like sands through the hourglass . . . so are the days of our lives.* As the actors' names skipped down the screen and the grains of sand dripped, dripped, dripped through the hourglass, Carleen was afraid it was all running past her, that the episodes of her life would end up in gritty, meaningless piles.

Chapter Fourteen

Rebecca

JUNE 1999

It had somehow got out that Little Peep was a representative of the entertainment industry, so, by the time they got to the Heart of Fire Pentecostal Church, the last thing anybody had on their mind was raising money for Eddie Ray Youngblood's casket.

At the time, Rebecca was in the dark herself, so she hadn't expected the place to be chockful of people. This was a development she couldn't wait to report to Olive, since her grandmother had predicted only a handful of mourners would turn up "fer the likes of a Youngblood." Rebecca'd also been expecting grim-faced men and ladies in black. But the crowd had been painted and perfumed: women in royal-blue pantsuits and big-bellied men in cowboy hats. Plus, everywhere you looked there were spangled children with musical instruments and batons. Two small girls twirled by in ballerina dresses and a gawky boy with velvety hair strummed a guitar and sang "By the Time I Get to Phoenix."

There was also a skinny, loose-limbed woman carrying a piece of luggage who billed herself as the Great Jasmina. She turned out to be a contortionist who could supposedly fit her body inside a Samsonite suitcase! Even some of the Youngbloods were swayed by the talent scout news. Eddie Ray's cousin, twenty-year-old Evelyn, was all set to sing "What a

Friend We Have in Jesus." Evelyn was a buxom brunette who had already caught Phil Bustamante's eye.

After a quick sales pitch for money and a suspiciously brief viewing service, the people practically broke their necks to get to the church basement. The large square room was awash in shamrock-green neon and set with banquet tables. On the walls were photographs of Bethlehem and Blue Lick, as well as a stag head with dusty Christmas ornaments hanging from its antlers. Draped over it all was a banner saying: IN MEMORY OF EDDIE RAY YOUNGBLOOD.

Little Peep and Big Dee had barely set foot on the last basement step when people began to rush forward. Someone shoved a plate of fried chicken and corn pudding at them, and another person handed them bourbon. The Kornkob Mountain Pickers started playing a loud, frisky version of "Dixie," the sort of rendition you hear when a presidential candidate visits a small town. Teenage girls with pink frosted mouths made goo-goo eyes and women with small children pushed them ahead and said, "Now don't be bashful, Roy Edgar. Say hello to Mr. Peepers."

Reverend Stagg, the bandleader, was also caught up in the talent scout confusion. He tapped the microphone and said, "Awright ever'one, let's give Mr. and Mrs. Peepers a big Kentucky welcome!" Then he urged everybody to "get out on the daince floor and show Mr. Peepers what ya got! Come on. Don't be shy!" He played the fiddle while another man, as sprightly as a leprechaun, blew on two ceramic jugs. Sheriff Burkle, who stood as tall and thin as a lamppost, was dragging a spoon down the side of his washtub.

The crowd was clapping and chanting "Whoopeeee!" and "Yippie-i-o!" There were square dancers and singers and a drum majorette in one big gallimaufry of activity. The girls in tap shoes were clicking up a storm and a boy in a tuxedo threw his juggling pins in the air. Even the contortionist had her ankles curled around her neck and a dopey, elastic smile on her face.

At first Big Dee, who was trying to make the best of it, gushed, "Isn't this quaint, Reggie!" He, also, was trying to take it in stride. But when there was no letup, the miffed couple asked Rebecca, who was still totally, completely stumped herself, if she knew why all the attention was on them instead of the dead man.

Although it did seem to Rebecca that people were overdoing it, she explained, "That's just Kentucky hospitality for you!"

While the atmosphere inside was at a feverish pitch, suddenly they heard a clackety-clack sound, one that caused everybody to drop what they were doing. The crowd—men, women, and costumed children—brimmed over the church steps and onto the lawn, their heads aimed toward the sky as if expecting the Rapture. Plus, Reverend Stagg kept saying, "It's Him! He's coming!"

When Rebecca dashed outside to check, she half expected to see robes and halos and Jesus Christ levitating on a cumulus cloud. It wasn't long before they realized that it was Horace C. Castle III. He was arriving in his thundering angel.

The helicopter had landed on the Cherokee Mills site and now hovered above the ground, the propeller whizzing around like a spinning saucer. Emblazoned across the plane was a variation on the infernal company motto: CASTLECO—YOUR FRIEND IN DEVELOPMENT. Underneath that, it said: TOGETHER WE'RE GOING PLACES!

"Yeah, we're goin' places all right," Rebecca snorted. "Straight to Hades!" For all her wisecracks, already her heart felt like a punching bag—throb, throb, throb.

The first to emerge from the glass bubble was a Lilliputian man, cherubic and rubicund, with a turned-up nose and twinkly eyes, like cupid grown up after a life of rich food and alcohol. He stood on the bottom step, the wind lashing his wavy white hair across his brow.

"So that's Horace Castle," Big Dee said, tapping her huge, bloated foot. "I've never met the man in person."

"I've always thought he wuz the spittin' image of that chicken fellow, Sanders," Maybelle added. "Don't you?"

As the other passengers exited, Castle rubbed the ivory knob on his cane. Like Cromwell checking his troops, he angled his body left, then right as he assessed the historical roofs and bucolic splendor. With a gentlemanly flourish, he extended his hand to a woman disembarking the helicopter.

"This oughta be interesting," Big Dee cracked.

"For Christ's sake," said Little Peep, clearly unhappy, "it's not exactly a moon landing."

Bustamante tapped his foot and said, "Can we wrap this up?" Evelyn Youngblood was leaning against him like a small timber resting against a building, and rubbing his tiger's eye ring, which now hung from a silver chain against her white neck.

The first thing they saw was the woman's shapely, bare leg, then a green satin flyaway skirt that quavered like a parachute right before impact. In one hand the woman was holding two apricot toy poodles in a goatskin train case. In the other was the brim of her hat. It sat atop hair as orange as the nearby Shell gasoline sign, and whipped around a face caulked with more makeup than a geisha's. She was having a devil of a time with the hat since her arm was in a sling. Someone in the crowd said, "That's her! That's Horace Castle's wife!"

The woman stood on the hillock spinning around like Julie Andrews in *The Sound of Music* as she pointed at a farm, and then the old Wells Fargo bank. She seemed to be saying, "Those are the ones I want, Big Daddy!"

The women were making huffy sounds and saying, "Get a load of that hideous outfit!" but Phil Bustamante purred like a kitten, "Boy, that's some dish!" and even Little Peep eyed the woman's near-bare bosom and said, "I certainly wouldn't call the police if I found her in bed with me!"

"You might not, but *I* would!" Big Dee slugged him in the gut and stepped on his foot.

Within minutes a panelled truck with the CASTLECO emblem came barreling up the hill, gears screeching and smoke belching. Four CASTLECO employees, moving as nimbly as paramedics, jumped out and began to set up shop, arranging chairs and standing umbrellas, even a campaign desk. Rebecca had seen a lot of extravagance and absurdity in her Hollywood years, but this took the trophy. It was also quite a display for someone who supposedly had a crumbling empire.

Practically spellbound, everyone watched as Horace Castle stomped and circled the hilltop, talking on a mobile phone, sorting through his desk and barking orders to a tall, distinguished black man who was jotting down his every command.

Castle wasn't moving as quickly as his wife wanted, so she began to pace and point and stamp until, finally, she grabbed his arm and shook it like a well pump. With that, the man finished his call and the two love-birds began to stroll down the hill. The woman was walking with her head crooked in the man's shoulder, fidgeting with her sling and trying to get the two poodles, who were bobbing in the case, to settle down. Castle was taking jaunty steps and breathing in the pure air.

Marching behind the couple was the black man in the houndstooth ascot and linen suit. Maybelle elbowed Rebecca and whispered, "That's Mr. Joe Lee Buttons, the director of operations for Castle's business dealings."

The minute everyone realized they were headed for Heart of Fire Pentecostal, they were like stampeding buffalo. Rebecca was dying to get a better look at the infamous couple, something that wasn't easy. For one thing, when they arrived at the church, they had two deacons push-ing back the crowd and for another thing, Rebecca wasn't about to give them the satisfaction of gawking.

For that matter, she was in no position to be scrutinized herself. Had she known about the run-in with public enemy number one, the shapeless shift was the last thing she would have chosen, and she would have definitely not piled and clipped her hair on top of her head. But, she had listened to Olive, who said, "Blend in sum. Ya don't need to be a big glamour-puss."

When the trio passed by Eddie Ray's coffin for a viewing, Mr. But-tons simply swiped his hand across the mahogany. Horace Castle patted his wife's back and said, "Now, now, sugah," while she sobbed and mewed like an injured cat and beat her fist against the brass handles. Only when Castle noticed the crowd gathered behind him, did he show any emotion at all. It was then that he tossed back his head, and, like a coyote braying at a full moon, let out a painful howl.

Rebecca said, "Oh, brother, they'll do anything to fit in!" Big Dee agreed, but most people seemed to have bought it. The woman next to them sniffled into a hankie and said, "That's the saddest thang I ever saw!"

After that the organizers took the Castles and Buttons down some se-cret staircase nobody even knew the chapel had, and everyone was encouraged to return to the recreation room via the regular stairs. By that time the Castles had been ushered to a small table where Mrs. Castle sat behind darkly tinted glasses while people brought her smelling salts and bourbon. The couple stayed there in the green shadows, exchanging murmurs shielded by Mrs. Castle's sling.

Rebecca, dying to size up the woman without being obvious about it, would steal glances in her direction. She couldn't be sure, but the woman also seemed to be interested in her. There had been one awkward split-second exchange, but they both quickly turned away, like two people who suddenly discover they're looking at one another through binoculars.

Since the Castles' arrival, nobody knew if they should impress Little Peep, pay homage to Youngblood, or lick the boots of the big time developer. But, after a small lull in the talent activity, the word started to spread that Eddie Ray would have wanted them to go on with their lives, so the Kornkob Pickers started playing "She'll Be Comin' 'Round the Mountain," a riproaring tune that had people slapping their knees, and once again buzzing around Little Peep. On top of the baton twirlers and girls in paper tiaras, even the grownups were playing up to him. Merva Jean Whitcomb showed up in a sequined crop top and skin-tight Wranglers and Janie Darnelle, batting her blue-powdered eyes, was decked out in harem pants. The worst of the bunch was Horace Castle's wife. Miraculously recovered from her coffinside grief, she smiled and made goo goo eyes at Little Peep from across the room.

"What's the matter with these women," Big Dee quipped from the sidelines, "haven't they ever met a little tyrant before? What's he wearing, anyway—catnip?"

"Huh," sniffled Maybelle. "When they find out who he really is, he'll be about as popular as a turd in a punchbowl!"

Rebecca cocked a curious eye at Maybelle and asked, "What do you mean who he *really* is?"

"You don't think they're after him to balance their checkbooks, do ya?" Maybelle puffed. "Shorty told them a Hollywood scout had come to Blue Lick Springs looking for fresh talent."

"A *talent agent?*" Rebecca shrieked and Big Dee smirked, "Ha! Watch 'em all drop him like a hot potato!"

When Rebecca asked, "Why in the world would Shorty pull such a stunt?" Maybelle, thrilled to be the bearer of bad tidings, told Rebecca it was all *her* fault. She had instructed Shorty to make sure the crowd was friendly.

During all this back and forth someone had overheard Maybelle say that Peep wasn't a Hollywood scout after all, and the word began to trickle through the crowd. First it was a low murmur, building into a loud, acoustical mess. Having heard the news, one girl kicked her baton across the floor and one tap dancer's mother said, "That'll be enough. You can stop now, Sally Imogene."

When the news reached Reverend Stagg, he declared, "Well, fer the love of Jesus!" He thumped the microphone with his fiddle bow and confirmed to the agitated crowd that there had been a mixup and that Reginald Peepers, the one they thought had industry connections, was just an accountant.

Everyone was giving Peep dirty looks and so many people groaned that Mooney banged on Jimmy Buzz's washtub and shouted, "Now, folks, let's don't get ugly. It ain't Christianlike!"

A perplexed Little Peep stood there hunching his shoulders, throwing up his palms, like a homicide suspect explaining his whereabouts to the police. Just as Big Dee predicted, all of his admirers were gone in no time.

Seeing a golden opportunity to seize control, Joe Lee Buttons exchanged a few words with Mr. and Mrs. Castle, then he lifted up from the table. He had a long hook nose like a snorkel mask which he pushed high into the air as he walked toward the stage. He tugged on both French cuffs of his shirt, then whispered something into Mooney Stagg's ear that caused the man to beam. "Ladees and genna-men," said Stagg, flagging an envelope around like Jerry Lewis at a telethon. "You just heard the *bad news* about Mr. Peep. Now listen to the *good news,* some *very good news.* Mr. Joe Lee Buttons jest delivered this here check for $10,000 made out to Butch Youngblood—a doe-*nation* from Mr. and Mrs. Horace Castle!"

"Amen and hallelujah!" people roared. A man with square yellow teeth said, "Castle must be a purty nice feller." Someone else said, "Oh, yes, he's a large contributor to charity."

Until then, nobody had seen hide nor hair of Butch Youngblood, which had been a godsend to Rebecca, who was dreading a showdown. But now he suddenly appeared just in time to collect Horace Castle's money. Even his cheerless eyes had perked up and a teardrop of a smile hovered on his lips.

Rebecca punched Little Peep and said, "You don't think it looks bad, not buying the coffin for someone who died in my restaurant? That's the kind of goodwill and PR that money can't buy."

"We're not looking for goodwill; we need a good legal position," snapped Little Peep. "How would that look in court if we start acting out of guilt?"

"I say we cross that bridge when we come to it," Rebecca said. "We're here now. Regardless of what you say, that should have been us up there."

Instead, it was Mr. and Mrs. Horace Castle who were, slowly but surely, collecting hearts and minds. While the Kornkob Mountain Pickers played the Virginia Reel, an excited crowd had formed around Joe Lee Buttons and the Castles. Buttons stood there with a seraphic smile, acting like the man who delivered the check on *The Millionaire*, while Horace Castle passed out candy bars and five-dollar bills to the children. One little girl asked to pet Mrs. Castle's dogs but one of the poodles nipped at her. To make up for it, she let the girl try on her earrings, two diamond disks jangling from her earlobes like tambourines.

As the merriment mixed with general hurly-burly, a feeling deep down in Rebecca's gut gained momentum. As she studied Mrs. Castle, the pouty, plump lips, the impudent slash of her chin, there was the ghost of familiarity about her. There were the eyes—playful but ruthless—and the quick, sudden movements of a theatrical actress. Rebecca said yes, there was positively something about her. When she asked Maybelle, "What did you say Horace Castle's wife's name is?" Maybelle floored her by saying, "I think she's changed it since she lived in Blue Lick, but—"

"Horace Castle's wife is from *here?*" Rebecca yelped.

"Where you been, girl?" Maybelle drew her brows into a puzzled arch and studied Rebecca. "She got a big award and scholarship to a fashion school in New York and left Blue Lick when she was real young. Her name's Coco or some such."

"Coco? Fashion school? Wait just a minute." Rebecca took another long, hard look at the woman. A notion began to develop, an embryo of a thought so far-fetched that she kept sledgehammering it before it fully formed. It just couldn't be and yet . . . and yet. Finally, when the undeniable presented itself, she whooped, "Coco, my foot! That's Cookie Youngblood!"

If she was a fashion prodigy, then Rebecca was the Queen of England. In fact, Cookie's only fashion connection had more to do with the removal of clothes than the design of them. As for an award, the only honor Cookie Youngblood ever held was the Blue Lick Springs town strumpet. By the ripe old age of fourteen, she had climbed up and down almost every man in town like a fireman slides down a pole. There was also her life of petty crime: the front-page photo of a harlequin-eyed, handcuffed Cookie fresh from her shoplifting arrest at Klink's . . . the stolen pickup truck retrieved near Boone's Creek littered with empty bottles of Wild Turkey and Esther Herman's handbag. Even after the Wootens moved to California, they kept tabs on the Cookie Chronicles all through her stints at St. Agnes's Home for Wayward Girls, all the way to Rome, Georgia, and Miss Canary's Beauty College, and during her marriages to this one and that one. There was also a catfight with Darlene Eversole over Frank Snow, the son of a Louisville Cadillac dealer, a brawl that left Cookie with a black eye and Eversole missing a front tooth.

And now, Cookie Youngblood, Eddie Ray and Butch's wayward sister, the hussy who was run out of town on a rail, had turned up with an expensive but flashy wardrobe, good jewelry, oodles of plastic surgery, and a wealthy, property-hungry husband, one who was determined to take Blue Lick Springs by storm!

In a state of disbelief and indescribably peeved, Rebecca watched from the wings, bunching her eyebrows together in a scowl. All the people she so desperately wanted to keep Little Peep away from were in a cozy swirl! There was Little Peep and Jimmy Buzz, the latter shaking the former's hand like he was playing with one of those test-your-own-strength arcade games. "We're gonna feed this man some world-class barbecue!" Jimmy Buzz slapped Peep on the back. Little Peep jumped forward as if reacting to an overzealous Heimlich maneuver, and said, "You'd better have all your paperwork together! There's wheeling and dealing to be done!"

Next it was Joe Lee Buttons and Little Peep, exchanging toothy smiles and arranging meetings. Rebecca overheard Little Peep say, "Yes, yes there was a bit of confusion there earlier, I'm the business manager for the St. Clairs . . ." Then Joe Lee Buttons said, "I see, I see, the Castles are interested in purchasing *all* the property on Main Street," and Little Peep chimed, "Of course! Of course!" When he suggested a meeting the next day, Buttons's lip dropped like a flap door and he said, "No, no, not until after the funeral. . . . The Castles have been hit very hard by this." Little Peep, Phil Bustamante, and Joe Lee Buttons tipped their bourbon glasses upside down, and Mrs. Castle joined them, saying they'd meet at Miz Becky's two days later.

The last thing Rebecca wanted was an unexpected tête-à-tête with Cookie Youngblood, but she ended up bumping into her anyway. Mere feet from the front door, there she was, face to face with the enemy, a fake smile planted on her lips, figuring she'd greet the woman who used to grit her ten-year-old teeth and hiss, "I'm gonna cut your gizzard out," like a long-lost friend. So, she said, "Hi, Cookie! It's Becky Jean Wooten!" Instead of playing along, the woman pursed her lips into a self-satisfied knot and said, "If you're talkin' to me, I'm Coco." She patted her chest to punctuate each syllable and looked at Rebecca with eyes like little black stones. Then she said, "I don't mean to be rude, lady, but I have *never* laid eyes on you." She paused to draw in a breath, and added, "Unless you were from that poor family over on Honeysuckle."

By the time Rebecca said, "Huh! I'm actually the one who owns all the property *you* want to buy," Coco had slipped her arm through her husband's and drifted into the crowd.

Knowing Coco, Rebecca didn't expect charm-school manners. But she also didn't expect to be standing there with a dropped jaw, totally humiliated, and armed with an unspent arsenal of ripostes. Oh, she wanted to wring the woman's neck! Why did she not pounce first? What made her think that success would have tamed Cookie Youngblood?

More than ever she wished she'd worn her new Valentino jacket, a few baubles from Cartier or Van Cleef & Arpels, something to let Miss Hotshot know she wasn't the only hometown girl who had hit the big time. But there she was looking like Little Orphan Annie with sweet sixteen jewelry: a thin bangle bracelet and small pearl-stud earrings.

As Rebecca made her way out, people started bombarding her with comments. A man massaged his biceps and said, "I'm gettin' my bowlin' arm ready!" Another man patted the top of his fringed head and said, "Can you do sumthin' with this mop?" One woman said she hoped to celebrate her birthday at Miss Lila Mae's. With her brain in some semi-catatonic eclipse, Rebecca stumbled around the room like a sleepwalker rendering monosyllabic responses, "Thanks . . . Okay . . . Great."

As they exited the chapel, Coco, Horace, and Butch were standing beneath Eddie Ray's photograph. Coco, back to her old weepy self, kept pecking at her eyes with a black lace hankie and exclaiming, "Oh, Eddie Ray!" while Horace and Butch held her elbows to keep her from collapsing. Rebecca knew it was her brother and she also knew the shooting had been a tragedy, but she still thought Coco was overdoing it. Rebecca also noticed that both Butch and Horace weren't all that put out, and she even heard Horace grumble, "For Gawd's sake, Butch, how'd you let things get so out of hand?"

Not that Rebecca had expected to have a rollicking good time at Eddie Ray Youngblood's casket fund-raiser, but what hideous luck to have the Castles show up. In her wildest dreams and zaniest nightmares, Rebecca wouldn't have predicted this turn of events.

Chapter Fifteen

Irene

JUNE 1999

To begin with, Irene was not a huge fan of funerals, but she definitely had no intention of attending one for a total stranger. This was against the Wooten family tradition of showing up at every funeral parlor and cemetery this side of the Mississippi for people they didn't know from the man in the moon. As the baby, Irene had missed Lila Mae's glory days of ambulance chasing in Kentucky, when her mother spent much time skidding down the hallways of Blue Lick Springs Memorial Hospital, always the first to arrive at an emergency room and a reliable fixture on the funeral home circuit.

In any case, Olive had said that if Irene wanted to start off on the right foot in the community, she'd better get herself to Silkes Funeral Parlor on the double. When Irene asked why Rebecca didn't have to attend, Olive said, "She already paid her respects at that casket sales pitch."

Olive offered Irene some pointers on what to wear, telling her to "put on that nice pink blouze" of hers and to have Maybelle lend her something to cover her head. "Don't let her go overboard, though, she's got herself sum doozies!"

Olive, who didn't have it in her to actually attend Eddie Ray's services, decided to stay home, but she told Irene to keep her eyes open so she could report anything fishy to headquarters. "Them two," referring to Shorty and the she devil, "never let me in on nothin'." She also told her if she ran into Butch, she should give him a dirty look for Olive and tell him that she knew who else was involved in the Mishap.

Inside the humid chapel, a metal fan whirred and the wooden floors creaked. There were women in black crepe dresses cooling themselves with Jesus fans and men in dark gabardine suits and tar-spattered shoes. The tang of Kentucky bluegrass, musty oak, and disorder were in the air, the sort of commotion that reminded her of an art gallery opening where people are stirring in the lobby after a controversial exhibit.

At first Irene thought the melee had to do with the corpse itself—especially since the coffin was open and, according to Olive, "Eddie Ray had his head nearly clean blowed off!"—but most of it was caused by Coco Castle. Standing in a spear of sunlight, near a stained-glass cross, she looked like a red flame. The dress floated around her like scarlet petals and on her head was a pillbox hat with red netting that fell down her back like a bridal train. Also, her arm was in a sling—not just any sling, but one that had her arm sticking up at an odd angle, sort of like a prancing chicken. Horace was nowhere to be found, and neither was her brother, Butch. Supposedly, the latter was in "seclusion," tucked away in a side room where he could smoke and, people speculated, save himself from putting on a big front. As a result, Coco spent most of her time wiggling her heart-shaped bottom at any man wearing an unsoiled shirt.

For more reasons than one, Irene was trying to resist the temptation to snoop. The fact that both Olive and Maybelle had talked her into wearing an idiotic concoction of straw and ribbon and clumps of grapes, a hat that dipped and swirled and sat on her head like a giant fruit compote, was enough to keep her in a dark corner of Silkes's. But, finally, she couldn't take it anymore, so she pulled herself up and made her way to the front. Although she had never laid eyes on Eddie Ray Youngblood, she looked at his bloated salmon skin and features that seemed to have been rearranged to one side, trying to look heartbroken and solemn, the same phony act she'd seen Lila Mae put on dozens of times.

After the service, the mourners gathered at Reverend Mooney

Stagg's home for a feast. As the guests spooned vegetables and cornbread onto their plates, the temperature soared to 102 degrees and the tubs of iced tea began to drain. Irene stayed close to the banquet table, which was near the sweets, and also next to two women who seemed to have the scoop—or, at the very least, strong opinions: Letty Bookbinder, a DAR officer who had also been at Miz Becky's the night of the Mishap, and Ruby Pearl McCracken, her boss's wife. It wasn't long before Irene realized Olive wasn't the only one who was suspicious of the recent events.

Bookbinder, a bosomy woman with a gray topknot, wore thick yellowed glasses and had goggly eyes that were constantly adjusting to accommodate her curiosity. She took one look at Butch and said, "I've seen better acting jobs at an elementary school play!" Ruby Pearl agreed, telling them to look at him, he was cracking jokes like he was in a carnival arcade. Bookbinder said Coco Castle wasn't much better, that she looked like a lady of the evening with that loud outfit and her loose, seductive ways. Sheriff Burkle, who had joined in, said, "They're Youngbloods! You can't change a leopard's spots." Irene said she hated to be a blabbermouth, but they weren't alone. "My grandmother said there was something peculiar about the whole mess, too."

The leading man in this drama, and the cold-blooded killer in Olive's crime scene theory, was currently leaning against the metal clothesline, one foot tucked into his pant leg like a flamingo. Since Olive had referred to him as "that little runt," Irene expected him to be a creepy little critter. Olive had also added, "Butch Youngblood is a fine-lookin' feller, no one can deny him that." Since her grandmother had already tried to fix her up with Joe Guy Johnson, the muffler specialist at Rochester's Engine Repair, Irene had seen Olive's idea of handsome. It included anybody who didn't have a werewolf hairline and fangs. But Butch was actually good looking—hirsute and muscular with brooding, coffee-colored eyes. Stacked on his fingers were heavy silver rings like machine parts. Irene realized he was definitely the man she'd seen in her grandmother's garden on the day of her arrival.

Cigarette smoke rose all around him like steam from a locomotive and his eyes were moody and tentative, as he alternately chatted with the black man next to him and frantically searched the area for a nonexistent item, possibly Coco. Supposedly, she hadn't been feeling well and had gone into the Staggs' front bedroom to take a nap, but that was before anybody knew she had locked the door and was ransacking their purses and jacket pockets.

Irene was polishing off the last morsels of sweet potato pie, wondering if she should try the strawberry chiffon cake, when Shorty and Maybelle said they might as well pay their respects to poor Butch. It didn't look like the opportune moment to barge in, since Butch was in deep conversation with Joe Lee Buttons, a former city official who now worked for Horace Castle. Plus, with so much talk about how they all hated Butch's guts, Irene wasn't sure what Shorty had in mind. But he gave Butch's tattooed biceps a friendly tap, turning the tables on his previous attitude. "You need to get anything off your chest, Butch, you come visit us." He stared at the man with a look of heart-to-heart sincerity, then added, "Mom'll be all tore up if you don't. It just *killed* her that she cain't be here."

When Shorty introduced Irene as Rebecca and Carleen's younger sister, Butch jumped to attention, a moment Irene always hated—the one when the silent comparison between the blimp and the whippets was made. Although his eyes did register Irene's girth, he didn't say, "Hey, fatso!"

"Butch's the fella that keeps our trees lookin' so purty," Maybelle explained. "He knows his trees, that he does!"

"He might know his trees, but he knows his car engines, too. I never did see anybody change spark plugs as fast as Butch Youngblood." Shorty imparted this fact the way a Harvard Law School dean might endorse a brilliant graduate. "But his *real* talent," he paused, "is paintin'!" With the way Shorty was going on, lifting up on his toes, his voice plummeting and rising, you would have thought Butch was a frustrated Vincent van Gogh. But then, Maybelle said, "Butch painted Charlie Householder's carport and tool shed in thirty minutes!"

While Shorty and Maybelle convinced Butch that the world was his oyster, the bow-tied black man had been standing next to him like a cigar-store Indian. With his face clamped in a condescending smirk, he finally said, "Huh! I can safely say Butch won't be trimming any more trees or changing spark plugs . . . not if *I* have anything to do with it." Butch added, "You said a mouthful, Joe Lee!" With that, both men gave one another a big, insincere embrace.

Just about then, there was some ruckus inside the house. The minister's wife told everyone that when she came looking for her purse, there were strange noises coming from the bedroom. "I thought, 'What's all that racket?' "

Try as they might, nobody could coax Coco out of the room except Butch, who stubbed out his cigarette and yelled, "Coco, get your butt outta there!" Finally the woman burst through the door, stood there with the beatific stare of a Miss America contestant waiting to be judged, then flashed them a wide, red-lipsticked smile. She shifted her sling, took one gingerly hop across a sleeping dachshund in her path, then disappeared into the crowd outside.

Irene asked Letty Bookbinder if it was just her or did Coco Castle's sling look fishy and the woman said, "Fishy isn't the word for it." Then Irene wanted to know if anyone noticed how it bulged. "Who knows what she's able to put in there. Plus," Irene added, "when she went in the bedroom, her arm was sticking up one way, and now it's jutting off in another."

When she explained that she'd been a department store floorwalker, Ruby Pearl looked impressed and said, "Well, aren't you a smart cookie!" Then she turned to her husband, flashing him a "pride of ownership" beam and said, "You've got yourself a real jewel, Buddy Joe."

All this was before they knew that Coco had made off with a total of fifty-two dollars, a silk scarf and one tube of Elizabeth Arden lipstick.

Not everyone noticed, but a few minutes after Coco emerged from her hiding place, a man with a Cro-Magnon frown slipped out the bedroom door and darted outside. He looked both ways, ran his fingers through Brylcreemed hair the color of sunflowers, then opened the door of a Cadillac. Irene had never seen the man, but someone in the crowd said there was only person with bright yellow hair like that. It had to be that feller from up Goshen way, a Cadillac dealer by the name of Frank Snow.

Before they left Reverend Stagg's, Irene looked around to see what was up with Butch, but he had vanished into thin air. All that remained was the smoky silhouette of his cigarette fumes. Coco and Joe Lee Buttons were long gone, too. Someone saw the three of them drive off in the funeral hearse and they were headed toward Honeysuckle Way. That meant one thing: Coco Castle was wasting no time in getting her family's home and acreage in her clutches.

Right before the bereaved brother and sister disappeared, Irene overheard Maybelle—the absolutely imbecilic Maybelle—say to Butch, "Uh, I hate to bring this up . . . but you don't think your sister's husband had anything to do with this mess, do you? Mother Wooten swears up and down that's the case!"

When Irene reported all this to Olive, she screwed up her face and did the thing she usually did with her hands—flap them up and down as if to shoo away bad air. Then she huffed, "Now why'd that nincompoop have to go and do that?"

By doing her civic duty, Irene had pleased her grandmother, that much was true. But there was certainly more responsibility to small-town life than she ever guessed. How many more events would she have to endure, events that weren't mere fish fries and ice cream socials, but funerals . . . all to fulfill an obligation to a city she wasn't sure she would stay in?

For as long as she could remember, she'd listened to hymns of praise from besotted relatives and friends. "Kentucky, land of bliss!" Whenever her parents read about some horrible crime in Los Angeles, they would shake their heads and say, "This would have never happened in Kentucky."

Every other word had been: The South! The South! as if their life had been one big formal ball after another. First of all, Kentucky was hardly the Deep South and, second of all, Honeysuckle Way was anything but glamorous. Sure, it was the type of name that looked romantic as an envelope's return address. Except for a few old farms and Rosemont, which you couldn't even see from the road, Honeysuckle consisted of small, cubic houses and jalopies propped up on cement blocks. Instead of beautiful belles and handsome beaus, there were butt-nekked men staggering through the woods with a flask of bourbon in one hand, a loaded shotgun in the other. The women, many of them tubs of lard like herself, wore loud polyester dresses, and screamed their nicotined lungs out at runny-nosed kids named Jeeter and Babydoll.

All along, Irene was trying to be a trouper, but when she was picked up at the bus station, a faraway voice told her that Kentucky wasn't her cup of tea. During the drive to Blue Lick Springs, she tried to drown out the uncertainty with the mass of her wishful thinking, but the pounding of the telltale drumbeat only got louder. Behind the picket fences and the American Beauty roses, Irene suspected there were lonely hearts and broken promises and dreams darker than her own.

Olive had sent a friend to fetch Irene from the bus station, a man named Cecil whose pickup truck could not make it up Olive's long, bumpy drive-way. Irene had been shown to her room, a large, shadowy space with worn wooden floors and a crocheted-canopy bed. On the wall was a needlepoint of the Wooten family tree and a bas-relief of praying hands. One glass shelf had been cleared in the medicine chest for Irene's toiletry items, positioned above her grandmother's row of ancient cures and below the vulcanized Merle Norman age-defying creams and potions.

As Irene removed the shoes and dresses that Lila Mae had neatly folded for her, and spread them around the room, the hawkeyed Olive watched. There it was, the wreckage of her failed life: the Kama Sutra oil, her flea-market lamp shade, her motorcycle boots. Her grandmother scanned it all and said, "Lawsy, what all ya got thar, girl?" as if she might not have known how long Irene was staying. It would have been just like Lila Mae, who was big on getting your foot in the door, not to have broken all the news to Olive.

Her grandmother had stood, her keen eyes moving through the room, her fingers stroking the grips of her metal walker. "Yer sisters used to sleep in here, did ya know that?" Olive's eyes, misty, faraway clefts, seemed to be roving back to a glory days tableau. "Used to come stay with me whenever they could."

Irene hadn't known what to say, so she fidgeted with her clothes, folding them like they'd never been handled before.

"Yer my namesake, did they tell ya that?" Olive had said. "I wuz born Olive Irene Adams. See, yer mother and daddy, they already knew they wuz leavin' Kentucky, so they give ya my middle name. I figured if they really wanted to go that way, they would have done it with the first one. But oh no, Lila Mae got the name Rebecca in her head . . . Ya look a lot like yer daddy, ya know that?" Olive's quivering hand pulled back a sprig of Irene's hair and tucked it behind her ear. "Well, you come on out when yer ready." She grabbed her walker and clicked out of the room.

At dinner, they had folded their hands, bowing their heads in thanks. "Dear Lord," Maybelle had said, "for what we're 'bout to receive, we are truly thankful. In yer name, amen." Irene had even shut her eyes tightly and said "amen" with everyone else without peeking or making a big to-do. Over a dinner of pork chops and butter beans and a neighbor's heirloom tomatoes, Irene had filled them in on family news, most of it technicolor lies.

Out of nowhere, Olive said, "Tell me, what happened to that husband of yers?" Before Irene could ask "Which one?" Olive added, "What's the matter with you girls? Cain't ya keep yer men?" In Olive's books, a husband, even a worthless one, was a life raft, one to cling to through stormy seas. Olive couldn't figure why two of her granddaughters had run through several of them.

"Well," Irene took a big breath. "That's a long story, but basically, as they say in Blue Lick, he wasn't any count."

"Huh! Ain't that the way with most of 'em?" Olive retorted. They all laughed and chugged down more food and sweet tea. It was the laugh that had settled in some nice, warm spot in Irene's chest and made her feel at home.

And later, when she and Shorty and Maybelle and Olive were all bunched together on the veranda, with the praying mantis and the stars scrambled above them, they swapped tales and sang songs. Olive had closed her eyes, swayed back and forth, and sung, "Goodnight Irene, goodnight . . . I'll see you in my dreams. . . ."

This was it, Irene thought, the *Leave It to Beaver* American family, the precious portrait about which her parents and siblings always rhapsodized. Why then did she feel like Cinderella's ugly stepsister, cramming her foot into someone else's dream?

Irene knew what her grandmother probably thought of her. Even with rose-colored glasses, Olive knew she was a tormented soul. It didn't take a genius to suspect that Irene had been siphoning the apple wine. And when her grandmother casually mentioned that Irene had dropped a few pounds, Irene supposed she even knew about the diet pills she gobbled and the "nerve" pills that Irene could hardly keep from pinching. And, of course, all of them realized that every time her grandmother blamed society's ills on "alkie-hall" or "murray-wanna cigarettes," Irene had to restrain herself from asking if they knew where she might get her hands on some.

Certainly, Olive had been primed by Lila Mae, who sprinkled information the way a flower girl tosses rose petals in the church aisle. "Irene's not exactly like the other girls now. . . . she's, uh, different . . . but deep down she's a good girl."

Irene had to admit that Olive, the Wooten whose approval and love were important to have, the woman whose every utterance had been memorialized in Rebecca and Carleen's book of funny or wise proverbs, had given her a traditional warm welcome. And Irene forced herself to embrace Olive the way her sisters did, but their adoration sprang from a lifetime of intimacy and vivid memories.

Maybe Irene was being overly sensitive, but she suspected her grandmother was going through the mechanics of loving her, that there was no oomph to the ties that bind. Perhaps it was only the trickle of Olive's beloved son's blood that ran through Irene's veins that was the supply line for her grandmother's dutiful affection. Baby Sister had failed them by not being the Breck girl they would have wholeheartedly embraced.

The summer was still in full swing, and it was preposterous for her to even loathe the prospect of winter, but, in her soul, Irene was a sun-kissed California girl. Sure, she admired Currier & Ives prints of winter splendor, but she could think of nothing worse than being trapped in it. Even though the thermometer was still in the high nineties, and the owls hooted into crackling hot nights, Irene could see the hoarfrost of February on the fat, green leaves of Olive's trees, just as if she were looking through a frosty windowpane.

Chapter Sixteen

Rebecca

JUNE 1999

It dawned on Rebecca, after it was too late to do anything about it, that she had gone overboard with the Miz Becky's cash giveaway scheme. When Little Peep, Bustamante, and Big Dee showed up for their dreaded meeting with Jimmy Buzz and the Castles, a mob scene had developed outside, the type you see on the news when Bruce Springsteen tickets are going on sale. "Well, for heaven's sake!" Big Dee exclaimed. "Is this the place you want to close down, Reggie?" She rested the back of her hand on her husband's forehead, pretending to take his temperature.

Evelyn Youngblood, who had tagged along with Phil Bustamante, hit the nail on the head when she said, "They usually ain't this busy. You'd think they were giving the food away!"

It would have been one thing if it was just an unrealistic volume of people stampeding the place, but most of them were madder than hornets. The proprietress of the Helen of Troy's Tanning Salon came fluttering through the crowd like an injured butterfly, her arms flapping like she was trying to get off the ground. "I don't care if it *is* free," she stamped her foot. "I gotta get back to the salon. I got customers!"

There was even some guff about the cash giveaway. Rebecca heard one man, a fellow with a black triangular beard, gripe to the man behind him. "I only got a ten and I gotta wife and two kids to feed, yet he give you, a single fella, a twenty? That son of a gun!" The man's wife said, "We got rooked, Harlan. And that ain't right!" as if she was urging the man to take some action.

Little Peep's head was moving like a ball bearing, so Rebecca could tell he was impressed with the place. He seemed to love the old-time counters and the step-back cupboard with antique crockery. He even grabbed Big Dee's arm, pointed to Madame Serena and the jukebox and said, "Look at the nickelodeon and the gypsy fortune-teller!"

Obviously, he didn't say, "Maybe I was wrong about Miz Becky's; let's don't sell it after all," but he was far from the raving lunatic he'd been in David's office. Rebecca didn't have any set game plan, just the hope that by the time Little Peep got back to Los Angeles, Rebecca twisted David's arm, Big Dee larruped her husband, and Olive seduced him with her apple wine and bourbon balls, that mixed emotions would plague him.

While they were waiting for the Castles to materialize, Sheriff Burkle, Little Peep, and Bustamante were sitting in a comfortable corner booth eating ribs. They seemed to be getting along, mostly because Sheriff Burkle asked Little Peep and Bustamante if they wouldn't like a nice cold beer to go with their meal. Then a few things happened to turn the tide: Burkle said, "Now tell me somethun', Mr. Peep. Did you come all the way from Los Angel-eaze to check my police notes? You wanna see 'em?" Then he hit his temple three times with his forefinger. That was one thing. After that, Little Peep told Jimmy Buzz that he needed to see Miz Becky's books; Phil Bustamante said especially the cash receipts, since activity means nothing on a spreadsheet and it's all about the bottom line. Next, a woman named Betty Harp who owned the laundromat, said, "I hate to complain, bein' that it's free and all, but . . ." and she told Rebecca that her meal had been lukewarm. Then two rough-looking teenage boys wearing studded bracelets like bronze manacles wondered why they and others like them hadn't heard back about their bowling alley applications.

When he heard that, Little Peep's mouth pursed and wrenched and he said, "You mean the bowling alley is for real?"

"Oh, for God's sake, Reggie! You've never liked any investment that wasn't suggested by you." Big Dee turned to Rebecca and said, "You could offer him the White House for one hundred thousand dollars and he'd say it was a bad deal on account of a limited-use clientele!"

"Look, these people pay me to keep them out of financial trouble. I'm here to shut down, not expand!" Little Peep pumped his fists. "Now let me do my job!"

"Well, Mister Hotshot Accountant, open your eyes. This town is hoppin'. Horace Castle's a shrewd businessman, so you sell anything now and in six months you'll be on suicide watch."

"In six months, there might not *be* a ready buyer!" Little Peep punched the table and wheeled around as if checking for the Castles or Buttons. "Strike while the iron is hot!"

Evelyn Youngblood said it was none of her business, but she agreed with Little Peep. "Horace Castle could go ice cold. See, he don't give two hoots about Blue Lick. Cousin Coco, she's the one wantin' to dress the place up."

Delighting in her newfound prominence as a Youngblood, Evelyn had them where she wanted them—spellbound. Little Peep scooted his chair closer and his greedy eyes perked up. And with the prospect of inside information, regardless of its total accuracy, even Rebecca was all ears.

"Coco wants all that land north of town—her old house where she growed up, all Honeysuckle Way, and more. They're gonna buy what they can buy from the owners and git the city to condemn what they cain't git the regular way. They got people thinkin' it's for some new airport." Looking perplexed, Evelyn said, "Hey, your grandmother's on Honeysuckle. Ain't she sellin', too?"

"Not that I know of. Not that *she* knows of either." Even as Rebecca responded, the words *airport* and *condemn* terrified her. "This is the first I've heard about an airport!"

"See, Cousin Coco's in thick with the city," she bragged. "First the city designates the land they supposedly need for the airport, then once everyone's sold their property, the officials'll let the Castles do whatever they want. Coco wants thousands of acres and she'll git it, too!"

"Huh! I might want to live in Buckingham Palace," Rebecca snapped. "But that's my tough luck."

"Even if they don't condemn," Evelyn added cheerfully, "they's something called em-nent domain." Phil Bustamante was nodding his head enthusiastically. "She's right!" he said.

When Rebecca asked Little Peep if such a thing was really possible, he said, "Of course! It happens all the time."

"They can condemn for *no* reason?" an incredulous Rebecca asked. "They can take my grandmother's house, just like that?"

"Of course, not for *no* reason," Peep said. "It doesn't happen overnight . . . but in certain cases it *can* happen."

"I, I'm not supposed to let anyone know this." Evelyn leaned toward them and lowered her voice, something that caused everybody in Miz Becky's to cock their ears. "But I just heard that Cousin Coco's fixin' to buy Rosemont, too."

"Rosemont?" Rebecca yelped and Big Dee, feeling the pangs of possessiveness, said, "That can't be, the house isn't for sale!"

"It might not be for sale, but Castle's gonna git it anyways!"

Although the girl could be dead wrong or simply spreading rumors, just the mention of eminent domain and Rosemont's sale put Rebecca in a panic. What an idiot she had probably been, thinking Castle couldn't possibly get Olive's farm. And who would dream, that after generations of the status quo, the Youngbloods could get their mitts on Rosemont? But, through the cacophony, came David's voice, the voice of rationale and calm. Who knew if it was *really*, *officially* for sale? Here she was letting some greenhorn Youngblood get her worked up over information that was probably exaggerated. For all Rebecca knew, there could be antique dealers across the county who were saying the same thing about her: "Yes, Rebecca St. Clair bought the chandelier and settee for Rosemont!" But, what if the Castles knew something she didn't know or pulled some trick she hadn't pulled? Honestly, though, she really hadn't *pulled* anything, only mooned over the house like she used to swoon over Frankie Avalon or Fabian.

A leaping bolt of illogical thoughts overwhelmed her. She would drop everything to hound Hamilton Montgomery to accept a huge offer, cash under the table if that's the way it had to be, to sell Rosemont and all the surrounding acreage. If she owned *all* the property, surely they couldn't condemn it overnight. Even Little Peep admitted that. Surely there was a technicality or stall tactic or something to derail even the most concrete plans. Oh, she just wished the horrid Castles would disappear off the face of the earth! How unsettling it all was!

Suddenly there they were, two golden silhouettes, two yapping poodles in tow, hovering in the doorway like gunslingers before a shoot 'em up. Knowing what Rebecca now knew, she despised them more than ever.

Mr. Castle surveyed the crowd with a kingly air, and said, "Hello ever'body. We're here to have us some BAR-BEE-KEW!" For some moronic reason, half the room burst into applause.

Milking the warm reception, Coco said, "Everybody, this is my husband Horse Clarence Castle the third!" She was dolled up in orange capris and white clip-clops. The slingless arm had a wristful of platinum bangles, which slid up and down and clanged like Jimmy Buzz's washtub.

Determined to reverse her previous Plain Jane look without being gaudy, Rebecca had on her slim Gucci pants and a chunky gold chain belt slung low on her hips. She tried not to overdo it with the jewelry, but she couldn't resist wearing her huge diamond stud earrings and a Cartier watch.

With everyone looking, Coco placed a bouquet at the spot where her brother had fallen, while Castle yelled to the waitress, "Honey, bring us some ribs and red velvet cake, would you?" Then he ran his hands over his convex belly and asked, "Where's the owner? We've got ourselves a little meetin'."

Little Peep, acting like a buzzard circling fresh meat, said, "Hello! Hello!" Castle gave his hands a cavalier toss and swaggered toward their table.

Since the Castles had made such a big stink with the Roman numerals, Bustie placed his reddish hand to his chest and said, "I'm Philip Raymond Bustamante of San Marino, California, and this is Reginald C. Peepers Jr. of the San Fernando Valley, California," as if their forefathers had signed the Declaration of Independence.

"I'm Dolores *Hicks* Peepers originally from Franklin, Tennessee," Big Dee announced. "I think you know my father, *Lyman Crittenden Hicks* of the Hicks Corporation."

Castle, smelling of clove and tobacco, said, "Yes, of course!" as if they were best buddies. Then he leaned toward Rebecca and Big Dee and, in a sissy Southern drawl, said, "Horace Clarence Castle the third, of Chawl-ston, North Carolina. Ladees, the pleasure is all mine."

"Honeeey . . ." Coco tugged on his sleeve and muttered through a slot of her mouth. "Chawl-ston's in South Carolina."

"Oh, that's right; it is, isn't it." The man tried to laugh it off, but Rebecca and Big Dee exchanged glances.

"Sometimes he gets things mixed up." Coco gave her head a dismissive toss.

"Of course!" Little Peep said. "It can happen to anyone!"

When it was Coco's turn she shrugged her shoulders, and said, to no one in particular, "I suppose you've guessed, I'm the Mrs." She offered her hand which dangled at the end of her sling like a just-caught catfish.

Big Dee glowered at her and said, "We know who you are."

Rebecca added, "Cookie and I are already acquainted."

Coco, her eyes set in half-shut gashes, mumbled, "Now don't start that again." Then she turned to everyone and said, "Yes, we met *a few days ago*." She tried to change the subject by *ooh*ing and *ahh*ing over all the antiques, but her husband cut her off.

"So you're Olive Wooten's granddaughter," Horace Castle mused. "She's got herself a right nice piece of land."

"Yes," Rebecca said coolly. "It's been in the family for several generations."

"Oh, that's your grandmother?" said Coco, her lip curled into a self-righteous sneer. "Her place is part of that property we're wantin' to buy . . . the one next to Rosemont, isn't it? Gee, I'm surprised she didn't mention that we were there. Fed us homemade cherry pie and everything! We were made to believe that place's for sale, right, Horse?"

"Yes, that's what we were led to believe," Castle said.

The Castles could tell from Rebecca's white-faced reaction to the cherry pie comment—one that also caused a cold breeze to run up her back—that their visit was all news to her. She gave them a honey and arsenic smile and said, "Well, you can *believe* anything you want, but the property really isn't for sale."

"Maybe it is and *you* don't know about it." Coco had nonchalantly turned to tend to one of the poodles. "You didn't even know we visited the farm. Nobody told you *that*."

"Now that I think about it, my grandmother *did* mention it, but she referred to the person as Cookie *Snow,*" said Rebecca. "I told her she had to be mistaken because the only Cookie we know split up with Frank Snow ages ago . . . She forgets things easily . . . she's old. I reminded her that Hasty Taggert came after that and, the swimming pool contractor was in there somewhere, too . . . plus a few other husbands I can't remember. So, then, you *are* Cookie, Butch's sister, right?"

"Listen," she said, dropping her purse with a purposeful thud. "I am a Youngblood . . . I never claimed to be otherwise . . . but my name is Co-Co. Plus, I swear on a stack of Bibles, I've never heard of Taggert or Frankie Snow." Horace Castle had reared back suspiciously, and even the dogs, two high-strung pom-poms, started barking at their own mistress. "Now that's the gospel truth . . . Evelyn Anne!" Coco hollered to her cousin, "Get me my pills! *Now!*" When Evelyn produced the orange tablets from a straw bag, Coco put four of them in her flat palm and shoved them into her mouth.

It looked like Horace Castle was ready to leave because he told the waitress to change their order and to make it snappy. Seeing this, Coco lifted her elbow and gave her husband a blow to the kidneys, something that made him lurch forward and sputter, "So, h-how much do you need for this place?"

Little Peep, who was balancing up and down like a toe dancer in warm-up exercises, was thrilled to be discussing business. He said, "Two hundred thousand for *both* buildings!" Horace Castle feigned shock and even one poodle barked at Little Peep as if he, also, thought the price was steep.

Coco threw out her lower lip and pouted, "Don't forget, Horse, I still want that candy store building, too." She stomped her foot like a spoiled child. "I mean it, now."

"We'll see, sugah, we'll see." Castle was doing the same thing David sometimes did to Rebecca, sending her a signal to cool it, if only for the sake of negotiation. And Coco was doing the same thing Rebecca usually did: totally ignoring him.

Coco began to quarrel with her husband, bunching up his sleeve and giving him the evil eye. "Now, Horse . . . you said I could!"

"I *said*," he emphasized each word. "We'll *see*." With his big bulging eyes doing one thing and his tight, smiling mouth doing another, he looked like a demonic ventriloquist.

A nervous Little Peep said, "How does one hundred *seventy* sound?" Big Dee, who had been in the background making snide remarks, lifted up and said, "Hell, I'll pay *that* price! I'll pay three hundred thousand!" Little Peep said, "Oh, no you *won't!*" Coco hollered, "I might pay more than *that,* but Rebecca said the property wasn't even for sale and Little Peep didn't own it anyway, so don't listen to him."

When she added, "Why don't you get *Frank Snow* to buy the place for you?" Coco took a step closer to Rebecca and threatened, "Just *stop* with this Frank Snow business!" Then she thumped Rebecca on the shoulder.

Rebecca said, "Hey! Stop that!" and thumped her back.

Coco stepped on her foot and said, "You're just sore because you didn't know about your grandmother's farm."

"So what?" Rebecca said. "Your husband doesn't even know what state he's from!" Then she stepped on Coco's foot back.

Coco said, "You're just jealous because I've got a rich husband," but Rebecca said she and *her* rich husband, who was handsome to boot, could probably buy and sell the Castles . . . But Coco said she didn't believe a word of it, because why was she selling everything?

The poodles were all worked up, barking and yipping and squirming inside the bag. Horace Castle said he'd had it up to here and went for the door. Little Peep was bobbing back and forth like a heavily guarded basketball player, trying to pass his business card to Coco who kept saying, "NOW GIVE ME THAT CARD GOD DAMN IT!" Big Dee had gotten the first one and was holding it in the air like someone who caught the winning ball of the World Series.

Jimmy Buzz, who was wedged between the three women saying

"Ladies! Ladies!" finally shot two blanks into the ceiling. The poodles let out a high-pitched yelp, so Peep bent over to keep them from going bananas. One of the dogs calmed down, but the bigger one didn't. It craned its neck forward, and took a flying leap for Little Peep's necktie. Burkle tried to lift it off, but the dog hung on for dear life, baring its teeth at anyone who got close.

Phil Bustamante went for a broom and one customer yelled, "Grab its hind legs!" A waitress suggested that they get some scissors and simply cut off Little Peep's necktie, which everybody thought was a good idea, but nobody knew what to do about the other dog. It had also gone haywire and was working its way up Little Peep's trouser leg.

Peep was shimmying like a burlesque dancer and Big Dee was yelling, "For God's sake, do something! They're just poodles!" The one person who could have helped was Coco, but all she did was raise her voice slightly and say, "Now, Wildfire! Pinky! Stop that!" Horace was a little better. He would lunge forward and bat the dogs with a rolled-up menu, then jump back.

Sheriff Burkle offered the dogs some beef ribs, but they even turned their noses up at the food. After that, Burkle finally yelled, "Someone call 911!"

It seemed like an eternity and involved practically everybody in the place but they finally managed to peel off the dogs. With so much turmoil, it was a miracle that there wasn't more damage. The one who got the worst of it was Little Peep. He was crumpled on the ground, sprawled this way and that. He had a big bloody gash on his forehead and scrapes and bruises all over his body. When they tried to get him on his feet, he stumbled around in a daze, like one of those boxers right after a TKO. His side might have been injured, too, since he was clutching it and moaning, "Jesus, Mary, and Joseph . . ."

While everyone else was tending to Little Peep, the Castles slipped out the side door. Coco was trotting behind her husband, saying, "Horse, I twisted my arm in all that mess! My arm's in a bad way. Horse? And poor, poor Pinky, she'll never be the same. This place is *bad luck!*"

Revving up in the background was the familiar clackety-clackety sound of the helicopter. When Rebecca looked around, there was no evidence of the two Castles except their business card and the scent of Coco's vanilla cologne. On the back of the card Coco Castle had written "I'm ready to do some business."

While they were waiting for Thomas Percy Justice and his ambulance to carry Little Peep away, somebody had given him pain pills and bourbon to wash them down, so, in one of his rare attempts at being charming, he looked up at Evelyn Youngblood, who was still hanging on to Phil Bustamante like a barnacle, and mumbled, "Now what does a nice girl like yourself see in an onery ole cuss like Bustie?"

Evelyn, her face as blank as a chalkboard, surprised them all when she said, "Why, I want him to git me on at the candy store!"

"Candy store?" Little Peep said in a swoon of nausea. He lifted his silver-rimmed glasses and rubbed both eyes, as if he had taken just about all that he could take. Phil Bustamante didn't look so hot either. He threw out his lower lip, and cracked, "Huh, *I'm* only seeing *her* to keep the Youngbloods from suing Miz Becky's!"

Later, they got the bad news about Little Peep's dislocated shoulder and bruised ankle and internal injuries and all sorts of other medical problems that had popped up during some routine testing. The doctor took Big Dee aside and told her she might want to rent an apartment or house in Blue Lick, that it would be quite some time before Little Peep could travel. Bustamante, glancing at Evelyn, said he didn't see any good reason for him to stick around; he'd return to Los Angeles and keep the home fires burning. Big Dee, sounding like Florence Nightingale, said she would stay where she was needed most, with her husband, but the minute she was out of earshot, she gave her hands one clap and said, "Goody! Now we've got time to get into Rosemont!"

Normally, Rebecca would have gone along with Big Dee but Rosemont was the last thing on her mind. The mere possibility that Olive's farm could fall into the hands of that money-grubbing businessman and corrupt city officials hiding behind the mask of airport expansions and rural redevelopment made Rebecca sick to her stomach. How could this happen? Was it really possible, in the United States of America, for the city to condemn and snatch any land they wanted? They weren't living in Communist China!

As soon as she got home, Rebecca opened her laptop, starting a new page with the title "Blue Lick Springs Preservation Project," something that looked simple and manageable enough. Her fingers flew across the keys, moving the listings around, combing two or three items, then giving them headings. There was a priority list and categories of property to save—Olive's farm, Miz Becky's, Rosemont. Spread out in perfect formation as they were, all the letters on the page looked so docile and malleable, all of them knaves with slavish devotion to their mistress. All Rebecca could do was keep her fingers crossed that the project itself was half as cooperative.

Since Rebecca and Big Dee looked like victims of a barroom brawl, they had managed to sneak inside the house, and, they thought, away from the curious gaze of Olive. But soon, Olive stood in the doorway of Rebecca's bedroom with both hands on her hips. "What in tarnation went on down thar enyways?" she asked. "The whole town's already talkin' about it, Maybelle and Shorty's all tore up cuz they missed out on all the doin's. And that poor Mr. Peepers stuck down thar in that hospitul that'll take out the wrong part if ya don't watch 'em . . . Yer gonna make a bad name fer yerself . . . Mercy, mercy me."

When Rebecca told Olive not to worry, that the incident was all for a good cause and she would have the last laugh, her grandmother stared at her with skeptical eyes and said, "Jest don't make the big mistake ole Haman made with Mordecai. He hanged himself on the same gallows he built fer someone else."

Chapter Seventeen

Rebecca

JUNE 1999

It was like pulling teeth, but Rebecca finally got Olive to cough up more details about the developers. When Rebecca asked her to wrack her brain to remember if a woman who looked like a streetwalker, smelled like a Youngblood, and hung out with a man who looked like a tipsy Colonel Sanders showed up at the farm, Olive floored her by saying, "That's them, that huzzy ya said and that Sanders feller . . . They brung Joe Lee Buttons, stuck his ole, shiny Florsheims right in the door. I sez, 'Now Joe Lee, I knowed ya since ya wuz a boy, ya ain't gonna scer me none.' Buttons sez, 'Miz Wooten, I work fer Castle, I'm the die-recter of the whole shebang; I ain't no hit man!' "

"You don't happen to remember when this was, do you, Grandma?" asked Rebecca.

"Oh, it wuz quite sum time ago. Way before the she devil got me that fancy chair. Ask Maybelle, she invited 'em here!"

"Maybelle?" Red clouds of anger towered before her. "Grandma, that woman is Cookie Youngblood, Butch's older sister! She's going by Coco Castle now, but she's trying to get Rosemont, your farm, her parents' house back, and who knows what else!" Rebecca grunted, "This doesn't sound good at *all*."

"Well, it ain't!" Olive shouted, twisting a lace hankie into a wet rope. "Nobody lissens to me. I been tellin' ever'body."

While Maybelle showed the intruders around, Butch and Joe Lee Buttons had encouraged Olive to sign a paper. "They tole me they's nothin' can be done 'bout it! I shoulda tole ya they wuz here, but it wuzn't in my hay-ed to bring it up. Enyway, what could I do? Maybelle and Shorty's all fer it, too!"

"Shorty also wants you to sell?" Maybelle was one thing, but Shorty owned a share of the farm, giving him a legitimate say-so. "Well, don't let him fast talk you. You're sure you didn't actually sign anything?" Rebecca was a nervous wreck, muttering to herself, "Let's get *ooonnn* with it!"

"Oh, I played 'round, jest to let 'em think I *might* sign up. I even picked up the pen, but I ain't no fool."

"Do you know what this means, Grandma?" Rebecca crouched on her knees in front of Olive's chair, looked squarely into her eyes, and enunciated carefully. "This means that Maybelle and Shorty are trying to talk you into selling this place, to a *Youngblood*, no less."

"I wuddn't put it past them two, wud you?" Olive stared ahead like she was reading an eye chart. "I knew when Shorty married Maybelle we wuz in fer it."

In the past, Rebecca had dismissed Maybelle as a mere annoyance, but in her mud-brown eyes, Rebecca suddenly saw hostility and gluttony and a big, fat real-estate commission check. Shorty, for all his bluster, would cave into Maybelle's pressure faster than one of Castle's demolished buildings.

Shorty and Maybelle got more than they bargained for when they showed up for Olive's devil's food cake. Here they came, slamming the screen door, Shorty clutching the mail, and Maybelle, a vision in cold cream and jumbo rollers, yoo-hoo-Avon-calling her way into the parlor. The granite-faced Olive and Rebecca caused the couple to freeze in their tracks. "Did someone die?" Maybelle let out a jittery squeal.

"No, but someone's about to," Rebecca quipped. "Grandma's been filling me in on Horace Castle."

Cutting right to the chase, Shorty said, "They don't have to take the house, girl, just the property! They'll leave half an acre, if we want it."

He sniffed dramatically, his nostrils flaring to drink in his own importance. "You take care of this lawn and you'll know that's plenty to deal with."

"So, this boils down to mowing a lawn?" asked Rebecca, a strain in her voice and a look of disgust on her face. "That's *it*? They're going to leave one single house in the middle of a supposed airport runway, an airport that probably doesn't even exist? You must be kidding!"

"Now what good would that do?" Olive grumbled. "Me a-sittin' here nekked as a jaybird, dodgin' them jumbo jets."

"With all these long, drawn-out conversations we've had about this, nobody ever told me the Castles actually *came* to the house!" Rebecca said. "I know more about Butch Youngblood's farm and Raydeen Harper's situation than I do ours!"

"THERE AIN'T NOTHIN' YOU CAN DO, IT'S PROGRESS!" Shorty screeched, his voice cracking like an alto with soprano aspirations. "I don't wanna sell any more than you do . . . but AIN'T YOU EVER HEARED TELL OF EM-NENT DOMAIN?"

"I'M NOT WORRIED ABOUT EMINENT DOMAIN," Rebecca hollered. "I'M WORRIED ABOUT SHORTY AND MAYBELLE WOOTEN!" Ten to one, they didn't even know what eminent domain was, couldn't even check the right box on a multiple-choice question. For that matter, Rebecca didn't know how it worked either. She just knew it was drastic.

"If we don't sell now, then, uh, see, we outsmart ourselves," Shorty said. "Then the government gets it and you got no position. They pay you peanuts!"

"Fer cryin' out loud, Curtis," Olive snapped. "Don't get all sturred up. This is still my land as fer as I know."

"IT'S PART MINE TOO, DAMMIT!" Shorty screamed. Looking at him, Rebecca wondered if it was *really* possible that someone could just blow their top! "IT AIN'T GONNA BELONG TO EITHER OF US FOR LONG!"

"Just tell me one thing." Rebecca's desperate eyes scanned the room. "Has anybody *signed* anything? Jesus!"

"No, and I don't intend to. And they don't scer me none, neither.

They kin break my winders and who knows what all, but I ain't sellin'!" Olive speared her hickory cane into the floor and announced, "I still got my stinger, yes I do!"

Olive struggled to grab the last word, but with the slam of the screen door, Shorty was gone. Without missing a beat, Maybelle pushed the waste-can lever with her foot and daintily dropped her empty Pepsi can inside. Then she followed her partner in crime out the door.

"Ya see how his temper flares up? Might as well be talkin' to a brick wall," Olive snorted, pushing away a small bowl of chocolates. "That's the Wooten in him. The Adamses wuzn't lak that. They wuzn't lak that at all."

That was the thing. If Rebecca could just reason with Shorty and Maybelle, maybe she could penetrate their dense, gullible skulls. She'd let them know that they didn't have to be swept away by the rhetoric. They didn't have to take all the eminent domain propaganda at face value. They didn't have to be victims of the momentum Horace Castle had managed to create.

But, Olive hit the bull's-eye with her assessment of Shorty. He was a classic Wooten hothead, one who fought every debate with fists, not logic and eloquence, one who hit the roof before all the possibilities were even exposed.

Maybe Rebecca had it wrong, though. Perhaps they were caught up in the avaricious sell! sell! sell! Maybe they were anxious for new appliances and aluminum siding. But what did they have in mind for Olive? Were they going to cart her off to some foul-smelling, old-age facility where the highlight of her day was bingo, telling themselves that she was happier than ever?

What a crime that because of their obstinance and greed, Olive, almost a century old, woke up every morning, scanning the countryside for surveyors and tripods, scouring the newspapers for public notices of zoning changes, never knowing how much longer she could hang on.

And Olive's land was so much more than mere acreage. Beyond the cottage, past the minnowed streams, behind the deer-populated woods, was the sawmill operated by her father and her grandfather and her great-grandfather before that. From the leftover squares and circles of pine, her father's carpenter hands had created doll cradles and a hope chest decorated with hearts and flowers for his beloved only daughter. All from trees on this land.

As a gangly young girl with Irish-pink cheeks, Olive had dipped water from the well with her wooden pail, had gone *sangin'*—gathering ginseng from the jagged hillside. At sunset, she snapped Kentucky half runner beans on the porch for dinner. With the whippoorwills chirping and the water moccasins restless, the land was only one poisonous snake away from Shangri-la.

It was also on that farm where Olive Irene Adams, a princess in white tulle with rosewood-hued hair, had married Clayton Dawes Wooten. A handsome rogue with chiseled cheekbones and a five-hundred-watt smile, he had trotted up the horseshoe driveway in a brass-wheeled carriage. After a wedding banquet of roast pork and cider, he had carried her across the threshold of her own home, a chamber in which they lived unhappily ever after.

On this very farm Olive had given birth to her five sons, toiled from dawn to dusk, her pink, callused hands tending yarn, pumping rusty well water, stripping tobacco. With her heart-shaped face set in compliance, she would darn socks and mend shirts, sprinkling orange-blossom water on the linens she'd kept in her dower chest. Tied in white satin ribbons, she'd stack them in her mother's walnut linen press, her last grip on refinement. She would refashion her own crepe dresses until they were threadbare and slide box cardboard into her holey work shoes while her Beau Brummel husband sported pin-striped suits and a rose-gold pocket watch.

And when times were unspeakably bad, there would be a house brimming with boarders, men with eyes the color of bad whiskey. During the day, when all respectable types were at work, her lawn was overrun by these prurient strangers in soiled gabardine. For two dollars a week, Olive fried eggs, brewed coffee, swabbed toilets. In the shadows of narrow corridors, she would avoid their nicotined grasp as they pressed their bulk against her slender body.

In the evening, these same men would scatter across the wooden porch, settling into a glider or dangling their legs over the railing, their cigarettes like orange rocketships arcing through the darkness. They would nuzzle the bottle of Hiram Walker to their lips, passing it to their new gambling pal, someone named Jimbo or Buddy or Say, friend! Sometimes the evening would end in spirited song—"Jimmy Crack Corn" or "Flat Foot Floogie"—or just as often in fisticuffs.

"Alkie-hall . . . the devil in a bottle!" Olive would grunt. Then she would watch with a slow leak in her heart as her own husband joined the wassailers.

With the crying babies in the background, Olive would glare through the dull Irish lace on the window, past the willow tree, beyond the veranda stairs, the moonlight blazing across her parlor. She would watch as Clayton, his poker cards squeezed to his vest, frittered away the few coins she'd managed to save. Then she'd furl her taut fist at her husband. "Ya better straighten up and fly right, ole fella!" Afterward, she'd climb the staircase and slip between the sheets of her twin bed, waiting for the racket to subside and the Kentucky sun to rise.

When Rebecca was a girl, she and Olive would enter the woods, a giant evergreened tabernacle, where they chased runaway pets and picked berries. They would wade through ponds percolating with crawdaddies. Olive would point to the water and tell her bright-eyed, but wary, granddaughter, "You put a hair from a horsetail in that pond over yonder and it'll turn into a snake . . . It'll do it, too. You watch!"

Rebecca just couldn't picture the farm without her grandmother. Olive Adams Wooten, the Queen of Honeysuckle Way, inhabited every tree branch and each flower petal.

"Sumday you'll bur-ee me on this land." Olive's freckled hand would ruffle the top of Rebecca's head. "Who knows, maybe I'll turn inta somethin' else, too. Ya never kin tell, can ya? But this is whar I'll always be."

If Rebecca just had the luxury of time, she could finagle something. It could be years before this big, devastating hurricane of a project would see fruition, regardless of all the current activity. As for Rosemont, what made the Castles believe Hamilton Montgomery would suddenly sell the plantation? And it wasn't as if Rebecca didn't have connections to help. She knew there was growing resistance to

CASTLECO's tactics; perhaps if the town protested, it would cramp the developer's style. And what in the devil was going on with the so-called crumbling empire?

All Rebecca knew was this: If it was the last thing she ever did, if it took every penny she had to her name, if she had to pull strings, or if she had to resort to something shady herself, tactics that could take years and involve half the population of the Southern hemisphere, she was going to make sure Coco and Horace Castle did not get their paws on her grandmother's property or Rosemont. Yes, it would be a very cold day in hell before Rebecca would let that happen.

One evening, on her way back to Olive's house, Rebecca passed a tower of red, blinking lights and smokestacks, neon skeletons, rattling their bones in defiance, staking their claim to the sky. She didn't remember seeing them before. Overhead was a moody, dark yellow moon, a moon that had clouds like Spanish moss drifting across it, the same moon that David would be looking at in a few hours. She could visualize him now, still behind his desk, patching together deals, making his world spin around on double overtime. She wondered if Ava had packed for ballet camp and if David had eaten his dinner yet, as if it were she who provided packing services for her daughter and gourmet meals for her husband every evening. Being there, as she was, so embroiled in local politics and family and menacing developers, it was easy to forget that there was an Ava and a David. Then she'd imagine her daughter's sweetheart face and her husband's big, warm syrup of a smile and long for them.

Whenever Rebecca stayed in Kentucky for any length of time, she'd be swept up by melancholia, and she'd want nothing more than to spend Saturday afternoons with her husband and daughter, days when they ate hamburgers and pie at the Apple Pan, shopped for books and ski clothes in Century City, and saw a movie in Santa Monica. She would long to get a whiff of her daughter's skin, the skin that smelled of ripe pears, or the lemony-lime aroma clinging to David's cashmere sweaters. She wondered how this was all going to work out. From now on, would she always be yearning for her daughter and husband when she was in Kentucky, then dreaming of Olive's parlor when she was back in California?

Along her grandmother's drive, the tree branches swept the ground like heavy drapery. Lightning bugs, the sparkling insects they used to catch and store in Smucker's jelly jars, hovered midair like miniature spaceships.

Since the news of the robbery and shooting, Rebecca's heart had been heavy. Looking into the starless night, she remembered afternoons when she and Carleen would sneak over to the Youngblood place . . . the mischievous Eddie Ray who used to blush and tell Rebecca and Carleen they were the "purtiest gurls on Honeysuckle Way." She thought of his pesky sister, Cookie, who wore Rebecca and Carleen's hand-me-down dresses and who, instead of being grateful, gave them dirty looks and pelted them with dirt clods . . . and Butch who broke the handlebars off her first Schwinn, and of Jesse, his father, who fixed them. She found herself humming, "On top of Old Smoky, all covered with snow . . . I lost my true lover . . ." A few moments of madness and confusion, a few clicks of a rifle's trigger . . . and that was the end of Eddie Ray Youngblood.

As Rebecca crept slowly down the lane, with a forlorn feeling clawing her bones, she tended to blame the very beloved land on which her feet were planted.

The name Kentucky, according to folklore, was an Indian one that meant dark and bloody ground. In the daytime, the atmosphere was sweet as honeysuckle perfume, but at midnight came the graveyard shift, when it spread its nocturnal poison. From some mysterious berth came three-legged animals, and feral men with glass eyes. They clutched guns and harbored grudges in a place where all your dreams and even some of your nightmares came true.

Chapter Eighteen

Carleen

JULY 1999

For some reason, Carleen had expected Joshua Beaton, the chairman of Beaton, Richardson and Bardwell, to be grumpy and grandfatherly, so when she and Roddy Berlin, the *Chesterfield Bay Sun* editor, met him at the private airport in San Francisco, she was shocked to see a dashing, fiftyish Prince Charming descending the stairs of the corporate jet. He wore a gray pin-striped suit and loosened paisley tie, and there were little accents of understated elegance: an Italian briefcase and a gold chronograph watch. His wavy black hair had a self-confident tumble to it, but best of all were his eyes: peacock-feather blue with warm, crinkly laugh lines. He was the kind of man she could see escorting an actress in white mink to a movie premiere, someone she and Rebecca used to refer to as a top-notch dreamboat.

Two things came to Carleen's mind as Beaton strode toward her: the first was that she was sorry she'd made such a big deal about McDonald's grouchy employees, and the second was that she wished she'd already had the facelift she'd been thinking about getting. On the plus side, she had made a good outfit choice: a slim black dress, slingback pumps and her Jackie O. sunglasses. And thank God for the Gucci handbag Rebecca had given her, a black clutch with a gold clasp, so much better than the worn bucket bag she usually carted around. Even her hair had co-operated, hanging to her shoulders with a playful swish and twinkling in the afternoon sun.

"Carleen Carlyle?" Beaton cupped her hand and gave it a firm shake. "Pleased to meet you. Joshua Beaton."

The first thing she did was check for a wedding band, which Beaton wasn't wearing, but that didn't mean anything because Nelson never wore one either. For obvious reasons, that shouldn't have mattered. After all, Carleen was a married woman and this was a business meeting, wasn't it? He must have pictured some crotchety mule-faced spinster who had nothing better to do than hang out at McDonald's, then write complaint letters, because Joshua Beaton, too, seemed pleasantly surprised.

With him was Edgar Manning, the head of McDonald's marketing division, a large, wavy-haired man with a round, ruddy face who gave her a curt smile and said, "Hello." Given Carleen's long history of complaints against the company, it wasn't surprising that Manning was cool toward her.

The strategy had been to schedule a cordial get-together with the city officials, but they would arrive early for a surprise attack, visiting Chesterfield Bay's McDonald's franchise as ordinary customers. Carleen and Beaton would actually stand in line while Manning and Roddy Berlin would watch the shabby treatment from afar.

When they got there, behind the cash registers were six zombie-eyed people of all varieties, employees who didn't say please, thank you, or I'm sorry, only cracking smiles when they were blabbing with their coworkers about upcoming dates or problem skin. In contrast to that, the restaurant was crammed with happy-face mobiles which bounced from the ceiling on colorful twine. Carleen pointed out that they were trying to accomplish with signage that which they were unable to do with their stubborn employees. "Surely the genius who dreamed up that ad campaign has never been a McDonald's customer," she said to Beaton. "Honestly, a smile is the *last* thing I'd promote. These people don't even know the meaning." Of course it wasn't until after she said it that she forgot that Joshua Beaton himself could have been the so-called brainiac behind the creative misfire. But he lifted his brow and, as if to suggest that he was on her side, said, "Believe me, I know the situation all too well."

They had almost reached the counter when Edgar Manning came rushing out, flashing his business card to let everyone know who he was. Then Tracy Williamson, the mother of one of Cassie's classmates said, "Are you writing another column on bad service?" After that a teenage boy who looked like Mr. Clean with a shaved head and one hoop earring, pointed to Carleen and said in a loud voice, "Hey, you're the goat lady!" So that was the end of that. The grouchy employees had caught on and now looked as cheerful as their happy-face signs.

The only thing that was going right was that Beaton placed his palm on the small of her back and steered her away, a gesture that gave her butterflies.

After that, the newspaper photographer took dozens of pictures in front of the restaurant as they stood with their arms draped around one another and exchanged lifelong-friends smiles. By now, the manager, a nervous little fellow named Ray Esposito, had joined them. Mayor Ogden had shown up with two keys to the city, one each for Beaton and Manning, and a speech depicting Chesterfield Bay as the most perfect spot on the entire planet. Ogden also praised Carleen Carlyle for her "humorous and pointed essays" and for "'embodying the spirit of the Chesterfield Bay community."

Finally, they took one last photo of everyone drinking a supersized Earthquake, a new frozen milk-shake product they were launching that day, which was probably what the get-together was all about to begin with. They unrolled a plastic sign saying: EARTHQUAKE, AN EARTH-SHATTERING EXPERIENCE with a drawing of a drink surrounded by zigzags to make it look like the cup was shaking. Mayor Ogden said, "We are delighted, as well as honored, to have been chosen to host this most auspicious occasion!"

Carleen was ecstatic when Roddy Berlin said he had a deadline and had to dash back to the office. But Beaton and Manning had time to kill before their departure, so the three of them ended up in San Francisco at Ernie's for an early dinner.

All the way there in Beaton's limousine and all the way through the restaurant, Carleen kept pinching herself. As they were shown to their table, a tufted U-shaped red leather booth, Carleen walked through the room as if she were in a flower garden, savoring the red velvet walls, roses in silver urns, and glass-candled lamps . . . all that plus a pianist who played Gershwin. The sommelier, who knew Joshua Beaton, came to suggest a Cristal rosé champagne for an apperitif. As opposed to Nelson, who would have blurted out, "How much is it?" Joshua Beaton asked him what year it was. He must have been pleased, because minutes later, a waiter brought icy crystal flutes and beluga caviar.

Dinner with Nelson, when it wasn't something she'd slaved over, usually consisted of a hand grabbing a paper sack from a takeout window. On the rare evening when they did dine out, Nelson always asked for the check before Carleen had taken her last bite. Dinner with Joshua Beaton was a langorous affair, filled with bubbly champagne and tiny, elegant courses of seafood bisque and veal and truffles, and spun sugar desserts.

They even managed to discuss the different public relations choices, somewhat of a real eye opener for Carleen. She was so used to regional papers like *The Busy Bee* or *The Gadabout* that she couldn't believe her ears as they bandied about *People*, *Us*, even *Time* and *Newsweek* as possibilities for articles. The champagne gave her a shaky confidence so when Manning said, "What do *you* think, Ms. Carlyle?" Carleen said, "Well, there are two ways of going about it: Either the big-hearted corporation cares enough to send the very best—that would be you two, or my personal favorite, the David versus Goliath angle. *I* would be the heroine in that one . . ." She paused. "Actually, there's a way to do both . . . small town fights back, big corporation takes note, then takes action!"

When she set her champagne glass down dramatically, the two men were peering at her like she was an extinct animal. "I know the beat-the-system part might be overstating it," she backpedaled nervously. "After all, it's just a hamburger, not the Internal Revenue Service or city hall, and it would probably be better to focus on the big-hearted corporation, but still . . ."

"No, you were right the first time." Beaton's eyes caught Carleen's and he seemed to edge toward her, as if her good idea bound them closer together. "I was just startled by how you hit the nail on the head. I think we should unite the two themes."

"That's right!" A ruddy-faced Manning, who was drinking Grey Goose martinis, added, with a chuckle, "You can make anything work— you're a journalist!" But then a realization hit him and he yipped, "But what's that got to do with the Earthquake? How do we work that in?"

By the time they got around to everyone's life stories, Carleen was feeling like Barbara Walters and Joshua Beaton was looking more and more like Adonis. Carleen didn't give a hoot about Edgar Manning's vital statistics, but she did learn that Joshua Beaton was from Richmond, Virginia, had gone to Princeton, was divorced, and had a daughter who attended Vassar.

"If you've never been to Virginia, you'll adore it." Joshua said "Virginia" lovingly, the way she and Rebecca always talked about Kentucky. When Carleen mentioned her home state, he said, "You know, the two are very similar. You'll have to visit and see for yourself." In a split second of craziness, she began picturing Beaton and herself strolling through their colonial mansion in Virginia, the one with silk-papered corridors and white-plank fences. There would be parents' weekend in some New England bed-and-breakfast visiting his daughter, an English Literature major, who after months of family therapy sessions, finally accepted her stepmother and got along great with Cassie. Carleen couldn't wait to tell Nelson she was leaving him for a man who had graduated from the college that had rejected him!

When Beaton asked Carleen about herself, she was stunned when she said, "There's not much to tell, really," going out of her way to hardly mention Nelson and Cassie! At the thought of them, she panicked, realizing that she was supposed to be at La Fonda having Mexican food.

By the time they left the restaurant, all the red velvet and Cristal and "Someone to Watch Over Me's" had taken a toll. Carleen felt like Cinderella, transported to one of those magazine ads where special people, happy people, were living life to the fullest. The three of them rode along in a white limousine, all crammed together, watching the blue-black night through the skylight, the smells of champagne and Carleen's

White Rose perfume and Joshua Beaton's faint citrus and Edgar Manning's martini fumes all clashing together in one small bubble. Seated next to him, with their legs slightly touching, Carleen was in such a swoon she almost rested her head on Beaton's shoulder. She noticed the flexing of his leg muscle beneath his suit and wondered how it would feel wrapped around her own slender thighs. She had no idea from whence this urge came and she hoped against hope that the sensation was a case of temporary insanity, one which would vanish when Beaton left town.

But there was fat chance of that, especially considering the person she was married to, the person whose every little habit rubbed her the wrong way—the way Nelson jiggled his ice in a paper cup during the movies; the way he drove, flooring the accelerator, then removing his foot, making the car lurch like an angry bull. She couldn't even stand the way he ate his food, and too many other things to even count.

While they were standing on the tarmac outside the limousine, everything was in motion: flags whipping and coattails flapping, the plane's propellers creating gusts of wind. Beaton leaned toward Carleen, so close she could see the luminous gray flecks in his eyes. "I really dreaded this trip. It was one of those necessities when you're in the public-relations business. But I had a great day."

"I wasn't looking forward to it either. You know, you write that stuff, then you panic when you're confronted. I flipped when Roddy told me someone from McDonald's was coming to Chesterfield Bay. I was thinking knockdown, drag-out fight."

"Instead, it was quite the opposite." Beaton took one baby step forward. "For me, anyway." His hair was going every which way, giving him an exciting, rakish air.

"Yes, I really enjoyed it, too," Carleen murmured, trying not to read too much into Beaton's words and giving him a look that she hoped landed somewhere beyond casual acquaintance, but a millimeter away from sexual predator.

"Here, take this." Beaton scribbled a number on his business card. "Just in case you ever want to leave your husband, abandon your daughter, sell all your belongings, and move to New York! I'm only kidding . . .

a little. You'd be great in advertising. By the way, that's my private number on there."

"Oh!" Carleen stared at the card as if it were a valentine.

"Listen." His eyes were as intense and deep as the endless sky around them. "I really hope to see you again. I'll be back next month."

"You will?" Carleen asked incredulously. She prayed she didn't sound like her whole world balanced on it.

"Yes." He rested his hand on her bare arm. "I'm looking forward to it."

She looked at him in a last gasp of flirtation and said, "So am I."

The moment seemed to stand still, preserved by some canopy that separated it from all the other motion in the world, as if all life existed only in those few square feet. Somewhere "Rhapsody in Blue" was playing and a sensation from long ago, a feeling of warmth, blossomed inside her.

When Manning approached and told him they had to get a move on, Beaton said, "Well . . . we're off to Los Angeles." When he got to the top of the plane's staircase, he turned around once and wagged his fingers good-bye.

Instead of departing right away, Carleen sat in her car with her hands curled around the steering wheel, humming, "Leaving on a jet plane . . . don't know when I'll be back again . . ." Then she watched until the aircraft's blinking lights climbed past the Golden Gate Bridge, over San Francisco Bay, into the sky headed straight for Ursa Major and a big bronze moon.

There had been moments like these in her life before, those starlight, star-bright encounters that shot rocket ships and cold chills through her, ones that resulted in a phone call to Rebecca when she would say, "Guess what, Rebecca? I'm in love!" But this time things were different; there was no way Carleen could be in love, she was married!

It was a warm, moon-drenched night, with the fragrance of eucalyptus and redwood in the air. With the car windows down, she zoomed across the Bay Bridge, past the Berkeley hills, noticing all the McDonald's arches as if they were the entry gates to seventh heaven. She sang to the silvery planets, "Some enchanted evening . . . you may see a stranger . . . you may see a stranger. . . ."

Ten miles from home, whizzing across the Carcenas bridge, she began singing along with Aretha. "R-E-S-P-E-C-T . . . Find out what it means to me." When she exited the freeway, she was belting out, "These boots are made for walkin'. . . ."

By the time she passed through the Mount Olympus Park gates, a mounting anxiety hit her. As she pulled up to the Poseidon, everything on Apollo Drive seemed normal enough: garage doors battened down for the night, the flashing metallic squares of televisions through bedroom windows, dogs barking, cats meowing; there was also the inevitable rustling of Anita Roundtree's bedroom drapes.

And then she saw it, sticking in Ebraim Agajanian's yard: the RE-MAX Realty ANOTHER ONE SOLD! sign. "Shit!" Carleen sighed, hitting the brake. The Agajanians just put the Atlas on the market, for goodness sake! Surely they didn't get the asking price: double what they paid and an amount the Poseidon couldn't fetch if Michelangelo gold-leafed their walls and ceilings. Now she *really* didn't want to go inside.

Like someone shouting "Surprise!" at a birthday party, the second she opened the door, Nelson pounced on her. It was ridiculous to believe Nelson and Cassie had spent five hours eating Mexican food, but she would have been ecstatic if they weren't home yet. "Where the hell have you been? It's 11:00!" Downstairs was the smell of burnt popcorn and beer and the clatter of a basketball game on ESPN. From Cassie's room upstairs came Britney Spears.

"I told you I had that, that thing today . . . that meeting with the marketing people from New York." In a court of law, Carleen could have honestly said, "Your honor, I am totally innocent of the charges," nonetheless, she felt guilty. There was also the champagne to consider. She riffled through her purse, making a huge production out of putting away her keys. She took forever to slip out of her sweater, too.

"That was this morning, wasn't it?" It surprised her that Nelson had even remembered. "Cassie and I went to dinner alone! Weren't we all going out for enchiladas?"

"Well, I'm sorry. I don't hound you when you're not here every night, which, by the way, is most of the time." She was thinking . . . luckily. "I left a message with Rhon——"

"Well, I didn't get it."

"Well, then you need a new secretary. This was an important meeting for me, Nelson." Trying to impress him, Carleen mentioned the possibility of the *People* or *Us* articles. "These were the hotshots from New York."

"It took all day and half the night to discuss one article? Those things never come through anyway." From his position slouched on the couch, Nelson sized her up with one dubious eye and switched the television to another sports channel. "You look like you've been drinking."

"Aren't you the one who always says, 'more business is accomplished over a cocktail than a conference table'? So, yes, I had a, a few."

"With you, all it takes is a few sips. By the way," he said slyly. "Do you have a confession to make? Is there anything I could have found out by accident?"

Since "by accident" was the way Nelson discovered most things, it was Carleen's least favorite trick question. He had also been patting a stack of mail at his side like a puppy dog, so who knew what the incriminating envelope held. Could it be a Mayfair Memorial residual check—something that usually totaled a whopping $1.32? Or, could it have been the "you are over your limit" letter from American Express? Maybe it wasn't that bad . . . maybe it was about the realtor's sign.

"Are you talking about Eb and Suha selling their house?" Carleen asked. That's how things changed with Nelson. The dreaded topic became the favored one when facing the unknown.

"No, I'm talking about *this!*" He jumped up and poked the paper under her nose, like he was asking a key witness to verify their own signature. It was the sample invitation for her mother's birthday party, a party she hadn't yet mentioned to him.

"Why didn't you tell me about this huge, inconvenient, out-of-state event for hundreds of people?" Nelson's voice lifted and fell from fortissimo to piano and then back again.

"If I told you weeks ago, you would do what you always do and forget and accuse me of not telling you, anyway." Carleen pumped her hip and tried her hand at her husband's specialty, putting the blame on the other person. "Gee, I'm sorry my mother's birthday party is a big inconvenience."

"Every time I turn around, you people are throwing another huge fiasco. Carleen, you're up to your eyeballs in nonsense—school events, baby showers, that leech of a next-door neighbor. All you do is gripe about spare time, about not being able to take your column to some 'higher level.' Can't you ever say no?"

"If my mother's seventy-fifth birthday is your example of something I could have avoided so I could write *Anna Karenina*, boy, do we have a communication problem!" No wonder Carleen never told him anything. She felt like an animal trainer trying to put meat in the cage of a ferocious animal. "Brother!"

"You know precisely what I mean." Nelson narrowed his eyes. "You'll end up doing all the work. Now that's just assinine, particularly since Rebecca could hire someone and Irene is permanently unemployed."

"Would you rather pay for the whole thing?" She knew that would hit the skinflint right where it hurt. "Besides, Rebecca's taking care of everything . . . it's all under control."

"Ha! With *your* family, that can change in a heartbeat. Is the whole idiotic bunch going to be there? Irene and your brother? Is he still missing in action or will he suddenly pop up? Oh, let me guess, you're in charge of tracking him down!"

Carleen wasn't any happier about the situation than Nelson, especially since she *was* the one who would actually pound the Berkeley pavement looking for Billy Cooper, but there would be hell to pay if Nelson knew that. So, she spun around, and stood with her back to him, mumbling, "I, I can't imagine that he would be there . . ."

"Well, thank God for small favors. Just know that I might not make it." Then, probably because the basketball game was back on, he took another sip of his Corona, and said abruptly, "Now go spend some time with your daughter!"

She stood stiffly as if addressing a drill sergeant and said, "Yes, sir!" Already, the encounter with Beaton seemed like it had happened in another galaxy.

Knowing that the subject of her brother—her "totally disgusting, intolerable brother"—would spiral out of control, Carleen had been thrilled to curtail the birthday conversation. By the time Nelson found out about Billy Cooper, if she was successful in locating him, Carleen hoped they'd all be in a room singing "Happy Birthday" with the glow of champagne to keep everybody from blowing their stacks.

Years ago Carleen would have never imagined such a disparaging conversation or believed Nelson's change of heart toward her family. How charmed he had been by the eccentric clan! How delightfully different they were from the fuddy-duddy Carlyles! He was enthralled by their escapades, always patting Carleen's leg lovingly when she was the focal point of a particular crazy yarn.

Then ever so slowly—and for reasons that remained murky—the tide began to change. Oh, it was all in good fun, Nelson insisted, when the anecdotes about the looney Wooten family became knee-slapping material for their friends and his business associates at Brown, Carlyle and Whittingham.

"Let's face it," he told his spellbound staff huddled around a party punchbowl, "every one of them is nuttier than a fruitcake. Carleen compares her whole life to an *I Love Lucy* show. She must say 'This reminds me of the time Lucy did so-and-so' ten times a day. Her brother's a weirdo who sings and juggles for a living—Frank Sinatra one day and Marcel Marceau the next. Then she has one sister who got the nerve to leave her second husband after watching that nun in *The Sound of Music* sing 'Climb Every Mountain!' Somebody cracked, "Thank God she wasn't watching *Texas Chain Saw Massacre!*"

But Nelson, who could dish it out but not take it, smoked with anger when Carleen retorted, "It's not like *you're* a Rockefeller!" Everybody else laughed. "That'd be funny . . . Nelson Rockefeller . . . Ha, ha, ha."

The only person she'd ever shared her dismal marriage details with, the one she always consulted right before she stuck her second foot in the nuthouse, was Rebecca. It seemed ridiculous, but after so many decades of self-sufficiency, Carleen was still in a one-hundred-yard dash to the safety of her big sister's arms. During their infrequent get-togethers, Carleen would squeeze in dozens of questions: "Believe me, it's not *The Burning Bed*, but do you think Nelson will ever calm down? Do you think I can get him to change?"

Although Rebecca was comically overstating the issue when she'd say, "Oh, just leave the bum!" Carleen now wondered if separation might be the inevitable option.

She wanted to soar off to some exotic place, some other place, any place far away from Nelson. Suddenly that place had crystallized, had become more than some undefined, Kodachrome dream. Now she knew it was Kentucky. For years, Carleen hadn't given it a second thought, but now that she felt so stuck out on this godless edge of the continent, all she did was reminisce about the hot, muggy summers in Blue Lick Springs when she and Becky Jean were young and full of hope.

How lucky Irene was to be back in Blue Lick Springs! Each time Carleen spoke to Baby Sister, she could sense her clutch on the world Carleen craved for herself. And now Rebecca was there with her, too. With all their lively tales of country ham and cherry-pie dinners, of wine and song on the veranda, the cottage sounded like a cabaret. Worse, now Irene and Olive had conjured some sugar-free chocolate and Irene seemed to be horning in on Miss Lila Mae's Confectionery. Every time Rebecca mentioned the subject, Carleen wanted to say, "Hey, I thought you wanted me to run that candy store!"

But, Nelson continued to make her feel like a circus freak for her family yearnings. Way too often, when he was in his Wooten-bashing mode, she felt like saying, "Don't you get it, Nelson, it's *you* I need to escape from?" It was only in their company—this so-called severely flawed family unit—that Carleen felt whole.

But what else could she expect from a man who didn't nurture his own family ties? Although she supposed he loved Cassie, she wasn't even sure Nelson was a great father, wasn't even sure he'd forgiven her for being a girl, particularly one who resembled the wrong side of her genetic tracks. When Cassie was a toddler, Nelson panicked every time she made goofy faces or drew abstract sea creatures. Carleen assured Nelson that all kids do that, but he had cracked, "Oh, no they don't. She's a Wooten all right!"

In the last months of her pregnancy, Carleen had bizarre nightmares about her unborn child. She begged her mother to stop telling her about some tabloid oddity, but Lila Mae always managed to slip in a gem. "Listen to this one," she would howl in delight, describing the Guatemalan woman whose baby boy was born with an elephant's trunk instead of a nose, or the proud couple whose daughter had twelve fingers and toes and who smiled for the camera and said, "She's perfect!"

There was also the farmer who was so vile that his own family killed him, then fertilized the crops with his rotting corpse. "Supposedly his cornfields were the envy of every farmer in the county!" Lila Mae exclaimed.

Even though Carleen said, "Mother, now I won't be able to sleep!" her insomnia prediction was wrong. Unlike other evenings when she tossed and turned for hours, she fell into a deep slumber, dreaming about the farmer who had been done in by family members. She imagined his wife, a watermelon slice of a smile on her face. She saw the farmer's daughters, pigtails thumping against their pinafores, as they hopscotched through the cornfields. Only in Carleen's dream, it wasn't the farmer from Sioux City, Iowa, who was a goner. In her dream—a recurring one, appearing more and more often—the cornfield ashes belonged to her own husband, Nelson.

Chapter Nineteen

Rebecca

JULY 1999

Nobody could believe their eyes when they showed up at the hospital to visit Little Peep and found him covered in bandages from stem to stern. They just stood outside the door, trying to figure out what happened, or—in the beginning—if they were even at the right room. Both legs were wrapped up in a sling and connected to some contraption that looped around a couple of times, went off like a forked road, then attached to two cables hanging from the ceiling. His arm was also taped up and it was dangling from another steel pulley that came out of the wall. It was the sort of treatment a skier in an avalanche might require.

Big Dee stood gawking through the small chicken-wired window and said, "What in Sam Hill?" and Rebecca said, "My God, was it really *that* bad?" A bunch of other people who didn't even know Peep felt the situation wasn't right, either. One woman asked them, "He's not that feller in Jessamine County that got clobbered by that freight train, is he?"

When everyone was told that Peep's accident involved two dogs, not a train, a man with muttonchop sideburns said, "All that from toy poodles? Somethin's rotten in Denmark!"

At first, Big Dee refused to believe the bandaged patient was her husband, until Irene pointed to the penny loafers under a chair and the plaid jacket hanging on a door hook. Then another woman, who was part of the crowd that had collected around Peep's hospital room, said, "Tell the nurse to bring you his wallet, that'll tell ya somethin'!" They could see it sitting on top of a metal chest.

Big Dee took one look at the billfold, curled her mouth into a knowing snarl, and said, "It's him all right!"

Only a few days before, Rebecca would have been snapping her heels with joy. Finally she had Peep where she had wanted him in the past, down on his luck and flat on his back, unable to strut around David's office with his high-and-mighty expression and his financial statements to torment her. But she no longer felt like knocking his block off.

Big Dee went straight to the nurse's desk, and said, "Would someone please tell me why my husband looks like he's ready to croak?" Rebecca was appalled, too, adding, "Yesterday, he was walking around with a shoulder sling and now he looks like mobsters got to him!" Big Dee kept saying, "We want some answers!"

Hearing the complaints, a supervisor escorted them into Dr. Roy K. Hand's office to calm them down. "Ladies," he said, "Mr. Peepers's getup is out of the ordinary, but there was more to that accident than meets the eye. The situation is *very* serious!" Dr. Hand leaned toward Big Dee, his thick-boned arm touching hers, and spoke confidentially, "Now here's the good news, Mrs. Peepers—if there is sucha thang in this tragic sitch-ation—yer husband has one helluva lawsuit 'ginst the owners of them dawgs!"

If Big Dee wanted to make sure justice was done and they got their fair share, she should contact the law firm of Sharpsteen & Sharpsteen. "They'll get you what you've got coming . . . and then some!" He clenched his jaw, opened his lips, and smiled as if showing his teeth to a dentist. "You won't believe how much a jury would award someone in your husband's condition."

Irene, hearing that the physician who'd taken over the case was Dr. Hand, the same doctor responsible for most of Bohannan's insurance claims, said, "I'm not surprised in the least."

Neither was Olive. She said, "Why, that's the kook from Arkansas who dressed Edna's wounds a while back! And Baby Sister sez his name's on ever' insurance claim at that place whar she works. I wouldn't trust a thang that man tole me . . . even advertises hisself on the television set!"

Normally Olive's disdain for doctors plus her hunger for fresh guinea pigs made her judgment and motivation questionable, but nobody was defending Roy K. Hand in this debate. She got Big Dee riled up when she said, "That's the same hos-pitul that took Edgar Whipp's gall bladder when he wuz jest in fer cataracts . . . got the rooms mixed up or sum such . . ."

So, it was a shock to no one when, after a few days in the hospital, Olive insisted that they all go pick up Mr. Peep, bring him to her place, so she could "fix 'im up real good."

They had a task actually getting Little Peep out of the facility until Sheriff Burkle told the hospital he had orders to release the patient. By the time they got him back to the Cottage, Olive had already assembled the tools of her trade: witch hazel and plaster of Paris, dull-bladed scissors, foul-smelling poultices, and apothecary jars burgeoning with curative herbs.

From the looks of things—that is, the way he could almost put all his weight on his left leg and nearly make a tight fist, Olive said, "I'd say ya sprung a few thangs, and they might be sum ligament problems, but nothin' to keep ya in the hos-pitul." As for his tender shoulder and the assorted gashes and bite marks, Olive applied a hot compress which she fished out of a blistering pot of medicinal herbs. She also gave him a honey-and-kerosene cough remedy for his sore throat.

Olive, who said Little Peep's getup was "the most ridic-alus thang" she ever saw, set him up like Prince Charming in a four-poster bed filled with yellow roses and homemade chocolates. After three hot toddies, Little Peep said he felt better already. He paddled his arms like an outboard motor and said, "Hell! I don't need any therapy or cast!"

"Ya see," Olive bragged, "they's not a thang wrong with that man that a little common sense and home remedies cain't cure. It just takes sum tender lovin' care!"

When Big Dee realized, several days later, that Little Peep couldn't hear a thing out of his left ear, they were forced to take him back to the clinic. That's when they learned about the broken eardrum, something that could cause "serious inner ear damage." The physician on duty warned Little Peep to stay put and not to travel by air until further notice. Rebecca tried not to sound overly anxious when she asked, "How long will *that* take, doctor?" She also hoped nobody heard her mumble, "Shit," when he replied, "It could be ages."

Little Peep wasn't thrilled about being stuck, either, but he refused to go along with Big Dee when she suggested that they drive down to Tennessee to stay at Heaven Hill. Little Peep, baa-ing like a sheep, said, "Oooohhh nooooo, you don't! You're not sticking me with *your* family." Shortly after that, he told Big Dee to get him his laptop computer and his ledgers and he'd stay in Blue Lick Springs for the bare minimum.

Rebecca, who had been rooting for the Heaven Hill idea, figured his presence would put a serious cramp in her style, but Big Dee disagreed, saying it would give them an opportunity to outsmart Horace Castle and to get into Rosemont. "Reggie comes on strong, but he's as wishy-washy as a rose petal in a Kansas tornado. You watch, he'll be wearing coveralls in no time!"

Every day, Rebecca made a point of passing by Rosemont, thrilled that there was no FOR SALE sign or unusual activity. The latest gossip was that the Castles had shown up out of the clear blue sky on Rosemont's doorstep, waving their checkbook. They were kicked out when the Montgomerys, who were embarrassed to tears to be caught in their robes and slippers like that, slammed the door in the startled couple's faces. Horace Castle took the snub in stride, but Coco said, "How dare you!" to Mrs. Montgomery and started beating on the door and windows. Finally, Horace Castle told Coco she wouldn't get anywhere with that kind of behavior. So, she tramped down the brick walkway, flailing her arms and kicking flowerpots, then gave the house one last scornful look, and barked, "Ha! I wouldn't have this dump if you paid me!" Then she ordered their limousine driver to step on it.

They knew all this because Sammy Swannett, Maybelle's third cousin, a UPS driver, was delivering Ramona Montgomery's medication, like he had been doing once a month for several years, which is why Rosemont's gate was open to begin with.

"The Castles is lucky they didn't git thar heads blowed off," Olive said. "Serve 'em right if they did!"

Not prone to defeat, Coco had inquired about the Sawyer home, a nineteenth-century Colonial brick, and said if that didn't suit her, she would get her husband's contractor to build her the most spectacular house in the country, something like those Irish castles or French chateaus, one that would make Rosemont look like a chicken coop. "Who wants that creepy old house, anyway!" Coco told Penny McBride, who mentioned it to Jeannie Charlene Shoop.

After sifting through the dust and soil and grit of the town scuttle-butt, the end result was this: Coco Youngblood might have her sights set on Rosemont, but so did a lot of other people and that was *their* problem. As far as anybody knew, Hamilton Montgomery didn't want to sell and if his rifle hadn't convinced Blue Lick Springs of that, he didn't know what would.

Their efforts to keep Little Peep halfway civil and his mood in fine fettle, while making progress on the property battle, was a full-time job. In the afternoons, when Little Peep was napping, Big Dee and Rebecca studied the checklist given to them by Big Dee's father, Lyman Hicks, huddling over maps and papers and zoning regulations for preservation strategy. They made phone calls to attorneys and consultants, always dreading the moment when they would hear the familiar "Miss Olive?" coming from the parlor—their signal that Little Peep had stirred and it was time to disassemble shop.

Their strongest weapons in the battle for Little Peep's sentiment were the carafes of apple wine and the Southern meals that they fed him each day: oval platters of fowl and gourd vegetables from Olive's garden. There were stuffed peppers and spiced shrimp and a cornucopia of desserts: toffee cookies, chocolate icebox pies, and lemon coconut cake. All of them were baked by Irene who had been experimenting with sweets that were high in taste and low in calories. Irene's secret ingredient was *stevia*, a natural low-calorie sweetener that Olive said "wuz the latest rage." They had planted it in a back pasture, and it was flourishing, trailing across the grounds in buoyant plumes. "That

Martha Stewart lady ain't got nothin' on Baby Sister!" Olive announced proudly.

When Little Peep's ankle was better, he and Big Dee toured the grounds each afternoon, bringing with them Olive's wine and Irene's praline nuggets. They snapped pictures of themselves beneath dogwood boughs and on stone benches while Big Dee twirled a silk parasol and read passages from William Faulkner and Tennessee Williams. They collected plums and green apples from Olive's orchard and zucchini from the garden. Capitalizing on Little Peep's new outlook, Olive played up the glory of farm life, rhapsodizing about the herbs and white lavender, echinacea, and other crop possibilities that could turn a profit. "So there's money to be made on herbs?" Little Peep's ears pricked and he pulled at his suspenders.

"Ya ain't kiddin', only trouble is to keep the integrity of the crops ya need yerself land—*lots* of it. . . ." Olive's sharp eyes lit up.

"Several hundred acres, at least," Rebecca jumped in. "This land was all part of Rosemont years ago, when it belonged to the Adamses. As far as the eye can see there were corn and cattle, beans and tobacco."

Yes, Olive explained, vegetables, livestock, spices, and holistic herbs would all thrive on the farm. She said they currently had planted an herb garden for their personal use, but it could easily be expanded and marketed and exploited to make multimillionaires out of them all!

"President Roosevelt said 'what we do to our soil . . . we do to ourselves,' " Big Dee spoke like a presidential candidate on a whistle-stop campaign. "So then, we must plant and replenish!"

With that, Little Peep thrust out his wineglass for more of Olive's nectar. "Yes, replenish we must!"

"By the way, Miss Olive," Big Dee asked. "Where would one buy this wine? We'd like some for Los Angeles."

Olive knocked her cane against the ground and said, "Ya git it right here on the farm! Yessireebob! Right outta my orchard. We got ourselves an apple press, then they's, uh, other thangs we do to it. That's sumthin' else; if ya wanna really make it big, a vineyard's the way to go."

"A vineyard?" Little Peep wriggled in curiosity. "Will a vineyard work in Kentucky?" Inside Little Peep's head there seemed to be Ferris wheels in wild spirals—highfalutin' notions of him strolling the grounds of his own vineyard, poking a walking stick at Merlot and Zin-fandel vines.

"Of course," Rebecca confirmed. "There are already vineyards oper-ating, not far from here either."

Everybody was thrilled when Little Peep said, "Ummmmmm, I might have some investors for this one!"

Rebecca began to invite first one person, then another, to the Cot-tage. She got Jasmina, the contortionist, whose uncle was an officer for the Kentucky Heritage Society, to show Little Peep yoga stretches, and brought Sheriff Burkle's cousin, Tiny, a barber and a zoning board mem-ber, to groom his hairpiece and polish his shoes. Letty Bookbinder showed up with Civil War bullets she thought Little Peep might be in-terested in. They had come from the Perryville Battlefield, not very far from Blue Lick Springs, and she brought a book to tell him all about it. As a Colonial Dame and officer of the Daughters of the American Rev-olution, she wanted him to own such things. "Just a little memento of our area!"

Little Peep held a small brass pellet in the air, turned it around like an antiques expert studying a silver chalice, and said, "Dee, take a look at this! It's from the Civil War!"

Jimmy Buzz brought him juicy ribs and orange freezes from Miz Becky's, which Little Peep ate while looking at pictures of cannons and dead, bloody soldiers.

After Rebecca got Little Peep accustomed to socializing with the Blue Lick folks, she shifted the emphasis, inviting more town leaders and bankers who could help in their preservation battle. At first, she kept them at bay, taking pains "not to bother" Little Peep, but always making sure there was joke-cracking and delectable chocolates. Soon, Peep started asking, "Who were all those people in the parlor?"

Once, when he overheard them discussing strategy, from the next room came a toneless voice, "Call the FAA, they'll know." Pretty soon, Peep was inching down the corridor where he stood at the parlor door like a wallflower pining for gaiety.

He was still on his mission to sell, though, because he spent hours on the phone with Phil Bustamante in Los Angeles and kept asking, "Did those Castle people ever call about the barbecue building?" When Dee told him no, he made a notation on his laptop to follow up, but at least he didn't pound the table, like the wild man of old.

Just as their days had burrowed into a predictable groove, in the evenings, they would gather on the porch, creaking their rockers, catching the golden sunset. "Don't you just love the South, Reggie?" Big Dee would enthuse, arranging her chiffon polka-dot outfit around her. "You never gave it a chance before."

"You have to admit these people are easier to deal with than those stuffy Southern highbrows down your way." Little Peep tucked his chin to his chest indignantly. "I even prefer this land itself to Tennessee."

"Yer right, sir. That's why it just kills me to see all this vanish right before our eyes." Olive shook her head, and told him when he had time, to check the binoculars for all the new development surrounding them.

After the crockery was dirtied, the women would all congregate in the kitchen for cleanup detail, with Little Peep perched on a toile wing chair ready to assemble the Monopoly board. Long after Shorty and Maybelle had returned to their cottage, there the rest of them would be listening to the snapping cicada outside, and sipping peach tea.

Olive would wait until she landed on a high-priced square—New York Avenue or Park Place with houses and hotels situated on it—then use the unfortunate roll of dice as an opportunity to once again discuss Blue Lick.

"Wuddn't ya know it, I gotta end up on a spot with more development than a Hearst Castle project." Olive would lick her thumb and peel off the counterfeit one-hundred-dollar bills and hand them to Little Peep. She would start slowly, then, like a revival-tent evangelist, build her argument to a sizzling high, attempting to make a nexus, however feeble, between Park Place and Blue Lick Springs.

"Ain't it a shame they're gonna redo the mill, remodel the courthouse. Ever'thang's gotta be fancy-schmancy or it ain't no count! I'm with that Perot fella that wuz runnin' for president . . 'if it ain't broke, don't fix it!' " Olive would stamp her cordial glass against the table, making the Monopoly board pieces jump to neighboring spots.

"With so many other problems to tackle, you'd think people would get their priorities straight!" Rebecca would provide kindling for Olive's fire. "I don't understand why Blue Lick Springs needs five hundred more houses. Even if there were only two people to each house, the population of Blue Lick would have to double *overnight!*" Then, because she knew Little Peep was big on infrastructure, Rebecca would add, "What's going to happen to the infrastructure of the town?"

"Well, I suppose none of this concerns me," Olive sighed dramatically. "I'll end up in sum nursin' home sumwhars . . ."

"And what about Rosemont?" Irene asked.

"That'll fall into the wrong hands, too!" Olive *tsk-tsk*ed. "Now that's the real shame of it all. Fer years no amount of money could get Hamilton Montgomery to part with that place, and now it might be up fer grabs. That huge plantation house, it's the finest to be found enywhere."

Big Dee said wasn't that sad, because a house like that would cost millions in Los Angeles, and anyone with a good business head could fix it up and, if worse came to worst, sell it for double, too. "What an *investment* it would be." Big Dee had thrown the dice and advanced six spaces to land on Free Parking.

"No wonder Horace Castle is interested." Rebecca would straighten her piles of pastel money. "A house with hundreds of acres for only two something. Who wouldn't jump at the chance?"

Big Dee said, "Two something? Two hundred thousand or two million?"

"Two hundred thousand, silly!" They had to come up with some number and Rebecca had heard through the grapevine that if the City condemned the property, they would offer the Montgomerys around $300,000, and two something could be rationalized as $299,000, and two anything sounded better than three.

"Why, that's dirt cheap, isn't it!" Big Dee, like a union organizer, rallied to get all on board. "You should have that house, Miss Olive. That'd be a real pity if you lose that."

By now they had all expected Little Peep to have one hoof in their trap, but he didn't, so Big Dee finally lifted up. "Surely you're not going to stand by helplessly and let the City or that Castle man buy everything in sight now are you, Reggie?" The woman stood with one hand on her hip, looking like a teakettle as she glared at her husband.

Then, when everyone had offered their vociferous objections and they moved the plastic hotels from Virginia Avenue back to North Carolina, and well after Little Peep's face shone like a used-car-lot bulb, Olive finally turned to the man and said point-blank, "What do *you* have to say about all this, sir, this mess with Hearst Castle that's a-goin' on in our town?"

"Well . . ." Peep drew the word into his barrel chest and scanned the penetrating eyes before him. "I agree with you, Miss Olive, I think it's a shame . . ." he knocked his fist against the table as if christening a boat, "a doggone shame!"

Chapter Twenty

Rebecca

JULY 1999

Regardless of all the pros and cons and warnings and good news and bad news from one person or another, Rebecca woke up on that particular day with one goal. She was going to hunt down Rosemont. It was an especially beautiful day, one that God seemed to have designed with Honeysuckle Way in mind. All around her was the blaze of sunlight and fluorescent green grass. Olive's peacocks, perched high in the beech trees, moaned their mournful *meoowww* like a falsetto Persian cat. The morning glories seemed to stir in the flower beds. Everything appeared to be plugged into neon. Rebecca slipped on her running shoes, determined to get to the bottom of things as well jog off the apple charlotte she'd had for breakfast.

More than anything, the excursion was triggered by all the contradictory rumors about Rosemont. First there was the champagne-popping news about Coco being kicked off the property, followed by a wave of eyewitness reports and gossip that left Rebecca unhinged. The most disturbing was that Coco and Horace Castle had flown over Rosemont in their helicopter and found it in such obvious disrepair that, as much as it broke her heart, Coco saw no other choice but to tear it down and start from scratch. Then someone else said, no, that wasn't right, they heard that Coco was going to buy the house and fix it whatever it took. It was also reported that the roof had caved in. It was so bad, you could even see inside the house from the helicopter! Yet another said no, that was an exaggeration, too, that it was only the back wing that was affected, that all the bricks suddenly caved in. There was still another report that the house was fine, but all those three-hundred-year-old trees were gone—all felled by lightning. Finally, someone else stated, and this was the version embraced by Rebecca, that Hamilton Montgomery was so disgusted with the hurly-burly that he had shot the CASTLECO helicopter right out of the sky!

Rebecca knew the stories were tantamount to the two-headed humans at carnival sideshows. You see the claims, you listen to the barker . . . AN ODDITY LIKE NO OTHER! A MEDICAL SCIENCE PHENOMENON . . . ! knowing it will be some silhouette behind a thin curtain or a rubbery form floating in a jar. Still, you pay your twenty-five cents.

Jogging along the old railroad bed, streaking past trees with star-shaped leaves, Rebecca was nervous and excited. The cedar that rinsed the air, and chocolate mint flourishing along Boone's Creek overwhelmed her. She loved the crunch her Nikes made against the evergreen needles as an old teenage song grooved in her head, "I hear the cottonwood whisperin' above. Tammy, Tammy, Tammy's in love!"

By jogging, Rebecca had hoped to dissuade Big Dee and Irene from joining her, since she really wanted the experience on her own, but they were on a health kick, and tagged along. In the distance they were calling for her like some faraway ghostly tintinnabulation. "Hey, wait up!"

So many scenes took flight as she dashed across Olive's land . . . days when Rebecca would settle in the backyard, her iodine-and-baby-oil brew and movie magazines next to her. After sunning until her shoulders blistered, she would slip into her daisy thongs and walk to Klink's for a cherry Coke. There were the family picnics with the sound of crackling beef gristle, and the banquet tables with blueberry pie so hot the juice still gurgled beneath the lattice crusts.

Half an hour later, Rebecca had found herself wading in bramble bushes and wondering what possessed her to take off with no pointers.

She had already passed the old milking barn and trampled through Olive's north pasture, a pasture, by the way, that looked nothing like the agricultural masterpieces Butch had described, and one which he also used as his excuse for not keeping up the front acreage.

"I only got two hands, Miss Olive!" Butch always barked at her. "I gotta tend to the crops or they'll die on me. Ya wouldn't want that now, would ya?" A few puny rows of soy beans and exotic herbs were all that seemed to be growing.

The other two women had caught up, so the three of them trudged along, passing the brick carriage house, finally reaching Boone's Creek. They pushed through shoulder-height grass until Rebecca had a feeling. "I'm not sure, now," she hesitated, "but I think we're getting close."

"She thinks," said Irene, panting and doubled over. "All right, smarty pants. Now what? Where are we?"

A sweating, shrimp-colored Big Dee was picking off cockleburs from her cargo pants. "I say we pack it in. I've had enough."

Rebecca said they could do what they wanted, she didn't go through all that to poop out. She also told them to shush. "Why don't we just make an announcement 'Hello, Hamilton Montgomery! We're here to spy on you!' Besides . . . I'm almost positive we're here."

Soon, they saw the torn barbed wire that separated Olive's farm from Rosemont, a spot Rebecca still recognized. She crept forward, taking very careful steps.

Standing there, poison ivy to her left and a caterpillar gliding across her foot, Rebecca felt as she had so many decades ago when she roamed the farm in pedal pushers and Persian Melon lipstick, trying to track down this same spot. Having come all that way, she was petrified that Rosemont wouldn't be there at all, instead, there would be a charred hole, like the ruins of a gigantic campfire. It didn't help matters that Big Dee and Irene were yanking at the binoculars hanging from a cord around Rebecca's neck. Irene grabbed them first, pausing and saying ta-da! before placing them over her eyes. Rebecca stood over to the side, pacing in figure eights, and hollering, "Don't give me any details. Just tell me if it's there."

It was an eternity before Irene said, "Holy smoke, that's *it?* You've *got* to be kidding. I can't even *see* anything." Big Dee was chomping at the bit, wiggling her fingers and telling Irene, "Come on, give me those." She put the binoculars to her eyes and moved slowly from one section to the other, then back to the bull's-eye where she let them rest for a moment. She wasn't much help either.

A frustrated Rebecca listened as the two women assessed what they had seen. Irene wanted to know why in the world someone didn't get rid of those vines and Big Dee agreed, saying, "The place is a dump . . . what you can see of it."

"What do you mean?" Rebecca whined. "Can you see it or can't you?"

"Look for yourself," said Irene, patting her shoulder like a grieving relative outside a dying person's room. Then she added with a good-natured mock, "We'll leave you alone with Rosemont." The two women sat on a whale-shaped rock, swabbing their brows while Rebecca had her turn.

She lifted the binoculars, aiming them right and left, moving them from the smokehouse to the tobacco barn to the fruitless gardens. From that angle, Rosemont was almost invisible. But from behind layers of jungle greenery, she finally spotted it: a big, smashed, once-grand wedding cake of a house. And not a crinoline or julep in sight . . . only the vines, vines that stretched across the fields, trailing up one side of the house, then down another. They bulged over the gardens, turning trees and statuary into bestial limbs and haunches. It seemed that, year by year, they were staking their claim to more of Rosemont, inching so close to Olive's land that even a tendril or two had climbed the divisionary barbed wire. Nonetheless, she still had goosebumps.

Over to the side was the abandoned classical gardens with overturned statues, then the porch. Its pots devoid of flowers, its furniture blistered, it was, unbelievably, still tended by the same supine figure, this time in a brown flowered dress. Ramona Montgomery sat with her slatternly arms and legs thrown across a chaise longue like a mannequin, one that seemingly hadn't moved for decades. Again, one quivering brown eye switched back and forth in a wild, unpiloted pivot before turning toward Rosemont's property line. Suddenly, Rebecca loosened the binoculars and simply said, "Let's go."

On the way back to Olive's house, Rebecca's chest burst with excitement and fear and a tangle of so many other unspecified emotions. Her head was throbbing with questions and strategies and possibilities. Rosemont's worth was built up, then torn down. The women covered all universes, explored every burg and borough of flummery and logic. It would take backbreaking work and tons of money to restore. It was a diamond in the rough, but a nightmare still. It was foolhardy and pure folly but Rosemont was the Adamses' fate.

"Oh, we don't need to tell her any of that, Dee, she's gung ho," Irene sighed. "I'm her sister and I know. There could be a double-wide underneath there and she'd insist it was Rosemont! Yes, yes, Miss Scarlett's gotta have her a big house with columns!"

"Doesn't every woman want a house with columns?" Big Dee asked. "I'll take mine standing up, though!"

"Go ahead," said Rebecca, giving the women an impudent toss of her head. "They laughed at Bugsy Siegel, too!"

Rebecca wasn't the only one whose head was in the clouds. All the talk of dream houses and Southern life flung its spell on Big Dee. She had money burning a hole in her pocket, the much ballyhooed Rosemont out of her system, and a husband she wanted to spite. She also had one eye cocked at the Ferguson home, a big brick Federal on the edge of town, one she'd spied the first day.

So when Rebecca said, "Are you guys thirsty? Do you want to go into town and have a Coke?" Big Dee clapped her hands together and said, "Yes, let's have a Coke! And, let's take a drive and see the Ferguson house."

Irene perked up and said, "Let's go right now, shall we?"

On the way to Main Street, they bumped into Edna, who reminded Irene about her hair-frosting appointment, and Haldeen Pike, who said, "Keep up the good work! They just voted against that zoning change!" After that, they slipped into Miss Lila Mae's to see if the wooden booths and stove had been delivered on schedule. The spot was coming along nicely: The marble fountain had been polished, the varnished cases were filled with paisley teacups, and the Edwardian chandeliers had just been installed. It was the exact look Rebecca and Carleen had imagined, only better.

They crammed into a small booth, drank frosty bottles of Coca-Cola and nibbled at pie, and took the copy of the *Gazette* so they could read the editorial Rebecca wrote responding to Horace Castle's latest building permit application:

> It is sickening, preposterous, idiotic, and a few other things that can't be printed in a newspaper, that some Kentuckians continue to view the destruction of our natural resources and historic properties as progress.

> Developers assume that they have a God-given right to the land and it's only a matter of time until it's theirs. According to them, anybody who doesn't succumb to their pressure is living in the Dark Ages. We must wise up and end the rampant destruction of Blue Lick Springs.

They scanned the paper, thrilled to see other such letters to the editor, celebrating the changing tide in public opinion. "See," said a beaming Big Dee. "It's really catching on."

What Rebecca didn't tell them was that three of the other letters were actually written by her under a nom de plume, but if both Big Dee and Irene fell for it, everybody else would, too.

Rebecca and Irene slapped one another's hands in congratulations and Big Dee shook her arms in the air like a pentecostal preacher as if embracing not only the entire room, but all of Blue Lick Springs, perhaps the entire state of Kentucky. "Oh!" she breathed in rapture, "this is so much fun, isn't it?"

Perhaps it was the visit to Rosemont, maybe it was just a magical alignment of the planets, the same choreography that inspired the lunar eclipse, that found Olive and Rebecca in the parlor just after the grandfather clock struck midnight. Rebecca inched the needlepoint footstool to the Queen Anne where her grandmother sat. All around was the aroma of walnuts and Olive's pink dusting powder.

"Grandma, I've been thinking. What would happen if we contacted

Hamilton Montgomery? I don't mean to barge in or anything. We've been tiptoeing 'round the tulips, afraid of our own shadows, imagining this and that, like he's the wild man of Borneo or something. What do you think?"

Usually, when Rebecca mentioned what she had in mind to Olive, she would say, "No, don't call that one, call this one instead," or "That might be how they do it out yer way . . . but in these parts," and so on.

"Well," Olive took a deep breath which fluttered out like a gust of stale summer air. "Ya know I've been wonderin' the same thang . . . I been wonderin' that too."

Olive told Rebecca to get a piece of her paper, the one with her name spelled across the top, that they were going to write Mr. Hamilton Montgomery a note, a proper note.

Rebecca turned the small brass key in the mahogany drawer of the Hepplewhite secretary. She pulled out an ivory parchment, spearmint-tinged paper. At the top in script was the name: Mrs. Clayton Wooten. She fetched a fountain pen from her purse and curled up at her grandmother's knees, waiting.

"Let's see, uh, Dear Mr. Montgomery . . . no, dear Hamilton. I don't wanna git too buddy-buddy . . . now don't write that, that's what I'm a tellin' ya . . . but Hamilton sounds better to me . . . so, dear Hamilton. I would be intra-sted in speakin' with ya about a private matter . . . make sure ya put that in thar, the private part. . . . he don't lak his business bein' circa-lated ever'whar. It is of utmost . . . now underline that three times . . . utmost . . . importance to both of us. Maybe ya should underline private, too, jest so's he knows we ain't no blabbermouths. Please let me know if ya are also intra-sted.

"Now read that back, will ya?" she took a sip of wine and sank into her pillowy chair, her eyes, like polished silver buttons, directed toward the ceiling molding as Rebecca repeated:

> "Dear Hamilton:
> I would be interested in speaking with you about a <u>private</u> matter. It is of <u>utmost</u> importance to both of us. Please contact me at your earliest convenience."

"You changed that last line sum . . . I reckon it's okay, though. Now, let's see, sign it . . . Sincerely yers, Olive Adams Wooten . . . let's add sumthin' to that. Put Olive Adams Wooten, yer neighbor fer over fifty years . . . yeah, make shore ya put that in thar . . . and, and keep the sincerely yers . . . so it would be sincerely yers, Olive Adams Wooten, yer neighbor fer over fifty years . . ."

"I think it's perfect, Grandma. It doesn't have too much information, just enough to make him curious. Yes, I, I really think it's just right."

"I jest thought of sumthin', though. What happens if Ramona gits aholt of it and reads it instead? Ya don't think I should put her name on thar, too, do you? I don't want her sore at me."

"No," Rebecca said, "no, she probably won't read it. Just leave it addressed to Hamilton Montgomery."

"I say we send it to 'im, first thing." She fingered around for her cane, lifted herself up, and said, "The ole codger cain't shoot me if I jest send 'im a letter now, can he?"

When Rebecca lay in bed that night, under her woven coverlet, it struck her why she hadn't been using the gangbusters approach in getting Rosemont. Yes, it was partly because of David and the roof-raising Little Peep. But there was another reason she had been so patient. Some distant corner of Lila Mae's gene pool, one Rebecca had tried so often to leave behind, the one whose Atlas strength often trumped logic and courted danger, came swimming to the surface. After all the talk about Rosemont needing to be back in Adams' hands, Rebecca actually felt sympathy and compassion for the Montgomerys. She didn't want to do the same thing to them that Horace Castle was attempting to do to Olive.

It was painfully obvious why Hamilton and Ramona Montgomery stayed at Rosemont, why, in spite of the offers and pleading, they still vegetated in the house that was eating them alive, and why they still tried to recover in the same spot that caused their ailment. Ramona Montgomery was dwelling in Rosemont, but she was really tending to her daughter's bones.

No, Rebecca didn't want to crouch in the wings with Coco Youngblood on the prowl, but she hoped the hand of providence would push Rosemont in her direction.

Chapter Twenty-one

Irene

JULY 1999

Although the Mishap and general commotion with Little Peep and Big Dee kept her distracted, Irene was still waiting for the other shoe to drop. Almost every week she'd get a plain white envelope that said DO NOT FORWARD containing threatening letters and plastered with hot-pink stickers. In a sick twist, the court had ordered her, not her rat ex-husband, to pay the lion's share of their debts. This included Albin's Liquor Locker and a car upholstery shop, both of whom were threatening to sue.

Worse than that, any day she half expected to get fired from her job. To land the position, she'd fibbed about how many words per minute she could type, when, truthfully, she could hardly type at all. How ridiculous that Irene was employed by the one business in the entire United States that still required typewriters. McCracken had told her, "I don't believe in that newfangled compooter stuff."

One afternoon the doomsday call came from her boss. No, she didn't have great skills and yes, she had made some big booboos, but she had also kept Mr. McCracken's coffee just the way he liked it, with three sugars and lots of cream. Often she'd volunteer to do personal work for Ruby Pearl, picking up their sheepdog from the groomer or stuffing envelopes for the United Way canned-goods drive.

How would she hold her head up at the dinner table that night if she lost her job? With the speed at which information traveled in Blue Lick, by the time she got home they'd be waiting for her, a CIA squadron, demanding an explanation. After that, there would be many I told you sos and finger-pointing. If only you hadn't overslept that one time . . . if you'd let Edna do something with your hair . . . things would have turned out so differently. They'd cap it off with advice on how to handle the rest of her life.

Mr. McCracken took his good, old sweet time, straightening reports and clearing his throat while Irene slumped in the leatherette chair, staring at the macrame wall hanging and twirling the globe, halfway searching for some other exotic spot—Madagascar or Belize or New Zealand—to consider.

Finally he leaned between the two stacks of file folders and managed a faint smile. "Miss Wooten, I've been keepin' an eye on you and I'm not sure you're cut out for office work."

Irene had to hand it to the man, no beating around the bush with McCracken. At least it was a swift, clean death. "Well, I'm trying my best." She shifted and coughed and drummed her fingers.

"You also know about the financial trouble here . . . these medical claims is gettin' way outta hand," he said, his foot jittering. "So, I hate to tell you this because you're a fine woman, but I have to cut expenses so, I need to make some changes."

Usually Irene beat her boss to the punch, saying, "I quit!" but suddenly, like those horror movies where someone's talking in a normal voice one minute, then some gutteral monster tone the next, she found herself saying, "Mr. McCracken, I've been thinking about the claims situation and I can help you."

"Help me, uh?" McCracken was rubbing his whiskers and narrowing his eyes in skeptical thought. "How you gonna do *that?*"

"Look, I come from a big city where there's a scam a minute. Most of those claims are ridiculous," Irene said. "People could never get by with this before. Nuisance claims used to be five hundred dollars, now they're thousands." She was waiting for McCracken to ask, "And how is it that you come to know so much about these shady dealings?"

"I used to pay ever'thing, too, but I cain't if it's a counterfeit. It ain't so easy to deny claims in a small area, though. A big town like where you're from, heck, you just send a form letter." The sweat began to gather on his brow. "I gotta go to church and Kiwanis and, I, I see these people every day! But, I've got pressure to weed out the good from the bad . . . a *lot* of pressure."

"Listen, I'd be more worried about your job than some swindler filing illegitimate claims. I can tell from just reading the forms that most of them aren't legit. I mean, it's called L-I-F-E! It's called 'that's the way the cookie crumbles.' Every time you trip on a carpet, you don't have to get paid. These cheats can be nailed, and," she paused before she announced some strategy she had never worked out, "I know how to do it."

"You *do?*" McCracken braided his hands behind his neck, put the toe of his shoe against the desk and rocked way back. "So how would you go about something like that? Is it simular to detective work, you think?"

"Detective work? That's probably not what I would have called it but, yeah, I guess." Irene didn't want to commit to a career label if it wasn't what McCracken had in mind.

" 'Cause, see, that's what I need here. I was gonna call that agency in Lexington and see what I could come up with. I need someone who could move around some, hang around the claimant's place of business, church, recreation halls . . . wherever you can find them, and see if they're water-skiin', huntin', hot-roddin'—anything out of the normal . . . that's how you catch them."

"By the way, I have photography experience, too. You know what they say; a picture is worth a thousand words." Since she had worked in Ready-Stop Photo Lab, Irene thought it was okay to tell McCracken that; he didn't have to know that she ran errands and was fired after one week.

"Take this one, this guy over in Sulphur Lick, he says he's got a herniated disk. You cetch him puttin' a roof or the like on his house and you've got yourself a phony claim." McCracken licked his wide, flat thumb and flipped through the documents. "Sally Swinton Monroe says she almost died from a free cheese sample from the market over in Maudville . . . Raymond Victor Beezel severed artery . . . claims the doctor removing his cast overdone it and sawed right down to the bone . . . and so on."

"Let's see how bad the arm is when he's pitching softballs to his son or carrying groceries for his wife," Irene snorted.

"Tell me about it," McCracken puffed. Then pulling in a noisy breath, he continued, "I also got that situation with Coco Castle's bad arm, you brought it up at the fooneral, remember? Well, it started off as one thing—a sprunged wrist. It wasn't 'til that scuffle at Miz Becky's that it got serious. Claims someone egged her poodles on and everything went berserk."

"Puleeeze! That's the exact opposite of what happened!" Irene jumped up. "They're lucky Mr. Peepers isn't suing *them!* The hospital had him wrapped up like the abominable snowman!"

"You and I both know what's going on, but Mrs. Castle's got that big-wig husband and a fancy medical report from Dr. Hand . . . then with her losin' her brother and all, juries are sympathetic to that. She claims Miz Becky's has it in for the Youngbloods since both accidents happened in the same place."

"That's ridiculous!" Irene grunted. "Like the restaurant knew her brother was going to rob the place? And what about the poodles? I suppose that attack was planned, too? All of these are coming from Dr. Hand, aren't they?"

McCracken was drifting, biting his lip, and mumbling, "You're good with customers, and . . . I know Ruby Pearl thinks a lot of you . . . I tell you what." He suddenly sat upright. "You're not well known in these parts so you might be able to get by with this. How about you get your regular salary and a bonus for each successful claim. Then if it doesn't work out, no hard feelings. Ms. Wooten?" He changed to a more serious tone. "You pin that Castle woman down and there'll be somethin' real big in it for you." Then he gave Irene two thumbs up, like a double hitchhiker.

"That would be greeeeat!" said Irene, in a heel-clicking moment. Already visions of anklet pistols and cloche hats and faraway cafes where she would hide behind the *Herald Tribune* waiting to trap her prey, came waltzing into her head.

"Remember, all you've done is paper and telephone work. And you could be dealing with some rough characters." McCracken had his hands on his hips and his head tipped down in a last-chance stare. "You do know that, don't you?"

"So . . . are you saying it's really dangerous?" Irene asked.

"Dangerous?" McCracken took his hand and rubbed his whiskers like he was checking for a clean shave. "I don't know that it will be that bad. I just thought I'd mention it."

"Well, then . . ." Irene gave her hands a festive toss and said, "Let's get *ooonnnnn* with it."

The proposition, if she could handle it, had great timing. On top of Darrell's obligations, she was up to her beak in delinquent bills of her own. Plus, there were suede jackets to be bought, garnet bracelets to fetch, excursions to Cumberland Falls to take! She had never given investigative work a second thought—a real shock with the record-breaking number of careers to her credit—but the mere idea sparked excitement in her soul.

Since it was a beautiful summer twilight, Irene decided to walk to her grandmother's house, something she'd been doing for exercise. She had even started cutting Olive's grass when Butch didn't show up, which was practically all the time. Besides, she found it calming to march through town and down Mayfield Drive, waving to Edison Hatt, the old man with the shoe-leather skin who repaired outboard motors. She knew exactly where everything would be, the RAY FINE FOR COUNTY JAILER sign: YOU CAN'T GET FINER THAN FINE!; the Donut Shoppe with the billboard: COMMON SENSE AIN'T SO COMMON. She smiled at a sign outside the Heart of Fire Pentecostal Church: WAL-MART ISN'T THE ONLY SAVING PLACE.

By the time Irene had passed the stone fences of Rosemont and arrived at the Cottage, the North Star was already twinkling. As she walked the final half mile up the drive, bunny rabbits and butterflies scampered across her path. Somewhere in the distance was a madrigal of hoot owls and cicadas and tree frogs. As she took a heavy breath of honeysuckle, Irene found herself humming, "Summertime and the living is easy . . . Fish are jumpin' and the cotton is high . . ."

How exciting it would be to have some substantive information to impart at the dinner table! How satisfying it would be to participate for once, to have something other than "oh, thank you" to say when they complimented her on the kiwi tart! What a pleasure it would be to own the conversational limelight.

The minute she entered the house, Irene realized what a Pollyanna she was. Olive, who had been pressed against the door, huffed, "We wuz jest 'bout to call Jimmy Buzz. We wuz afraid ya wuz in a pool of blood sumwhars, weren't we, ever'body?"

When they sat down for dinner, Irene told them she actually had good news, something she thought would shift the tide. But now that she was alive, they were holding her responsible for the cold food. Olive listened to the news, drizzling red-eye gravy over her roast beef, then said, "If Buddy McCracken has ya runnin' all over the state, you'll git lost . . . This is a *big place* . . . Git him to hire someone knows the lay of the land!"

Little Peep said it sounded interesting, but she might want to check her health insurance first. "Miss Olive's right. You could be headed for something."

"Is McCracken that same fellow you wuz tellin' us about . . ." Shorty slapped butter across his cornbread. "Claims his ancestors come over on the Maytag or some such?"

"Why, they wuzn't no black people *on* the Maytag, wuz they?" Maybelle's pearly pink mouth twittered in confusion.

"Come on, Maybelle, ya know better than that," Olive grunted. "The Maytag's that warshing machine with the repairman who twiddles his thumbs. Why cain't the man do his own dirty work?" Olive looked at her granddaughter, her eyes two bright, inquisitive pools. "Tell me that, would ya please?"

"Ruby Pearl's been helping him out some, but she starts teaching in a few weeks and he needs someone to take her place," an already glum Irene told them.

"Ruby Pearl, that's his wife, ain't it? That's how the blacks do their chil'run. They name all the girls fer jewelry and the boys after presidents. Ruby Pearl, she got two fer the price a one!" Olive passed the cauliflower to Shorty. "You'll hear the most ridic-alus combinations—

George Washington Mudd, Franklin Delano Roosevelt Bobblett. Why, they's a man works down to the funeral parlor named Abraham Lincoln Grumpp. He's a nice enough feller, but I'd like to ask his mother, I'd say, 'Now why would ya go and do that to yer boy?' "

Suddenly they were so far off the track with their "What to name the baby?" conversation that it wasn't even funny. But Irene should have known she'd only be allowed split-second stardom before they trotted down some serpentine road exploring back alleys and tunnels and dead ends.

Noticing Irene's despair, Olive said, "Now cut it out, ever'one! Let's congratulate Irene on this new position of hers. Maybelle, pass me that coconut cake . . . and let's say a prayer askin' the Lord to watch over Baby Sister."

That turned out to be a long, drawn-out plea begging Jesus to keep "our precious Irene Gaye out of harm's way . . . to watch over her with Yer guidin' light and all-encompassin' hand and keep her from danger's doorstep" and all sorts of other requests that made it sound like Irene had enlisted for World War III.

When that was over, Rebecca told everybody to raise their wine glasses to Baby Sister. "Congratulations! Let's hear it for Ireeeen. . . ! Just think." Rebecca leaned forward, her eyes spinning with intrigue. "You'll meet so many people and go so many places. I really envy you!"

Irene knew what Rebecca's enthusiasm meant: Her sister would inveigle her way into the matter, showing up with a special page on her list entitled, "Instructions and Detailed Pointers for Poor, Helpless Baby Sister." Already, she had shifted the subject to Horace Castle, telling Irene that as long as she was in the snoop mode, she should dig up some dirty laundry on the developer and everybody else involved in his empire. Olive piped up, "What about that contortionist, Jasmina? I heared tell she kin fit her whole self in a suitcase! If that's true, then set her up somewhars close to the Castles, have her spy on them two. Heh, heh! They won't know what hit 'em!"

Little Peep was beside himself, whooping "Brilliant!" and "What a scheme!" He vowed to call his friend who owned the finest spy paraphernalia business in the country so he could FedEx the necessary equipment for such a covert operation.

With the fumes of strong coffee and delusions of grandeur elevating them to some higher plane of megalomania, they sat up until all hours mulling over all the choices. Rebecca kept saying, "I just *love* this sort of thing. I must have been Agatha Christie in another life," and Olive added, "I ain't too bad at that mystery stuff, myself." Little Peep said he was always up for a challenge, too, and Big Dee slapped her fingers together and exclaimed, "Oh, I can't imagine anything more fun!"

So, in split seconds, the spotlight had been tugged from Irene and whooplash claims, and shifted to Rebecca and her strategy to crumple Horace Castle, put his wife in her place, save the town of Blue Lick Springs, if not the entire county. Heck, why stop there when civilization in general was at stake? In this—and other such sessions—where anything of global alarm was hammered into some manageable pulp, Irene was the blob sitting at the end of the table, nibbling on peanut-butter cookies, wishing her iced tea was spiked, listening to the effervescence of a half-dozen amateur Columbos talking about races with the clock and high-tech and low-tech tactics and high-speed chases and solutions involving limber women with tape recorders hiding in suitcases. And they thought Irene was the lamebrain!

But for the first time in ages for as long as her memory was able to calculate such faint things, Irene's heart was bursting with hope and faith . . . even the prospect of happiness.

Irene figured the conversation ended on a note as optimistic as possible, when Olive said, "If yer gonna take McCracken up on that Sherlock Holmes business, then ya better change that hairstyle. Someone sees that purple stuff and that's the end of yer detective work. Ya need to blend in, girl." She told Irene to get over to Edna's Beauty Box, that they'd "fix her up good."

Then just to dismantle Irene's equilibrium, with a half twist of the blade and one granule of wound salt, Olive added, "You be careful, now, Baby Sister, no job is worth *killin'* yerself over."

Chapter Twenty-two

Carleen

JULY 1999

Nelson's prediction had come true—the garage was falling apart post by post, rafter by rafter. Strewn across the cement floor were fir splinters and drywall, and they had removed all the contents in anticipation of total ruination. There were other spots, too, places that Nelson didn't even know about that Carleen managed to vacuum before he found them. Every other sentence out of Nelson's mouth was, "When the *hell* is the extermination? You're not still on this environmental kick are you?"

"Dead Siamese cats, birds falling off tree limbs," said Carleen, pulling back one finger for each catastrophe. "Our grandkids, if we end up with any, will be laughing at us for using these toxic chemicals."

"Carleen, you go to those meetings with a bunch of Birkenstocked losers who spend hours reading the fine print on labels," he lectured. "If you want to talk toxic, how about those Diet Cokes you're addicted to?"

When she told Nelson there was some confusion about the origin and the type of termite, he said, "I don't care if they're from the South Pole or Pluto, just get the damned house exterminated, *period!*"

"I'll do it when I feel like it, *period,*" Carleen barked right back.

As Carleen watched her husband in a real spin, his face shining with anger, she was aware of a strange development: all of the buttons he so expertly pushed in the past, the ones that invariably shook Carleen into action, were on the blink. This blossoming wrath toward Nelson, the years of inability to get even, had developed into a striking monster. Now she had one mission: to do everything in her power to spite him.

Wasn't it ironic, idiotic really, that even their arguments weren't normal? Carleen could see them in divorce court pleading their case to a kindly, silver-haired judge. "Well, your honor, it all started with a spat involving fumigation. The ex-con jewel thief said the problem was Vietnamese termites, the actor/contractor claimed it was dry rot." "Irreconcilable differences," the judge would announce.

Despite the supposed upper hand and detachment Carleen had on her side, she was still stuck with the in-depth inspection. Since Nelson knew he couldn't count on Carleen, he called Mr. Slidell himself and told him to show up "On the double!" At least this time Slidell was coming without Smitty.

What she had planned to say to Lenny Slidell, very quickly, before he could get a word in edgewise, was, "Mr. Slidell, this is probably going to surprise you, but we're going to postpone this indefinitely; our daughter has an allergic reaction to chemicals."

But when she opened the front door, there was Slidell already hunched over like a biologist knee-deep in a scientific project. Before she could speak, the man unfolded a silver knife and lifted up a shard of the porch planks. One knick and dozens of bugs squirmed onto the knife. Mr. Slidell held his knifeblade midair like someone offering her a just-sliced apple. He didn't say a word, but he looked at Carleen with deep, knowing eyes.

"Those are termites?" Looking at the vermin in Mr. Slidell's magnifying glass, they appeared almost as menacing as the plastic termite on top of A-1's van. Carleen wasn't going to admit it, but she, too, was shocked by how many of the horrendous critters had turned up in just a random checkpoint.

It was a wacky thought, one totally out of line with the scene she'd just witnessed, but maybe Slidell brought the insects himself. After all, there was plenty of time for him to cut the wood, plant some termites, pat the wood back in place, then make the "big discovery" just as she opened the front door.

As if reading her mind, Slidell said, "Let's see if they're over here, too," and right before Carleen's eyes, he dug into a brand-new spot! Once again, the demons scurried every which way. This was something that made her clap both hands to her face and exclaim, "My God! We *do* have termites, don't we?"

"You think I've been whistling 'Dixie'?" Slidell looked puzzled, then his eyes blinked and batted nervously. "Uh, I've got more bad news for you, Mrs. Carlyle. We sent the sample to Marietta, Georgia, for analysis."

"Are they Vietnamese?" Carleen's heart plunged.

"Yes, Mrs. Carlyle." Slidell's head dropped to his chest as though it were in a hangman's rope. "I'm afraid your termites are from overseas."

Slidell narrowed one eye and bit his fingernail in bewilderment. "Here's what stumps me, though. Smitty, too. Every Vietnamese we've ever seen comes from Louisiana. There's an area there in New Orleans? The French Quarter? Why they're afraid it'll be gone in no time with this epidemic they got. The termites came in on a freighter with some Italian antiques—"

The French Quarter? Carleen remembered the bartender at the Napoleon House in New Orleans who had mentioned this very thing. "Oh, it's just horrible!" the man kept saying, as he cleaned the bar in small, Cloroxed circles. "All the city's treasures down the drain . . . *gone!*" As for the antique part of it, Carleen had bought a drop-leaf table at Rolfe's Antique Junction, next door to the bar! A peculiar orange color began to spread across her face. She looked around, wondering if every single solitary stick of furniture was crawling with the foreign termites!

It was noon, way past her column deadline, as well as her self-imposed deadline for kicking Mr. Slidell out. But now that Carleen knew about the antiques, she was in between the devil and the deep blue sea. When she got to thinking about it, the paper *still* didn't pay her dime one, so she could skip turning the column in just once. Wouldn't that be something if there was a big blank space where "That Just Gets My Goat" usually was? Maybe the public would riot, stampede the *Chesterfield Bay Sun* offices. That would show those suckers at the newspaper!

"Say, is that your column there?" Slidell pointed to the stack of papers and files. "I don't mean to be forward, but I been wantin' to ask you why you don't write a book . . . you know something that takes it a little further."

"Well, I used to think about it," Carleen said. "I just wasn't sure there was a market for it."

Slidell said she had to be joking, that she got down to the nitty gritty, everyone he knew thought the columns were the greatest and as a matter of fact, he even thought she could do stand-up comedy. "I ain't lyin'!"

"Stand-up comedy?" shrieked Carleen, as if the idea had never occurred to her. "You have *got* to be kidding!"

"I'm telling you, Mrs. Carlyle, you're talented! You could go places!"

Carleen stood there speechless, wondering why her own husband couldn't see what the termite inspector saw. She'd only met Slidell once, hadn't even brought up the subject, as opposed to conversations she'd had with Nelson where she did everything but ask him point-blank if she had what it took. And, here he was, this perfect stranger, an ordinary exterminator, resurrecting so many of her dreams.

Not wanting to hog all the attention, Carleen asked, "What about you, Mr. Slidell? Do you ever miss the violin?" Slidell shook his head like an overactive child and said, "No! No, I've got my hands full!" as if she had plucked a wound, so Carleen didn't push it.

By the time Carleen and Slidell checked out the rest of the house, examined every closet, and moved the last few pieces of furniture they'd been rearranging all morning, it was already 2:15. As she offered Slidell more raspberry doughnuts, she eyed the signature line on her household checks.

Carleen couldn't have lived with herself if she didn't mention alternative treatments, so she asked one last question. "Didn't I hear about some new organic product? Dr. Zollinger's something or other?"

"You might have, but it's all a big racket, Mrs. Carlyle. Just like those fruits and vegetables the stores sell. They'll tell you they're organic and people buy 'em 'cause they're full of wormholes. Come to find out, the big companies sell their rejects for natural."

Chapter Twenty-three

Rebecca

JULY 1999

It was a good omen for Rebecca when some of the financial papers for the barbecue, bowling alley, confectionery, and a few other things that she still hadn't gotten around to telling anybody about were plucked by a brisk breeze, went flying into the branches of a weeping beech tree and Little Peep, taking a sip of apple wine and rippling his pudgy fingers in the air, said, "Oh, to hell with 'em!"

He was sitting where he usually did in the afternoon, in a wicker settee on Olive's porch at the makeshift desk he had set up with papers and blueprints and a pencil cup with a dozen ballpoint pens he hardly picked up. When he leaned too far to one side and almost fell off his chair, Olive said, "We'd better start waterin' down them drinks. He's higher than a Georgia pine!"

"Yes, and that's just the way Big Dee wants to keep him, too," Irene said. She was in the kitchen tethered to a marble slab, shaping soft chocolate into clusters and dusting her fingertips on a coarse, white chef's apron. On a shelf above her were jars of strap molasses and butterscotch. On her marble candy table were bouquets of fresh-picked chocolate mint from the garden. Between Irene's desserts and Olive's apple wine, Little Peep, not to mention Big Dee, was a goner.

"I'm supposed to be on the Zone Diet," Big Dee declared. "This isn't exactly part of my plan."

"It is the Zone Diet," Irene joked, patting her newly reduced belly. "We're eating everything within a ten-mile radius."

Curiously, and in spite of all the food and sweets, everyone, including Irene and Rebecca, seemed to be losing weight. Rebecca was down to ninety-nine pounds, barely enough to qualify for a low-grade fever, something that caused everyone to say "EAT!" Irene had dropped thirty pounds and even Big Dee had lost ten which elicited a "Good for you!" from the table. Long, challenging walks and fresh, home-cooked food were being given the credit for this unanticipated—but welcome and healthy—turn.

As for Little Peep, when he wasn't touring the grounds, he sat in his chair like a pharaoh while friends and townspeople came bearing casseroles and upside-down cakes. When Olive's catfish and hush puppies and Irene's chocolate cakes failed to satisfy Little Peep's cravings, Sheriff Burkle brought beef brisket from Miz Becky's, as well as the rumor that Horace Castle had backed out of the Cherokee Mill project! Better yet, they learned that the zoning board was requiring Castle to install special sewer systems at Castle Heights. CASTLECO had argued that the natural topography of the land made such a requirement unnecessary.

Lyman Hicks told them to call the National Trust for Historic Preservation, the ultimate weapon for that very situation. "Also, if there are any Civil War battlefields," Big Dee's father told them, "nobody can touch those with a ten-foot pole."

All this good news was nothing compared to what Walter Westmoreland divulged. Westmoreland, the Fidelity Bank manager, mentioned that Castle had a few uncovered checks floating around. "The thing is, Castle ain't a man of his word and around these parts, that's all a man has!"

"That's not just around these parts," Little Peep added, his voice clanging with authority, "but *all* parts."

Letty Bookbinder, who brought Little Peep a canteen and bronze belt buckle for his burgeoning Civil War collection, told the group the DAR had saved more than one grande dame from ruination and offered inspirational homilies about recent successes: the Dawson Manor in Maysville, the Spencer County train station and even a two-hundred-year-old ash tree in Covington!

"Before those bulldozers get the Cottage or Rosemont or anything else in Blue Lick Springs, they'll have to mow down the Dames and the Kentucky Daughters first!" she vowed.

"Hear! Hear!" They all gobbled bourbon balls, clinked their wine-glasses, and leaned into the calico pillows for the remainder of the sunny afternoon.

Rebecca knew she was overdoing it, but she told Little Peep about the "Reginald Peepers for Mayor" campaign, a grassroots effort that had "sprung out of nowhere and was gaining steam." The man had contained his Cheshire grin, tugged at his clothes as if testing them for durability, then feigned modesty, "Oh, for Pete's sake!"

Bookbinder had also offered one more interesting tidbit: Coco Castle had applied for membership to the Daughters of the American Revolution, a perish-the-thought notion that sent the women into a tizzy. "Can you imagine? A Youngblood in the Kentucky Daughters?"

One perfectly glorious day, a morning when the robins lounged on persimmon tree branches and the aroma of candied pears and coffee stirred from the kitchen, when they had begun to believe that Horace Castle was short on funds and the airport project had lost steam and when Little Peep seemed the least of anybody's problems, there it was on the front page of the *Blue Lick Springs Gazette*, an article causing Rebecca to realize that inaccurate "inside" information, Little Peep's apathy, and long, glorious afternoons with a few friendly officials had fostered a false sense of security.

AIRPORT PROJECT GETS OFF THE GROUND

After a slow start and many interruptions, the Blue Lick Springs Municipal Airport expansion is set to move forward. Hiram Peabody, a city zoning board official, said work will resume at an escalated pace to compensate for the long and unnecessary delays. "There's been enough dawdling!" Peabody was quoted as saying at an emergency city council meeting called last evening. The venture has not been without its detractors, with particularly staunch opposition coming from the Colonial Dames Historical Society and the DAR. In one recent encounter, Letty Bookbinder was arrested for disturbing the peace at a ribbon-cutting ceremony for Castle Heights.

Joe Lee Buttons, the spokesman for CASTLECO, the company contracted to do the airport work, said Horace Castle was pleased with the announcement, one which will pave the way to begin "this exciting and much-anticipated project."

When pressed for details about the purchase of land from resistant sellers, Peabody said, "The City might have to exercise its power to condemn such properties and exercise it, we will! But, most homeowners have been very cooperative. They know this is good for the economy of Blue Lick Springs."

Mr. Horace Castle agreed with Peabody, saying, "Blue Lick is on the threshold of great things. I think most of their citizens realize that." Mr. Castle's wife, Coco Renée (nee Cookie Youngblood), is a native of Blue Lick and is in the process of purchasing a home in the area.

Rebecca dropped the paper with an irritating rattle, looked at the group and said, "Well, now what?"

"We can't say this is a surprise," said Irene.

"Yeah, we knew it wuz a-comin' all right!" Olive agreed.

Maybelle clapped her hands together like an enthusiastic seal. "Ya know, Mother Wooten, ya might get a new lease on life." She pinched her mother-in-law's cheek and shook it back and forth. "Might do ya some good to get away from this ole place." Olive snapped her head away and screwed up her face.

"That's right, Mom," Shorty chimed in. "Don't knock it till ya try it!"

"I'll knock sumthin' else if ya don't watch out," warned Olive. "Dee and Rebecca both sez there's still ways. I'm not givin' up so easy and neither should you!"

"It says right in the article that they'll condemn all this land—Rosemont and yours, Grandma—and once we're all out, you just watch that airport project fall apart," Rebecca said. "There's no telling what Rosemont will look like if that tramp Coco gets her hands on it! She'll have all the rotten apples there . . . The Youngbloods, of *all* people! What happened to that Irish castle Coco was going to build?"

"Where's all this activity a-comin' from, anyways? Ya'd think ever' person in the U.S of A. is movin' to Blue Lick!" Olive said. "What happened to the quiet town I used ta know?"

"WHO KNOWS, MOM? IT'S PROGRESS! WE BEEN OVER THIS A MILLION TIMES!" Shorty was balleting across the room, his temples crackling in anger. "THEY'RE PUTTIN' IN AN AIRPORT AND YOU CAN EITHER SELL OR WAIT FOR THEM TO TAKE IT FROM YA!"

To keep the peace, Olive, who had been taking shallow breaths and nervously twisting her hankie, said, "Curtis, ya know how I feel about the subject and I'd 'preciate it if ya didn't get our guests all upset. Now the matter is *closed!*"

Maybelle had been nestled in an armchair like a Persian cat, rubbing and filing and sliding her emery board like a violinist playing a frisky tune on her fiddle. Suddenly, she tapped Shorty's shoulder with her nail file and said, "Come on, honeybun, let's go." Outnumbered, they slammed the screen door and stomped down the flagstone pathway.

"IT'S A WONDER WE AIN'T BEEN BURNT TO A CRISP, CURTIS!" Olive yelled. It had been six years since Shorty's shoddy electrical job, but Olive still used her predictions of a devastating electrical fire to needle him. She waited until they were out of earshot, then said, "Good riddance . . . to hear them tell it, my farm is theirs and all the cash it'd bring. Huh! Ya know how long that money'll last in Maybelle's hands?"

In the thank-God-for-small-favors category, at least the writer got the story straight about Cookie Youngblood. What Rebecca wouldn't have given to see the tramp's face when she realized that her flimsy

"Princess Coco" disguise was done for, blasted across the front page of the *Gazette*.

That night at dinner, Rebecca and Irene made Little Peep's favorite dishes: fried chicken, spinach souffle, and banana cream pie. The plan was to wait until Little Peep was in his normal, postmeal good mood before they resuscitated the sempiternal topic, this time with some strategy from Big Dee.

"Every chance, I'll talk about how there's no way around a brilliant, shrewd businessman like Horace Castle. I'll throw my father in there, too," Big Dee suggested. "Reggie's never quite matched up to Daddy's expectations and he's waited for years to outsmart him!"

After the dishes had been cleared, they bided their time, discussing possibilities for saving Olive's farm and this and that until Big Dee walloped the table. "This is absurd! We really have to contact Daddy. He'll know *exactly* how to handle this! He's gotten some *amazing* things accomplished, Daddy has."

"Yeah-sure-huh!" Little Peep answered with cynical snorts. "They're not *that* amazing. He couldn't stop that country club deal and the amusement park is still on the drawing board."

"That's not exactly true . . . Daddy got them to scale everything back, *waaaay* back!" Big Dee countered.

"Huh! If he had the Midas touch you're claiming, he could have prevented it altogether!" Little Peep turned to Rebecca. "Have you ever met a grown woman who still calls her father 'Daddy'?"

"What would *you* have done, Reggie?" Rebecca, her chin in her hand, cocked her head and moved forward to demonstrate singular interest in the business manager's answer.

"Yeah, Mr. Big Talker!" Big Dee challenged. "How would *you* stop someone like Horace Castle or the City from, well, buying Mrs. Wooten's farm and Rosemont, for example?"

They watched as Little Peep reclined and crossed his leg, swilling the apple wine and taking a slow, imperial sip. "First thing *I'd* do is create some group to protest . . . You know, storm the property, wave a few signs . . . make sure the newspapers and television are out there to get it all . . ."

"But Daddy says the media's a waste of time. Supposedly, you can talk until you're blue in the face and—"

"Now wait a minute, Dolores." Rebecca faked a disagreement with her friend. "Reggie might have a point. It couldn't hurt to get some turmoil like that going, could it?"

"Besides, that's not *all* you do, Dee . . . for God's sake!" Little Peep made his eyes twitch in disbelief and turned to Rebecca. "As I was saying, before I was so rudely interrupted: You start a Coalition to Save Blue Lick Springs, make the City do impact studies, then you urge the owners of the property to fight the project. Remember!" He paused and pointed his finger like an exclamation point. "Some people might be selling because they've been told there's no way around it."

"You mean, tell them there's a credible fight, even if there isn't? That might work in a big city, but you can't trick people in a small town. You have to produce something," Rebecca said. "All they hear is 'condemnation' and 'eminent domain.' "

"You see, Reggie." Big Dee dropped her hand against the table, "Daddy knows how these small Southern towns work."

"The *hell* he does! People are people, Dee. I don't care if they're from Rabbit Switch, Tennessee, or New York, New York! There is always a way to finagle something. Besides, I'm talking concrete plans and action, not tricks. We're smart people, for God's sake! We can get this done."

"I'm sure you're right," Rebecca said, switching a surreptitious look with Big Dee. "If we all pitch in."

They stayed up until 3:00 A.M., dreaming up tactics starting with a before and after campaign, photos showing Blue Lick at the turn of the twentieth century, its current state, and a computer generated picture of the destruction that would occur if the Castles and corrupt politicians had their way. They hoped to scare everybody stiff, so they overdid the drawing of the future, making Blue Lick Springs look like a *Star Trek* set.

Rebecca added to her list people to recruit and organizations who offer sponsorship; she would consult with the Frankfort zoning attorney recommended by Bookbinder; and Jimmy Buzz Burkle could help them with an organized protest, maybe even rough some people up, if need be. They also toyed with slogans for bumper stickers: PROGRESS KILLS

BLUE LICK FOREVER or BLUE LICK CITIZENS WHO WANT TO LICK DEVELOP-
MENT or STOP THE HASSLE . . . GET RID OF CASTLE.

Irene said she was already unearthing some dirt on Castle, and Big
Dee insisted Lyman Hicks was the panacea to all their problems. "I'll get
the pertinent information from Daddy's secretary." Rebecca also made a
note to call Tiffany; maybe she could come up with something incriminating on the Internet.

Then, in a break from their enthusiasm, Rebecca leaned her palm
against her forehead, pretending to be exasperated and weary. Since Little Peep was in such a malleable mood, she decided to throw in the un-
mentionable projects. "Oh . . . I don't know, Reggie, I just don't
know . . . maybe I'm dreaming . . . bowling alleys, barbecue restaurants,
candy shops, plus protest marches. Just as you always said, it would take
Albert Einstein to make these projects worthwhile."

"Well." Little Peep grimaced. "I wouldn't say it's *impossible*." You
could tell the roll call of businesses completely jarred the man; but anxious to prove his worth as a genius, he added, "It *can* be done with some
cunning and fortitude and foxy maneuvers. We're on the right track
here, people." He thumped the papers on their work table, and lectured
them in a gruff, but motivational, voice, "Let's just keep our noses to the
grindstone!"

For all Little Peep's amazing, unprecedented signs of compliance,
Rebecca walked around in a state of worry and agitation. As they cod-
dled and manipulated, pampered and tricked the man, the ticking
clock of disaster boomed before her. Each day, they would get a parcel
of good news, but it was like having beautiful weather on the day of a
funeral.

In her head was a rat's nest of complications: Miz Becky's, which she
still struggled to keep open; Horace Castle; Rosemont; and her grandmother's farm. Miss Lila Mae's Confectionery was the only new enterprise that showed immediate promise and activity, that is if you could
call Irene's nightly forays in the kitchen, kneading dough and ladling low
calorie chocolate into mint nougats, progress.

Every day Olive and Rebecca waited for a letter or phone call from

Hamilton Montgomery, like a spotlight skittering around for a no show performer.

None of this fracas took into consideration her husband and daughter. When Rebecca talked to David, who was in Paris on business, he seemed irked not only at her, but at Little Peep as well. "This was supposed to be a short business trip!" he said.

"It isn't my fault that Reggie can't travel. With the eardrum and his ankle, it not a pretty picture, believe you me!" Even though Little Peep's yoga sessions with Jasmina were coming along nicely—she had him doing the downward dog and the cobra—Rebecca had heard Little Peep telling David, "I'm still not feeling great, plus my doctor won't release me to fly." It was true that Peep went around on doddering legs, but Rebecca figured that was on account of the wine more than anything else.

"Actually, there are some robbery details that have popped up, a bogus liability claim, and the airport project," Rebecca said. "That involves my grandmother's farm, so we're trying to come up with a strategy. It would be a shame to dismantle everything after all the work."

"That could take forever!" David yelped. "You need to read that article I sent you. It'll give you some insight into Castle's operation. You can't just huff and puff about the deterioration of everything and expect to change it. Create some stumbling blocks. Get the city disenchanted with him, then he'll become disenchanted with the town."

"Some of that's already happening," Rebecca said.

"See? Believe me, this guy's no more in love with that city than I am. He's just a man with money to burn and a wife who's got her sights set on something."

Rebecca said she didn't see anything wrong with that. "I wish I had a husband like that."

"You usually get what you want, don't you?"

"Welllll . . . sometimes." Rebecca put on her coy little-girl voice, something that, at her age, should have been utterly absurd and pointless, but it seemed to work with her husband, which is all that counted.

"Do you really think I'm interested in owning a restaurant and bowling alley and whatever else it is you've got going on in a one-horse town in Kentucky?"

"Bowling alley?" Rebecca couldn't play too dumb, since David had received an invoice from Buck McGill's Ten Pin Equipment for twenty pairs of ladies' bowling shoes and twelve dozen score pads. "That must be a mistake of some sort."

"Yeah, Miz Becky's was a 'mistake,' too, as I recall."

"Well, it didn't turn out to be such a big disaster after all. We're going to break even this month . . . that's what Reggie said, anyway."

"You're kidding?" David sounded genuinely impressed and, better yet, sort of off the bowling alley topic.

"Nope, it broke even! Peep said that's almost unheard of for a restaurant that new."

Rebecca had carefully avoided telling David the entire picture: that the favorable report was due to the infusion of her own cash, and she certainly wasn't going to tell him that the restaurant had taken in a mere $1.14 more than it had paid out.

"So, what's the plan?" asked David, sounding very nuts and bolts. "I send Reggie to keep tabs on you and now you *all* disappear!"

"We haven't disappeared, and Phil's back, isn't he? And, besides, you're not even in Los Angeles right now."

"I bet I get home before you do. All I know is, you're spending too much time there. That place is a trap!"

Although Rebecca managed to get off the line without an FBI interrogation, she wouldn't have blamed David if he had grilled her. After all, his wife had been weaving back and forth from Blue Lick Springs to Los Angeles as frequently as most people go from their kitchen to their living room, paying skimpy homage to her wifely and motherly duties.

At the moment, her vagabond ways were easier to get by with than usual because of David's European travel. Plus, Ava was in Lake Arrowhead at dance camp. But, the minute David returned to Los Angeles, he would pour it on thick, asking, "So, when are you going to wrap things up? When are you coming *home?*" And there it would be, the dreaded discussion about leaving Kentucky.

As for Ava, Rebecca could sense the tide changing. Her daughter, the porcelain-perfect, lily-beautiful daughter, might finally be demonstrating signs of rebelliousness. When Rebecca called her at camp, instead of saying "Hi" or "Hello, Mama," Ava said, "Hey! Mother! What's up?" Rebecca said, "Hey? What kind of expression is that? Hay is for horses." Rather than laugh, Ava snapped, "It's also for young people. You're getting old, Mother!"

On top of her sassiness, there was the "mother" thing, and the formal, remote tone, admonishing Rebecca as if it were Ava, not her mother, who had all the power. What was next, the full teenage catastrophe?

But how could Rebecca fault her family for traveling their own paths or for not sharing her devotion to Kentucky? Ava, whom she kept trying to lure to Blue Lick, said she had no interest in county fairs and quilt festivals. "I'm a California baby! I get nostalgic for the Sunset Strip and movie billboards!"

Sometimes, even though Rebecca would fight to keep the shameful thought from fully blossoming, the reality was that her family's welfare was not always her top priority; times when the Los Angeles she once adored was so sketchy to her that all she could picture was chestnut haze and neon squiggles.

She even had a hard time recognizing the California Rebecca. When she looked in the mirror, there was no trace of the woman who dashed from luncheons and business meetings to black-tie affairs, who switched from cashmere sweaters and Opium perfume to plumed slippers and Yves St. Laurent cocktail dresses. What happened to the Rebecca who had manicures and massages and visited beauty salons where they served Veuve Clicquot and serenaded customers with *Madame Butterfly*?

Now she was the Kentucky Rebecca, the one who sometimes spent the entire day in the same running clothes she'd jogged in at dawn, the one with salty skin and hair reined in by a tortoise clip, the one who spent evenings slipping preservation flyers under doors and into mailboxes. Instead of her black sports car, she whizzed around Blue Lick in her red pickup truck, with a Coca-Cola at hand and a crooning Johnny Cash in the CD player.

And while her husband was in Paris sipping Chateau d'Yquem with Pierre Guillot, a French cosmetics heir, Rebecca sat at her grandmother's table, feasting on scalloped potatoes and ham and plumping her glass with chilled apple wine. Underfoot and dueling for table scraps would be a snaggled-toothed cat named Mammy and an old spaniel named Geronimo.

Just when David arose, calling for his croissants and espresso, Rebecca would be retreating to her four-poster bed. With her laptop propped on her knees, papers left and right, she would turn the tables on her 1950s world, crash-landing in the twentieth century with all the calamity and insomnia it dragged with it.

The black cloud du jour was still Lila Mae's birthday party—one lousy line on Rebecca's list, but an item that generated hundreds of phone calls and errands. Initially, Lila Mae had low expectations of the event and begged her children not to put too much pressure on themselves. But now she said, "This party means *so much* to me, honey . . . to have *all* my family and friends together. Oh, what a wonderful time we'll have!"

With most of the people on the guest list either dead or locked up, hunting them down was still the biggest challenge. Rebecca hadn't expected all that much from these far-flung acquaintances, but there was fallout even from people they took for granted. Carleen mentioned that Nelson might not be up for the event, which was good news, but it also demonstrated how little support the party had. And who knew if you could even count on Irene? On the surface, Baby Sister was better than ever, but it wouldn't be the first time she'd inexplicably gone astray. Shorty and Maybelle weren't sure they could come either. There was an Avon convention in New Orleans around the same time.

Every time Lila Mae asked how many guests had responded, Rebecca strung her along by stressing that they'd *sent out* over three hundred invitations, not mentioning that they only had forty-three confirmed guests.

"Dear me . . . three hundred people," said Lila Mae, faking alarm. For her, each warm body was a medallion for her popularity plaque, and it comforted her to know the situation might create a space problem. "Where will we put them all?"

Another thing to dread was something Rebecca used to look forward to: Carleen's phone call. With her legendary bad timing, she usually

red man in a white caftan holding a cardboard
oman dressed like Goldilocks covered in daisy
had had no luck, something that caused her im-

s easy as pie, not nearly as simple a check-off as
caterer," but Carleen promised to do it nonethe-
y to Rebecca when she asked, "What do you *mean*,
How could she face her family as they stood there,
rvest from their efforts—the musicians, cakes, and
s—when she, Carleen, the one who lived a few
ly Cooper, showed up empty-handed?
and moan to herself about how unfair her family was
ream at the top of her lungs, "Let them see how easy
s nothing new about this dilemma of hers. From the
obably forevermore, the task of finding and coddling
always fallen on Carleen's shoulders.
teenth birthday, the days when his eyes were wild and
amily like a cocked pistol, their fed-up father had told
o mend his ways. The drugs they suspected he'd been
alcohol they knew he'd been drinking simply had to go.
was time for him to hightail it. Nobody realized he would
sappear, or that the guilty relief they all felt when he de-
turn to fright and the inevitable, desperate mission to lo-
him back in. It was only years after Billy Cooper left home
s an occasional card or sighting, but those simply deepened
ry except the one proving his sheer survival. Lila Mae fret-
ly Cooper had fallen in with a bad crowd, but secretly prayed
ealistic message with news of a loving wife and a Wall Street
en one day came the fateful call from Lila Mae with exciting
e's not far from you," she had told Carleen. "Honey, see if you
him down, could you?"
s the last thing in the world Carleen wanted to do; she had
her teeth and clutched her temples in frustration, wondering,
Why? Of all the places in the stupid country, was Billy Cooper
miles from *her?*" Why was *she* the one sent to rescue him from the

called when Rebecca had one foot in the shower or her key in the door-knob. Obviously, Carleen was dying to talk, saying provocative things like, "All systems are haywire," adding that she had a "crush" on an advertising executive.

"Crush?" Rebecca had said. "Are you still married or did I miss something?"

Carleen said, "I'm married all right, but that's another story. Call me, *soon*. I've got *lots* to tell you."

As much as Rebecca wanted the lowdown, she cut the conversation short. After Carleen told her tale, there would be the feared moment when she would ask Rebecca about Miss Lila Mae's Confectionery, the business Baby Sister had taken over. They'd also decided to drive to Kentucky together—a re-creation of their Route 66 trip—to attend Lila Mae's party, but that was planned when Rebecca thought she'd be in California. So, now, Rebecca would either have to talk Carleen out of the trip, which was an event her sister had placed on an altar and worshipped as her only hope in life, or stop what she was doing in Blue Lick, fly back to Los Angeles only to drive back to Kentucky in time for the party, all in a two-week period. All these were small problems in life, she kept reminding herself, nothing like the examples Lila Mae always used when she wanted to show her ungrateful kids what lucky dogs they were. There were always tales of poor, poor crippled children born with no feet or hands who, on top of it all, had lost both parents in a train wreck. So, no, it wasn't that dire, but the mere thought of all the unnecessary hubbub was exhausting.

When Rebecca asked about Billy Cooper, Carleen said, "I can't seem to find him," and she felt the familiar panic, a swirling, light-headed anxiety, grazing every organ before settling into some indigestible clump. "Hire a detective; he couldn't have vanished into thin air, could he? Just, just *find* him." Rebecca threw a blanket over the subject, leaving it like the furniture covered in summer houses, waiting, waiting for a cloud-less, sunny season.

Yes, Rebecca's head was swollen with tasks. But, despite all the ruckus surrounding the fate of Blue Lick, David's edginess, Ava's mercurial new phases, the nowhere-to-be-found Billy Cooper, and the constant maneuvering and pampering of Little Peep, she loved the mess she had made of her life.

Best of all, seemingly—and unbelievably—David's attitude was shifting, even cheering her on. He'd also opened up the door of opportunity, mentioning "whatever else" as if he knew the multitude of her sins as well as the tricks she might have up her sleeve.

The only thing that kept Rebecca from sleeping like a log was something Sheriff Burkle had overheard in town. He said his wife's nephew, the boy with one arm who worked at the John Deere factory in Dog Walk, had a friend who was dating Donnetta Ellen Pew, a Youngblood by marriage, and the friend claimed that several days ago Horace Castle's helicopter had landed on the back lawn of Rosemont.

Sam on stilts, the whiske
JESUS SAVES sign, and a w
jewelry. But, so far, she
measurable anxiety.

Certainly, it wasn't
"order balloons" or "ca
less. What could she s
you can't find him?"
surrounded by the ha
HAPPY BIRTHDAY sig
lousy miles from Bi
She could gripe
being. She could s
it is!" but there w
beginning, and p
Billy Cooper ha
After his eig
aimed at their
Billy Cooper t
using and the
Otherwise, it
completely d
parted would
cate and ree
that there w
every myst
ted that Bi
for an un
career. Th
news. "H
can trac
It w
gnashe
"Why
mere

If her life were a road tr
caution signs: DIVIDED RO
that she was hanging on to ev
tional words of wisdom for car
keep from befriending this same
her of Billy Cooper, were all bad
of Joshua Beaton's lapel and the so
wasn't so hot either. It also wasn't s
ing Cassie's backpack, that she hadn'
months after she discovered her asthm
amount of cigarettes missing from the c
her, but she couldn't even remember if
Caldwell lawsuit.

Worse, every day she was more and m
she hadn't come through with the *only* respo
becca for Lila Mae's birthday party. It wasn't
Several times a week she would drive to Berk
graph Avenue to see if she could spot Billy Co
sidewalks and studied every peculiar character

depths of some unknown despair? But Carleen had been the dutiful middle daughter, the one whose chief virtue was that she waited on her mother hand and foot, the one who, like a mourner who piles supermarket flowers at the scene of a horrible accident, always supplied alms for the bereaved victim. Number one on the hit parade! She put on a perky voice and told Lila Mae that she could count on her.

With much apprehension, she had driven to Berkeley, searching the quaint streets for months on end for someone who looked like the Billy Cooper she remembered. She tried to imagine how he might appear, this brother who'd let the drugs and years of street life pound him into some unrecognizable ghost. Finally, one cool November day, she spotted a curvy shadow between Patterson's Storage and Cora's Bakery; a form with hair that hung like animal pelts, sitting cross-legged on a threadbare blanket. Placed on it like garden pebbles were a backpack, woolen gloves, and a milk carton. There was nothing to suggest it was her brother except some visceral tug that told her it was. She put her hand to her mouth to contain the gasp, then swerved to the roadside.

Carleen slumped in the car across the street, calming a heart that felt larger than the space it inhabited. She watched in peculiar fascination as he magically pulled origami animals and soiled tarot cards out of thin air. He juggled fruit and played an old mandolin, serenading a hippie couple with "Stairway to Heaven." When they left, they handed him a few coins.

She sat there revving up, contriving the nerve to move. After all she went through to find him, she *had* to take action. There would be hideous consequences—catastrophes of biblical proportions—if she simply sat there, then drove way. Then, too, there would be Lila Mae to face. Finally, with her heart jumping, she crossed the road. With a cheery wave of her gloved hand, she called him, hoping her high-spirited greetings would establish a tone and tame her own anxiety. "Billy Cooper?" She stood over him, her shadow slanted like a tree trunk against his blanket. "It's me, Carleen—your sister!"

He looked up slowly, like a winter sun rising. "Heeeyyyyy!" He revolved his head like someone trying to iron out a kink. "How ya *dew-in'*?"

For years, Carleen thought she had prepared herself for this moment. How odd could it be? After all, this was her own flesh and blood, the person whose Cheerios she'd poured and whose bottom she'd talcumed. Surely Billy Cooper would be anxious to hear news, to wax nostalgic, wouldn't he?

Petrified that Billy wouldn't know his own kin, Carleen had been ecstatic with his greeting. She began to distribute the gifts she had come bearing: argyle socks and Timberland boots, a tin of homebaked muffins and sheepskin gloves. He sat patiently, just as they used to do when Lila Mae removed the deviled eggs and chicken from their Fourth of July picnic basket.

But, as she stayed kneeled on his blanket, the gifts strewn around her, the cars and pedestrians streaking past, she waited for a crack in the fog that never arrived. When Carleen handed him the items, he had taken each one, saying, "Oh, thank you!" and when she left, he had said, "Good-bye." He had even stretched ever so slightly toward Carleen, but he didn't ask about his mother or his other sisters or for pocket money. He didn't beg her for jam cakes and fresh linens or for Carleen to take him with her to someplace safe and warm.

It was only when Carleen was leaving, when she watched the Berkeley shoppers and merchants and sightseers stroll past Billy, that she heard her brother say to each and all, "Heeeeeyyyyyy, how ya *dew-in'*?" First to the robed African woman, then to a FedEx delivery man, next a jogger and after that . . . and after that.

Regardless of his condition, Carleen had come home that day with the wonderment of a person who'd seen a dead man risen. At long last, she admitted to Nelson that for several months she'd been hunting for Billy Cooper. "Guess what?" she said, flushed and breathless. "I found him!" Nelson had given her his alien look, and said, "Why? Carleen, don't you realize that the beauty of maturation is that you don't *have* to see your family?"

In spite of Nelson's tough talk, for a time Carleen had struggled to integrate Billy Cooper into her world, a pursuit of mixed yield. Although he had long ago shunned drugs, the brew of hallucinogens had left a permanent and debilitating stain. Whenever she was in San Francisco, she'd drive to Fisherman's Wharf, where he sometimes visited, relieved when she spotted him near the Ghirardelli chocolate factory juggling or singing "Duke of Earl." Often she'd invite him to Cassie's birthday parties or Thanksgiving or Christmas dinners. When she went to pick him up, more than once there had been a blank space on the sidewalk where he usually sat. Days later he would sometimes appear on his own, having hitchhiked to Chesterfield Bay. He would confuse one holiday for another, popping up two days after Thanksgiving with handmade Christmas gifts for Cassie—paper lanterns or metal birds. Or he'd appear the week after Christmas expecting turkey and cranberries.

Cassie, who had always loved the way Billy made cards disappear down tattered coat sleeves and moth-eaten trouser cuffs, finally complained about her bizarre uncle. "Mom, he smells so weird . . . and he's always crying and he looks at me funny."

"I know, honey, but do me a favor . . . don't tell Daddy that, okay?" Carleen found herself playing one against the other, hiding this from that one and something else from the other one.

Finally, one Thanksgiving, Carleen was balancing a pumpkin pie and dessert platters, moving carefully from the kitchen to the dining room. She was quite the perfect hostess in her russet silk shirtwaist dress, the opera-length pearls. When the doorbell rang, she hollered, "I'll get it" and set down the pie. She had no idea who in the world it could be, but there stood Billy Cooper. He was stiletto thin, with haunted eyes that looked like a full, naked moon. "Billy Cooper!" she gulped. With a table of guests waiting in the next room, including Noah Whittingham, a founding partner of Nelson's law firm, she almost collapsed.

He stood under the yellow bulb, his arms dangling like spiritless wings, leaves of rain falling from his buttonless coat and a one-hundred-and-three-degree fire burning his body. In spite of all that, he had hitchhiked fifty miles to their suburban home.

Try as she might to shepherd him into the den without anybody noticing, she could hear the chink of silverware against china, then silence as the guests craned their heads in curiosity.

"Who is it, honey?" Nelson's joyful, founding-partner voice, the one saved for special occasions, billowed from the dining room.

Before Carleen could make something up, Cassie curled her lip and announced, "Yuck, it's Uncle Billy."

Carleen dug her nails into her scalp, hating that she had a husband who never gave her any leeway. She even resented Cassie for smarting off. She was furious that her brother put her in this awkward position. Why couldn't he have been a normal drug addict, one who had his fun for a few years then lived to talk about it? Billy Cooper's damage was done. She kept thinking, "Why? Why? Why?" More than anything, she was worried about the Whittinghams. Surely, they would think it was bizarre to conceal an uncle when they were only a few rooms away. And impressions were of utmost importance to Nelson.

"For Christ's sakes!" Nelson came skidding into the hallway and hissed at Carleen. "What the hell is going on! We've got *company,* Carleen, *important company!*" His eyes were so heated in anger, that they seemed to melt into one another.

"I've got it under control, Nelson . . . don't worry! Your guests will never know." A million butterflies were beating in Carleen's chest. Knowing Billy Cooper, he'd want to sing "Glow Worm," then "Side by Side." That's all she needed. Already, he was humming "Yellow Rose of Texas."

Nelson hadn't said a word until the flowery platters and eggnog mugs had been washed and stacked and Billy Cooper was asleep on the wheat-colored carpeting. Praying that she was off the hook, Carleen was snapping off the lights, when Nelson started. First it was a hum, sounding like a low, growling machine, and finally, the explosion. "That's *it.* Cassie and I, not to mention our guests, don't have to put up with that, that *nutcase!* Let Rebecca handle him. Ship him off to Los Angeles, take him back to Berkeley, send him to Timbuktu for all I care, but get him out of here *first thing tomorrow.* I mean *out.*"

"Okay, Nelson, fine." Carleen never even defended Billy Cooper. Nor did she point out that his precious guests never got a clear look at Billy, that she had managed to occupy him with turkey and dressing and a videocassette of *The Towering Inferno* while sponging the fever from his temples. For all the Whittinghams knew, the phantom guest was a perfectly presentable Greta Garbo type, someone who just wanted a little privacy.

It made Carleen sadder still to know that her brother would be happy, even cooperative. Even if she said, "Billy Cooper, my husband thinks you're disgusting and you have to leave," her brother would stare at her with those innocent, startled eyes and reply, "Okayokayokayokay," and begin gathering his belongings as quickly as possible.

They had gotten undressed with the sounds of a ticking clock and the charging rain filling in the silence. Carleen had slipped into her flannel nightgown and thick cashmere socks, setting the alarm for 5:30 A.M. She and Billy Cooper would tiptoe out, drive into town where they would have bacon and eggs in Betty Anne's cafe; then she would give him money or perhaps get him a hotel room, even fly him to see Lila Mae if that's what he wanted. Before they left, she would rummage through the garage, collecting Cassie's old sweatshirts and Nelson's used jackets for him. Even when he was a little boy, he would often have to wear hand-me-down tennis sneakers or T-shirts, never complaining even if the shoes were too small or had belonged to Becky Jean and Carleen.

As Nelson lay in a deep, dead slumber, Carleen had drawn the fleecy blanket around her as if it was the only warmth and protection available. As she listened to the thumping of a branch against the window, she silently cried herself to sleep, brokenhearted to think of future holidays when her brother would wander around the sidewalks of Berkeley looking at Christmas wreaths or Thanksgiving turkeys with no particular place to go.

Since then, Carleen had endured the secret burden, trying to tend to Billy Cooper, still waiting for a breakthrough. She watched and watched as he flickered and dimmed like the flame of a candle being carried through a drafty hallway. All Carleen could do was cup her hand around him to preserve the spark.

Through it all, she tried not to rock the boat, waiting for some magical, nebulous event to turn Nelson around. But Billy Cooper was still her husband's favorite touchy subject, the one that he carted out when mere spite wasn't enough, one that tapped all the hair triggers for the entire family, and made for riveting, if not downright unbelievable, cocktail chatter for total strangers. Nelson wouldn't be happy until Billy Cooper was spread-eagled on the hood of a police car. Because of it, Carleen began to resent every bone and muscle in her husband's body.

Maybe if she walked in Nelson's shoes she would see that he wasn't the only one. After all, Billy Cooper's own kin, herself included, couldn't even face the situation. That was even putting it mildly—often, they practically disowned him.

Hadn't they shown their true colors when they were organizing Lila Mae's seventieth birthday party? Yes, she and her sisters decided, if Billy Cooper was in Berkeley as he usually was, it was feasible to cart him to Los Angeles for the evening, but there were other things to consider: the explosions that were nerve-wracking and humiliating. It was also possible that they'd bring him to Los Angeles and he'd become so jittery that he wouldn't show up at the party. Or, they could wake up on the Big Day and Billy Cooper would be off collecting puka shells or grunion on Venice Beach.

"To put it mildly," Irene said sarcastically, "he just doesn't fit in." With her spiked hair and black slumberous eyes, she was the pot calling the kettle black.

Normally, Rebecca would have been the one to do the straightforward, logical thing, and to make the final decision. It would have been a sanitary choice, one executed with military precision, one honoring the ease and enjoyment of the general guest list versus Lila Mae's personal happiness. This time, though, Rebecca was voting to include Billy Cooper. "It won't be *Father Knows Best,* you can bet on that. Still, I really can't imagine it without him, and Mom would definitely want him there. It is *her* birthday, after all."

But Carleen, the swing vote, and the one they all expected to melt into a hundred sentimental pieces said, "He'll make us all nervous wrecks. It'll be a full-blown disaster."

So, in the end, they lied to Lila Mae, who would have wanted her son at the party under any circumstances, telling her they looked high and low but found "no Billy Cooper."

"You couldn't find him?" Lila Mae stared at her lap as if revisiting her son's cradle. "Did you call those nice people at that bakery? There's also that health-food store in Berkeley, did they know anything?"

When Carleen said, "We tried everything," Lila Mae looked melancholy and utterly despondent. But, finally, she had patted Carleen's hand and said, "Well, that's okay, honey. I know you tried your *very* best."

One sunny October day, weeks after the party had taken place, Carleen drove by Billy Cooper's regular spot. She left him a writing tablet and asked if he would contribute a note for an album of memories they had assembled for Lila Mae. He said, "Okayokayokay," and took the paper. Thrilled if he had even been able to sign his name with an X, Rebecca and Carleen were stunned when he actually returned a dozen single-spaced pages. Contained in them were fractured recollections involving stormy nights and lost loves and the flowers their mother wanted on her coffin someday. None of the memories had any relevance to Lila Mae's birthday, but they demonstrated a lucidity that shocked them all.

At the end of the letter, scribbled in royal-blue ink with his writing peaking and dipping like a dangerous mountain range, he wrote: "I feel in my head I have lived one hundred years . . . but it's been a good life."

Included in the envelope were darkened, stained papers and a poem by Edna St. Vincent Millay: "My candle burns at both ends; It will not last the night; But ah, my foes, and oh, my friends—It gives a lovely light!"

The thought that her brother was within ten miles of her crouched on a sidewalk, clutching a money jar, singing "Spirit in the Sky" while she was worried about standing up to the exterminator and her chintzy Mother's Day gift, made Carleen sick to her stomach. If it was the last thing she ever did, Carleen would make sure Billy Cooper made it to Lila Mae's seventy-fifth birthday party.

Chapter Twenty-five

Irene

JULY 1999

As a freelance field agent, Irene, her lavender hair now tobacco brown, a supply of Ace bandages and crutches in tow, had already nabbed a woman named Hester Moses for lying about an injured leg. Irene got friendly with Moses at a bus stop and pretty soon, the chatterbox woman noticed Irene's wrist guard. "If that there's on account of yer work, you can git a bundle!"

"Is that so?" Irene played dumb and let the woman do most of the talking.

"I got me a sizable settlement comin', and it weren't nothin' but an Ajax can fell on my big toe." She kicked her foot in the air, turning it from side to side, to show Irene her cast. "My attorney and doctor told the insurance company I wuz permanently disabled! I ain't supposed to take this off fer several more weeks, so's we can build it up more." The lawyer, a fellow by the name of Ira Sharpsteen of Sharpsteen & Sharpsteen, even told Moses which physician to visit. "You git yerself over there. Ira or his brother, Abe, they're Jewish boys but they know what they're doin'. I stand to collect twenty thousand dollars!"

Irene said, "Well, I declare!"

She also caught Jeanette Whiteburn and Hewey Ed Seaton, both victims of a "brutal" motorcycle accident, sans their neck braces at Fayette Multiplex standing in line to see *Enemy of the State,* and a man named Charlie Dean Arbuckle whose torn knee ligament kept him from his sales job at DeeDee's Shoe Carousel but didn't stop him and a busty blonde from careening across Tucker's Lake in his Chris-Craft. They all had Sharpsteen & Sharpsteen for their attorneys and, sure enough, Dr. Roy K. Hand as their doctor. Needless to say, Irene was despised by all when their claims were denied, but over the moon when her investigation became the straw that finally broke the camel's back. Dr. Hand, under investigation by the insurance commissioner for two years, closed his office and hightailed it back to Arkansas.

Thrilled as Bud McCracken was by these victories, there was one outstanding and all-important case: Coco Castle's. The insurance claim was for a whopping $1,000,000, enough, McCracken swore, to close his branch and cause Miz Becky's insurance to skyrocket, if not make the business totally uninsurable.

Day after day, Irene had hunted the woman, checking her haunts and hangouts; she had trailed Coco to fancy shops in Lexington and to the Crestwood Inn Tea Parlor. She had tracked her to the private airport in Louisville where she put Horace Castle on their Lear jet, then sipped mint juleps with a girlfriend at the Seelbach Hotel. She sat outside the offices of Daniels & McCoy, the architects who were either redecorating Rosemont or designing her European castle. Irene had even spent hours parked near the Youngblood house on Boone's Creek watching the various comings and goings. Coco never once took off the sling.

The one day she could have had Coco in the palm of her hand, she made the mistake of stopping at the Bluegrass Hills Mall in Lexington after work. When she returned home, a police car was sitting in Olive's driveway, its red lights revolving, its door swung open.

Lately, none of this was unusual, since Irene's new job had turned Olive into a real worrywart. Even if she was only five minutes late, she would see her grandmother's head peeking behind the undulating lace drapes, just inches away from requesting an all-points bulletin.

But along the driveway and on the porch, there was a general air of topsy-turvy: rubbish containers and stray dog bones and upside-down zinnia pots. Irene threw down her belongings and flew into the house, praying she wouldn't find her grandmother in a near-death sprawl.

"Well! Ya sure picked a bad day to go gallivantin'!" Olive, flushed and discombobulated and sitting in her Queen Anne chair, huffed her standard response. "I wuz jest 'bout to call the po-leece on ya, then all *this* . . ."

Sheriff Burkle was standing in the parlor, his neck swiveling from side to side as he surveyed the situation.

"What happened, Grandma? Are you okay?" Irene's heart did fishtails as she noticed the displaced rugs and furniture and knick-knacks, plus the horseshoe-shaped scratch on Olive's forehead. Everything was oddly quiet. A freezing cold ripple of fear overcame her, as she wondered if the rest of the house had police outlines galore. "Wh-where is everybody?"

"Who knows?" Olive tossed up her hands. "Usually the place is swarmin' with people, but Dee and Peep's out, and, and Curtis and Maybelle is whar they always is when I need 'em—nowhere to be found. Maybelle, she's gone to a mod store to buy herself a dress and yer sister'll never tell ya what she's up to."

"So, so, what's wrong? What happened?" asked Irene.

"I got in a tussle with that biddy . . . that Coco Castle."

"Coco Castle came *here?*" Irene shouldn't have been too shocked, since she had detected vanilla, Coco's signature scent.

"That's what I'm tole." Burkle had his hands in both pockets, jiggling change.

"Butch Youngblood showed up here sweet-talkin' me . . . 'Hi Miss Olive!' he sez. 'How are ya today?' . . . He brung all his rakes and lawn mowers. Then here come that hel-ee-copter of Castle's, swoopin' down, spinnin' lak a top right over the roof here . . . pretty soon, there it wuz . . . sat it right down on the lawn."

"This is just unbelievable!" Irene stiffened her fingers and shook her palms in the air. "This takes nerve and, and, I'm not even sure they can do that . . . was Horace Castle in it?"

"It wuzn't him . . . it wuz Coco, that sister of Butch's. She dragged along Joe Lee Buttons. First thang I sez wuz, 'I know yer here to size the place up, ain't ya?' I asked Buttons 'How many times ya gonna come this way before ya git the message? Don't ya speak plain English, mister?' "

"They won't let up, will they?" Irene said.

"Then I asked Butch, what about all them garden tools ya brung, ain't ya gonna fix the place up while yer here? He sez, 'I'm workin' my way up to the front property, Miss Olive. I got them back pastures lookin' *real fine*.' I tole Butch, that's all fine and well, but next month I want that *front* yard lookin' good. He reared up and sez, 'Now you know Miss Olive that I cain't trim no trees in August. It's Time of the Heart. That job's gonna have to wait till fall.' "

"He's right 'bout that," Jimmy Buzz Burkle confirmed. "He goes messin' 'round next month? One little cut on a tree and you can lose yer whole yard."

"So I sez, 'Even if I wuz to believe all that *Farmer's Almanac* hocus pocus, what's yer excuse the rest of the time?' That's when he gives me a sneaky ole smile. He sez 'What good's it gonna do ya with Castle ready to buy ya out?' Sez, 'Castle don't care what the place looks like when he steps in, ain't that right, Sis?' Stood right over thar when he said it." Olive pointed her crooked finger to the spot, as if identifying the guilty party. "Yeah, Butch's a big shot now . . . acts like the kinga England."

"Can they *do* that?" Irene turned to Sheriff Burkle. "Just barge into her house? The helicopter is bad enough, but the house itself is really off limits, isn't it?"

"I don't like it any more than you do," Burkle said, "but you let 'em in, Miss Olive."

"What else could I do?" Olive turned her palms over like a beggar asking for coins. "Of all days, I'm in that stupid ole thing. I shoulda throwed it in the junk heap by now." She glowered at the therapeutic chair as if it was partly to blame. "Well, pretty soon Butch sez he and Joe Lee had sum business dealin's that wuzn't gonna take long. Onct Butch and Buttons went off snoopin' around, they stuck me with Coco. I told her, I knew ya when ya wuz Cookie Youngblood, missy, so don't try nothin' on me. I also said I ain't much on chitchat, but I did offer the woman sum lemonade. But it wuzn't no lemonade she wanted."

Jimmy Buzz fingered his gun, then asked her what she supposed the woman was after. "Did she tell ya, Miss Olive?"

"Oh, she didn't beat 'round no bush! First thing, she asks me, 'Ya take nerve pills doncha? I *know* ya do.' And I said, 'That's whar yer wrong, Missy.' She took off fer the bathroom lickety-split, and I sez, 'Hey, Miss Priss, whar ya goin'?' "

"She was looking for pills, Grandma?" asked Irene. She turned to Sheriff Burkle in shock. "Can you believe that?"

"Next thing I know here comes Coco limpin' around, showin' off that arm brace of hers, rattling that pill bottle over my head like them things cheerleaders shake. 'I thought you didn't have no nerve pills,' she sez. I looked her square in the face and sez, 'And I thought yer arm wuz all tore up. It don't look so bad to me if ya kin move it lak a hootchy-cootchy dancer.' She come close lak she wuz gonna pop me one. So I took a swing at her."

"Grandma!" Irene yelped. "You're unbelievable!"

"I didn't git too far cuz she slugged me back. That's when I tole her that I know what I know."

"And what's that, Miz Olive?" Jimmy Buzz's monotone, robotic voice sounded like a cheap electronic toy.

"I told Coco that she might git away from me, but she won't git away long. 'I got one of my girls who's on to ya, Miss Priss, she's trailin' ya ever'whar ya go and ya won't git far,' I tole her."

"Great," sighed Irene, letting her arm fall to her lap. The detective work was hard enough to begin with. "Maybe you shouldn't have said anything, Grandma."

"Don't you worry. She's scerred now. See, I tole her I knew who the other robber was at Miz Becky's. Oh, Coco knew what I mint. Coco and Butch'll have it in fer me now, they will!"

"Your granddaughter's right, Miz Olive. You let us take care of this sit-chation." Jimmy Buzz chewed his gum in a lazy counterclockwise motion. "This is official *po-leece* business."

"Is that so?" Olive snapped. "Well, I know what else I know!"

"What's that, Miz Olive?" Sheriff Burkle's eyes had the disinterested glaze of a man who was already wondering what his wife had cooked for dinner.

"What makes you think Butch wuzn't in on it, too? I have it on good authority that he wuz no more with Billy Ray Cyrus in Branson, Missoura, during that robb-ree than I wuz."

"That could be," Burkle said, giving it some thought.

"It ain't as simple as this robb-ree neither. I've said it till I'm blue in the face; I'll say it again. That developer is in on this. Git ya a pad, make yerself three columns—one fer the property, then say if it's fer sale or not, then put whether they wuz eny BB guns or burglaries and such. In that last column, mark down who owns it now and you'll see!"

Sheriff Burkle was tugging his collar and coughing nervously.

"Whatever it is, ya connect all that and yer gonna see Castle's name smack-dab in the middle. You watch! They're tryin' the same with yer sister's rest-rent . . . this place, too . . . the whole town!" Olive glared at Sheriff Burkle. "You wuz even at the robb-ree that night. You cain't tell me that one of them fellers wuzn't Butch Youngblood. Why Miss Bookbinder hit the other robber on the head and she sez it wuz Butch all right. She said, 'Ya kin smell a Youngblood a mile away!' I got testimony from sum others, too. Ya cain't deny that thangs is fishy around here . . . You fellers down to the po-leece department must be blind if ya don't see what's a happenin'."

"Now, Miss Olive," Burkle coughed. "They's things you don't know . . . privileged information! We still got some avenues to pursue. You just leave all the detective work be."

After Burkle left, Olive peeked through the sheer curtain. "I wuz fakin' sum of that stuff I tole him, but he's lak a big ole pimple, ain't he? Squeeze him a little and all sorts of interestin' stuff spurts out. Ya see, none of this is as cut 'n' dried as ever'body makes it out, is it?"

As a result of all this commotion, although not exactly the ingredients for Utopia, Irene's unhappiness lifted like a heavy fog, something she would have never guessed possible. Every morning she would wake up thinking: I'm gainfully employed! I'm on the road to self-improvement! I feel like a million bucks! So far, Irene had walked, gardened, and dieted herself down to one-hundred-and-forty-five pounds. She loved the yoga sessions with Jasmina and Little Peep, and the long, vigorous walks she took down wooded lanes. Her hair was no longer

Crayola red and lilac, it was dark brown and shiny and she wore it like Rebecca's, slightly turned under and just brushing her shoulders.

Even Darrell was off her back. Now that she had paid his delinquent bills, the annoying calls had stopped. How silly of her to think he had been phoning to beg her to return. And, everybody was beginning to think it wasn't even Darrell who had been calling. They suspected it was Joe Lee Buttons instead, since other resistant property owners, people who didn't know Darrell James Armbruster, had received similar menacing calls.

After dinner, Irene loved returning to her bedroom, a frosted tumbler of sweet peach tea and crystallized ginger slices with her. There she would make neat stacks of her papers, turning all the notes and chicken scratch into reports. She would check and double-check all her facts, scanning her brain for some insignificant detail that could make all the difference between a legitimate and bogus claim. For inspiration she would glance at the gift-shop plaque, the one that said: BEHIND EVERY GREAT WOMAN IS . . . HERSELF! When she was finished, she tucked it in the burgundy leather briefcase her grandmother bought her at Bacon's, feeling accomplished and content and on the road to success.

She was also pleased with her other side, the Mother Earth Irene who came to them all each night with mincemeat pies and crème brulée, who put a smile on their hungry lips and who was always rewarded with rousing applause. That such huge benefits could be reaped from these small tasks wouldn't have seemed possible to Irene. But how would she have known? Irene had never completed anything, not even a crossword puzzle.

Naturally, though, Rebecca, as supportive as she had been, occasionally turned into a spoilsport, quizzing Irene's progress, suspicious that Irene had a fatal flirtation with calamity, and all sorts of other ultradramatic accusations. Down every hallway Rebecca would trod, at every table she would sit, sniffing around like a U.S. Customs dog.

"What is it with you?" Irene asked. She was perched on a Windsor chair, her knees on the seat, her hands on the spindled back, tipping forward precariously. She remembered being yelled at by Lila Mae for this same thing when she was a girl. "I'm not allowed to be sleepy or glassy-

Chapter Twenty-six

Rebecca

JULY 1999

A fter all the fuss and feathers about the Montgomerys not selling Rosemont or letting anyone within ten miles of it and after all the tall tales about trespassers being gunned down, Rebecca and Olive ended up getting inside after all. One afternoon, they all watched in suspense as Olive answered the phone and nestled the receiver to her shoulder. Finally, they heard her say, "Now listen, Hamilton, they's sum thangs ya probably ain't aware of . . . Maybe we should fight this so-called airport project together. I'm gonna bring my granddaughter, the smart one from California. She's got sum good idees!" She also told Mr. Montgomery that she'd heard that Ramona had "sum sortie an attack," so while she was at it, she said, "I'll come over and doctor her, if need be." Montgomery must have refused her offer because Olive asked, "Are ya shore? It wouldn't be no trouble!"

When Olive hung up, she winked one silvery-white eye, and said to Rebecca, "Let's get *oooonnnn* with it . . . we got places to go and things to do!"

A sky dappled with sunshine and low charcoal clouds and a crack of thunder slightly marred Rebecca and Olive's drive down Rosemont's allée of oak trees. As if in defiance of the neglect imposed on them, most eyed, no matter how tired I am. You stare at me, like I'm on something. You're like a narc!"

"I'm worse than a narc," her busybody sister said. "I'm a concerned relative. Irene, you live the life you've lived and people have an obligation to be suspicious. Besides, you're doing so well, I'd hate to see you slip up. You're going to break that chair if you don't stop."

Rebecca had also come to place her hand over Irene's glass when wine was being poured, something that irked Irene, who wasn't exactly a baby and who hadn't even been drinking either.

Even with the recent upswing in so many events, and the tunnel lights that Irene had never known before, there was still the realization that her white-picket-fenced dreams would never come true, that the babies she had always wanted were never meant to be, and that she'd never have that ubiquitous and obnoxious—MY CHILD IS AN HONOR STUDENT AT OAKVIEW ELEMENTARY bumper sticker on her fender. At this late date, she wasn't even sure she could salvage a relationship with her two nieces.

"Hi, Aunt Baby Sister!" the girls would tease, careful, Irene could tell, of not sidling up too close to their delinquent aunt. In their mothers' warning speeches, Irene was probably one ladder slot below the kidnappers who showed up with Hershey bars to tempt their quarry.

That night, when nary a light from the moon shone, when except for the click-click-click of the grandfather clock with the painted-moon face, the house was as still as Christmas Eve, Irene sat with her earphones and her *Cats* album and sang along with Grizabella. Being that the house was full of people, she couldn't sing out loud. But, even in her lung-wrenching whispers, she was absolutely positive she was hitting all the high notes, and doing so on the wings of joy, not despair, lifted by the abstraction that she was within striking range of some happiness that once upon a time she had known.

Through the bedroom wall, over the barking of Geronimo and the pecking of the cardinals at her window, sometimes she could even hear Olive singing, "Goodnight Irene, goodnight, goodnight Irene . . . I'll see you in my dreeeams."

of the trees still flourished. Here and there sprayed across this tattered Shangri-la were fence planks and broken iron settees like stray charms on a broken bracelet. Rebecca had never approached the house properly, so this was a different angle of her dream.

With her heart hammering, Rebecca thought to herself, "Who knows? Maybe if I see it, I won't even like it." But, one way or another, she had to shake the house out of her system.

As they moved farther up the drive, through boughs of greenery and the stranglehold of overgrown shrubbery, one spike of dark sunlight bounced through the trees and spotlighted Rosemont's columns.

"Well, good grief!" Olive, looking at the tangle of vines, exhaled a shock of a sigh. "Onct that kudza gits ya, it don't let loose. Sum sez it's purty, but it'll kill ever'thang it touches. Seems to me lak they cudda trimmed that back sum. But look at Rosemont, would ya? It's still a wonderful sight."

Before Rebecca knew it, they were standing on the lopsided porch, with its rusted chandelier and corniced doorway. Screwed to the brick was a small bronze plaque: ROSEMONT, BUILT IN 1810 BY THOMAS BRECK-INRIDGE ADAMS. Olive and Rebecca caught one another's eyes and smiled wistfully. It seemed an eternity, one accompanied by two hearts literally bursting out of their chests, until the door creaked open.

She expected Hamilton Montgomery to be decrepit and so much older than he was. Through Rebecca's teenage eyes, he had seemed prehistoric and possessed, like Moses on a rampage. In any case, so old that he couldn't have possibly still been alive if he had been the eighty years he seemed at the time. Olive told Rebecca she was way off. "Why Hamilton wuddn't no more than forty-five when ya seen him!"

The man had a tussock of white hair and the sad, deep-set eyes of a prophet who has seen the future and now has to live his lamentable destiny. When he reached for Rebecca's hand to say hello, he smelled like the decayed blossoms and roots of an old tree. Except for a medicinal vapor wafting from upstairs, there was no sign of Ramona. Montgomery told them she was confined to the house with some seemingly serious condition.

Olive said, "I pray to heaven ya didn't have that Hand feller lookin' after Ramona. Bring her to me. I already cured one of his."

Montgomery slipped around in burgundy house shoes and a shirt poked haphazardly into brown linen trousers. He motioned a large floppy hand toward the dining room, so they followed him through musty, uncarpeted hallways with sagging arches and shadowy nineteenth-century portraits. There were missing floorboards and broken windows mixed with medallioned ceilings and cherry mantels. In the kitchen were encrusted aluminum containers and cat food strewn across the checkerboard floor like pebbles. It all made Rebecca's heart plummet and soar with each measured step she took. As for Olive, she was moving with the slow-motion gait of a mother superior in a cathedral, the velvet drumbeat of her heart throbbing as she devoured it all.

They sat in a room with mint-green walls at a table with one silver candlestick and a blown-glass pitcher. Mr. Montgomery offered them lukewarm tea, which they drank from chipped, dirty teacups. They placed Irene's plum tart between them like a candied centerpiece. All of it was bathed in the caramel light of late afternoon.

"Well, Hamilton," Olive said tapping her fingernail against the mahogany, grasping for words to span several decades. "Ya still got yerself a nice place here, not that it couldn't use a little sprucin' up!"

"Ramona and I wanted to keep the place up. But things get away from you. I'm sorry it's not in better shape."

"Oh, no. It's *gorgeous,* Mr. Montgomery!" With her exaggerated compliments, Rebecca reminded herself of Lila Mae.

While the chitchat flowed, Rebecca knew they had business to tend to, but she wanted to roam the corridors, investigating every crevice and china closet. She wondered if the walnut bookcase and the marble Henry Clay bust could be purchased with the house. She placed furniture in her head, realizing that the one red Chippendale settee she'd bought for the sitting room would need some company. There were other orphan purchases, too: Hepplewhite chairs and sinumbra lamps, all squirreled away under Olive's various beds and in her attic. The silver tape measure jostled loosely in her pocket and she couldn't wait to take dimensions of floors and walls. As her eyes roved, Rebecca couldn't help but notice the renowned rifle propped against the door.

"You wait so long with some of your plans, that it doesn't matter anymore." Hamilton took a sip of tea and shifted one slippered foot over his long leg.

"Well, that's what we're here to talk to ya 'bout." Olive placed her hand on the table and squirmed. "I ain't gonna beat around no bush. Hamilton, this airport business . . . it ain't nothin' but a land grab."

"How's that?" Montgomery cupped his ear.

"Well, for starters it ain't no airport! That's what they want us to think, Hamilton! It's Jesse Youngblood's girl . . . Cookie . . . Coco, she calls herself now." Olive knew the name Youngblood left a vinegary taste in everyone's mouth. "That huzzy's got herself a rich husband and she's got her eye on yer property. My place, too . . . she wants the whole kit and caboodle! I tole ever'one the Hamilton Montgomery I know would *never* let the laks of that clan get aholt of Rosemont!"

"So you say the airport deal isn't on the up and up?" Hamilton cocked his head and rubbed his whiskers.

"What's Blue Lick need with a big ole airport? We don't need the one we got! This is a *land grab,* I tell ya!"

"It does seem like a big hoax, Mr. Montgomery. Believe me," Rebecca fibbed, "if the Castles were restoring buildings or preserving the farms around here, I'd be their biggest fan. Have you seen what Castle is doing right on Honeysuckle Way? They want to build dozens of houses where the old farms are."

"First they tell ya' they're puttin' houses galore, then they tell ya the airport's takin' it all. Either it's one or the other!" Olive said. "Coco'd have all them Youngbloods here. You know what I'm a-talkin' 'bout, Hamilton . . . Butch and Frankie, Jr. and them . . . right here on the lawn of Rosemont . . . all these hairlooms destroyed! Why, Dan'el Boone would be flippin' over in his grave if he seen all this destruction."

"Is all that really so?" Hamilton Montgomery, this citizen living among the ruins, so isolated from the world, and who Rebecca feared would be impervious to her sentimental preservation pleas, seemed genuinely concerned about the fate of his hometown. "It's that bad?"

"It's worse," confirmed Olive. She picked up a teacup decorated with fleurs-de-lys and took a sip. "Now, I heard tell it wuz the Castles who wuz *here,* flew right in on their own vehicle! And I heared tell it wuzn't the first time they showed their faces, neither. They come to my house too, rubbin' their grubby paws on ever'thang. If this wuz strictly the airport and city business, what wuz Hearst Castle and that Youngblood tramp a-doin' here . . . you tell me that!"

"Well . . . they, uh . . ." All of a sudden, he was drinking tea, lots of it. He took a gulp, then cleared his throat. "I can see your point, Miss Olive, but for me the sale would be a, a godsend of sorts. See, I've got Ramona in the sick girl's room and I need a medical facility for her and well, it's just time. You can only fight these projects for so long. And Ramona and I should have left this place after Babette passed."

Rebecca was stunned, hardly believing her ears at Montgomery's drastic change of view, seemingly just like that. "I can understand your wanting to leave," she said, "but don't do it because of this project."

They had come to discuss the airport and they were going to leave it at that, but Olive took a sudden veer. "That's all fine and well, but if yer set on sellin' this place, why don't ya name ya a price and sell to *us* instead?"

"You want to buy it?" Montgomery shifted uncomfortably. "You?"

As Rebecca faced Hamilton Montgomery, his eye held an unspoken message of familiarity, a few shared moments scattered through the ages like scavenger hunt clues. Did he sense that she was the pesky teenager hiding the day of the tornado, that day so many decades ago? And had Ramona Montgomery mentioned the presence she felt in the border trees only days before? What would Hamilton Montgomery think if he knew this woman before him had already purchased furniture for the very room in which they sat, that, if she had her way, his frayed couch would soon be replaced by a silk davenport and the wallpaper that broke away from the walls in sweeping, stained curls would be changed to Zuber's Scenes from Early America.

"Now, Rebecca's intra-sted in this place, airport or no airport. And, the way I see it, Hamilton, it would do ya sum good to sell to sumone who's gonna fight to keep it in the family!"

Since the cat had leapt out of the bag, Rebecca joined in. "It's true. I *am* interested in the house and I *would* restore it. I just can't imagine it being torn down. Like we said, this airport project isn't really going to happen."

"It hurts me to see it go, too," Montgomery said. "It really does. You hate to think your home meant nothing."

"It's like yer whole life wuz *worthless*," said Olive, sighing like Sarah Bernhardt. "A *total* waste! Hamilton, ya gotta join this co-lition we got goin'. I ain't gonna let sum Woolworth huzzy plow down ever'thang my family worked so hard fer . . . and neither should you! I heard the Young-blood woman's already changin' Rosemont's name to CASTLEMONT. Now how could *that* be if they want this place fer the airport?"

"Well, I—"

"And bein' that we're pillars of the community and all, it behooves us to stick up fer the town. So, ya sell Rosemont to us and we'll fight fer it. I'll say it again—it's a *land grab!*"

Rebecca tried to stall the conversation when Olive began talking of gentlemen's agreements, and good-faith deposits and all sorts of other things that urged Hamilton Montgomery to sell the property right on the spot! She said, "Uh, Mr. Montgomery, why don't you come for dinner or lunch? Yes, why don't you come for lunch? We could continue this then."

"Why shore, ya need a square meal, ya come to our place. I'll have Rebecca fetch ya whenever ya want."

The last straw was when Olive said, "I got a good idee. Why don't ya give Mr. Montgomery a check, Rebecca. I'd say it ain't no count right now, Hamilton . . . but it *will* be by the time it hits the bank." Olive let out a shrill whoop. "That Coco Castle ain't the only one with a rich husband, is she, honey?"

It was one of those rare occasions when Rebecca felt like wringing her grandmother's neck. The furniture and accessories she'd bought on the sly were one thing, but writing a check for thousands of dollars for a house David had never seen was out of the question . . . or grounds for divorce, well, maybe not divorce, but at the very least, a trial separation. Olive wasn't too happy with Rebecca either; she was perturbed that her granddaughter didn't know how to close the deal.

Not quite shooing them away, Hamilton Montgomery stood at the door, his leathery hand grasping the brass knob. "I'll mull all this over . . . I sure will," he told them.

They started down the driveway, cheered by the mere contact with Montgomery and all the possibilities, both sensible and insane, when Olive's face suddenly took on the mischievous glow of a child. She said, "Let's take the back way, why don't we."

"I didn't know there *was* a back way."

"Of course, they's a back way to ever'thang, don't ya know that? Turn here!" Olive said, pointing to a road that disappeared between ruptured branches. As they rumbled over rocky soil, her eyes skittered left, then right, studying fallen woodsheds and piles of old brick. Every few minutes and for no particular reason, she would say, "Well, look at that!" as if she were surprised by all the changes in the past fifty years.

The last thing Olive muttered before they left Rosemont's grounds was, "This place shoulda never fallen into the Montgomerys' hands."

Try as Rebecca might to temper her fervor, a strategy began to race in her head, one born from a clarity that only hindsight could give her: If the house was up for grabs, and it sort of seemed like it could be, she would buy it, even if that meant giving Hamilton Montgomery a big check, before the Castles got their mitts on it, and then pray that the check didn't stick out like a sore thumb on their bank statement. Instead of one lump sum, she could write several checks from different accounts to string it out. As she'd done in the past, she'd get Lila Mae and Olive and Irene to write checks of their own, then she would make checks out to them to pay them back. With the sale of some jewelry, the nest egg she'd kept aside, and the $200,000 sales price amount that was already out there in the universe and decreasing in outrageousness and deteriorating in monetary significance each time the number was mentioned, how far apart could the reluctant seller, the overzealous buyer, and the over-my-dead-body husband actually be?

Later, propped in the big four-poster bed, a mere six hours after meeting with Hamilton Montgomery, Rebecca was full of remorse. What an imbecile she was for *not* striking a deal with him. Why didn't she listen to Olive? She should have left behind a hefty deposit. But she'd fix that. Tomorrow, first thing, she'd take the suicide leap, she'd "sic 'em," she'd get *ooonnn* with it! Because, after all, she had places to go and things to do!

Falling asleep flat on her back, she traced the floor plan of Rosemont on the plaster between her bedposts. Let's see, there was the sitting room that was larger than she thought and the kitchen that, unfortunately, would have to be totally gutted and redone. And there were so many more rooms than she'd thought . . . and she hadn't even seen a fraction of them. She hadn't gotten to explore the cupboards and stone wine cellar and buttery and the keeping room where glazed bowls and porcelain vessels had remained untouched for three generations. There also hadn't been any sign of the gilded library with its rare Balzac novels. Nor did she notice any Duncan Phyfe furniture, and what about the ballroom, the grandest space of all, according to Lila Mae, who, Rebecca had to keep reminding herself, had never even set foot inside Rosemont!

All the men in her life: David, Phil Bustamante, and, especially, Little Peep would crown her. In some war-smoked room with their armor clinking, she could visualize it all: "I've *run* the numbers for this scatterbrained idea. I'll call you after I've *run* the numbers." She imagined sevens and eights and nines and tens with tiny arms and legs like those animated candy bars and popcorn boxes in movie theater ads running! Running! Running!

It wasn't until the next afternoon that the situation took a downward turn. Olive hung up the phone and looked at them with sad, vacant eyes. All the sunshine seemed to have drained from her face as she said, "That wuz Hamilton Montgomery. Claims we hardly let 'im git a word in edgewise. Enyways, he said he just couldn't break the news to ya on the spot, seein' that ya had yer heart set on the place and all, but Rosemont is already sold."

Chapter Twenty-seven

Carleen

JULY 1999

So, there they were, once again on their way to a retirement party for one of Nelson's law partners with an argument already under their belt. They sat in the front seat of Nelson's Jaguar, a sweet tawny moon hanging above the peak of Mount Tamalpais. A police car, siren singing, passed on the opposite side of the road. Maybe it's coming after our marriage, Carleen thought.

When they reached the Wildwood Creek Lodge, Carleen milled around the banquet room with its Virginia countryside theme: overblown, grainy photographs of racehorses and plantations. On the bandstand was a group playing Glenn Miller and suspended over a gazebo was a mirrored horseshoe saying GOOD LUCK, HAROLD! Harold Brown, one of the founding partners, was retiring and moving back to Charlottesville, Virginia. The mere mention of Virginia renewed thoughts of Joshua Beaton and the tranquil life the two of them could have back in his home state; it also reminded her that he would soon be meeting in Chesterfield Bay for more media hoopla for the *People* magazine article. If anyone knew how stirred up Carleen was about the upcoming liaison, she'd be on a cot in Our Lady of Peace with a white-capped attendant telling her it was time for her medication, but it wasn't all that crazy, actually. After one measly dinner, Beaton, unlike her own husband, made her feel like a million bucks.

Bumping her way through the room of party-goers, phony smiles and small talk ricocheted and boomeranged around her. Carleen put on her Stepford Wife smile and said her obligatory hellos to Nelson's business associates. All unpleasantry aside, she was feeling pretty good in her snug ivory dress and pearls. The evening seemed to get off to a pleasing start, too, when Harvey Rothstein, a new addition to the firm, approached Carleen, and said, "I know who you are! You're a writer!" Just when she was feeling like Edith Wharton, he added, "You're the one who writes about why slot A never fits slot B. Loved your latest column on dry cleaning."

Just as she suspected, Nelson had made a beeline to the nest of Brown, Carlyle and Whittingham partners, so that would be the last she'd see of him. Carleen had inched up to the bar and was talking with Loretta Brown, Harold's wife, when she spotted Anna Traminsky and Jordan Lampley. They were silked and buffed to cosmetic perfection and moved through the crowd like temperamental thoroughbreds.

Traminsky, the blonde-on-blonde femme fatale of Brown, Carlyle and Whittingham, looked like Big Bird. She had on a black chiffon dress with ostrich feathers swishing around her knees. Lampley had a mere thread of a body with hair like cinnamon tumbleweed and red, bowed lips. The attorneys, two of the firm's brightest, according to Nelson, twittered like pretentious, inebriated magpies, steeped in a conversation condemning the tactics of a rival defense attorney. Traminsky, holding her martini like a loving cup, told Lampley, "I cannot imagine what Corman was thinking when he brought his client into the courtroom dressed in those dirty chinos. I mean . . . *hellooo?*"

"It does make you wonder, doesn't it?" Lampley slipped a caviar-dotted potato in her mouth. "Talk about self sabotage! He should know better than that."

"The first thing *I* do," Traminsky pressed her bosom when she said "I," "is advise my client to get a good suit. If he doesn't have the money, I'll even purchase it myself."

"It's all about presentation," said Lampley, washing down her appetizer with a Manhattan. "Studies even show that."

As the two geniuses bragged about their techniques for swindling the jury, pure rage crept its way through Carleen's body. It wasn't just the attorneys' point of view that burned her up; Carleen had spotted a gold watch sliding up and down Anna Traminsky's slender wrist. It was identical to the one Carleen had purchased for Rhonda, Nelson's paralegal. And her earrings, baroque pearls crisscrossed with diamonds, were the ones Nelson had supposedly given to his mother for her birthday.

Traminsky, who just wouldn't stop, bragged, "I always pat my client's back, even if they're a brutal murderer, because that tells the jury that I'm not afraid of the accused and they shouldn't be either." Carleen couldn't take it anymore. She leaned into the duo and said, "That's just wonderful! You're all smoke and mirrors and psychological tricks. You claim you're trying to uphold justice, to protect your client's stupid constitutional rights. In the end, you're nothing but sleight of hand, Siegfried and Roy—"

"Oh, now the constitution's stupid?" Lampley half laughed and half coughed. "Hello, Carleen!"

By now the champagne was a roaring fire in Carleen's head. "All you're concerned about is a suspect's precious Miranda rights. You'd rather penalize the legal process and the police than the criminal who committed a heinous crime, wouldn't you?"

"Are you suggesting, *dear,* that a person shouldn't be given a fair trial, that they should be ripped from their bed and taken straight to the gallows . . . some procrustean tactics, is that what you're thinking?" That was Witch Number One, Anna Traminsky, who traded wicked smiles with Lampley.

"I love the way you twist it!" said Carleen, giving her head a haughty toss. "Even when they catch the criminal at the scene of the crime with a smoking pistol or bloody knife, which they often do—and believe me, I know, my husband is a senior partner of this firm—the crooks still get off, thanks to attorneys like *you*. Even Nelson says he couldn't sleep at night if he handled those cases."

"Believe me, *I* know Nelson very well . . . so I know he doesn't share your views on the matter." Ms. Traminsky dipped her lacquered finger into her drink, sucking off the alcohol. "We've had long discussions about this *very* thing."

Across the crepe-papered room, underneath the sequined GOOD LUCK, HAROLD! sign, was her husband, totally unaware of the skirmish. Standing in a huddle of gray-suited businessmen, his head was tossed back in roaring hilarity, an expression that would transform into a grimace when he got wind of things.

"The system isn't perfect, but it works most of the time," Lampley added her decisive two cents' worth.

"Actually," Anna crumpled up the cocktail napkin as if it were their conversation and handed it to a passing waiter, "it *does* work. Crime is going *down* in most areas." Carleen took another sickening look at the watch, her stomach rippling like a trip on a bad carnival ride.

"Yeah, inside your head, maybe. Believe me, most people see it my way." Carleen lifted her champagne glass in a mock salute. "Sleep tight! Try not to dream about all those slashers and rapists prowling around!"

"How's *your* career these days?" Traminsky taunted. "Your 'writing' career?"

"It's just *great!*" Before she was out of earshot, Carleen spun around and said, "By the way, nice jewelry." She waited until her back was to Traminsky to add, "Harlot." As she made her grand exit, Traminsky's eyes, two camel-colored darts, pierced her.

Soon after they were on opposite sides of the room, Carleen was in the Wildwood Lodge's lilac powder room, heaving and recoiling in embarrassment, and scanning the text of the ridiculous dry-cleaning article in her head; "Have you ever wondered why in the devil your clothes are stuffed like Thanksgiving turkeys? Are you just plain tired of pulling out yard after yard of tissue paper from one measly jacket sleeve? How many more trees does it take until . . ." Oh, she just wanted to roll into a ball when she thought about how inane it was!

Not only had she made a complete fool of herself, but she had done so with someone who obviously had a cozy relationship with her husband. What must the sirens have thought of her? What would happen when Nelson found out? A thousand fears flew around to torture her.

As for the watch, it was definitely the same one. And so were the earrings. It all seemed so shady now—the huge production Nelson had made, insisting that Carleen swing by a wholesale jewelry dealer in Oakland, the murder capital of the country, to purchase a gift for his assistant. Time and again, Nelson had assured her it wasn't unusual for his firm to offer extravagant perks for the staff. Lorraine Rockingham had received a new Lexus for winning a huge antitrust suit; Augusta Sorrenson visited Rome when she settled a class-action suit, Anitra Seligman got Oakland Raiders season tickets . . . and so on.

As Carleen reviewed the acrimonious exchange, there were so many lost opportunities. She wished she'd used the fancy words she'd just looked up; wished she knew what procrustean tactics were. Oh, how she had wanted to remember the statistics that placed attorneys on the bottom of the list of professions that the public trusted and high on the list of suicides.

Most of all, she wished she'd told the two flippant hussies that while they were cooped up in the musty library of Brown, Carlyle and Whittingham, Carleen was as free as a bird. She would tell them about the upcoming *People* magazine article, the one that would make Carleen the toast of the town.

And her mother-in-law's earrings were another story. Nelson had told Carleen that he had given them to her at a birthday lunch, one which Carleen was conveniently not invited to, a relief at the time. When Carleen asked him what Mildred had thought of the gift, Nelson said, "She didn't care for them." Knowing her mother-in-law, a woman who could receive a diamond tiara and exclaim, "What I really wanted were rubies!" this was entirely possible. The fishy part was that Nelson told Carleen he'd have his secretary return the earrings because, he said, "You've got enough on your plate, honey."

The trip home was an Evel Knievel joyride, causing Carleen to grab the car door and shriek at Nelson to "slow down!" But the more she harped, the faster he drove.

At home she kicked off her high heels and tiptoed into Cassie's room. They all look like angels when they're asleep, Lila Mae used to crack, and Cassie was no different with her golden hair radiating across the pillow like a fairy-tale princess and the flush of a deep, innocent sleep settling on her face. It broke Carleen's heart looking at her daughter, knowing what she knew and suspecting what she suspected about Nelson.

In the Poseidon's ice-blue bedroom, Carleen sat at her bureau and ran her hairbrush through her hair, giving it one-hundred halfhearted strokes, a leftover childhood routine. Then she unfastened her pearl necklace and set it in a porcelain dish. She unzipped her dress, her head rerunning the evening's vignettes. It was now obvious, as it should have been for months, that the late "work" nights were nothing of the sort. And Carleen had thought she was so clever slipping away for three years, disappearing one day out of the week to work on a stupid television show, when it just allowed Nelson more time for his dalliances. Obviously Carleen was a talk-show host's perfect guest for the "Last One to Know" episode.

While the last traces of Noah Whittingham's champagne toast were still with her, Carleen waited for the right moment to attack. Of course, it wasn't just about the watch; the situation was a messy, complex subject, one that alarmed her, one that made her hair stand on end, gave her migraines, one she was dying to get to the bottom of, and one she would desperately love to avoid. Priming herself, she took a deep breath and just let the words shoot out like steam from a high-pressure valve.

"Well, tonight wasn't a total waste of time . . ." Carleen sorted through her drawer, attempting to look preoccupied. "At least I got the theme for next week's column: 'Men Who Buy a Wristwatch Supposedly for One Person But Turn Around and Give It to Someone Else.' "

"What's *that* mean?" Nelson looked up from untying his shoe, his eyes pulled into two squinty kernels. As always, he removed the shoes and placed them neatly side by side, two obedient soliders, as if he were still standing at attention in them.

"You're always anxious to rewrite my columns, I thought you could give me some pointers." Finally, she swung around and blurted out, "That gold watch, the one you had me buy . . . Anna Traminsky was wearing it. What's going on, Nelson?" She hadn't planned on such a quick attack, but she couldn't hold it in.

"Anna won the Ry Hendricks case, the watch was for her. *You* knew that, you *always* get things wrong." He slipped off his onyx cuff links and clinked them together like dice, then whipped off his tie with the panache of a lion tamer.

"I see." Carleen pushed her evening bag against the cologne bottles. "So, *I* got it wrong."

She waited and watched as he delved into the cache of courtroom expressions, pulling out the beady-eyed arctic freeze. "Yes," he said. "Yes, you did." She watched him unhook his Patek Phillipe watch, probably the papa bear version of Miss Traminsky's. "You got it wrong."

"What about the earrings?" Carleen reached deep inside, groping for some cool, calm, collected reaction. "They just happened to be the same ones we bought for your mother, the ones you *returned*. What about those? Another *coincidence?*"

"How the hell do I know? I don't go around examining women's earlobes." He had removed his shirt and folded it, first the right arm, then the left. He flipped it over and folded it once more. Now it was finally ready for the laundry bin. "And what does *that* prove? Anybody can buy them, you know. Look, Carleen." Nelson shoved his closet door shut, and moved closer, standing over her like a bandit asking for all her money. "Where are we going with this? Or are you simply determined to keep us both up all night?"

"Just one thing." Carleen looked at him intensely. "Swear on Cassie's life that I was wrong about the watch and the earrings." It was a last-chance tone, like a travelers' warning sign that says: LAST GAS FOR ONE HUNDRED MILES.

Without batting an eye or skipping a beat, he said, "I swear on her life. You were wrong, *dead wrong!*"

Nelson turned as if the questioning was over, but Carleen grabbed his arm. "No, Nelson. Swear to *Cassie's* life. Say Cassie, say her name, not just *her*."

"I swear to her life, *Cassie's life,* God damn it!" Nelson slammed a drawer. "Now is that enough for you or what?"

Carleen grappled to take the remnants and fragments of thoughts and pound them into some brilliant response, but she was stunned into silence . . . and then the moment was gone, bounding away in a split second of squandered perfection.

Nelson had made a getaway into the bathroom, burying his anger and last unspoken words in the sound of running water and rattling drawers. All she could do was sit there on her aubergine vanity stool, staring at her glum face in the mirror, and holding her hairbrush as if posing for a picture.

Before long, Carleen lay in a debilitated puddle, the champagne throbbing away in some arrhythmic scamper. One more night when they slept in the same bed, two islands adrift in the same debris. Nelson rolled on one side, like a porpoise, his powerful back to Carleen, a daisy-embroidered sheet barely covering him, and was gone almost immediately. Even in this state his pattern never changed: the tugging of the sheet, whipping it into the air like a sail, the left arm that flapped first one way, then the other like a pendulum. She smelled the dying trace of musk, she knew the familiar whimpering breath that he sucked in right before he fell into a sleep that would go completely undisturbed until he was jolted awake by the ringing alarm clock.

Dotted around the room were the trinkets that were all so important to Carleen at one time. With one sweeping roll of her head, she took it in—her Limoges boxes and silver Tiffany vase, the big comfy Chippendale wing chair with the pillow her mother had embroidered for her: a scene decorated with the Leaning Tower of Pisa, the Coliseum, the Trevi Fountain, and Lila Mae's favorite saying: "Rome wasn't built in a day!"

Outside, she could see the vanilla moon, full and luscious, and a branch of their persimmon tree drooping against the house. The souped-up motor of a teenager's car rumbled in someone's driveway, and the Dobermans—Danny Boy and Liberace—were snapping and barking at some unknown assailant.

The day after the discovery, a coffee and sunshine morning, one that included an unexpected affectionate kiss on her shoulder from Nelson, Carleen's mind played tricks on her and she wondered if she *did* foul up the wristwatch information. Could Nelson be right? Had he told her the watch she picked up was for Anna, after all? Nelson was correct about one thing: Half of what he told her went in one ear and out the other. Plus, she had so many things on her list of stuff to do that she *could* have confused the names. Swearing on Cassie's life, something she'd felt guilty about asking him to do, surely wasn't a promise he took lightly. That was Nelson's genius, gathering her insecurities and uncertainties, adding a touch of pigment here, a dab of varnish there, and creating a museum-quality portrait, one of those cubist women painted by Picasso with one big crack right down the center.

Suddenly, her airtight scenario confused her more than ever. But, honestly, outside of the embarrassment and expenditure, she wondered if she even cared all that much. When she got down to the base metal of the issue, Carleen could hardly stand Nelson. There were days when she couldn't bear the sound of his car in the driveway, days when she loathed the way he brushed his teeth, like a janitor scrubbing a stubborn floor, days when she thought their marriage had only one destination: divorce court.

What she wouldn't give to confess to Nelson that right before their wedding she had gotten cold feet, that it was only the idiotic reality that the matchbooks and napkins had already been personalized in gold print that kept her from backing out. To think that two doves holding a ribbon banner in their beaks with CARLEEN AND NELSON emblazoned on it was all that stood between her and freedom! How utterly absurd that for the price of some party favors, probably two hundred and fifty dollars or so, she might have avoided entrapment.

Chapter Twenty-eight

Irene

JULY 1999

If somebody had told Irene that a few months after she left Los Angeles, she'd be crouched in the vinery of a lush tomato garden in Headquarters, Kentucky, waiting for a common criminal named Butch Youngblood and his sister Coco Youngblood-Castle, to leave Butch's trailer home so she could catch Coco without her sling, all because she needed extra money to pay her ex-husband's $2,314 bill at Seat Cover Charlie's, she would have told them they needed psychiatric help.

But when Buddy McCracken had called Irene into his office to ask Irene if he should hire someone else to take over the job, she said, "No! I want to do this."

Irene's mission, her last chance for concrete evidence for court, was to catch Coco out of her sling. She dreaded to think that Buddy McCracken would be pounding the pavement for a job, and that she would be beating a path to Silkes's Funeral Parlor. It wouldn't be so hot for Miz Becky's either.

So, there Irene was, fifty feet from Butch Youngblood's trailer home, tucked behind taxus groves and tomato vines, waiting for Butch and Coco to emerge. She had not come to this graceless position with ease.

The hunt began in a foggy dawn where she had followed Coco from the Seelbach Hotel, the Castles' Kentucky station, to a cafe on the banks of the Ohio River to an antiques auction in Maysville where Coco and a friend successfully bid on an ormolu-decorated recamier and Dresden urns. After they had a catfish lunch at Lake Herrington, followed by an aimless drive that could have been for pleasure or to shake Irene. There were more antique shops, then back to the Seelbach for an early—and quick—dinner with Horace, before hightailing it to Blue Lick. Irene was pooped, but well-informed on Kentucky geographics. She practically knew every loop and corner of the state.

Since she arrived, which felt like an eternity but was only three hours ago, the twosome's shadowy figures had crossed the small square windows of Butch's trailer home several times, but that was it. That meant she still hadn't used any of the supplies in her duffel bag—a scratch pad and tape recorder, three cameras—including a Polaroid, one with several fancy attachments that she wasn't even sure she knew how to use, and a miniature one like the cameras the tabloid reporters used to take pictures of Elvis in his coffin.

There hadn't been a soul around when she got herself situated. Since then, all sorts of people had popped up: a UPS delivery man, a housewife walking her terrier, and girls playing ring around the rosie. To speed up the tempo, and get closer to the action, she loped behind the vegetable garden, stayed there until the coast was clear, then dashed to the Dumpster just twenty feet from Butch's trailer. After waiting a minute, she galloped to the trailer itself, picking one of the huge shrubs that shot out of the ground all around the double-wide. If her knees didn't give out and the greenery and Coco's vanilla cologne didn't cause her hay fever to flare up, she could stay there for hours. It wasn't exactly what she was hoping for, but she was determined to get the job done.

It was those last few fleeting moments before the sky, currently streaked with orange, turned indigo blue. Plus, it was ninety degrees and Irene was burning up. There was nothing to see, but soon enough Irene's heart was pounding and she was muttering, "Oh, my God! Oh, my God!" as she listened to a conversation that was so juicy she wondered if Butch and Coco were toying with her. She lifted her arm, and stuck her tape recorder to the tiny screened window.

Butch started it when he asked how long he thought it would be until Coco and Horace tore down their parents' old house. Coco said it would be a while, especially since they were having a tough time with the Wootens. "I'm sore at Joe Lee. He told me he was gonna sweet-talk Ole Lady Wooten, but that old crow ain't lettin' go so fast . . . now they've got that granddaughter from California throwin' her weight around. I never could stand that girl."

"There ain't nothing she can do, is there?" asked Butch.

"She might slow things down some, but ain't no use foolin' with Horse *and* the Blue Lick officials. If it gets bad, the city'll condemn. There's no way around it! Did I tell ya that Wooten woman went for my sling? She's a feisty one, but you think about it, that old bat can't live forever, now can she? Her bein' near a hun-red . . . I give her six months, if that."

"There's some who've thought that for years." Butch grunted.

"Why is everyone around here so hell-bent for leather, anyway? I don't know which is worse, the Wooten woman tryin' to twist my arm off or Hamilton Montgomery." Coco paused. "I thought I was done for when that rifle went off."

"I tried to tell you that before you went nosin' 'round Rosemont," Butch said. "You knew what you were gettin' into."

"You didn't tell me I'd get *shot!*"

"I don't know *ever'thang* . . . I *did* tell you to watch your step, though."

"Well, it's no skin off our teeth, anyway, is it, Butch? In the end, these squabbles don't 'mount to a hill of beans, and I got my way. You'll get more cash than you ever dreamed and I'll have all the property I want."

"I guess so. I just wisht it coulda turned out different . . ." Butch was momentarily nostalgic; then he said, "Eddie Ray, that stupid idiot . . . wouldn't listen to reason."

"Now . . . now, don't go soft on me, Butch. You said you wouldn't; we're lucky we ain't dead and gone ourselves. Nobody wanted Eddie Ray to get hit. Things just got out of hand. It was all *your* idea, anyway!"

"I mighta gone along with some of it, but it was your husband's idea to shake up Miz Becky's. Plus, I wuzn't the one who showed up with a loaded weapon. Hell, we coulda gone there with a squirt gun and it would have been all the same. We wuz just lookin' for a little fun. But no, Eddie Ray's gotta take the real thing. Now what wuz that sheriff gonna do with that moron wavin' a loaded rifle around? What choice did he have?"

"And who knew the place would be full up with people that night? You said you'd be surprised if there were two people inside. You never told me it would have all those eyewitnesses. And that sheriff, he wasn't supposed to be on duty, either!"

"I ain't no fortune teller!" Butch hollered.

"Yeah, you ain't the one six feet under either! But you know we had no choice but to run. What we were supposed to do, stand over someone who looked like they were already dead? Eddie Ray'd jumped in that car, too, if that sheriff hadn't gotten him. Now, who'd you rather be having this conversation with right now—me or that stinkin' brother of ours?"

"I'm just thinkin' shoulda-coulda-woulda."

"Oh, well. This time next year you'll be livin' the high life in Cancun," said Coco dreamily. "And I'll bide my time for a while, until I get everything I can get, then bye-bye, Horse, you old codger, and hello Frankie Snow! I never did get over that man."

"You know what worries me more than any of this, Coco?" Butch asked. "Horace. I just hope you don't blow it."

"Blow it?" said Coco, as if she'd never heard anything so absurd. "In what way?"

"Oh, you know . . . you could overplay your cards with that ole husband of yours."

"I'd be a darned fool to do it," Coco chuckled. "Now do I look like a darned fool?"

"I don't reckon . . . I just don't think it's such a hot idea . . . you meeting Frankie Snow here like you do."

"Just mind your own beeswax. I know what I'm doing. Now here's my game plan, I'm thinking about—"

Curled in a fetal position, out of tape recorder cassettes, batting away mosquitoes and furious that a hot-rodder had zoomed by to drown out the last speck of conclusive conversation, Irene was wondering how she got herself in such an idiotic situation, when lo and behold Maybelle came along. She was hanging out her car window, and calling out "Baby Sister" like one of those loudspeaker cars that urge people to vote for one candidate or another.

"Shit!" Irene moaned, "what's that *moron* doing here?" Butch must have heard Maybelle, too. He had already opened the door, looked left, then right, like an outlaw checking before a fast getaway. Irene, panting and furious, made a dash for it, running on bent knees like a Russian cossack dancer until she reached a garbage bin several yards from the trailer. She waited a moment before heading for the crepe myrtles, only to have Butch turn the light on real fast like he was trying to catch the person off guard. Finally, she reached the car.

"Mother Wooten is just beside herself!" said Maybelle. "Beside herself. She thought your head was bashed in with a baseball bat or something. She thought you were *dead!* Big Dee and Little Peep are covering the west end. They're worried, too."

Great, thought Irene. She was over forty years old and every time she was five minutes late, somebody called the cops. How was she to know, when she parked Olive's car, that a busybody would call the police to tow it away? But if it hadn't been some concerned citizen, Olive would have still tracked her down—part of the agony and ecstasy of a small town. On top of that, Maybelle kept giving her sly glances and pelting her with questions and insinuating remarks. "What were you doin' over this way, anyhow . . . as if I didn't already know, heh heh!" At least Irene had a ride home.

On the way back to Blue Lick, they passed the old Cherokee Mill surrounded by CASTLECO cranes. In an empty field, they saw a big illuminated sign: COMING SOON—CASTLE HEIGHTS. Maybelle sighed, "There they go again!"

"There they go, all right," Irene said. "I can't wait for them to be going . . . going . . . GONE."

Maybelle hunched her shoulders girlishly and said, "I know so many are against them, but I really do think they're good for this place. I mean what's wrong sprucin' the town up some? Not everyone likes the old-timey look, ya know."

When Irene moved to Blue Lick, all the changes hardly registered. But Maybelle's endless twittering rubbed her the wrong way. "Sprucing up is one thing," Irene said. "*Tearing* it up is another. If money *is* the root of all evil," she continued in her best Rebecca voice, "then the Devil himself is kicking up his heels in glee over Blue Lick Springs."

Irene had tried to be civil, but she wished the woman would clam up so she could unscramble everything in her head. She also couldn't wait to call Jimmy Buzz Burkle and tell him that she'd cracked the case that everybody seemed to have on a back burner, one that nobody but Olive thought needed to be cracked. Her head was bursting with preambles and tailpieces of scenarios to craft together.

Let's see, Eddie Ray was dead, he'd gone "haywire" whatever that meant . . . both Eddie Ray and Butch were . . . wait a minute . . . Butch said Eddie took a loaded gun . . . which wasn't the plan . . . so, let's see, Butch was egged on by Horace and Coco to raise some ruckus at Miz Becky's, got Eddie Ray involved, maybe even recruited the person in the getaway car. But, it seemed to be Coco in the getaway car . . . or no, it didn't have to happen like that either. Maybe Eddie Ray *had* started it all at Miz Becky's, Butch tried to stop him from going nuts . . . and then Coco tried to save the day, and in the process of breaking up the fight between the two brothers accidentally ended up shooting Eddie Ray in self-defense, but that couldn't be it either because if it did happen like that, what in tarnation was Sheriff Burkle doing during all this, watching *The West Wing*?

Shit, Irene thought, *this wasn't as simple as all the crime shows made it out to be.* She wasn't sure it had actually come to her yet, that one chiming, Big Ben of a moment, or maybe she already had it right. Maybe the three Youngbloods—Coco, Butch, and Eddie—had gone to Miz Becky's with some plain, old-fashioned mischief in mind, the type of mischief Olive said Horace Castle was causing all over town. Things went wrong when Eddie Ray started waving a loaded gun around, Sheriff Burkle had no choice but to respond, and Coco and Butch managed to escape.

It irked Irene that one new reality gave birth to dozens. But, after all, there was only so much Irene could contribute . . . at some point, the police would have to pitch in and do their share. That was another thing, who knew how they would take all this? Sure, there were still blanks to fill in, but three things were certain: Coco and Butch were at Miz Becky's that night, the situation was definitely *not* an open-and-shut case, and it really was beginning to sound like her grandmother had been on the right track.

In any event, in Irene's carryall bag were stacks of notes and photographs, even one with Coco in her sling. She would assemble a dossier, including the Polaroids; she would listen to the tape of Butch and Coco, documenting all the twos and twos. She could visualize Bud Mc-Cracken's face as he heard the news that the arm Coco claimed was injured at Miz Becky's actually had a bullet hole in it, compliments of Hamilton Montgomery! All that would be reflected in her official investigative report.

As they drove through town, the sky was dark and starless and streaked with rain clouds. There was a hot, brisk wind blowing through all of Blue Lick Springs. At the intersection of Main Street and Maple Avenue the traffic signal undulated left and right. The newly installed awning at Miss Lila Mae's Confectionery and the sundresses of the little girls standing outside Miz Becky's were flapping like Fourth of July flags.

Along the way, they passed the Dairy Deluxe and one house with a dozen floodlit signs decorating its yard like lollipops: VOTE FOR OTIS BURR ATHERTON FOR COUNTY JAILER . . . SEND OTIS TO JAIL! Not too far from Olive's farm, the Heart of Five Pentecostal sign caught her eye: GOD IS LIKE G.E. HE LIGHTS UP OUR PATH!

Maybelle said, "I don't know who dreams them silly things up, do you?"

Right before they reached Olive's driveway, Irene told Maybelle to make a quick U-turn, that she had a feeling. Maybelle arched her brow and said, "All riiiiight, if you say so," then they drove three miles out of town to swing by Butch Youngblood's trailer once more, to see if something might have gone on after she left.

In this little partnership with God that Irene had going, she had come to believe that there was nothing happenstance about these random spottings of His word, not that there was anything in the Bible that referred to General Electric . . . but still, there must have been some relevance to the fact that the sign was in front of her nose.

That's why when they returned to Butch Youngblood's place, Irene was crestfallen to see that this so-called lighted path that God provided had led her to a spot where absolutely nothing had changed. The trailer light was still on, the spotted terrier still barked at strangers, and Coco and Butch were nowhere to be found. There was also no sign of Frankie Snow's fire-engine-red Cadillac.

Well, maybe the whole mess couldn't be wrapped up in one night, but it was just a matter of time until Irene was front-page news. She could see the headlines in the *Blue Lick Springs Gazette:* EXTRA! EXTRA! NEWCOMER INSTRUMENTAL IN CRACKING ROBBERY DEATH AND INSURANCE FRAUD RING.

Chapter Twenty-nine

Rebecca

AUGUST 1999

On their next visit to Rosemont—the one that they prayed would be the charm—nobody even answered the door for several minutes. Standing there, Rebecca thought she already detected the pungent fragrance of Horace Castle's Cohiba cigars and the putrid vanilla of Coco's cologne. Finally, from a high-reaching peak they heard the ecclesiastical pealing of a china bell, which could have been Ramona ringing for help or Minetta toying with their sanity. At long last, they spotted a head peeking through a porthole that looked like a tiny birdhouse.

In spite of Olive's lugubrious mood after the fateful phone call from Hamilton Montgomery, they had learned that the sale of Rosemont was not exactly sealed—that in any part of the world other than the South, where a handshake was Rock of Gibraltar solid—it would be considered no agreement at all. They hoped this, along with petitions and other new evidence against the Castles would sway Montgomery once and for all.

Rebecca and Olive agreed to visit in the spirit of bygones being bygones, using reverse psychology and other bargain-basement approaches they probably wouldn't be able to stick to. Even as they stood at Rosemont's threshold, waiting for Hamilton Montgomery to open up, Olive had warned Rebecca to keep her head about her. "A soft answer turneth away wrath, but grievous words stir up anger," she preached; "When a man's ways please the Lord, he maketh even his enemies to be at peace with him," and so on. Rebecca had said, "Okay, Grandma . . . I get the message."

It took several minutes until Hamilton Montgomery appeared through a half-opened door, wearing a robe and slippers. He smelled of charcoal and fusty leaves and his adamantine eyes gave his face a state-your-business expression.

They came bearing gifts—cookies, soft-centered fruit bars, and green-apple wine—which they plunked on the iron patio table where they sat trying to get satisfaction out of the man. They began the usual way, with charm and small talk, even pretending to adore Montgomery's shaggy Irish setter who was chained to a lawn chair and circled Rebecca's legs until they were both imprisoned in rusty links.

"Now, Hamilton," Olive said. "I know what yer a-thinkin', but I ain't gonna argue none. We really just come to leave ya this." She tapped the wine bottle and handed it to the man. "My granddaughter here got all fired up and she didn't mean to take this back the other day. My other girl made ya these." She pushed a basket of lemon sugar cookies toward him.

They bided their time, waiting for an opportunity to broach the inevitable topic. Finally, Olive said, "I say a person kin take this handshake business too far, Hamilton . . . Unless it's my hand doin' the shakin'!"

After hemming and hawing and coughing into a gray cloth, Montgomery astounded them both by saying, "Well, I probably should have told you first off but, I went ahead and signed—"

"You *signed* and it's f-final?" Rebecca stuttered. "Yesterday, you told Grandma it was spoken for, but none of the papers were drawn . . . you said it wasn't concrete, wasn't ironclad."

"I didn't mean to lead you astray. But things changed in the meantime; they, uh, put a gun to my head, so to speak . . . one of those now-or-never deals. So, now the sale is, is all set. It's subject to surveys, title searches, the normal contingencies."

"So yer a-tellin' me this place is *gone,* Hamilton?" Olive pinned him down with her scowling eyes. "Well, then yer right. This wuz jest a big wasta time."

Rebecca had battled to look unfazed, but all hope was trickling out of her. The nerve of the sadistic Montgomery to string them along like that! As if she didn't already know, she asked, "Who'd you sell the property to?"

"Uh, Horace Castle." The man seemed embarrassed.

"Ya see, Hamilton?" Olive slapped her palm on the table. "If it's really fer the airport, then it's the City shoulda bought it from ya, not an individ-ull!"

"Castle's the developer, and it's his holding company that's handling all the transactions for the city. That's why they wrote it up that way."

"Mr. Montgomery," Rebecca rushed to answer, "we've been investigating this project and something isn't right."

"You two got me to thinking, I'll give you that, so I made some inquiries and I was told the airport *is* happening. You keep saying it's a land grab, but it doesn't make sense—"

"It don't *have* to make no sense, Hamilton. The people who's tryin' to take yer land from ya, they's gonna tell ya it's all set." Olive thwacked the table so hard the dog growled. "I have it on good authority, it's as phony as a three-dollar bill!"

"I don't know how much they're paying you, but I'd pay you more," Rebecca, turning greedy and desperate, said. "Is there a way to get out of your deal?"

"Well," Mr. Montgomery's hand tugged at his thick beige ear, "I'd hate to do it, seeing that I gave my word and signed the papers and all. . . ."

"If the shoe wuz on the other foot, Castle and that Youngblood woman wouldn't think twicet 'bout two-timin' ya!" Olive set her nervous eyes on him. "A smart man lak you should see that."

When he seemingly mused and reconsidered the topic, crossing his legs and clearing his throat and dragging out the word "Welllll," for one split second—one that felt like an eternity—Rebecca prayed there was a chance. But, then, he cocked his head, scooted up to sit very tall in his chair, and said, "No, ma'am, I can't see myself changing anything at this point."

"If that's yer final answer, then this house is bulldozer food!" Olive hissed. "I'm sorry to see it turn out lak this."

It was all Rebecca could do to keep from shrieking or sobbing or crowning the old crow, but at least she didn't grab the wine bottle and the remaining sweets from Montgomery's table and stomp out, slamming the front door the way Olive did, rattling the nerves of the resident ghosts, and leaving Hamilton Montgomery licking lemon icing from his fingers and nursing a quizzical expression in his black, fretful eyes.

Even though Olive hadn't stuck to the plan to remain cool, calm, and collected, Rebecca wanted to end on a halfway decent note. "We know you made a deal, and we respect that," she said, carefully weaving her words together, infusing them with phony empathy. "But just in case anything falls through, let us know."

Hamilton said he would keep all that in mind, but he couldn't promise anything. He didn't tell them good riddance, but he did say, "These conversations are upsetting Ramona." Then he laced his large hands, spread like a lady's fan, against the table and pushed himself up. After cinching the bathrobe around himself, he shut the door.

Completely forgetting her own advice to leave on a high note, Olive left banging her cane against the herringbone brick, ranting her way back to the Buick. "Fer some reason Castle gives ya a bad check, JUST LAK THE SOB DONE TO SO MANY OTHERS," she hollered, "then you come to us, Hamilton. Yip, Castle'll do ya wrong, sure as shootin'!"

It was a windy, mauve dusk as they drove down Rosemont's gravel driveway. They passed the ancient Kentucky coffee tree and Minetta's fountain, cracked and filled with twigs and, according to Olive, dancing wraiths. "Shush!" she said, she heard something. "That'd be *her!*" Overhead were hundreds of birds hurling across the sky as if competing in a race with the fast-moving storm clouds. Maybe they were simply shooing them off the property.

How foolish Rebecca felt for her imaginary possession of Rosemont, one that skirted the fault lines of delusion. In her head, she had planned lawn parties where nimble-footed dancers would do the Virginia reel and all the Rhetts and Scarletts would sip mint juleps in chilled silver tumblers. How ridiculous that she continued to cradle her notions like a mother desperately clutches a doomed child to her bosom.

The sad part was that Rosemont's destiny wasn't to be bulldozer food at all. Like a cobra coiling upward to the notes of the flute, it would rise from the ashes, only to be turned into some godawful house that *Dynasty* built. Coco Castle would putter around with antique baskets and straw bonnets, picking long-stemmed roses from her garden. There would be Liberace candelabra and bathroom fixtures with gold swan's heads and all sorts of other ornamental monstrosities that would keep the town in exciting gossip and the house from ever seeing its potential.

When they'd gotten the first call from Montgomery telling them the property was sold, Rebecca had phoned David to shake him up. At the time she really didn't believe Rosemont was a lost cause, but she played it up like that anyway. "It's sold," she'd said, with a dolorous tone, "Rosemont's gone."

"Good, I was afraid you'd buy it!"

"Good?" she had whined. "I wanted that house! Now it's lost *forever!*"

"I'm sorry, honey . . . I know you're disappointed."

Although he hadn't come right out and said he always wanted her to have it and other malarkey that was only safe to say after the coast was clear, still David didn't seem as vehemently against the purchase of Rosemont as she had suspected. But now his fantasy compliance did her no good at all.

Suddenly, all of Rebecca's other Blue Lick projects diminished in importance. Even the good news they'd received just that morning, that the preservation board would prevent Castle from building on a Civil War battlefield, meant little. Sadly, the only thing that seemed to be going Horace Castle's way was Rosemont.

Years earlier, when Rebecca's world was flat, she believed this land flowed forever, that if she ventured to its edge, she would fall into some plumbless black pit. But now, as they toured the back gulches of Rosemont, they quickly reached the cusp of Olive's land. To the north of them was the vacant parcel soon to be Honeysuckle Acres and at night when Rebecca stood on the hill that used to overlook silos and tobacco barns, when the only light before her was the north star, she could now see the chain stores and towers that supplied water and cellular service to the onslaught of houses.

When, through the woods, Olive spotted some stone ruins, one of her girlhood hide-and-seek spots, she told Rebecca to veer off to the right. Her eyes hopscotched to the makeshift graveyard, where five or six headstones, all tilted this way and that like a mouthful of crooked teeth, were situated.

"Huh, I wonder who all they got in thar?" Olive twisted her neck like a swan, muttering, "Problee . . . Minetta and Babette and Dolly and them. I wisht I had me a camera."

They passed over a bumpy carriage trail dodging the hedge apples and ravines, driving in an awkward void as they approached the property line separating Rosemont from Olive's back pasture. As they kissed Rosemont good-bye, Olive stretched over her shoulder. As she took a last glance, her eyes glazed like the first frost of fall.

"Now I know where we are, Grandma," said Rebecca. "That's the Saint John's Wort and mint that Irene's been using. This is how we went a few weeks ago. I jogged through here."

"You wuz joggin' out this away?"

"Well, sure," Rebecca said. "I gotta make it to my nineties, like you, Grandma!"

"Well, ya won't git thar a-joggin'!" Olive leaned out in an analytical jut. "Well, lookee at that, wud ya. . . ? Wait a minute," she said, holding up her palm. "Stop, will ya?"

Opening the door slowly, she swung both legs out of the car. She kicked some hedge apples from underfoot, then plunged her cane into the soil. She lowered her eyes, and took one look at the object of her curiosity. "Well, I'll be," she grumbled. "That ain't no mint or Saint John's Wort or nothin' normal at all. That's MURRAY-WANNA!"

"Marijuana?" Rebecca squealed. "How did *that* get here?" Her first thought was that Baby Sister had something to do with it, but Olive had other ideas.

"So that's what that no good's been up to." She stitched her eyes into narrow slots as if piecing all the circumstances together like a crazy quilt. She looked upward as if addressing her thoughts to the white oak limbs and said, "I'm gonna skin that Butch Youngblood alive!"

Chapter Thirty

Rebecca

AUGUST 1999

Instead of burning the crops before anybody found out (which wouldn't have worked anyway, because before anyone could bat an eye, the information was smeared across the front page of the *Blue Lick Springs Gazette*), Olive said they should "turn themselves in before the law got to 'em."

Jimmy Buzz Burkle had assured them that the incident would be handled with the utmost sensitivity, so it was a complete shock when they woke up to the headline "Local Granny Lets Grass Grow Under Her Feet." Beneath the story was a fiend-eyed Olive with a varicose finger thrust in the face of Mayor Cheatham. The snapshot, taken years before at a heated city council meeting, also caught Shorty. He was in the background threatening some other fellow who was taking up for the mayor.

The *Gazette* article said the "drug ring has been cultivating the crop on property owned by Olive Adams-Wooten and her son Curtis, both longtime residents of Blue Lick Springs." The star witness was Butch Youngblood. He was described as the groundskeeper at the Wooten farm and here's what he said: "Miss Olive had me growing the marijuana crop for medicinal purposes. At least that's what I was told. I was just following orders."

"Medicinal purposes, my foot!" Olive lurched forward like a hungry lioness. "If Butch Youngblood kin say that, then I'll claim it's hemp . . . tell 'em we wuz gonna manufacture ropes and all." Rebecca pointed out that hemp was just as illegal as marijuana. "It might be," Olive countered, "but I seen people get off on less, ain't you?"

The article went on to state that Butch Youngblood had an obligation to the community to turn Miss Wooten in. "It's too bad she will lose that farm and have to sell all her property on account of this. I know how important that land is to her family, but the *law* is the *law*."

Since everybody assumed Butch was behind the whole thing, they got quite a surprise when Horace Castle appeared on *Good Morning, Kentuckiana!* According to the uberdeveloper, he'd been checking out some property and just happened to pass over the Wooten land in his helicopter. As a law-abiding citizen, it was his responsibility to alert the state officials, who ended up taking some infrared aerial photographs.

"I've met Olive Wooten and she seemed to be a fine lady." Castle blinked his eyes with the innocence of a newborn babe. "I am as surprised as the next one."

Coco, dressed like Audrey Hepburn in *My Fair Lady,* had on a canary-yellow hat with a coiled feather, and was standing with her good arm slipped through her husband's. The feather cast a shadow across her face that frolicked on her nose and lipsticked mouth like a sing-along dot. The poodles had on jeweled collars and were in a small basket to the side.

"I feel the same as Horse. We recently met with Mrs. Wooten and there was no indication *at all* that these type of goings on were," she stopped for a girlish giggle before continuing, "well . . . going on! When I grew up here, we knew of the Wooten family . . . even though we ran in different circles, and . . ." Coco would have gone on forever if an annoyed Horace Castle hadn't finally cupped his hand over the microphone.

Even though it had nothing to do with the case, another anonymous source piped up. "They was all kinds of comings and goings out to the Wootens. It was a haven for out-of-towners. Anytime of day or night you could find people galore."

"This is ridiculous!" Rebecca threw the paper to the floor in disgust. "This makes it sound like a hippie commune! I wonder who said that."

"I'll tell ya what I wonder. What makes Butch think I'm gonna lose my property?" Olive asked. "If anyone's responsible, it's that scalawag. He'd better not show his face 'round here and I mean it!" Then she turned to the sheriff and said, "I ain't planted eny murray-wanna, Jimmy Buzz, the one to go after is Butch Youngblood and ya kin print that in the *Gazette*, too!"

"I don't guess you did, Miz Olive," the sheriff said

"And Curtis, he don't have nothin' to do with it neither. He's a man of the law hisself." Olive paused, as if to rethink the situation. "Least as fer as I know. Son, ya ain't part of this, is ya?"

"*Hell, no!* I ain't guilty!" Shorty, who had been ashen with fear, popped up to defend himself. Mostly, he was scared stiff that they wouldn't let him leave town, and Maybelle had an Avon convention in New Orleans that was all the two had talked about. "Whoever is responsible, you tell 'em they'll be hearin' from Shorty Wooten! They'll hear from *me* all right!"

For a while, they thought Irene would be in hot water, too, because another source said, "Miss Olive's granddaughter cooks with it, calls it by some other name—*stevia* or some such."

"This'll be just *great* for the confectionery," Irene said sarcastically. "We'll be lucky to get *any* business."

"Ya never kin tell," Olive disagreed. "It could push it right to the top."

"What *is* that stuff, anyways?" Shorty said. "Maybe that ain't no herb you been a cookin' with, unless you call murray-wanna a herb."

"It's *stevia!* S-T-E-V-I-A. Don't you think I know what marijuana looks like? I *know* what I'm cooking with!" But when Irene turned to Olive and said, "I *have* been cooking with stevia, haven't I?" the old woman said, "I don't rightly know."

Initially they thought Butch was exaggerating about losing the farm, but Little Peep found out differently. "You see," he said, "the land could be seized by the government and there are heavy penalties to pay. You could really lose your property. Miss Olive, you couldn't have picked a worse state to grow marijuana in."

"I swear on a stack of Bibles, I didn't have nuthin' to do with the G.D. stuff!" Olive leapt up and pumped her fist.

One fact was clear: Olive had been right all along; behind each incident lurked Horace Castle. He and his wife were determined to get the property they wanted, regardless of what it took to accomplish it.

Rebecca went straight to the page on her laptop that said: BLUE LICK SPRINGS PRESERVATION. Out of all the pending leads on her list, somehow Baby Sister's name had inched its way up to the top. In her various cloak-and-dagger dealings with insurance records and claimants and whatever else it was that she did with her laptop in the semidarkness of her bedroom, Irene had come up with some very interesting information on Ms. Youngblood, more than information actually . . . a real bombshell. Nobody could get Irene to open up, not even Olive, who kept saying, "Come on, Baby Sister, tell us what ya got!" and not even Rebecca who said, "I can't believe this after all I've done for you. . . ."

Irene claimed she would have liked nothing more than to capture everyone's attention at the dinner table, to have them all leaning across the chinoiserie platters bending their ears for the scoop. But Irene wasn't being stubborn for the sheer joy of it. The walls in Blue Lick Springs had acoustical powers. One by one each gossipmonger would ask, "Can you keep a secret?" then swear the other person to secrecy and before you knew it, there would be several hundred people walking around with sealed lips. So Irene told them they'd find out all in good time. Whenever Irene was tempted to give a sneak preview, she remembered a quote from Benjamin Franklin, "Three can keep a secret, if two of them are dead."

Word had been circulating that the Castles were organizing a town meeting, one designed to muffle their critics, win over the skeptics, and instill renewed enthusiasm in their supporters. So, Irene decided to reveal her information with one dramatic yank of the theater curtain. She would unveil what she had at the town meeting and not a minute before.

Chapter Thirty-one

Carleen

AUGUST 1999

On the day of the actual spraying, the sun blazed like a copper kettle. Robins and wrens hopped from willow to willow and the fragrance of mint and garden roses mingled with an undertow of ether from a nearby industrial park. Three men from A-1 Pest whom Carleen had never laid eyes on before—Monty Doggett, the head technician; his son, Red; and Henry Pettigrew invaded the interior like locusts. The two Doggetts were cookie-cutter identical: rail-thin with concave chests and tangerine hairdos. Pettigrew was seal slick and reeked of a tangy cologne. He was swinging a radio that was tuned to a talk show.

It was bad enough that they had arrived thirty minutes early, right when every busybody in the neighborhood was leaving for work, but over a dozen foreign men milled around the lawn like wiggle worms. They were unloading the garish Ringling Bros. tent, barking at one another in some Tower of Babel chatter. Plus, there were hoses and metal canisters and all sorts of other junk.

Carleen dragged Doggett to the front porch and pointed to the hullaballoo outside. "What's next, elephants and lion tamers? A few harmless, magical poofs in the air . . . just leave for twenty-four hours, ha!

Where's Lenny Slidell, the snake oil salesman who sold me this bill of goods?"

"Slidell?" Monty Doggett raised his orange eyebrows and checked his two associates. "He got axed, didn't he?"

"*Axed?* How could *that* be?" Carleen griped. "I thought he owned the company!"

"Oh, right . . . he's retiring." Pettigrew traded glances with his part- ners. "Maybe he'll show up later . . . to *supervise*."

"Well, he'll get an earful from me. He *never* told me to remove *all* the food from my shelves and plants from the rooms. I don't have time for all this. I, I have a column to write!"

"Lad-ee," Monty Doggett purred, patting Carleen's hand gingerly. "Now it ain't no big deal. We do this ever'day!"

"I can't believe Slidell didn't tell you everything." Pettigrew was fum- ing, little spurts of menthol breath.

"Take my word for it, he didn't. And, what's this sick as a dog and woozy business I heard you say? My daughter has respiratory problems. All I heard was how *safe* Pantazine is."

"Well, not right after we spray, it ain't! Any *fool* knows that!" Doggett Sr. was getting testy, the type she'd written about in one of her columns on service people who, with their hot tempers, shouldn't be working with the public.

"It's not no Chanel No. 5!" Red Doggett howled, throwing his head back like a patient in a dentist's chair. Then he glanced at his father for approval. The trio got quite a kick out of that one.

"Excuse me while I get my dunce cap . . . ! Better yet, let me get my husband. He's an *attorney!*"

Nelson was in the last stages of grooming—slapping on cologne, knotting his tie, smoothing his brow—a process that brought to mind Victorian society ladies at their dressing table. He opened his cuff link drawer, choosing the Cloisonne dragons, and threaded first one, then the other through his French cuffs, probably all for Anna Traminsky's benefit.

"Wait until you see the madhouse downstairs," Carleen said. "You'll be thrilled, I'm sure!"

Without responding, Nelson picked up his briefcase, grabbed his car keys, and puckered his lips midair for his customary good-bye kiss. But Carleen crossed her arms like two blades and swiveled her face away from him. "I'm not a light switch that can be turned on and off."

"Is this what I have to deal with all weekend?" Nelson, shifting his briefcase, glared at her. "Your moods?"

"This isn't a *mood*; this is an *opinion*. I just wish you would hold your horses." Carleen swept her arm toward the ruckus downstairs. "I went along with this against my better judgment, but, but just look at that mess!"

"Jesus, Carleen. I don't have time for this nonsense. See ya!" he called cheerfully.

Several of the foreigners had dashed upstairs, taking the steps two at a time, whizzing past Carleen. The Doggetts were whipping the sheets and comforters off the beds; one man was in charge of the kitchen cupboards. Carleen streaked past the technicians, padding down the steps to catch her husband. "Nelson, that's *it?*"

"Look, you've been beating this dead horse for weeks. Some people don't have all day to chat. *Some* people have work to do." Nelson spoke like a parent lecturing a child. "But we're going to have a serious talk this weekend. I am worried about you, Carleen. You've been acting *very* strange lately."

"*I've* been acting strange?" Carleen made goggles with her eyes and punched her breastbone. "*Me?*"

"Yes, *you*. The office is still buzzing about your behavior at Harold's retirement party. There are other things, *many* other things. Anna Traminsky said she bumped into you a while back. She said you were performing . . . at Fisherman's Wharf."

"Performing? Fisherman's Wharf? That's ridiculous." Carleen could feel the familiar orange flush pumping into her cheeks. "You mean Anna the owner of the gold watch and Mildred's earrings . . . *that* Anna Traminsky?" Maybe she could distract Nelson, keep the A-1 gang involved; how bad could it get if Pettigrew and the Doggetts were in the picture?

"Carleen!" Nelson set down his briefcase. "Now that you have my attention, we might as well get the whole story out."

"I've gotta get a move on. I still haven't packed for the weekend . . ." Carleen was doing her Lila Mae wit's end routine, racing around like someone about to escape a burning house. "I've got my column to finish . . . I'm up to my eyeballs!"

"Carleen!" Nelson slapped one hand against the wall, slanting his body to make a small prison cell. "What's going on? Anna said you were singing with some bum with a tin cup. This is *highly embarrassing*."

"Highly embarrassing?" Carleen was cornered like a frightened animal looking into the barrel of a hunter's rifle. "It's highly mysterious. Tell Ms. Traminsky to have her eyesight checked."

Yes, it was true that months before—in fact the last time she'd seen Billy Cooper—they'd sung "Turkey in the Straw" for Japanese school kids, who had given Billy Cooper their spare change. So, yes, she had stupidly circulated through the crowd, snatching the dimes and nickels like an organ grinder's monkey. But, what pure, unadulterated bad fortune that Nelson's law partner, an archenemy at that, had seen Carleen in the middle of the day, particularly since that person was usually miles away preparing legal briefs to free vicious criminals. Oh, it was simply too embarrassing to imagine!

"Do you know how humiliating it is for my wife to be panning for pennies with a guttersnipe?" Nelson was gawking at her like a hypnotist stares at their subject. "I simply *won't* put up with it."

By now the A-1 technicians were huddling in a conspiratorial semicircle, watching the exchange through the banana tree leaves. Carleen grabbed the radio and turned it up full blast. "Just tell her I'm writing a column on panhandlers or street culture. That woman hates me. Besides, I'm sure she's lying."

"She has no reason to fabricate," said Nelson, in a very matter-of-fact tone. "Believe me."

"Ha!" Carleen snickered. "I suppose she saves her lies for court or the *bedroom*."

"What's gotten into you lately? Look." The punch of Nelson's finger boring into her shoulder felt like a knifeblade. "As I said, *some* of us have a career. We'll discuss this later. I'll see you and Cassie tonight at the airport."

"Maybe you won't, Nelson . . ." Carleen's voice trailed off. "Maybe you won't . . ." As she listened to the notes drift away, tumbling through the air like smoky curlicues, and watched her husband move farther and farther away from her, a fragment of their old relationship flickered before her, the husband that for a brief moment in time had been her confidant. She thought about running after him, pumping his sleeve and telling him that what they had to say to one another couldn't wait. But she was too slow to catch him, anyway. In that sparkle of a moment, she hated the sight of him. She cringed as the scuffed soles of his shoes took flight, wincing at her, and smashing the dichondra in his wild scramble for freedom. She hated watching as a jovial Nelson hobnobbed with the A-1 crew.

"Hey, guys," he yelled to Doggett and Pettigrew, "while you're at it, get rid of this antique crap, too. Ha, ha!" He pointed to the Chippendale chairs and a mohair settee. The confused men looked into the blank air, their hoses suspended before them.

She wanted to shout, "Just leave!" as he lingered at the door of the Jaguar. Finally, he gunned the engine and he was off in a puff of blue exhaust.

Inside, the technicians were at full speed. The radio was turned to a rock station, Bob Seger singing: "Roll, roll me away; won't you roll me away tonight? I too am lost, I feel double-crossed . . ." The driving beat of the song created a motivating tempo as their nimble hands shifted their gear, uncoiling and adjusting equipment. They hoisted perishable items from the pantry shelves and bided their time until the outside crew completed the tent.

Surprisingly, just having Nelson out of her hair was a relief. The upbeat music made the quarrel's acidic taste diminish and depression seemed to lift from Carleen's shoulders on the engine of the lyrics. The radio song was about a motorcycle driver and a waitress who had left all their troubles behind and were having a great time driving across America. . . . "and we rolled clean out of sight."

The words made Carleen buoyant, as if the life being sung about was her own. Anyway, very soon, that would be Carleen out on the open road, not a care in the world as she and Rebecca and Ava and Cassie rolled toward Kentucky. There would be Lila Mae's birthday party and lazy summer days with her grandmother's lemonade and sugar cookies and humid starry nights on the veranda.

Whenever Carleen remembered the upcoming weekend with Nelson, she felt the clamp of prison bars. She and Cassie were supposed to meet him at the airport that evening, when they would board a plane for Santa Barbara. During the next few days, they would stroll along the Pacific's jagged shoreline, eat brunch at the Biltmore Hotel, read classic novels, and have long, meaningful conversations with a fourteen-year-old girl who hardly uttered a word to them these days. Then, Tuesday morning, they would return to a spic, span, and healthy house. Sure. With Nelson gone, with some kernel of rebellious optimism rising within her, Carleen had half a mind to forget all about Santa Barbara. She'd pick up Cassie and they would cruise south, all the way to Los Angeles where they would stay with Rebecca until it was time to drive to Kentucky. In the meantime, they could lolligag in the Jacuzzi, shop at Neiman Marcus and lunch on jambalaya and Sassicaia at the Ivy. Ava and Cassie would prowl through the malls, buying glitter nail polish and the latest Adidas.

Then at night David would join them for dinner in some Mexican dive where they'd eat chips and guacamole, washing it down with icy Corona beer. Carleen would watch the way David and Rebecca mooned over each other like two teenagers in love, setting the standard for true love impossibly high. But just the fantasy of a weekend with her sister gave Carleen an unexpected boost.

When a car pulled into the driveway, dread enveloped Carleen and she said, "Shit!" realizing that once again, and just like he did almost every day, probably just to torture her, Nelson had forgotten his wallet or briefcase. With her husband there was no such thing as a clean getaway. But it wasn't Nelson at all, it was Lenny Slidell. He stood in the doorway, his small figure bleached by a beam of white sun.

"Mr. Slidell!" Carleen posed at the top of the staircase, her palm touching her chest in surprise. For some unknown reason, the sight of a familiar face cheered her up and on impulse, she flew downstairs. "I knew those men couldn't be right. They said you were *axed!*"

The man was looking very incognito, with a small tan cap pulled low on his head and oversized blue sunglasses that looked like two teacup saucers. His head slipped from left to right and he said, "Could we go into the kitchen? I need to let you in on a couple of things . . . uh, confidential things." When he said the word *confidential* his voice scraped rock bottom. All across his body, patches of sweat were cropping up.

"Uh, Mrs. Carlyle, you didn't catch *60 Minutes* last week, did you?" Slidell was balanced on a bar stool while Carleen brewed coffee. Before she could respond, Slidell told her the show was an exposé of the extermination racket. "I was that mysterious silhouette who blew the whistle on the whole mess. I was hoping you saw me."

"You were on *60 Minutes? You* were on *television?*" Carleen's eyes shuddered in disbelief. The fact that there was a whistle to be blown or that the words *racket* and *mess* were used, shouldn't have surprised her, but there was more to it than mere shock or curiosity. Rounding out the assortment of reactions was a tinge of envy. From a box being carted out of the house, she grabbed the vanilla wafers and two coffee mugs.

"You see, Mrs. Carlyle," he sighed, his shoulders rising and settling to demonstrate the heaviness of his millstone. "I was in a real pickle. I'm no squealer, but I gotta family to support and I got more aches and pains than Los Angeles has illegal aliens, and ailments the doctors don't even have names for. Plus, I'm no good at lying and that's ninety-five percent of this job." Slidell was coughing like a motor scooter misfiring.

"*Ninety-five-percent lying?*" Carleen asked, her voice cracking like a pubescent boy. "Wh-what *kind* of lying?"

"For starters, some places don't even have an insect problem. They send men out with live worms and termites, even give 'em a little bottle to carry 'em in. We're supposed to go into some hard-to-reach spot and then come back with something crawling inside our kerchief, like the critters caught us off guard. We also have a tin box with wood shavings. We shake 'em around chair legs and windowsills, you know, something the termites supposedly left behind."

Carleen's jaw went slack, and she said, "Are you kidding me?" As astounding as Slidell's gimmick was, what really shocked her was that she had told Nelson that Slidell was like those solitary confinement prisoners who train cockroaches and rats to do tricks, something like the Birdman of Alcatraz. Nelson had said she was off her rocker.

"So, are you telling me, after all this, we don't even *have* termites?" Carleen should have been relieved, but with so much water under the bridge, she was hoping the house was swarming with them. "Is that what you're saying?"

"Oh, you got termites all right, but they ain't nearly as bad as I had you believe and they ain't from Vietnam, either. You see, Mrs. Carlyle." He leaned toward her until they were face to face. "They're gonna recall Pantazine. You might as well drink strychnine as to breathe that stuff."

"Strychnine? Wait a minute." An alarm clanged in Carleen's head. "What about that liquid you drank, wasn't that Pantazine?"

"No, Mrs. Carlyle." Slidell rubbed his whiskers, sucking in a regretful breath. "That was tap water in that glass. I keep it in a metal drum, the same container Pantazine comes in. You see what I mean by crooked?"

"Yes, I am beginning to see it in twenty-twenty vision." Carleen sighed heavily, trying to assess all the stray puzzle pieces that were dropping from the sky like acid rain.

"There's something else . . . I'm not Smitty's son and I'm no musician." Slidell flicked his two thumbnails together and paused. "Mrs. Carlyle, I wouldn't know what to do with a violin if my life depended on it. That's Smitty for ya; he's got to embellish and embroider. Me and a fiddle—it never did seem right to me, but Smitty got it in his head and that was it."

"This is just unbelievable! Not that I want him here, but where *is* he, anyway? We haven't seen hide nor hair of him since that first appointment."

"Yeah, the old man gets himself in deep with this family-owned business crap. . . . 'Nothin' the public likes more than mom and apple pie, father-son,' Smitty always says. 'Makes 'em believe they're in good hands with Allstate!' He's my ex–brother-in-law but that's *it*." Slidell let out a sarcastic *ha!* "He's the front man, sets it all up, then leaves the dirty work for us."

"Oh, I am such an *idiot!*" Carleen snapped, hitting the counter with her fist. "I, I could just *wring somebody's neck*." When Slidell squirmed, Carleen added, "I'm not mad at *you* or anything, Mr. Slidell, Heavens, *no! You* were just doing your job!"

"Well, I guess that's one way of lookin' at it," said Slidell, twisting his coffee cup. "The way a nice lady like *you* would see it . . . so," he nodded toward the technicians, "now that you know, what do you want to do about *this?*"

"I, I, oh, I don't know." Carleen sat dazed, staring at a technician who was removing a Venetian glass beaker from her mantel. Another one was stooped over, connecting some spouts and cylinders. Already she could detect the odor of chemicals and they hadn't even plugged in their hoses.

"Mr. Slidell, this throws me for a loop, if you know what I mean . . . I've got some packing to finish, so you occupy yourself for a few minutes and I'll, I'll be back in a jiffy."

While the A-1 group fretted with this and that, Carleen marched upstairs to collect the duffel bag. Without even being aware of what she was doing, she found herself making clothing selections for Los Angeles, stacking cotton T-shirts and linen pants on the bed. She threw her hair dryer and cosmetics and a windbreaker into her suitcase. She still wasn't sure what to do about the extermination, but she'd decided to make up her mind by the time she got to the bottom of the staircase.

After one final sweep of the room, she noticed an open dresser drawer. When she lifted a gray cardigan that was causing the problem and started to flatten it, she saw a lump in a pocket. It wasn't like Nelson, Mr. Neatfreak, to leave anything behind, so she burrowed her hand inside and felt around the pocket, pulling out two items: a lapel pin and a Polaroid photograph.

"Oh," Carleen said. It sounded like an off-key note escaping from a musical instrument. She stood with one hand on the small of her back and the other one on her forehead, like she was taking her own temperature.

The pin said: DISNEYLAND—FRIGHT NIGHT and the snapshot, for all anyone knew, a portrait of the ideal American family, was of Nelson, Anna Traminsky, and a little boy clutching a red balloon and wearing Mickey Mouse ears. The three of them were on a small platform, posing with some Halloween monster. Anna's arm hung over Nelson's right shoulder and the boy, a detestable little thing who looked exactly like his mother, straddled Nelson's knee.

Carleen's hands felt for the bedside bench. She placed the picture beside her, her eyes peering at the two heads tipped together, the carefree smiles, the boy looking as comfortable in Nelson's lap as in an old easy chair.

Suddenly she leapt up, circling from side to side, hitting the walls like a bird trapped in a house. She searched under the bed and armchair. She dumped Nelson's overnight bag on the carpet. Then she pulled out all the drawers, yanking shirts and underwear and sweaters from their perfectionistic stacks. She pulled back the patterned drawer paper until, finally, her fingertips felt a package. At first she thought somehow her writing material had ended up in Nelson's chest. But this was an envelope, a large parchment bundle swaddled in lambswool, and it contained dozens of spice-scented letters. She ripped them in two, then again and again, flinging the letter bits into the air, and watching them cascade onto the carpet like colored ash. She kicked the door and a wastebasket. She swooped down, with one deliberate swat of her arm, a dozen bottles of Nelson's Creed cologne. She picked up a sterling frame and hurled it like a grenade, screaming in silence until she was hoarse.

Her arms, limp petals, fell to her side, and her back slipped downward. She began to cry, a sob that came from deep within, one that coughed up all the responses she'd swallowed over the years, ones that were all built up inside like a fortress of mismanaged emotions. "Nelson, you idiot!" she hollered, throwing a tennis shoe across the room. "You son of a bitch! You swore on Cassie's life!"

There it was all along, a secret life slipped under some cheap bureau paper, so many longings hidden in a drawer with socks and underwear and T-shirts, all the pieces now scattered at her feet like a shipwreck. All the happy moments of her marriage flickered before her, imposters each and every one of them.

And here she was imprisoned by a house full of strangers. Obviously, she could storm into Brown, Carlyle and Whittingham, waving the incriminating photograph, her linen dress flaunting the FRIGHT NIGHT pin, her voice resonating with the sort of tone she'd never been able to come up with before. But the red-handed approach would humiliate her and, frankly, took more belly fire than she had.

Plus, this wasn't the way she envisioned a showdown, that would be done with many rehearsals under her belt. They'd take place in the privacy of their own torture chamber, where all the poison-tipped arrows could bounce off familiar walls.

She called Rebecca, but Agostina, her Guatemalan housekeeper, answered and said, "Mrs. Rebeek-a, she no en casa," and her secretary said she wasn't in the office either. "Don't you remember? She's still in Kentucky." Even her mother's answering machine was on: "Hi! It's Lila Mae! I'm out gallivantin' but leave a message after the beeee-ppp!" Each syllable sounded like a happy, scampering child. Lila Mae was probably on a movie set somewhere, cantering across a meadow on an Arabian horse, with a makeup artist rouging her cheeks.

What if there was an explanation for that picture? After all, the woman wasn't wearing a negligee and they weren't pawing one another. And what else were two adults supposed to do with a six-year-old boy who insisted on being in the photograph, stand him there like a mechanical toy?

None of Carleen's ridiculously accommodating rationale took into consideration Nelson's presence at Disneyland or the letters. Like a photo developing in a tray, the image was undeniably clear. It *was* Nelson and this *was* the Exhibit A she always knew existed. Then why did she feel like she'd been smashed by a freight train? It was obvious, as it should have been for years, that the photo was the genuine article and her marriage obviously wasn't.

From the balustrade, Carleen could see men with bell-shaped heads and rubber coats struggling with the tent. She also noticed the steel clock had stopped on 5:31 A.M. and the warning light on the burglar alarm was flashing and other things that were on the blink. She grabbed a paper towel and blew her nose.

Carleen floated calmly down the staircase like Loretta Young, gripping the railing tightly. Chin up high, eyes fixed in some domestic-bliss glaze, she was going to be mature, be in control, tackle one issue at a time. When in doubt, she would take cleansing breaths and pause to think, instead of erupting.

Mr. Slidell, sitting in the kitchen, his hands folded patiently like a job applicant, said, "I see you moved your sectional back . . . you didn't like it in front of the fireplace?"

"*I* did, but my husband didn't." Through her throaty, teary voice, Carleen tried to sound jocular. "He's not happy unless he's making me miserable." With her back to him, Carleen removed the sugar from the cupboard and poured cream into a small pewter pitcher.

"That doesn't sound like such a good setup." Slidell lowered his head and fingered the bill of his cap.

"I don't know what to do, Mr. Slidell, I really don't." In spite of her efforts, tears suddenly rolled down Carleen's face.

"Now, now, Mrs. Carlyle . . . I hate to see a nice lady like you cry." Slidell pulled a stained hankie from his pocket and handed it to Carleen. "I don't mean to pry, but, this, this doesn't have anything to do with the fumigation, does it?"

"Not really . . . I, I wish things were that simple." Carleen blew her nose and pushed her hair behind her ear. "It's my husband. I'm not sure things are going to work out. I'm sorry, I've just got a lot on my mind . . . I shouldn't burden you with all this." For the life of her, Carleen couldn't fathom why she would even broach this topic to the pest-control man.

"I'm sorry to hear that, Mrs. Carlyle, I really am. It's not my place to say anything, but you should do what makes you happy. You're a really nice person." Slidell said it gently, like the voice a mother uses around a sleeping baby. "The last thing you need is all this turmoil. If you like, you can just shut this down. That's why I'm here."

"If I'd known this yesterday, I would have done just that, but now I don't know." Carleen looked all around her, remembering Rebecca's advice: "Here's the deal, Car. It's not as safe as the A-1 technician swears it is and it's not as harmful as the Environmental Watchdogs claim. Just blast the stupid place!"

From the corner of her eye, she saw two technicians moving a walnut chest from the living room into the entry hall. They had also taken the mohair armchair from the den. When she realized how much better the house was looking, she asked Mr. Slidell if Pettigrew and the two Doggetts could rearrange a few more things while they were at it.

When they were finished with the chest, Carleen asked if they could move the davenport . . . then the coffee table, and the china cupboard.

The house began to open up, leaving not much more than the hardwood floors and honey-colored walls. All the pieces had filled the entry hall and were trailing into the driveway like a line of congested traffic.

Despite the absence of logic, Carleen was feeling better. She began singing the song that was stuck in her head, "Roll, roll me away; won't you roll me away tonight? I too am lost; I feel double-crossed . . ."

Carleen strolled through the house, past the beige couch, an earthen lamp, the chrome breakfast table, and Nelson's high-tech chair with its levers and gear shift. It was the furniture that her husband, the minimalist, had been pleased with before Carleen "screwed it all up."

"So . . ," Mr. Slidell hiked up his tan trousers and snorted. "Have you decided what you're going to do?" He wanted to know if Carleen was going to put a stop to all the nonsense and just do the minimum, the spot clean.

"You'll think I'm nuts, Mr. Slidell, but let's go ahead with it once and for all. *Whole hog, full blast, the entire enchilada* . . . a *quadruple* dose of Pantazine, Chlordane, Malathion—anything that sticks to your ribs for ages! Ha ha!"

Mr. Slidell asked her, "You sure about that?"

"I am sure," Carleen nodded. She visualized Nelson barging in to check on Carleen and Cassie when they didn't show up at the airport. He'd flop his hands around like a philharmonic conductor and gripe, "Where the hell is she *now?* Can't she *ever* get it right?" All the while, his lungs would swell, his chest would thump. There would be the initial look of confusion, then the quickly escalating convulsions . . . the ultimate collapse to the floor . . . then one frantic arm reaching for his phone to dial 911. "I am absolutely, positively, one-hundred-percent sure."

"Well, if that's what you want, you got it!" Slidell snapped his fingers to the team. "Now you get the heck outta this place, you hear me?"

Carleen ambled through the house pulling down the shades, as if each one was a memory. Into one suitcase, she put the silver—the Colonial serving spoons and forks from her great-grandmother—carefully wrapping the sugar nippers and candlesticks in brown flannel. She added a family album and a wooden box with Cassie's grade-school art and dashed upstairs to grab her "Rome Wasn't Built in a Day" pillows. Yes, yes, it was all settled; Carleen was going to go rolling, probably clean out of sight.

Twisting the master key off her chain, Carleen handed it to Lenny Slidell. "Just leave the furniture where it is. I'll handle that, but will you do me a favor? If my husband happens to call, tell him that I just watched *The Sound of Music* and I'm going to Blockbuster video to rent *Texas Chainsaw Massacre*."

Slidell scratched his rubbery ear, and flipped her a peculiar look. Carleen said, "Believe me, he'll know *exactly* what you're talking about."

"Okay, that's what I'll say to him." Slidell paused, as if getting up his nerve, then he said, "Uh, by the way, Mrs. Carlyle, I don't want you to think everything I told you was a lie. I meant every word I said about that column of yours . . . I really think you've got what it takes. So, I'll be watching for you on the television!"

"But, Mr. Slidell, you old devil," Carleen gave the man a weak half shell of a smile. "You already beat me to the punch, didn't you?"

On the way out the door and along her path, she waved to the Doggetts and Pettigrew, then to the rest of the crew, bidding them hasta la vista, arrivederci, sayonara, au revoir, adios. She was halfway down the driveway when Mr. Slidell came flagging his arm. "Mrs. Carlyle, I forgot to ask you, will you be coming back here for any reason?"

"Gee . . ." She hesitated, squinting at the man. Carleen knew by the way Slidell was looking at her that he expected her to answer the simple question right off the bat. But her head was spinning with an array of details, all of them garnished and tinselled, all waggling their hands like showoffy schoolchildren with the right answer.

Of course, she could just open up her trap and ask, "What did you mean by that *for-any-reason* business, sir?" But she didn't want to make a rigamarole out of it. And who was going to cart her off to prison if she said one thing, then did another? My gosh, what if she left a diamond ring or something valuable behind? Did they expect her to just leave it . . . all because she swore she wasn't coming back *for any reason?*

She was about to say something all-encompassing, an answer that truth and shifting circumstances and the Wooten Luck could all embrace, something such as, "Well, I'm not too sure yet, Mr. Slidell, but maybe I'll come back." Then, after thinking about it for a moment, Carleen remembered that maybe was for wimps, that it suggested possibility.

Chapter Thirty-two

Carleen

AUGUST 1999

It was Carleen's favorite kind of day, a day when the air was fire hot, when the sky was aswirl with clouds like torn rags. All the bugs seemed paralyzed by the heat and the plump red American Beauty roses stood like obedient lieutenants. All around her was happy suburbia—neighbors clipping hedges and skateboarding children. Just behind Mount Olympus Park were the straw-colored hills rising like sombreros. And beyond that was San Quentin and a few miles up the road, Folsom . . . so many different perspectives of the same scene.

Carleen sat behind the wheel of her car, staring at the bug-dotted windshield, turning the key in the ignition one notch. She closed her eyes as the air conditioning blew her hair across her face like a silk scarf. She listened to the gentle *clang, clang, clang* of the safety belt warning sign. "Oh, shut up," she muttered to the stupid electronic device. The way things were going, everyone would soon be taking orders from a car dashboard.

The digital clock said 10:13 A.M. It was still too early to show up at the Chesterfield Bay Community meeting. That didn't start until 11:30 and she was only five minutes away. She wondered if she should make a last stab at Billy Cooper, but if she drove all the way to Berkeley, she'd be late. She swiveled the knob on the radio, then clicked it off, still sitting at the end of her driveway.

Next door, behind the chain-link fence, Danny Boy and Liberace were carrying on, their paws pummeling the metal, their snouts chewing at the BEWARE OF DOG sign.

Carleen took the manila envelope next to her and shook out the tabloids, skimming her mother's attached note: Here's the latest! All my love, Mom. She arranged them according to priority: first *The Star*, then *The Globe*, and last, *The National Enquirer*, scanning the items her mother checkmarked: the lawyer who was in a legal battle to save a squirrel and the spontaneous-combustion story about the New Jersey woman whose foot exploded while playing gin rummy. At the bottom of one page was an ad: "Do you have bone-chilling stories to tell? Something that's happening in your own neighborhood or someone who's had a brush with death? Let us hear from you!"

Carleen supposed it was the type of beautiful day her family had in mind when they had left Kentucky, headed for the promised land. What innocents they had been, expecting premiere lights and talent scouts at the border, perhaps some benevolent chap handing out gold sovereigns to newcomers.

All across the country Lila Mae had told everyone histrionic versions of their life story and spinetingling details about their road trip. They would pull into a motel or gas station and wait for the clerk or attendant to ask a simple question such as, "How are you folks today?" Lila Mae would shake and sigh and roll her eyes. "Well, sir, we're fine *now* . . . but we're lucky to be alive, ain't we kids?" It was what she called "something to break the ice."

"Goodness gracious!" the person would exclaim. "What *kind* of trouble did you run into?" It was just the response she'd hoped for, something that paved the way for long, drawn-out stories about tornadoes they'd outrun and close calls with criminals who almost got them.

Carleen would hear the grandiose tales, and say, "But, Mama, that wasn't——" Lila Mae, flushed from embarrassment, would shush her and say, "You know how kids is; they ain't happy unless you look like a dern fool. Anyways, how would *she* know what happened, she's just a little girl."

Once she had a captive audience, Lila Mae would flutter her hands and spin her eyes, making her predictions for their new life. Let's see, folks, her artistic, smart, and beautiful daughter, Rebecca, would "take California by storm." And William Cooper, her "bouncing baby boy" would "end up on the Top Forty . . . sure as shootin'." Number one on the hit parade! The jury was still out on Baby Sister, since she was only an infant, but Lila Mae prophesized great things, anyway.

Then after all the forecasts of fame and fortune, the topic would turn to Carleen, her middle girl. Lila Mae's giddy tone would screech to a dead halt. "Now I don't have too much else to go on, mind ya . . . but that girl would make a wonderful nurse. Why, you never did see anyone her age with such a compassionate side! She doesn't have a mean bone in her body." Then the bored stiff mechanic or grocery checker would hear how gifted Carleen was with wounded birds and small talk with old, sick people.

Once Rebecca gave Lila Mae a dirty look and huffed, "Maybe Carleen doesn't *want* to be a nurse. Maybe she's got other big plans and dreams."

"Dreams and plans, my foot!" Lila Mae glared at Rebecca, then turned to Carleen. "For Pete's sake, you don't have to be a nurse if you don't want to. I was just tryin' to tell people what a sweet, nice little girl you are. Someday she's gonna take care of her mama when she's old and gray, ain't you honey?"

Carleen turned the ignition and started the engine. It was time to get to the community meeting. Maybe she could still drop by the Dairy Kastle for a frozen limeade. She tucked some papers in the crevice between the two leatherette seats and waved to Timmy Jasper. He was flying east-west on his swing set, pushing his little body higher into the air, driving Danny Boy and Liberace to hop and howl and curse motion.

The foreign men were dressed like ghosts, cinching the tent around the house. Monty Doggett pulled a hose from a spool, lumbering from one spot to another. The hose jerked like an epileptic serpent, making him hop over the wayward tube like a child skipping rope. He waved his hands, lifted his white mask, and yelled, "Turn it off! Turn it off!" but nobody seemed to hear him. The hose shot blue quills skyward. The odor of gas and chemicals slowly leaked into the air.

Carleen set the car in reverse, glanced over her right shoulder, and pressed the accelerator. On her way down the street, she honked at Bonnie Goebel, her neighbor who lived in the Venus, now worth $85,000 more than the purchase price. She passed Hedda Roman, a bookkeeper who lived in the Aristotle, a model that recently sold for twenty-five percent more than Roman paid. There was a LOSE WEIGHT IN THIRTY DAYS advertisement stapled to a palm-tree trunk, and a white-haired girl with green-gold eyes who, as far as Carleen knew, didn't even live in that neighborhood. She was just standing on the side of the road, squinting at Carleen, looking like a marble cherub.

Right before she made a left turn onto Socrates Drive, Carleen adjusted the rearview mirror and took one last look at the Poseidon. When she was a little farther away and in a spot with better phone reception, she'd call Bekins van and storage and ask them how long it would take them to get out to 9844 Apollo Drive in Mount Olympus Park for an unscheduled pickup.

Chapter Thirty-three

The Blue Lick Springs Town Meeting

AUGUST 1999

It was the hottest day of the summer and the clock on the bell tower of the courthouse was striking 5:00 P.M. as the citizens of Blue Lick Springs spilled through the meeting hall doors. Heat lightning quivered in the moody sky, a sky the color of an elephant hide, and the roads were quiet except for an occasional big rig on its way to Oddville.

A week before, word spread that Horace Castle was prepared to make his case for the airport and housing projects. Since then, all through the county, like a cigarette dangling from a smoker's lips, was the question: Are you fer it or agin it? To make sure no stone was left unturned, there were fliers taped to the bus stop benches and stapled to all the telephone poles lining Highway 455. Pappy Bagler spun through town tossing leaflets from his electric lawn mower and yelling, "Hear Ye! Hear Ye!" and in the window of Edna's Beauty Box was a big poster:

IF YOU CARE ABOUT THE FUTURE
OF BLUE LICK SPRINGS, YOU MUST
ATTEND THIS IMPORTANT CITY MEETING
PLEASE JOIN HORACE AND COCO CASTLE
YOUR FRIENDS IN DEVELOPMENT!
TOWN HALL
FRIDAY, 6:00 P.M
REFRESHMENTS WILL BE SERVED

Flanking the courthouse door like ornamental shrubs, were the Castles. Coco was to the left, wearing a vanilla-colored linen suit and long, lacy gold chains that jangled every time she gave someone's hand a hardy shake. "So sweet of you to come, Regina," she cooed. "Horse, this is Howard Deeds Johnson, that nice man who . . . and his darling daughter, Clotilda . . . well hello there, Ida Lucille, don't you look pretty!"

"Horse" was on the right. He was dressed in a Panama hat and matching cream linen suit with a watch fob that hung against his protruding belly like a drapery cord. He really didn't know anybody from Adam, but that didn't stop him from doling out bosom-buddy slaps and chirps. "Thank ya for comin', thank ya *so* much for comin'."

Directly behind them was a black woman wearing a French maid's uniform and holding a silver tray of paper cups and heart-shaped cookies. She asked everyone if they wouldn't like some lemonade and gingersnaps.

If anyone bypassed the ropes at the front entrance, Joe Lee Buttons was inside to pick up the leftovers. He gave Olive a particularly warm hello, saying, "Well, well, Miss Wooten, you made it after all!"

"And why wuddn't I, sir?" Olive, cradling her carafe of wine, skinned him down with her feverish eyes.

When Buttons noticed the bottle, he said, "Now you know we can't have that in here, Miss Wooten . . ." and reached out for the decanter. "Let me have Rosario get you some lemonade."

"I don't see no badge on yer fancy suit, Mr. Buttons. I already cleared it with Jimmy Buzz, the shuruff of this here town." By the time Olive's words were out, she had grazed by Buttons, whose mouth was fixed in a disagreeable lump, and was overseeing two councilmen as they situated her Queen Anne chair in the first row.

The rest of Olive's troops had slipped through the side door to avoid the host and hostess and, in the case of Little Peep, Coco's poodles. Letty Bookbinder and the McCrackens were already there. So was Jimmy Buzz Burkle, who was wearing an American flag shirt and cowboy boots. Shorty and Maybelle were in New Orleans at the Avon convention, so that was one less worry.

Inside the big, musty meeting hall were ceiling fans on overdrive and walls decorated with photographs of prominent Blue Lick Springs citizens including Thomas Breckinridge Adams. As the crowd settled in their seats, women fanned their skirts and farmers patted their sunburned brows with hankies, grumbling, "Ain't that just like a derned city slicker to schedule somethin' smack dab in the middle of feedin' time?" Despite the gripes, in the air was the sensation of excitement and an incense of blooming summer flowers, armpits, and Old Spice.

Sitting on the podium along with several councilmen, was Mayor Cheatham, a dog-faced man with fierce, hollow eyes. He rolled a wad of tobacco around his mouth and inspected the crowd, rapping his gavel to get their attention. "All right, ever'one," he said. "We're here to discuss the ins and outs and pros and cons and all the other what have yous in between regarding this airport sitch-ation." You could tell by what he said next whose side he was on.

"Technically, we are all set to go . . . so this is actually just a formality. But Mr. Castle was nice enough to take time from his *very* busy schedule to answer your questions . . . and I think we should give him a *big hand*."

There was a bolt of applause as Horace Castle clasped his hands behind his back and strolled in dramatic, thoughtful sweeps. Then he paused to take a breath that he seemed to pull from the ground, one that slowly rose through his body, and became a companion to his inspirational thoughts.

"Ladees and genna-men of Blue Lick Springs, I am so pleased to be acquainted with your wunnerful town. As you already know, I have undertaken various beautification projects, projects that will—at least in the opinion of your humble speaker—put our city on the, uh, map, as they say. Soon, people from all over this great nation of ours, the United States of Amurica, will venture to Blue Lick Springs and say, 'Now, that's progress'!"

While Horace Castle stomped like Elmer Gantry, Rebecca checked the metal table behind him where six city officials sat like panelists on *What's My Line*. Coco was on the end, chain-smoking from an ivory cigarette holder. Her nails were painted deep red, like little firecrackers. Everybody was hoping to see something because she wasn't wearing her sling, but the mystery injury was hiding under long sleeves. Mayor Cheatham was next to her, and he had his chin in his hand with two fingers pointing to his temple. Every once in awhile, he would scribble something on a pad, then tap his pencil point against it.

"It is impordant, dear people, as we embark on our journey to make the Amurican Dream come true for so many deservin' home owners, that we keep step with our infrastructure. You see, what we're strivin' for is *more* than just a pretty picture, *more* than just a new-fangled toy with no battrees. We want the cake *and* the icing. Therefore, we *must* provide the services to encourage this growth. . . . We *must* develop the engine to keep it all goin' smoothly. . . . and these goals begin and end with access and availability, with the freedom to move to and fro and back and forth . . . we need ingress! we need egress! What I am talkin' about, *dear fellow citizens* of Blue Lick Springs . . ." He paused and wiped his hankie across his soaking brow like a window cleaner with a squeegee. "Is our proposed airport, the Blue Lick Springs International Airport!" At that exact moment, he jerked a drapery from some mystery object on an easel. When it turned out to be a fancy drawing, all necks in the crowd craned forward and everyone said, "Oh, my!"

Rebecca wasn't about to go gaga over the airport rendering the way the rest of the room did, but it wasn't the architectural grotesquerie she and so many had expected from Castle. It was actually a mini-Churchill Downs: a stately white clapboard building with steeples and spires and iron-hinged gates. That meant one thing: The tide that had been straddling the fence had belly flopped to Castle's side.

Sensing the crowd's enthusiasm, Castle removed his Panama hat, wagging it in his hand like a minstrel's tambourine. "Ladees and genna-men, I have traveled far and wide . . . I have looked high and low, but nowhere have I found a place whose charm is so infectious and whose people are so hospitable. Now, when we are faced with the choice between *stagnation* and *superiority,* when we stand on the very precipice of *wondrous* things, I assure you that with your support, I will take *great* pains to protect this special place that I proudly call my *home.* Ladees and genna-men, every dream has its day and Blue Lick Springs' day is *now!*"

"What's absurd is that this is occurring because a developer who had never set foot in Kentucky until six months ago has decided that it's time to brush the cobwebs off Blue Lick Springs, to plunge, feet first, one eye shut, into the twenty-first century . . . all to satisfy some frivolous dream of a woman who abandoned this town and a man who purports to adore it, but wants to change everything about it.

"How many times have we opened a history book or watched a television program that showed rural beauty or historical buildings that have been destroyed? We shake our heads and wonder what numbskulls would have allowed such a thing. Well, ladies and gentlemen, we are sitting in a room chockful of numbskulls if we merely stand back and watch it evaporate, one farm, one historical property at a time.

"So, I urge the council to honor the generations of families who will treasure our town's future, just as they have guarded its past. I beg them to protect the Cottage and Rosemont. I implore every person here to rise up and join the Coalition to Save Blue Lick Springs. Finally, I ask you to support my grandmother, Olive Adams Wooten, the woman whose love for the great state of Kentucky always taught me to leave my little corner of the world a better, more beautiful place."

As she finished, a scalding sun charged through the glass windows and a rush of honeysuckle came from an open door. Behind her, she could sense a scowling Coco and an indignant Horace Castle aiming burning darts at her back. But beyond the people in front of her, strung out like colorful necklaces, all the way in the back, was one man—a wild-haired, wrinkle-shirted man—who stood up and gave his hands a loud clap. It was Hamilton Montgomery. One by one, the crowd joined him in applause.

As a wobbly-legged Rebecca returned to her seat, Big Dee and Little Peep and Baby Sister were all bumping their paper cups of "lemonade." A small group had collected around them and this one and that one were shouting, "Amen, sister, amen!" When Rebecca sat down, Olive adjusted the summer shawl over her shoulders and greeted her granddaughter with a pat on her knee. "Ya done good, girl, ya done riiiil good."

If that had been that, they could have cracked open the champagne, but Joe Lee Buttons, trying to outrace momentum, jumped up, bounding back and forth on his long, spidery legs. He stopped suddenly, took a long drag off his cigarette, then threw his chest out like a bloated accordian. He angled his head upward and blew out a straight line of smoke. "Now, that's all fine and well, girlee girl," he said, "and it sure does tug at the emotional heartstrings, doesn't it, folks? But when you push all that gibberish off to the side, where it belongs, I hardly believe that the good people of Blue Lick Springs want their minds made up for them." Buttons paced and squinted as if studying the wood grain on the floor. "Now I can appreciate the circumstances of Olive Wooten, I really can, but this isn't the first time someone had to sacrifice for the *common good*. And do you know what? Most of the time those *very same people* send Mr. Horace Castle thank-you notes. Do you know what they thank him for? They thank him for openin' up their eyes to new possibilities. They thank him for *broadenin' their horizons*." Buttons paused to make contact with the audience. "And you speak so often of McDonald's and Wal-Mart, and yet, there isn't *one single* plan of Mr. Castle's that includes either of those. So *all* this talk 'bout bein' forced to sell to this one and that one, *all* this talk about Blue Lick Springs lookin' like some space-age monster, *all* these accusations about villains who are out to *git* ya . . ." He stamped his red snakeskin shoe and plunged forward to scare everyone, "Well, now, Ms. St. Clair, wouldn't you say that the clear-thinking, law-abiding, tax-paying citizens of Blue Lick Springs should decide for *themselves* what they want their town to look like? You see, girlee girl, this here is the United States of America where there isn't a soul who can tell you what you can and can't do with your *own property!* Now, I'm sorry, but that's just the way it is."

Whether you agreed with him or not, the skillful man had ambushed the crowd, insinuating that you were a moron if you didn't see it his way. He stood with a gleaming, open, knifeblade of a smile, trails of smoke curling around him like dancing spirits. People in the crowd were chuckling and saying, "Amen, Brother Buttons!" With Coco hopping around in gleeful little circles like the town's personal fairy godmother and Horace Castle sitting like a gloating tycoon, nobody heard Rebecca reply, "Ha! You're not giving my grandmother and Hamilton Montgomery any choice at all!"

Luckily, it was Letty Bookbinder's turn to speak, a smoking-gun presentation that had helped Rebecca to keep calm through all the swaying consensus and one she prayed would reverse Horace Castle's goodwill. Bookbinder tapped the microphone and said, "Good evening, ladies and gentlemen. I speak not only on behalf of the Coalition to Save Blue Lick Springs, but the Kentucky Chapter of the Daughters of the American Revolution. At one time, each and every one of these historical structures that you're about to see was scheduled for demolition. But for the determination of a few passionate people and organizations, much like ourselves, none of these jewels would be here today."

With that, the Daughters of the American Revolution came streaming to the front like contestants in a beauty pageant, each one hugging a photograph to her chest. They were the pictures that Rebecca and Big Dee had dug up from hundreds of old books and David had blown up, mounted, and FedExed to them just that morning. Joining the Daughters were Big Dee and Little Peep, Ruby Pearl and Buddy McCracken.

When Bookbinder held up a banner that said: A BLIND DATE WITH THE BULLDOZER, every Kentucky Daughter turned her photograph around, pictures that showed familiar regional property. Plus, Big Dee held a broken-down, abandoned Monticello. Little Peep was the Alamo, holding a photo of the famous structure right before it was scheduled for demolition. Ruby Pearl and Buddy McCracken displayed a poster of a ramshackle Mount Vernon.

Just as Rebecca had hoped, the crowd was saying, "That's Monticello? What a disgrace!" and "Were they *really* going to tear down the *Alamo?*"

Next Bookbinder held up an aerial photograph of Charleston, South Carolina, pointing her clear fingernail at the cobblestone streets and original brick and columned facades, a scene that caused a few to say, "Oh, how pretty!" Next to it, she propped up another photograph, this one of a bustling intersection, a bonfire of phosphoresence with lights and neon and plastic banners. In it was a super discount store, McDonald's, and Blockbuster video. Bookbinder said, "This shot could be Anywhere, U.S.A., right? Well, ladies and gentlemen of Blue Lick Springs, this picture is *also* Charleston, South Carolina. *Indeed*, it is the *exact same* intersection I just showed you. That photograph of the charming seventeenth-century setting was taken five years ago and here's what it looks like *today!*"

People were crying out, "For pity's sake, who would tear that down?" and "That's a crime!"

"Ladies and gentlemen, you will be interested to know that *this* was a project by Mr. Horace Castle. *This,*" Bookbinder grabbed the shopping center photograph and rattled it in the air, "is Horace Castle's idea of progress!"

Everybody was up in arms and all eyes switched to the podium. The carmine sheen of Horace Castle's round face was replaced by a sickly green color. All he mustered was a thin wire of a smile. Coco, sitting next to him, enveloped in curlicues of smoke, looked like a paper doll with her crimped smile and waxy eyes. She tapped her two-toned shoe against the floor and exchanged dirty looks with Rebecca.

After a bunch of nods and furrowed brows and bulging eyeballs from his sister, Butch Youngblood popped up, obviously just to switch the subject. He looked like a nervous elementary school student about to recite Kipling to a large crowd. He said, "I got somethin' to say and I'm gonna say it! If it wuzn't fer Horace Castle and my sister, Cook—, uh, Coco, makin' a difference in the place, the, uh, uh," he paused to stare at the small paper in his cupped hand, "the whole place could go right down the God-damned tubes. They gave me a bundle for my folks' place; who else is gonna overpay me for sumthin' like that?" He let out a nervous bray of a laugh and kept standing there until Coco drew her fist at him.

"Mayor Cheatham!" Olive raised her pointed finger. "What I wanna say is, is, Mayor, when are we gonna hear from Hearst Castle? Ya said in yer introduction that he wuz here to answer sum questions. Now I heared a lotta answers, but I didn't hear nobudy ask him nothin'." She crooked around to see if the crowd agreed with her.

Coco was giving her titian waves a nonchalant toss and fiddling with some evil eye fetish that dangled from one of her gold chains. Horace Castle sat like a dressmaker's mannequin.

To scare people off, Joe Lee Buttons stood at the edge of the stage, slightly forward in a half-lurch, his eyes darting down the aisles, like a Secret Service man who's been told there's an assassin in the crowd.

At first, nobody budged, then Big Dee stepped forward and said, "My father, Lyman Crittenden Hicks, has dealings with you, Mr. Castle. You're trying the same stunts in Blue Lick that you're trying in Franklin, Tennessee. Every time you get shot down, you come back for more. LADIES AND GENTLEMEN! HE WANTS TO CHOP UP MY FAMILY'S HEAVEN HILL PLANTATION JUST LIKE HE WANTS TO CHOP UP ROSEMONT AND—"

"THAT'S NOT TRUE," Buttons fired back.

"IT'S TRUE AND YOU KNOW IT!" Rebecca countered.

"Ask him about the robbery . . . find out what he knows about that," asked Ruby Pearl McCracken.

"I'd lak to see that Castle woman's arm, see what it looks lak now that that sling's come off," Olive snapped. "SHE ATTACK-TED ME . . . TRIED TO GIT HER HANDS ON MY NERVE PILLS."

Coco, stretching across the table like a panther, snarled, "WHY, YOU LIAR, YOU!"

"Change is *good* for ever'one," announced Evelyn Youngblood. "And that's why I'm for the Castles' way of doin' it."

Gladys Gaylene Horner said that's all fine and dandy what Castle wants, but how do they know it will all turn out the way he says?

"Some say the airport's gonna bankrupt the town," Buddy McCracken said. "They say the numbers don't add up."

"NUMBERS DON'T LIE," Joe Lee hollered, "according to the *statistics* the airport project is economically sound."

"There are three kinds of lies," Little Peep pulled himself up, stretched his chest, and replied, "REGULAR LIES, DAMNED LIES, AND STATISTICS!"

All along Horace Castle had been harumphing and Coco had been stamping and coughing, barely held back by her husband, who kept sticking his arm out like a tollbooth gate. Jimmy Buzz, who wasn't even on duty, was trying to shoo people back to their seats, and all the while Mayor Cheatham kept tapping his gavel and hollering, "PEOPLE, ORDER! ORDER!"

So far Irene hadn't participated, mostly because things hadn't been going the way she planned. Before they left the farm, she had consulted the tea leaves for advice, opening her Bible and hoping the first passage that caught her eye would give her some notion of the near future. She was stunned when there, right before her, was Psalms 6:10: "All my enemies will be ashamed and dismayed. They will turn back in sudden disgrace."

Since nothing could have been more conclusive, an excited Irene had packed her briefcase with all the goodies, the valuable evidence that would have chased all issues into their coffin. But now her turn as star witness was threatened by another verse in Proverbs, one that was being played out before her eyes: "The first to present his case seems right, 'til another comes forward and questions him."

Plus, now, the hour was late. Through the window, there was a liver-colored twilight and sterling silver stars; inside was the edgy, weary crowd who swayed first one way then the other. Irene feared she had overplayed her cards, waiting for the phantom perfect moment. But it wasn't the end of the world if she simply presented the tape to Sheriff Burkle the next day. She didn't have to make the front page news! But, if that was the way she was going to handle it, then what good did her new yellow Donna Karan suit do her, the suit that made her look slimmer and better than she had in years?

While Irene sat there in a stupor, Olive egged her on. "Onct Baby Sister's story is out," she whispered to her row, "it's lak squeezin' toothpaste back in the tube." Soon the word spread and they all were saying, "Come on, Baby Sister," and Rebecca added, "Yeah, what happened to that 'explosive' information?"

Except for the meetings where every speech began, "Hi, I'm Irene and I'm an alcoholic," this was the first time she had faced a crowd. As she mounted the stage, her heart was beating like a captured baby bird. She stood there like a deaf-mute in a police lineup, her mouth in a half-open snore, her eyes skimming the sea of runny-nosed urchins and broad-faced women and sunburned farmers. She could have easily been there for another five minutes, but Olive yelled, "She ain't got nothin' to say, but they's *plenty* to hear!"

Irene removed the tape recorder from her pocket and popped the cassette inside. She'd already decided against a long song and dance and she was way too jittery, anyhow, so she said, "This conversation should shed some light on the issues discussed here today." She was about to press the play button when Joe Lee Buttons shoved his palm toward Irene and said, "Not so fast, lady." Without even knowing its import, he complained to Mayor Cheatham that this was no place for tapes that came from who knew where and served who knew what purpose. "Now that's fair and square," he said.

Although the mayor was ready to put an end to it, one councilman, Hiram Peabody, went against that, saying, "I don't see no harm in listenin' to the tape, jest as long as you people know it could be a fake."

Everyone in the crowd said that would be fine with them, so Irene was told to start the tape. Within seconds, the unmistakable sound of Coco Castle's baby-doll voice radiated through the room. Coco, both stunned and fascinated, cocked her head and declared, "Why, that's *my* voice!"

In no time, Buttons was prowling across the stage, pitching his arms in the air like a javelin-wielding native. "You see, Mayor, this is just what I was talking about! I can't have the Castles exposed to this. They came here on good faith. Now haven't we taken this charade too far?" Buttons insisted that Irene "*stop that tape immediately,*" which the mayor made her do.

Cheatham told Irene, "I'll take that whole set up, the recorder, the cassette . . . all of it."

"Wait. This is mine," said Irene, pulling the recorder to her chest. "If you won't play it, that's one thing, but I shouldn't have to give it up."

Little Peep rose and said, "Now, Mayor, I don't profess to be any expert on the law, but I believe the lady has a right to her say-so . . . just like everybody else."

Jimmy Buzz said they should take a vote so before the Mayor could butt in, he said, "All those *fer* it, raise yer hand and if yer *agin* it, don't." After dozens of hands shot up, Jimmy Buzz said, "The *fers* have it!"

While all this was taking place, word of the mysterious tape had gotten around, so by the time they were ready to press the Play button, people from all over the place had poured into the room. Flint-eyed men in porkpie hats took nips of bourbon, housewives dragged in sailor-suited children eating cotton candy. There were radios blasting and crop-topped teenage girls drinking Coca-Colas and two women who said they'd been told there was food and those ginger cookies weren't their idea of refreshments. Coco was barking to her maid, "How'd you let that lemonade run out, Rosario?" Big Dee was running back and forth from Miz Becky's for ribs and onion rings and more apple wine, which Olive said they should offer to anyone who saw things their way.

While they waited for the crowd to settle down, Irene held the tape recorder to the microphone and watched for the signal from the mayor. When he nodded to Irene, everyone, believers and skeptics alike, swayed forward. Then, after one flick of the button, there was the undeniable boom of Coco and Butch's voices, rising over the low drone of anticipation:

"I'm sore at Joe Lee. He told me he was gonna sweet-talk Ole Lady Wooten, but that old crow ain't lettin' go so fast . . . but ain't no use foolin' with Horse *and* the Blue Lick officials . . . She's a feisty one, but you think about it, that old bat can't live forever, now can she? I give her six months, if that . . ."

"There's some who've thought that for years . . ."

"I thought I was done for when that rifle went off . . ."

"I tried to tell you that before you went nosin' 'round Rosemont."

"You didn't tell me I'd get *shot!* It was all *your* idea, anyway!"

"I mighta gone along with some of it, but it was your husband's idea to shake up Miz Becky's. Plus, I wuzn't the one who showed up with a loaded weapon . . . Eddie Ray's gotta take the real thing. Now what wuz that sheriff gonna do with that moron wavin' a rifle around?"

"You never told me we would have all those eyewitnesses. And that sheriff, he wasn't supposed to be on duty, either!"

"I ain't no fortune-teller!"

"Oh, well. This time next year, you'll be livin' the high life in Cancun. And I'll bide my time for a while, until I get everything I can get, then bye-bye, Horse, you old codger, and hello, Frankie Snow! I never did get over that man."

Through the crackling silence, Coco let out a piercing shriek. "I'd like to see that hold up in court! They won't get far with that! I saw a program about those fake tapes, said they could fix it so the person said anything they wanted them to. With technology being what it is today, well, hell, it'll make your head spin what they come up with! Butch? You'll stand up for me. Won't you?" She let out a wild piglet of a chuckle and pulled a cigarette from her gold case. Her hand was shaking so hard, she kept flicking the small wheel, and all she could get was sparks. When she broke her thumbnail, she said, "God damn it to hell!"

With so much going on, nobody knew what to do next. The poodles were in the vestibule yapping their heads off. Coco was threatening to leave, saying, "We called this meeting and we can call it off, too!" Butch was all the way in the back now, ready to make a getaway, and there was Jimmy Buzz, the stars on his chest, the stripes on his arms, telling both of them, "Oh, no, you don't!" As for Horace Castle, who'd been smiling like a marionette and ho-ho-ho-ing like it was all a big joke, his tune had changed. Coco was petting his sleeve like a woman stroking her first mink coat, cooing, "Horse, honey, you believe me, don't you?" But his stony, colorless face stared straight ahead.

Irene had never really visualized the aftermath; it had been beyond her imagination to even picture herself in the spotlight. She had been like a concert pianist whose fingers are simply playing somebody else's composition. But now she was having a hip-hip-hooray of a moment. The Kentucky Daughters were hoisting her in the air, Sheriff Burkle was telling her that tape was all the evidence he needed to solve his case, Rebecca was hailing her as their savior, and they were all thrusting their cups toward Olive, asking for a fill-up of apple wine so they could toast Irene as Queen for a Day.

Mayor Cheatham let the crowd get everything off their chest, then he lowered his head like a charging bull, slapping his gavel against the table. "Now listen, everyone. This is all very dramatic, but it is also unsubstantiated and, I might add, irrelevant. This was a *zoning hearing*, not the Salem witch trials! Now, this meeting is *adjourned!*"

Except for her outbursts, they hadn't officially heard from Olive. Rebecca could see by the way her grandmother was fingering her silk jabot and batting her cloudy eyes in thought, that she still had something bottled up, so she said, "Mayor! You can't adjourn the meeting yet . . . my grandmother wants to say something."

Mayor Cheatham looked straight ahead with the glazed, distant eyes of a museum stuffed animal. He bared his stubby teeth, marinating in tobacco juice, and said, "All right, but let's make this snappy."

Rebecca, Irene, and Little Peep took Olive by the elbows and escorted her to the podium. She turned to the room, ground her cane into the hardwood, and pushed her lips toward the microphone. "Don't worry, ever'body. This ain't gonna take me long. I reckon ever'one already knows my name, but I'll tell it to ya enyways. My full name is Olive Irene Adams Wooten . . . and I been lissenin' to all this back and forth . . . I been watchin' ever'one be fer it, then agin it, and then back the other way. But here's how I see it: We don't need no city that looks lak Chicago, Illinoise, or Mo-beel, Alabama. We don't need no town that's got skyscrapers and jumbo jets and what have ya. We don't need no city that's lak a cheap streetwalker advertisin' its goods. If ya want that, then they's plenty to have up the road twenty miles in eny dierection. So, I say these bright idees this Castle feller has ain't so bright after all. Ya see, bad decisions don't march into the room wearin' no name tag or label . . . Fool's gold don't tell ya that's what it is!" She let out an ironic cackle. "But you lissen to me and you lissen good. When the almighty buck is kinga Kentucky, when ever'thang's got a price tag on it, then nothin' will be worth anythin'. They's sumthin' else we been forgettin' too, sumthin' I ain't heard no one mention yet: This here is God's land we're tinkerin' 'round with. That's all."

It was obvious from the corpselike figures sitting on the podium, that the men had their heads set and that was that. What did it matter that the crowd cheered Olive Wooten and reviled Coco Castle? The good old boys' network had worked it all out in some Marlboro-filled, bourbon-soaked tavern . . . probably days before the town meeting. Rebecca could almost hear Mayor Cheatham's silent heckle as he shuffled papers that were probably headed for the incinerator.

"Thank you, everyone," the mayor said, directing his eyes, hard as granite, at the crowd. "I think we have all the information the committee needs to make our final decision. So, we appreciate your interest in this important matter, which we'll take under *very* careful consideration. Now, once and for all, this meeting is adjourned!"

Olive, her foot on the bottom step, suddenly reared up and aimed her cane toward the council. "Mayor Cheatham, I got one more thang to say. Now I know ya fellers think it's *allll* up to you, that it don't matter a hilla beans what wuz said here. But, do ya know who took cer of these problems ya seen, the pitchers Miss Bookbinder showed ya—George Washington's place and the Alamo and all . . . do ya know who started all them groups and organizations that saved 'em from the bulldozers and *total* ruination?" Olive wheeled around the room, her eyes like small candle flames as they settled first on Rebecca, then Baby Sister, and after that Big Dee and Letty Bookbinder and all the other Daughters of the American Revolution. She paused and then, like an archer drawing her bow, said, "Wimmen . . . ever' single, solitary one of 'em wuz saved by wimmen."

Chapter Thirty-four

Rebecca

AUGUST 1999

On the same day that Oscar Percy Allbright's tractor overturned, crushing his left arm and killing his coon dog, Curly, and two days after the town-meeting fiasco, they found out through Lyman Hicks that Horace Castle wasn't from Charleston, South Carolina, after all. He turned out to be a scoundrel called Horatio Castelli of Garden City, New Jersey. Far from being from a family of land barons, Castelli was actually a crook with a slew of assumed identities and illegal activities to his discredit—everything from blackmail to Ponzi schemes. After he burned all his big-city bridges, he recently switched to one-horse towns. The law had been trying to nail him for years.

"Why, I figgered Castle wuz one of them fake names," Olive said. "I never heared tell of another one, have you?"

None of this surprised Letty Bookbinder, who said, "Coco and Horace Castle are two of a kind. She never even bothered to divorce her second husband, that Frank Snow fellow, let alone the others. Why, she's worse than Zsa Zsa. Oh, the likes of her in the Daughters!"

Irene had managed to locate one Scooter Clarksdale, a stock-car driver and another ex-husband, who claimed to have recently spent the weekend with Coco at the Caesar's Palace Riverboat in New Albany, Indiana.

Although the walls protecting Horace Castle were finally crumbling, the man deserved credit. Through charm and chicanery he had managed to worm his way into Blue Lick. How clever he had been, forming alliances with the untold dozens in town who had practically handed him their property on pedestals, all before the escrows had closed or his rubber checks had cleared. The only stray puzzle piece was the status of Rosemont.

With so much going against Horace Castle, it stood to reason that Rosemont would fall apart too. Perhaps, though, Castle would put all his eggs in one basket, retreating to Rosemont for a peaceful, agrarian life. Unfortunately, nobody knew anything about it and despite Hamilton Montgomery's fleeting support for her town meeting speech, Rebecca wasn't about to trample the welcome mat yet.

That evening Olive, Rebecca, and Dee prepared a feast of roast chicken and cabbage, and Irene baked a fig tart. They weren't calling it a celebration, but in the air was a feeling of accomplishment. Grace, delivered by Olive, was a long pep talk/sermon. She chattered on and on, telling them, "The simple inherit folly, but the prudent are crowned with knowledge . . . there's a season and a time to every purpose under the heavens . . ." all the while thumping away tiny orange insects with a clockwise and counterclockwise sweep of her freckled hands. More than once Rebecca looked up and caught Big Dee's eye and Irene mimicked Olive, saying, "Let's get *ooonnnn* with it!"

For Rebecca's sake, there was much talk around the Cottage about hope springing eternal and other platitudinous hogwash that did little to vanish the looming ebony clouds. Big Dee said, "That's right! It's not over till the fat lady sings!"

"I've heared tell of that." Olive creased her brow and scratched her neck. "But I never did know what it mint, did you?"

"In this case," Little Peep chortled, "it means keep your damned trap shut, Dee!"

All the women ganged up on him, tossing their napkins and saying, "That wasn't very nice, Reggie." What Little Peep and Big Dee didn't know was that since her weight loss, they referred to her as Medium Dee.

After dinner, they moved to the moonlit porch, sipping wine and dipping strawberries into the chocolate fondue pot. "Ain't it funny, how thangs work?" Olive mused. "If it wuzn't fer Rebecca's rest-rent, then Hearst Castle and that huzzy wuddna come in, then Peep wuddna got attack-ted by them poodles, and ya wuddna been a-helpin' us do Mr. Castle in. Yes, we got Hearst Castle to thank fer his own downfall."

"And your apple wine, Grandma!" Irene said, then muttered on the sly to Rebecca, "*Mostly*, the apple wine . . ."

"And your desserts, Irene, your delicious desserts . . . Not to mention your Academy Award–winning talent with a tape recorder!" Rebecca said. "And, Dolores . . . *you're* the one who knew all about Horace Castle."

"*Please*, let's give credit where credit is *due*." Medium Dee pushed her glass into the air. "Miss Olive is right; if you hadn't restored Miz Becky's, then those hoodlums wouldn't have robbed it and, and *none* of us would be here." Speaking of none of them being there, Rebecca said she wouldn't have been born if not for Miss Olive, so she deserved a big hand, also.

Realizing that Little Peep had been left out, Rebecca said, "Last, but not least, I think we should give Reggie a round of applause. He has been the guiding light and the financial wizard who has made it all work. Without his numbers running and brilliant leadership and business savvy, where would we be?"

"Pleease! Pleease!" He flashed his hands and puckered his lips in artificial modesty. "I say we *all* deserve credit!"

As the tumblers clinked and mirth and good cheer abounded, behind Olive's gaiety was a crushed spirit, one mirrored deep in those eyes of hers, the eyes that kept pedaling and pedaling on a journey to some moonless melancholia with no walls or architecture or hope bordering it. How utterly heartsick she must be knowing that one more generation of Adams heirs had missed the boat on Rosemont. And so the Adams legacy was to meander down the same convoluted path, hanging on to the coattails of an hallucination, still yearning for emancipation.

As they were tidying the porch, Rebecca got a phone call from Jimmy Buzz Burkle with more bad news for Horace Castle and additional cause for celebration for them. In a tight vote, the city council zoning board had decided to require an impact study to be done by an independent firm before proceeding with the airport project. "The mayor tells me that's their way of puttin' this in the deep freeze. And you can tell your sister and Miz Olive, too, that Miz Becky's happened just the way she thought it did—all three Youngbloods in on it and Horace Castle behind it."

"That's great, Jimmy Buzz!" Rebecca exclaimed. "That's absolutely unbelievable! Uh, you haven't heard anything about Rosemont, yet, have you?" With Rosemont out of her picture, all she could muster was half-hearted enthusiasm.

"Well, I don't have anything conclusive right now, anyways, so as far as I know the deal is still on. But, are ya sittin' down? I've got something else for ya." Then Jimmy Buzz told her that he'd just gotten the news that as a result of this and that and the other, the rumor was that Horace Castle had finally left his philandering wife, Cookie Youngblood Castle, high and dry!

Although the feeling in Rebecca's bones was heartening, and the room boomed with hurrays, she didn't dare make deductions or predictions. Besides, at the terminus of all the crisscrossing information was Olive who had said, "It's all in His hands now."

Later, as they swung on the porch savoring their victory, a diorama of thunder and lightning quavered in the sky around them, breaking open like a purple theater. "Well," Olive muttered out of the blue to no one in particular, "I guess ole Bessie Belle's in like Flynn . . . I heared tell on the TV set this mornin' that she's pulled away from Spicer in them polls." Then, bunching her crocheted shawl around her shoulders, she turned her face to the clouds and said, "It looks lak we're gonna git that bad weather they been a-talkin' 'bout."

While they were removing the swing pillows and shutting the windows for the upcoming storm, Rebecca felt the warm flutter of déjà vu. She could remember steamy, turbulent nights like these when she would slip away from her mother's prying eyes. Even now she could picture herself and Glen cuddling there on the wicker, aswirl in young love, with their Coca-Cola bottles at their side. They would turn the knob on

Rebecca's transistor radio, waiting for "Only the Lonely" or "Tears on My Pillow." With their heads tipped together, she would point out her own secret constellations: Santa's Sleigh and Cinderella's Slipper.

Those were the same days when Rebecca thought a Ferrante and Teicher theme would accompany all the important moments of her life, when all she wanted was a boyfriend who would give her the look William Holden gave Kim Novak in *Picnic* while they danced to "Moonglow." It was back to the time when she and Carleen preened around in bouffant hairdos and tulip-shaped dresses the color of ballet slippers.

It was so long ago and far away from the time when Rebecca entered what her disgruntled parents called her "doomsday" phase, the days when she dressed in head-to-toe black and glared at the world through kohl-rimmed eyes. With her face gathered into a moody scowl, she'd stay up until dawn reading T. S. Eliot and Jack Kerouac, listening to her father gripe, "She's turned into a God-damned beatnik!"

Much later that evening, hours after midnight, they awoke to the sound of Geronimo howling. Then the choking rush of smoke and a vortex of black clouds billowing through the hallways. Somewhere from a dark crevasse of Rebecca's memory came scenes of Sunday fire drills. Lile Mae would wrap them all in blankets on the ground in "position" and shriek, "*Fire!*" They would roll down Olive's hill like logs, stamping out the imaginary flames, waiting for Lila Mae to pump her arms and rejoice, "Thank the Lord. You're alive!"

None of Lila Mae's emergency training or school drills or anything logical came to Rebecca as they raced through the corridors with their hearts in their throats, flying in and out of rooms gathering what they could, bundling Olive in wet towels and all of them—Baby Sister and Big Dee and Little Peep—linking hands, as they stumbled their way out the pantry door and onto the grounds, and waited for the Blue Lick Springs volunteer fire department to materialize.

On the lawn, far away from the house, they stood drinking coffee from paper cups. They listened to the thundering of hooves and the screeching of the forest varmints. In the trees were all their feathered friends—doomed trapeze artists—jumping from limb to burning limb.

As the last flames tumbled through the oak treetops, Olive's rib cage, like fragile architecture, moved up and down fighting for oxygen. Her blank eyes, searching for something familiar, moved from the rootless earth to the barren sky. All that remained were the silhouettes of her old dreams.

From out of the pink boiling earth came a crackle and a belch, one final hallelujah. It was all going slowly, but magnificently, downhill.

Olive pressed her blue fingertips to her face. "Dear me," she said, sighing deeply as if everything inside her was oozing out, "yer grandfather's gonna be so upset 'bout this." Rebecca looked at her and wondered, "Grandfather, what grandfather?"

The next day all everyone in Blue Lick Springs could talk about was how heartbreaking it was that Olive Adams Wooten's farmhouse, the one the old woman had grown up in and the one everyone had always referred to as the Cottage, had burned to the ground.

Epilogue

Rebecca
One Big Almost Happy Birthday Celebration

LATE AUGUST 1999

The ponds, as they did once a year, had turned. In a peculiarity of nature, their bottoms inexplicably switched places with the top, leaving the surface murky and alight with mosquito larvae. All over town the creeks ran bone-dry, long poisonous serpents where dandelions and dead rodents collected along limestone banks. And the bluegrass was so parched that it crackled like shattering glass. Only weeds flourished, engulfing the CASTLECO billboards with brambles and the forsaken bulldozers with monstrous stalks of sticker bushes.

During such a time—a time when Kentucky cardinals with soot-streaked feathers swooped low to the ground, and laborers buckled over the spoiled tobacco fields—to be precise the *Time of the Heart*, Southern legend and the *Farmer's Almanac* warn that a simple nick of a fingernail against bark could kill the mighty oak.

On this particular evening during such a time, a night with a vampire moon and temperatures so hot everything seems to melt before my eyes, I find myself where I often have—chasing a dream from behind the wheel of my car.

In the backseat, sequined mask over her eyes, enveloped in White Shoulders perfume, and squirming like a toddler on Christmas morning, is the birthday girl. "I almost didn't make it," Lila Mae moans, as she has all day long. "I'm as sick as a dog, *sick!*"

To the naked eye, her complaints are nonsense, for she is a sprightly and trim seventy-five with a face as dreamy as a valentine card. She rubs the calf of her "almost-amputated leg," reminding us that she's in the same distinctive boat as Richard Nixon. Her physician, Dr. George Poindexter, had proudly informed her that the ex-president had died of the exact same thing! For good measure, she coughs just to let us know it's more than the leg.

She is flanked by Carleen, who, in her black tulle cocktail frock, looks like a funereal ballerina doll. She pats Lila Mae's knee and tells her to, "Settle down, Mom. We're almost there." Also sharing the backseat is Ava, who is checking her reflection in the chrome seat-belt clamp. She applies another coat of vixen-red lipstick. It is the perfect dramatic accompaniment to her black velvet nails.

Next to me, cell phone clamped to his ear in an effort to wrap up business for the day, is David. His head shifts east and west, scooping up the allée of filigreed black oak trees and the sweep of bluegrass. Just ahead of us, in all its splendor, is Rosemont.

The remodelers have done what everyone in Blue Lick had said would be impossible: In a matter of a few weeks they have basted the house together, buffing and burnishing it beyond recognition. At the moment it glows against a tempestuous, unpredictable twilight. But I will get to that.

From the twinkle in David's eye, he is about to exclaim something, for this is his first visit, but I press my finger to my lips, and Ava motions "No!" with her small pink hands, warning him not to spill the beans.

Great care has been taken to make sure the location of this wingding is a surprise. All along, we'd been planning on the Kon Tiki, Lila Mae's peculiar choice. In its heyday, the Kon Tiki was way beyond the financial reaches of the Wootens and probably the reason for Lila Mae's unrequited need to celebrate there. In any case, she is in for a shock.

The location switch is not the only thing that's top secret. Little does Lila Mae know, but the Moby Dick of funnel clouds has been galloping its way through Alabama, Tennessee, and central Kentucky, a threat that has taken its toll on our nerves, affected the guest turnout, and eliminated all possibility of the tented event we'd had in mind.

But, Olive tells us, the storm is a tiny brush stroke on this big haphazard canvas of life. "Ya take the good with the bad, the bitter with the sweet," she chants. In case the platitudes fail to arouse calm and level-headedness, she is quick to add, "Enyways, them dumb weathermen jest tell ya what happened after it done happened."

We have grown up with Olive's sayings, most of Biblical derivation, many of them in varying degrees of vernacular and grammatical disorder, all of them proposing the theory that minor victories are sabotaged by major defeats.

How perfectly fitting then that this evening, which would have been the Mount Everest point in my life, is marred by much more than a summer squall and presents a dilemma that is far beyond the colloquial limbs of my grandmother's proverbs.

Finally, we guide Lila Mae to the front porch—David holding one elbow and I the other—counting the six brick steps for her. In each window is an Argand lamp, and peach roses tumble from wire baskets bordering the entrance. The band strikes up a stanza of "For She's a Jolly Good Fellow" and the guests, already gathered in the entry hall, shout "Surprise!" In a *voila!* of a moment, we untie the mask and watch as Lila Mae's face twitches. She had been expecting torches and fake thatched roofs and waitresses wiggling their tanning-bed bottoms.

"Wh-where in tarnation *are* we, honey?" Since Lila Mae has made a second career out of romanticizing Rosemont, she should know the house like the back of her hand. "Don't you *know*, Mom?" I ask.

Reacting like the brunt of a dirty trick, she frowns and says, "*This* isn't Rosemont, is it? You got *Rosemont?* Well, I swannee! *Honeeeey!*" First Lila Mae embraces me and then, her face blaring with dissatisfaction, she self-consciously slides her hands down her torso, aware of the inappropriateness of her theme garb. "Oh, I wish I'd known."

With the Kon Tiki in mind, she is dressed like Dorothy Lamour—a loud sarong and coral hibiscus in her newly tinted chestnut hair. Her nails are painted watermelon pink, a hue that would have looked great wrapped around a piña colada.

When the delayed impact of Rosemont hits her, Lila Mae exclaims, "I declare!" and her eyes, like silver-blue propellers, circle the room, taking in the winding staircase from Charleston and the tromp l'oeil wallpaper. She cranes her neck, searching for the Henry Clay library where the statesman introduced the mint julep to Blue Lick Springs.

I realize when she asks, "Do you think they'd let us take the grand tour?" that it still hasn't sunk in. Finally, I tell her, "Mom, we didn't rent this place for the night. I *bought* it, we *own* it, Rosemont is *ours!*"

On her face is a Sasquatch-sighting of an expression and her hand gropes for a chair. "*Good lordy!*" she yelps. Looking to the ceiling and the blazing chandeliers and all the glittering ormolu in between, her teary blue eyes are like the mouth of a hungry babe. "So, Rosemont is really ours?" she mutters.

The band is playing "My Old Kentucky Home" and there are white-tuxedoed waiters holding trays with pâté and shrimp. There are catering stations with sweet tea and a punch bowl with a frothy pineapple-champagne concoction. Here and there are pale green mints and white almonds tied in tulle like wedding favors. Outside, in the newly planted garden, are stone cupids and a tent that it's too windy to pitch.

Placed around the house are photographs of Lila Mae in braids with missing front teeth and wedding frocks and pregnant bellies. There is Roy with his brilliantined hair and pilot's uniform and Mr. and Mrs. Wooten's fortieth-wedding-anniversary portrait. There are children and granddaughters and nieces and nephews and pets of yesteryear, even an ex—son-in-law or two.

Lila Mae scans the group of friends, greeting Lurlene, the alive twin, then the parakeet man from Sparks, Nevada. She spots the Fuller Brush salesman, to whom she still owes twenty-three dollars from 1957 and barks, "I don't care what you say, Cecil Owen Mitchell, I'm paying you before the night's over!"

She hugs Bones Burford, a car mechanic who saved her life one icy February evening when her car flipped over near Boone's Creek. Surrounded by many fawning gentlemen is Mary Beulah Clark, the owner of the Lucky Horseshoe Motel, where Lila Mae and Roy honeymooned, who, after some work by a Lexington plastic surgeon, looks better than Lila Mae had hoped.

Lila Mae even rushes to Little Peep and Medium Dee, whom she has never laid eyes on. Dee taps her big buffalo foot and clinks her champagne glass to Lila Mae's, says, "Cheers!" then whispers, "We probably shouldn't be here, though." But Lila Mae exclaims in a typical response, "Why, of *course* you should. It wouldn't be a party without you!"

Sounding just like my dramatic mother, I say, "Mom, we wouldn't be here tonight if it weren't for Dolores and Reggie. They bought a house here, too! And, they were *so* much help in getting Rosemont back."

"Yeah, Hearst Castle, we run him outta town on a rail," Olive cackles, punching her little gladiator fists. "Him and that huzzy of his. We're gonna git this town back lak it wuz, ain't that right?"

"The *poor* man!" Lila Mae does her sympathy for the devil routine. "Did Mr. Castle have *anyplace* else to go?"

"I gotta hand it to you, Rebecca." Little Peep's eyes are dollar signs as he calculates the untold numbers that are running around like chickens with their heads cut off. "You really put this place together." What he doesn't know is that behind the scenes, there is decayed plaster and walls stuffed with deteriorating horsehair and that, if it rains, we will all be dodging the pinprick holes in the copper roof.

In contrast to all this fraternity, Lila Mae eyes the mandrill-faced Maybelle with skepticism. "The Mousers of Egypt." Maybelle extends her hand, then curtsies. Lila Mae, Olive's original daughter-in-law, has never heard anyone call Olive "Mother Wooten." She manages to say, "Well, I'll be doggone, Maybelle!" Wait until she bumps into other Kentucky Egyptians whom we needed as fill-in guests.

And Shorty, lucky to be on speaking terms with any of us, says, "Lila Mae, you look right purty!"

Despite the probability that Shorty's electrical handiwork caused Olive's fire, an act for which there is no forgiveness or remedy, I see him in his little gentleman suit, no bigger than a fourteen-year-old boy, and emotion tugs at my heart. The official report lists the cause of the fire as "Unknown," with a footnote raising the possibility of lightning or faulty electrical work. An act of God or a screwup by

Shorty. Since the latter is a more accessible scapegoat, Shorty has carried this two-ton, mammoth loss on his fragile shoulders and, even in celebration, his face is a road map of deep trails that snake across his forehead and down the slant of his jaw.

Assessing the room, Lila Mae places her palms to her throbbing temples and rattles her head as if she were overwhelmed by it all. "My, oh, my! How did you come up with all these people! I just can't believe it."

"Ain't this what ya wanted, Lila Mae?" Olive, a tigress in repose, wears a navy suit and sapphire brooch and cradles a bowl of vanilla ice cream in her lap. She looks at the colorful guests, a scene she claims looks like police headquarters on a Saturday night. "She better watch herself . . . she'll end up dead in sum dark alley runnin' with characters lak that, she will!"

"I don't know, Grandma," I say with a quizzical shake of my head. "She always comes out smelling like a rose!"

Distrustful of the lashing wind, Olive ventures to the veranda, dragging along a few guests. They stand with their mouths open, their heads tipped backwards like onlookers witnessing an outer-space invasion. Olive twirls her finger like a spiraling bird across Cassiopeia and the Archer and all the starry hosts, demonstrating how the clouds over Goose Rock way are moving in from Crystal Falls. "If it hits, I'd say Maudville'll git it," she announces. "That's my expurt opinion, enyways."

"I'm sure it's nothing," I assure the wary guests. Standing in my peach mousseline slipdress, balancing on one sore Louboutined-foot and holding a champagne glass in my hand, I am mindful not to use the word *tornado*.

I watch from afar, a demilune smile on my face, as Lila Mae sweeps through the room charming her guests. Bound by similar medical experiences, they describe glaucous eyes and tumors the size of basketballs. I know Lila Mae has joined the club when out of the conversational fragments, I hear, "Flee-bitus or some such" and then the name Richard Nixon. Soon enough, Lila Mae pokes her bad leg forward, moving it from side to side like a hosiery model. Her friends are scratching their jaws and brows, like museum goers figuring out abstract art. "Yes," she sighs, "I'm afraid my Charleston and Dipsy Doodle days are over!"

For a time Lila Mae plays coy about her showbiz career, but soon enough, she is wreathing her ringed fingers, sharing details about the horseback-riding commercial for Aleve and her latest—a Polident spot. The latter features an auctioneer who's confident that his false teeth won't fall out during a spirited auction. Lila Mae is the bidder in the front row. But she really has her guests by the jugular when she tells them that she almost drowned during a scuba-diving commercial. "I was afraid to tell them I couldn't swim! But when they put me in that rubber mask and showed me that tub of water, I thought I'd die a thousand deaths!"

"Lila Mae, go on!" Mary Beulah exclaims in disbelief and Cecil, the Fuller Brush man, adds, "You cudda got yerself in too deep, woman!"

Olive, with her own story to tell, says, "I had me a little scrape myself. They almost had me in the pen fer murray-wanna!" A small crowd begins to gather around her.

"Oh, Mom . . . you tickle me so. Isn't she great everybody?" Lila Mae, Cinderella for a day, turns to the roomful of guests, not sure she should give too much attention to the ninety-five-year-old mother-in-law. After all, the clock is galloping toward midnight.

This trail that leads from mother to daughter, the one that through the years has narrowed and widened and sometimes almost disappeared, expands and retracts all evening long and in the midst of all the hoopla, we find ourselves huddling over one thing or another. Where are the silk drapes and Kentucky cherry sideboard and the Gilbert Stuart paintings? And where's the ballroom and that Sèvres porcelain? What happened to all that, Lila Mae demands, as if after all those years of neglect, it had been Rebecca who had turned up to neglect Rosemont.

"Mom, the house is old, what do you think happened to everything. It's *Gone With the Wind!*"

"Honey, you are *so* funny!" As usual, Lila Mae overreacts to the mildly amusing comment. As her eyes skim the guests, she asks, "How many are here, honey?" I give her my standard line, "We *sent out* over three hundred invitations."

"Three hundred?" Lila Mae hums. "Oh, my!"

Hunting for a project, Cassie and Ava, who is thin as a swizzle stick and looks nothing like the future heir of Rosemont, climb the staircase, counting heads. "Mom, there's nowhere *near* three hundred," Ava reports. I tell these two blabbermouths in magenta cowhide to just keep it to themselves.

I assess Ava and wonder why all this hard-metal and spiky trinkets after years of cotillions and museums and high English tea at the Helmsley Palace. All that and Ava ends up with armadillo hair and jewelry like the stopper chains in old claw bathtubs, not exactly the stuff of a Gainsborough portrait. It serves me right, I think; she has been a rudderless ship. Before ballet camp, she had been coming and going as she pleased, existing on TV dinners and Mrs. Smith's deep-dish apple pie. Now we're told she is a vegan, meaning she doesn't eat dairy or meat or much else, it seems. But it is so sudden, this switch of Ava's, like the swift jerk of a curtain and an announcer saying: and now, contestant number two!

When I tell David, "She's just not finished yet," he says, "You make her sound like a cake!"

David, so ferociously protective of his stepdaughter, fetches a sweater for a summer cold she's nursing and brings her a white china plate of food she barely eats.

But at least Ava is better than Cassie, whose once sparkly eyes are now the color of pond water. And she is coughing, a choking, raspy noise, that causes her baby lungs to struggle for life and undoubtedly comes from her three-pack-a-day Virginia Slims habit.

When no one is looking, Ava still clings to me like a frail koala, wrapping her long arms around my waist and burrowing her head into my chest. I smell her familiar and exquisite scent of ripe pears. She dangles a necklace charm before my eyes and says, "Look what I got at camp." It is a pink enamel ballet slipper, one tiny memento of the last few weeks spent in a flurry of arabesques and pas de deux, and a symbol of the little girl I can obviously kiss good-bye.

Two late arrivals—a man with a Prince Valiant hairdo and his petite Asian wife—lumber into the room, causing quite a stir. "Who in the world is the geisha girl?" Lila Mae murmurs.

"Mom, don't you know who that is? It's Benny . . . Benny Featherhorse! He wasn't in prison, either!"

"Benny? You found *Benny?*" Lila Mae hammers her chest and screams like a passenger in a roller coaster. She cries at the sight of him, then goes to the man with open arms.

"Everybody, this is Benny Featherhorse! *He saved our lives!*" This exclamation, a frequent one for Lila Mae, surprises the roomful of other heroes and heroines, many of whom have been credited with the same rescue operation.

But, like sole survivors of a fatal crash, there is a special category for Benny. He is festooned in turquoise jewelry with a spectacular squash-blossom necklace. His wife has earbobs of abalone and agate, and Ava and Cassie are enthralled. "Cool jewelry," they say.

Medium Dee states the obvious when she says, "Your mother certainly has some interesting friends!"

"Boy, does she!" snorts Irene. The newly spiritual Baby Sister, a wafer of her former self, has a psalm on her tongue and a gold bauble saying JESUS IS THE ROCK AND YOU ARE ON HIS ROLL around her neck. Gone are the days when Baby Sister's eyes were like little glass stars, when her head would bob in woozy spirals. At long last, she has a cornucopia of possibilities: Sherlock Holmes, Martha Stewart, or Aimee Semple McPherson. But, we have coveted high hopes before, so we cross our fingers and pray for continuity.

As much as I savor this merry reunion, I am anxious for Rosemont to empty of guests. I can't wait to fetch Olive so we can limp through Rosemont, room by room, hallway by hallway. I want to see her face as it lights up and be close to her heart as it settles into some slow, satisfying, unsyncopated rhythm. And I want to watch her as she imagines what it might have been like, this life of luxury she would have led, if the gambling James Butler Adams hadn't sabotaged the Adams destiny.

And then I will sip port in the big sunshine-yellow parlor with David. In those hours between midnight and a rose-sparked dawn, when the temperature still soars, we will drift through room after room and I will point out all those details that surprisingly mean so much to him. He'll want to know about the Worcester and Chinese Export porcelain; he will ask about the Adams silversticks and the ancestral portraits. With the first sprigs of a Kentucky sunrise drifting through the windows, we'll clink our glasses and thank the gods for our good fortune.

David leans into me and half-teases, "How much is all this costing me?"

"The house or the party?" I give him a playful slap. "The house you don't want to know about. By the way, you haven't told me what you think of Rosemont."

"It's amazing, just amazing. I knew it would be." He gives me a William Holden–Kim Novak look, only hundreds of times better.

I move through the rooms and gather everyone into the entry hall. Around the rosewood table, under the chandelier that suspends like a crystal headdress, we all wait for the waiters carting the Eiffel Tower–shaped cake, a lemon confection made by Baby Sister. The band plays "Happy Birthday" and white balloons are released. They float to the ceiling like hundreds of peace doves.

"Happy birth-*dee* to you . . . happy birth-*dee* to you . . ." Carleen and Baby Sister and I sing, making sure Lila Mae hears us above the others. "Happy birth-*dee*, dear Lila Maaaae, happy birth-*dee* to you."

"Oh, you girls!" Lila Mae flaps her hand to dismiss us. Applause and congratulations and dozens of rented champagne glasses are hoisted into the air.

As Lila Mae mounts the circular staircase to address her subjects, I cross my fingers and hold my breath, praying she won't unearth the beast of a topic that's been shadowboxing with us all evening. Standing at the balcony, a torch of moonlight bounces through a transom and settles on her, like a lagoon of limelight. Behind her is an urn filled with cream roses that seem to bloom from her bare shoulders. "Well, everybody," she sighs in a voice like bubbling champagne. "After so many generations, here we are at Rosemont, of all places! Of course, we're sick, just *sick* about losin' Mom's place." And so the words are out, hanging in the air like skywriting.

"Well, anyhow, we're all here now . . ." She has stopped for a moment and takes a shuddering gasp of a breath, one that seems to come from the fiery core of the planet itself. "All of us that's still left, anyway."

And then Olive and Lila Mae embrace, these two remaining links to Roy and Billy Cooper and all the other vanished souls they cherish in common. There are tears, huge drops like pear-shaped diamonds, that roll down their cheeks. Lila Mae dabs her watery, mascaraed eyes with a cocktail napkin. "Oh, dear me . . . I'm sorry everyone."

"That's okay, Lila Mae." Olive, her voice sounding like crunching autumn leaves, pats her daughter-in-law's saronged back. "That's okay."

All evening long one spot on the wall devils me, but now my eyes catch Billy Cooper's photograph and I, too, am trapped in a weepy moment. The picture—a grainy black and white of a boy with an angel's smile and crushed-blue-velvet eyes—is a memento that stirs fond memories of a disaster.

"I tried to find him," Carleen releases a ponderous moan. "I tried my best." With her dreams of a Madison Avenue Prince Charming still squirming with life, but her nightmare with Nelson just beginning, she is having a bad health day, and later she will blame her lethargy on her fibromyalgia, a condition that leaves her as limber as our friend Jasmina and as unpredictable as a drive-by shooting. It is also one that Olive is itching to doctor. But, for the first time in decades, Carleen has her fists curled around ambition. She has moments of pure bliss and fairy dust that gambols all around and seems to sprinkle her with silver light. At long last, and just like Baby Sister, she has choices before her: Miss Lila Mae's Confectionery, advertising maven at Beaton, Richardson and Bardwell, or simply, newly divorced bon vivant.

We gather in the parlor for the feature attraction and wait for the projectionist who fiddles with buttons and levers and knobs, while outside the roaring wind makes a sound like discordant bagpipes. Rosemont's lights suddenly flutter on and off. In spite of the three possible causes—the tornado, Minetta's ghost, or old, faulty electricity—I realize that Carleen is way too close to the projection equipment. We usher her to the front row, telling the guests not to fret. "It's just Carleen. Don't worry everybody!"

In moments, Lila Mae is displayed before us on the huge screen. She is a small-town princess with gardenias sprouting in her hair, mahogany silk that puddles around her shoulders like a queen's robe. But the image is upside-down and pictures flash on the screen, moving like Charlie Chaplin. And then the projector makes a sour, winding nosedive.

"Now what?" I jump up, steaming, furious that after all the dress re-hearsals, we can't quite get everything right.

The projectionist, a man with a friar haircut and an all-too-lackadaisical mien, moseys out to assure us, saying, "Give me a minute to figger out the derned thing."

"Have you ever operated one of these?" I huff to the man. "Listen, momentum is a very delicate commodity and——"

"Go on, honey, sit down." David pats my arm like the baby I am being and says, "I'll handle this."

For years I have had pastel-tinted dreams of Rosemont; for months I have planned this evening, phoning, faxing, and tracking down hard-to-locate friends. That doesn't even count the hundreds of remodeling tasks just to get the house ready. My fear is that I won't get this right, that a few hours from now I will be reviewing it all from the four-poster bed in a near-empty upstairs room with David at my side, wishing I hadn't forgotten this or that. All evening, the fear that I will soon be critiquing that which I have just finished bungling keeps me vigilant—I have made introductions to strange bedfellows—linking the parakeet man to Little Peep, Benny Feath-erhorse to the living twin. I have spoken to a Mouser or two when their eyes search for a friendly face. I have dashed to the kitchen making sure the cake is presented at the precise moment when we sing "Happy Birthday." I have done all this with the hope that Lila Mae will clench her hands together and say, "Oh, honey! It was just like something out of a movie." And now this, this totally unnecessary botch-up!

When the anxious projectionist tells us the repair might take longer, a waiter brings Asti Spumante to soothe our ruffled nerves and someone—maybe Carleen, perhaps Lila Mae, or maybe even my Ava—suddenly shouts, "Let's sing songs!"

Lila Mae, an enthusiastic volunteer, leaps to the front of the room, crowding out any other potential songstress. Standing with her chin tipped up, almost as if auditioning to some faceless man upstairs, she brushes back the coil of stray hair that hangs like a graduation tassel on her forehead. Without skipping a beat, she begins the family anthem, not in the spirited manner we are used to—fists pumping like a power walker, lungs thumping like Ethel Merman's—but a misty-eyed rendition that her pure, strangely childlike voice delivers like a glee-club soprano.

> *California, here I come*
> *Right back where I started from*
> *Where bowers of flowers bloom in the sun*
> *Each morning at dawning,*
> *Birdies sing an' ev'rything*
> *A sunkissed miss said, don't be late*
> *That's why I can hardly wait*
> *Open up that Golden Gaaaate.*
> *CALIFORNIA . . . HERE I COME.*

With that, I am spirited back to 1959, where I see four rambunctious, sassy children and a woman, drunk on her visions of Eden, lured by some fanciful notion of happiness. Traveling across the country like gypsies, singing along with Elvis and Tennessee Ernie Ford, we are searching for a shard of the great American Dream.

When I close my eyes, I see teepees and freight trains and clouds that look like pink castles. In front of it all is a narrow road. Sometimes this path is as straight as a rifle barrel; often, it simply bounces and twists and disappears between jagged mountain ranges. Through it all, this group pushes forward.

In this dream there is a row of burning candles all marching in step, their torches raging. With their jaws clenched in resolve, they are trampling grass so green it looks blue. They are running toward the palm trees, these artless flames, so blinded by glitter, they do not see the gathering clouds.

Then I imagine another scene of such peculiarity, one in which these same seeds that have scattered across the land, are all reunited, frolicking on clovered Kentucky soil. There is a mother, so many years older now, still with star-filled eyes and a story to tell. She is leading her daughters through freshly minted dreams, still coaxing them this way and that. Trailing behind the women is one lone pilgrim, a raggedy, bearded man with a mandolin in hand and a melody in his heart. Joining this fractured group, and keeping a special eye on the musician, is the father, who wears a smile he has saved for years.

As they roam their newly claimed paradise, there are fragrant summer berries and ruby-bellied insects lighting the sky. And there is Minetta and all her ghostly playmates who leap through Rosemont's garden. If I listen carefully, I can even hear Johnny singing in the background: "I hear the train a comin' . . . it's rollin 'round the bend . . . and I ain't seen the sunshine since I don't know when . . ."

There is another woman, this one ancient, with wise crystal-blue eyes. With her shaky, loving arm, she has raised her glass of wine to the impulsive family who long ago forsook her for fool's gold. But in this dream, she is still pink-cheeked, sassy-tongued, and swift of foot. And her rusty spine is once again sturdy and arched as she gathers the lilacs from her garden.

And down the road apiece comes a rawboned hank of a man with grizzled familiarity and eyes darker than Bordeaux wine. He is walking with the injured swagger of a man who can account for the minutes of his life, but doesn't know what happened to the years. The crook of his bones and the faded sparkle of their grandfather's smile are destined to attract their sympathy, and for a time, this mirthful group spies him with a wary regard. But eventually, he will join them as they stroll across country fields, watching for Indian arrowheads and high-flying cardinals.

If they should stop and look to the east, just over Rosemont's smoke-daubed treetops, there is a transparent shadow reminding them of a God who toils in mysterious ways and who believes that, after all, some parades deserve a little rain. But they are careful to avoid the spot, not yet knowing the value of blank spaces.

And, all the while, as these images come and go, and the wind whips around us in unpredictable spirals, we wait for Lila Mae's suspended photograph to take flight. And all the belles of Honeysuckle Way sit in the same row in the semiblackness, seven flags flying from the same pole.

Soon enough, Olive, her patience now at its rope's end, lifts up. Instead of lecturing us on the virtues of tranquility or quoting a Bible passage to cool our brow, she gripes, "What in tarnation's the holdup? I cudda fixed that G.D. thang faster then that myself! Let me talk to that slowpoke!"

So, I watch as Olive tears off, this frail, humped spirit, limping her way through the guests, toward the back of Rosemont's big, pink-wallpapered sitting room. She is on a mission; she is going to get to the bottom of things; she will get this show on the road. I watch as her figure grows smaller and smaller almost until it disappears altogether, but even all the way from the front row, I can still hear her saying, "Let's git on with it. We got places to go and things to do."

Acknowledgments

Thanks to all those who lent a helping hand and who deserve much limelight: Lynn Nesbit, whose worth is immeasurable; Diane Drummond, a wizard at all things; and Laurie Chittenden, whose sage advice I sometimes wanted to ignore, but didn't . . . fortunately. More thank-yous to Karen Butler, Bob Bookman, Michael Lynton, Natalie Ungvari, Larry Greaves, Kim Riback, and Bob Philpott . . . so different in every way from you know who.

Affection and gratitude are extended to my big, zany, inspirational family, especially my mother, Virginia, whose heart of gold is unequaled and whose antics still keep me in stitches. Don't worry, everybody. The names have been changed to protect the guilty.

Special thanks and love go to my lovely and unbelievably wise daughter, Alexandra, and my ever-supportive and near-perfect husband, Jerry. He, like my grandmother, taught me to keep my nose to the grindstone, my feet on the ground, and my head in the clouds.

Linda Bruckheimer is the author of the national bestseller *Dreaming Southern*. She divides her time between a farm in rural Kentucky and Los Angeles, California, where she lives with her husband, film and television producer Jerry Bruckheimer.